A BRIGHT FUTURE

Christine walked over to stand beside him, her eyes widening. "Oh my, I had no idea what this part of the property looked like. I bet it'll be beautiful this spring when all the trees get their leaves," she said, pointing ahead of them. "Can't you just imagine your Clydesdales grazing on this ground over here—with your barns on this side, and your house right here on this rise?"

"I can see everything just as you're describing it, sweetheart," he whispered as he slipped his arm around her shoulders. "It's the picture of horse farm heaven—and I'm hoping you'll be my angel in residence."

Christine's mouth dropped open. "Are you sure you want—even if we'll have no children to—"

Monroe punctuated her sentence with a soft kiss. "I want," he replied. His face was shaded by his wide-brimmed black hat, but his eyes shone warmly as he gazed at her.

Weddings
at PROMISE
LODGE

**Charlotte
Hubbard**

ZEBRA BOOKS
KENSINGTON PUBLISHING CORP.

http://www.kensingtonbooks.com

ZEBRA BOOKS are published by

Kensington Publishing Corp.
119 West 40th Street
New York, NY 10018

All Kensington titles, imprints, and distributed lines are available at special quantity discounts for bulk purchases for sales promotion, premiums, fund-raising, educational, or institutional use.

Special book excerpts or customized printings can also be created to fit specific needs. For details, write or phone the office of the Kensington Sales Manager: Attn.: Sales Department. Kensington Publishing Corp., 119 West 40th Street, New York, NY 10018. Phone: 1-800-221-2647.

Zebra and the Z logo Reg. U.S. Pat. & TM Off.

First Printing: July 2017
ISBN-13: 978-1-4201-3945-7
ISBN-10: 1-4201-3945-2

eISBN-13: 978-1-4201-3946-4
eISBN-10: 1-4201-3946-0

10 9 8 7 6 5 4 3 2 1

Printed in the United States of America

For Neal, for 42 fabulous years of marriage.
Where would I be without you?

ACKNOWLEDGMENTS

Many thanks to my editor, Alicia Condon, for your constant encouragement, and to my agent, Evan Marshall, for your friendship and publishing savvy. I'm ecstatic that we three are working together on this series as it continues.

Special thanks to Vicki Harding, innkeeper of Poosey's Edge B&B in Jamesport, Missouri. Your assistance has been invaluable! Thanks and blessings, as well, to Joe Burkholder and his family, proprietors of Oak Ridge Furniture and Sherwood's Christian Books in Jamesport.

Matthew 19:4–6 (KJV)

Have ye not read, that he which made *them* at the beginning made them male and female,

And said, For this cause shall a man leave father and mother, and shall cleave to his wife: and they twain shall be one flesh?

Wherefore they are no more twain, but one flesh. What therefore God hath joined together, let not man put asunder.

Chapter One

As Christine Hershberger sat on the front pew bench, close enough to bask in the glow of her sister Mattie's joy, she smiled brightly. At long last, she was attending the wedding that should've taken place years ago, when Mattie Bender and Amos Troyer were young and so deeply in love—before Dat had insisted that Mattie marry Marvin Schwartz instead. Now that Mattie and Preacher Amos had outlived their original mates, they were standing together, hand in hand, repeating the age-old vows after their new bishop, Monroe Burkholder. Christine, who'd lost her husband a couple of years ago, found it encouraging that at forty-five and fifty, her older sister and Amos had taken up where their youthful romance had left off, to enjoy a second chance at love that would see them through the rest of their lives.

Beside her on the bench, Rosetta grabbed Christine's hand and squeezed it. *This is so exciting!* she mouthed.

Christine nodded, returning her younger sister's squeeze. She had to admit, however, that the glimmer in Bishop Monroe's green eyes eclipsed the happiness she felt for Mattie and Amos. Was it her imagination, or did Monroe glance at her as he led the happy couple in their vows, as though he hoped to be exchanging these sacred, binding phrases with *her* in the near future?

It was too soon to contemplate a wedding—the handsome bishop had only arrived at Promise Lodge a week and a half before, on Christmas Eve. Yet Christine's pulse thrummed with the distinct possibility that widowed Monroe Burkholder was as attracted to her as she was to him. Her soul took on the sparkle of the snowy, sunlit hills outside. Hope blossomed in her heart, because it felt absolutely wonderful to believe that such a prosperous, upstanding man might be interested in becoming her husband.

"Amos and Mattie," Monroe said, his resonant voice filling the room, "I pronounce you husband and wife."

The wedding guests sprang to their feet, their applause resounding like thunder in the lodge's large meeting room. Mattie blushed prettily as Amos turned her to face the crowd. When he slung his arm around her to kiss her, a loud *whoop* went up from the men's side.

Rosetta laughed, linking her arm through Christine's. "And they'll live happily ever after," she said wistfully. "Maybe there's hope for us, too, sister."

Christine nodded toward Truman Wickey, their neighbor, who—along with Allen Troyer—had been Preacher Amos's side-sitter. "Here comes your hope as we speak, Rosetta," she said. "Now that our new bishop has performed his first wedding at Promise Lodge, it's a *gut* time to ask his feelings about an Amish woman hitching up with a Mennonite."

"That's only a part of what's on my agenda," Truman said as he came to stand beside them. His hazel eyes held a special glow as he grasped Rosetta's hand. "We'll speak with Bishop Monroe, *jah*, but we'll also celebrate this special day with Mattie and Amos. Lots of food to eat and lots of fun to be had, the way I see it."

"We're grateful to Floyd Lehman, too," Rosetta murmured as she glanced toward their former bishop, who was now confined to a wheelchair. "It was *gut* of him to turn over the reins to Monroe. I thought Floyd might insist on remaining our bishop even though he can't talk anymore."

Christine nodded. A serious fall and a concussion had incapacitated Floyd the previous fall, after he'd tried to catch Preacher Amos, who'd tumbled from the roof of the shed beside Rainbow Lake. Amos had wisely followed the doctors' instructions and taken physical therapy, or he would still be confined to a wheelchair, too. Floyd hadn't been as receptive to his English doctor's advice. He was a mere shell of the blustery bishop who'd come to Promise Lodge claiming God had declared him the new colony's leader before they'd even met him.

"*Jah*, we can thank God for giving Floyd the wisdom to step down," Truman said. "I see it as a fresh start for your whole colony now that Monroe has come—and a fresh start for Amos now that he's married Mattie and his twins have decided to move back here to Missouri, as well."

"I believe Sam and Simon Helmuth's nursery and greenhouses will be a boon to our other businesses," Christine remarked, smiling as she watched Amos's identical daughters congratulate their *dat*. "Barb and Bernice have always kept things lively—and when their babies arrive, Amos and Mattie will have grandkids to spoil."

"And I bet they'll have fiery red hair, just like Sam and Simon," Rosetta teased.

"Unless I miss my guess, Allen Troyer plans to live at Promise Lodge, as well," Truman remarked as Amos's dark-haired son clapped his *dat* on the back. "He was telling me he plans to take his license exams to become a plumber and an electrician, and then he'll be set to help build the new houses his sisters and Bishop Monroe will need."

"It's amazing, how much our colony has grown," Christine said. "Just last May we were purchasing this old, run-down church camp, and now we're really picking up steam. It's a dream come true—"

"And we have Mattie to thank for turning our dream into reality," Rosetta put in.

"My dream," Truman said with a mischievous wink, "is to stuff myself with wedding food and have you all to myself for the rest of the day, Rosetta."

"I can't argue with that," Rosetta said playfully. "Let's see if our cooks need any help carrying their heavy pans of food to the dining room, shall we?"

Christine smiled as her sister and Truman made their way through the crowd, following Mattie and Amos to the dining room. It was such a blessing to see Rosetta blooming at last, after devoting most of her adult life to caring for their parents until they passed. Truman Wickey was a wonderful man—and with his landscaping equipment, he'd felled trees, cut the underbrush from the orchard, and cleared the paths that would become the roads between their homes and businesses. She had a feeling Rosetta and Truman would be marrying soon, if Bishop Monroe decided their colony would agree to interfaith marriages—a more progressive belief than many Old Order Amish settlements condoned.

"You look lovely in that deep red dress, Christine. It was all I could do to keep my mind on marrying Amos and your sister."

When Christine turned, Bishop Monroe was standing so close she nearly bumped into him. She smiled up at him a little nervously, for he was tall and broad and extraordinarily handsome—and his dimples had come out to play.

"Mattie wanted Rosetta and me to have new dresses with some color to them," she explained. "And since Christmas was only a couple of weeks ago, we decided this red would be more cheerful than, say, the usual dark blue or gray or teal."

"Mattie's a wise woman—with admirable taste in color, and in husband material, as well," he added. He held her gaze with his glowing green eyes. "May I have the honor of sitting with you at dinner, Christine? And spending the rest of the day with you, as well? Once we're alone, I'd like to discuss some important decisions."

Christine wondered if Monroe could hear how rapidly her heart was beating. Was her face as red as her dress? "I'd like that a lot, Monroe," she said breathlessly.

The crowd around them seemed to disappear as he offered her his elbow. All Christine could see was Monroe's attractive face, framed by wavy brown hair and a neatly trimmed beard—and those deep green eyes that focused so intently on her. What decisions could he possibly want to discuss with her? Did she dare hope he wanted her to become a permanent part of his new home, his new life, at Promise Lodge?

Monroe might've remained rooted to the spot, gazing at Christine's flawless skin and the glossy brown hair pulled neatly beneath her *kapp*, and those green eyes as serene as an evergreen forest—except the happy folks around them had other ideas.

"Say there, Bishop! Better head into the dining room before you eat Christine alive!" one of the men teased.

"*Jah*, I've been inhaling the aromas of our meal all morning," another fellow said as he clapped Monroe on the back. "Ruby and Beulah Kuhn and the other gals have whipped up quite a feast, I'm guessing."

"No doubt about that," Monroe said. He winked at Christine before turning to reply to these men, whose names he'd learned but whose voices he didn't yet recognize. "Ruby and Beulah and the others have put a few pounds on me this week—and if I go through the buffet line before you, Eli and Marlin, you'll be lucky if there's enough food left to fill your plates," he teased.

Monroe was pleased that two of Promise Lodge's preachers felt comfortable enough to joke with him. Eli Peterscheim was a welder who'd followed Amos and Mattie and her sisters here from their previous Amish community, while Marlin Kurtz had come from Iowa with his married son, daughter-in-law, and two teenagers to reestablish his barrel factory. Marlin had agreed to serve as the colony's deacon, because Eli and Amos had already been established as the two preachers.

But Amos was *not* particularly chummy with Monroe.

Monroe figured on giving Amos time to settle in with his new wife before he questioned him about his misgivings. It was true that he'd arrived at an unexpectedly opportune time to become Promise Lodge's new bishop, yet he sensed Amos doubted his intentions and his background. He wanted nothing to interfere with the relationships he would establish with his new flock—and especially with his preachers.

His past was behind him. And Monroe intended to keep it there.

He smiled at the folks who'd gathered around him and Christine—men and boys mostly, because the other women and girls had gone to the lodge's large kitchen to help set out the meal. "It's a happy day, and I'm blessed and grateful to be here amongst you," he said as he met their gazes. "Every one of us came to Promise Lodge for a fresh start, and I look forward to the new future God will provide for us."

"Let's eat, Bishop Monroe!" a boy in the back piped up.

"*Jah*, we're hungry!" his friend chimed in. "It's been a long morning in church!"

Monroe laughed out loud. Lowell Kurtz and Lavern Peterscheim were the two boys who'd walked and stabled his Clydesdale after he'd arrived during a snowstorm on Christmas Eve. At twelve and thirteen, they were ruled by their stomachs. "You boys have your priorities in order," he agreed jovially. "I think you need to go on ahead, to be sure the food's fit for the rest of us."

The lanky boys, all decked out in their best black pants and vests with crisp white shirts, didn't wait to be asked a second time. As Lavern and Lowell grinned at him before entering the dining room, Monroe recalled his own boyhood with the uncle and aunt who'd taken him in after his parents died in a house fire. It did his heart good to see young boys taking an active part in their new settlement, for they were the future of Promise Lodge. He looked forward to hiring these two and their friends after his Clydesdales took up residence in the large barns he would have built for them.

A tug on his coat sleeve brought him out of his musings. Christine was smiling at him, making his heart thrum with longings he hadn't felt since his wife had died.

"My sisters and I consider you our guest of honor at this wedding feast," she murmured. "Shall we go?"

Monroe was momentarily tongue-tied. *Shall we go?* If Christine knew what that simple question, spoken in her soft, flowing voice, did to him . . .

But then, Christine was forty, and she'd given her husband two fine daughters before he'd died in a barn fire two years earlier. Her wistful, hopeful expression told Monroe that she did, indeed, know the effect she had on him—and that she had no intention of letting him off easy. At this point in his life, he found women who spoke their minds a lot more enticing than he had when he'd been a young man exchanging vows the first time.

"Yes, dear," he replied playfully as he tucked her hand into the crook of his elbow again. "Whatever you say, Christine."

Chapter Two

Rosetta clasped her hands, gazing around the dining room with a full heart. Because Amos and Mattie had wanted to marry before his kids returned to their homes out East, she and her sisters and the other women had baked the pies and the bread the day before. They had pressed the white tablecloths that graced the worn tables and chairs that had remained at Promise Lodge from when it was a church camp. Rather than hold the wedding in Amos's house, they had all agreed that if the service was conducted in the lodge's meeting room, no one would have to tromp through the snow to eat dinner. Beulah and Ruby Kuhn, who rented apartments upstairs, had directed the preparation of a fabulous feast—which Truman and Mattie's sons, Noah and Roman Schwartz, were wheeling out on carts. They began arranging the large metal pans on a buffet table set up along the wall.

The air was redolent with aromas of chicken baked with stuffing, creamed celery, fresh bread, and mashed potatoes—traditional wedding dishes—as well as many other favorites, including the baked venison roast Amos had requested and the corn casserole Mattie had always adored. Fruit salad and slaw rounded out the menu.

The Kuhn sisters had outdone themselves making a tall white wedding cake with the newlyweds' names on it, which sat proudly at the *eck*—the corner table where the wedding party was gathering before they filled their plates. The cake they'd frozen after Amos had fallen during their engagement party graced the dessert table, along with dozens of pies and bars. Christine's daughters, Laura and Phoebe, stood behind the table to cut and plate slices of pie, while Marlin Kurtz's daughter-in-law, Minerva, was arranging the bars on platters.

"Bishop Monroe says we can eat first!" Lavern Peterscheim crowed as he and Lowell Kurtz burst into the dining room. "We're starving!"

Minerva gazed purposefully at the boys. On ordinary weekdays she was their schoolteacher, so she was adept at dealing with them. "You know that members of the wedding party are the first to fill their plates," she reminded them. "They won't be doing that until all the food's been set out, so cool your heels, gentlemen."

"But the side-sitters are all busy," Lowell protested as he watched Truman set the large metal pan of creamed celery on the serving table.

"Shall I find you fellows a job?" Minerva countered. "You could help fill the water glasses."

With loud sighs, Lavern and Lowell went over to where Amos and Mattie were talking with Amos's son. "Bishop Monroe said we could go first," one of them murmured—and Preacher Amos heard his plea.

"Tell you what, fellows," Amos said as he reached across the table to shake their hands. "This isn't like a wedding where it's two young people getting married, and we older folks are liable to chatter all day while you boys wither away. When Truman says everything's ready, you can load your plates."

Rosetta chuckled when a couple other boys slipped into

the dining room to await Truman's signal, as well. Including Truman's mother and some longtime friends from their former home in Coldstream, nearly seventy people were present for this happy occasion—and everyone could be seated for dinner at the same time. Rosetta was pleased that her lodge building could be the center of social life at Promise Lodge, because its meeting room and dining room—and its commercial-sized kitchen—made it much easier to accommodate everyone at special gatherings.

"Come on in, folks," Truman called out over the men's conversations. "Soon as our cooks join us, we'll be ready to eat this fabulous feast!"

A few moments later, the women brightened the room with their warm smiles and lively chatter. When Truman handed a plate to Lowell Kurtz, the boys rushed over to start the buffet line. Amos and Mattie followed them, and Rosetta waved Christine and Bishop Monroe toward the line before joining Truman and Amos's son.

"Might be an advantage to being in the wedding party," Allen Troyer remarked as he gazed at the food on the serving table. At twenty-three, he was taller than his *dat* and wore his black hair a little longer then most Amish fellows. "A crowd like this can go through a lot of food."

"Never fear," said Rosetta. "Ruby and Beulah have more of everything ready to serve. From the amount of food I saw this morning, we'll probably be eating leftovers for days after the guests leave."

"I hope I'm invited to help you get rid of those leftovers," Truman hinted as he picked up a plate and his silverware.

Rosetta's stomach fluttered when he held her gaze with his soulful hazel eyes. "Don't wait for an invitation, dear," she murmured. "You're welcome here any time you care to come."

"Ooh—sounds like there might be another wedding soon," Allen teased as he followed them through the line.

"Might be," Truman affirmed, and he didn't miss a beat tossing the topic back at Allen. "How about you? Got a special girl in Indiana you're bringing back with you?"

Allen laughed. "Haven't felt the need for any such entanglements," he replied breezily. "The bachelor life has its advantages—"

"But if you change your mind," Rosetta interrupted, "you've known Laura and Phoebe Hershberger all your life. Gloria Lehman's single, as well."

"You sound like Mattie, trying to match me up," Allen protested. "From what Dat's told me, I'll have plenty to keep me busy when I move here, what with building houses for my sisters, as well as the Helmuth Nursery buildings and Bishop Monroe's house and barns. No time to fiddle-faddle around with the women."

Rosetta took a big scoop of mashed potatoes and a large portion of the chicken and stuffing, then spooned creamed celery over everything. The ladies in the kitchen had been speculating about Allen, too, and it was no secret that Gloria Lehman had her eye on him. As Rosetta recalled the way Gloria had gone all out to win Roman Schwartz's heart—until he'd proposed to her younger sister, Mary Kate—she had a feeling Allen would receive a lot more attention than he anticipated.

She wondered if Amos's son was staying single because he hadn't felt compelled to join the Amish church, but it was a topic she didn't feel comfortable asking him about in the presence of all these people. Rosetta was pleased that Barb and Bernice had talked Allen into moving here with them. Younger folks were the key to Promise Lodge's growth.

When she sat down at the *eck* table beside Truman, the light in his eyes made her hold her breath.

"Honey-girl, if your new bishop allows us to marry,

when do you want to tie the knot?" he murmured as he grasped her hand. "I fell head over heels for you the moment I met you last summer, making dinner in that big kitchen—"

"*Jah*, the way to a man's heart has always been through his stomach," Rosetta teased. Her heart was hammering in her chest, and she suddenly felt like a tongue-tied teenager. It still surprised her, the way Truman made much of her and waxed so romantic, considering he was somewhat younger than she was.

Truman smiled. "I have no fears of going hungry after we marry," he murmured, rubbing his thumb over her hand. "But my clock's ticking. I'm thirty and I want a family—I can't wait to watch you grow big with our children, Rosetta."

Rosetta held her breath. She, too, had dreamed of mothering a large family, but the years after losing her first fiancé and then caring for her aging parents had slipped by. Even though God granted children to women who were older than she, at thirty-seven, Rosetta was concerned about getting such a late start. "My clock's ticking, too," she murmured. "I—I hope I'll be able to have healthy, normal babies—"

Truman squeezed Rosetta's hand, gazing at her until her worries disappeared. "We'll do our best," he stated. He smiled playfully. "Maybe we should slip away and start practicing right now—and keep at it until we get it right."

Rosetta felt her face flushing. Truman's way of making her feel desirable was only one of the reasons she loved him. "We'd better speak with Monroe soon," she teased. "And, gee, since the tables are already set up for a crowd—and we'll still have lots of food—maybe he'd marry us tomorrow."

Truman picked up his fork. "That would suit me fine,

time-wise, but you deserve better than someone else's leftovers, Rosetta. We should have our own special day. Soon."

She gazed at her loaded plate, blinking back happy tears. Truman's gentle voice and his way with words had always made her feel especially blessed. Although Rosetta loved living in the lodge and renting apartments to single Plain women, she suddenly knew that for Truman, she would leave that life to live in his home up the hill. "I love you, Truman," Rosetta whispered as she dipped her fork into her mashed potatoes.

"I know," he replied with a soft chuckle. "I love you more with each passing day, pretty girl. My heart's in your hands."

Rosetta's heart swelled. She'd prayed about it often, and there was no way around it—she loved Truman so much she would leave the Old Order and become a Mennonite if Bishop Monroe refused to marry them. For Truman alone she would endure whatever separation and censure the folks of Promise Lodge dished out if she left her lifelong religion behind.

"You're looking awfully serious, considering we're at a party, Rosetta."

Rosetta smiled at Mattie, who sat on her other side, and she realized her fears were unfounded: her sisters and the new friends who'd come to live here all adored Truman. The strictest Amish settlements believed that if a member left the Old Order to marry a Mennonite, the deserter would lose all chance of the Lord's salvation—and that family members should no longer associate with them.

But Rosetta knew her sisters would never shut her out. She and Mattie and Christine had sold their farms to buy Promise Lodge, to start a colony where spousal abuse wasn't tolerated and peace was part of the promise of living here.

Rosetta smiled as she slipped an arm around Mattie's shoulders. "It's the best party ever, too, seeing you and Amos together at last," she said. "Never fear, sister. I may look serious, but I'm planning for happiness in a big way—and it'll happen soon!"

Chapter Three

Christine couldn't recall the last time she'd felt so happy. Even though she and Monroe were seated at the end of the *eck* table with the wedding party—on display for all of the other guests—she forgot about being nervous when the handsome bishop smiled at her as though she were the only person in the room.

"What say we slip away for a while?" he whispered, his breath tickling her ear. "Those slices of pie are tempting—but not nearly as tempting as the chance to spend some time with you when folks aren't gawking at us."

Christine smiled. "*Jah*, I can tell that our friends who came from Coldstream—where we used to live—are curious about you and me being . . . together."

Monroe's eyes sparkled. "Well, if they're gossiping about us, they're giving somebody else a rest," he joked. He focused intently on her. "I've got a surprise for you. Give me a few minutes, and then wait for me out on the porch, okay? You'll want your coat and boots."

Her eyes widened. Before she could quiz him about his plans, Monroe excused himself by congratulating Amos and Mattie again before exiting the crowded dining room.

As he slipped out through the kitchen, Mattie leaned forward to look past Amos and down the table at Christine.

"What's Monroe up to?" she asked. "He hasn't had his pie yet."

Christine shrugged, wondering if her smile appeared as giddy as she felt. "He says he has a surprise for me."

Preacher Amos let out a laugh. "*Jah*, I know a little bit about that, too, but my lips are sealed. Behave yourself, Christine," he said, playfully wagging his finger at her. "You're the mother of two young women who'll model their behavior after yours."

"I hope they do!" Mattie blurted. "Laura and Phoebe couldn't follow a finer example."

"Have a *gut* time, Christine!" Rosetta rose from her chair and walked behind their table, placing her hands on Christine's shoulders. "You're due for some love and laughter—and meanwhile, I'll save you back some pie. What kind do you want?"

Christine glanced toward the pie table, where a few of their guests were gathering to choose their desserts. "Rhubarb—and I want a slice of that chocolate cake we didn't get to eat at Mattie's engagement party, too."

"And for Monroe?"

Christine looked up into her younger sister's glowing face. "I have no idea."

"I say that any man who leaves before dessert should have to settle for whatever's left," Amos teased as he stood up. "But really, how could you choose the wrong pie for him? Monroe impresses me as a man who would enjoy whatever kind you gave him—and he'd be too polite to complain if he didn't."

"That's probably right," Christine murmured. There was a bit of an edge underlying Amos's remarks, but she didn't feel like challenging the preacher on his wedding day. "If you save back a piece of pecan and a piece of lemon meringue—and some of that chocolate cake—that should keep him from fainting away with hunger. *Denki* for thinking of us, Rosetta."

Her sister leaned down to hug her. "Anything for you, Christine. Go have a *gut* time."

Was it her imagination, or did everyone in the dining room watch her leave? Christine hurried through the kitchen and up the back stairway to her apartment to fetch her wraps. She buttoned her black coat and tied her black bonnet over her *kapp*, unable to stop smiling. Monroe's secret felt like such an adventure! Her apartment was on the back of the lodge, so before she went downstairs she stepped into Rosetta's apartment, because the large windows looked out over the snow-covered garden plots and Roman and Noah's new houses, as well as Amos's place—

Christine squealed. Monroe was leading his Clydesdale out of Amos's stable, and he'd hitched up the preacher's wonderful old sleigh!

She hurried down the back stairs and into the mudroom to put on her boots. Ruby and Beulah Kuhn turned from the oven, where they were removing more food, to smile at her.

"Looks like somebody's mighty excited," Ruby remarked.

"Who wouldn't be excited about Monroe Burkholder?" Beulah said with a laugh. "Why, for him, I'd almost join the Old Order Amish church and give up being a willful, opinionated *maidel*. Almost."

Christine laughed along with them as she pulled her boots over her shoes. The two sixty-something Mennonite sisters had livened up the days at Promise Lodge ever since they'd left their brother's home last summer to pursue life on their own terms. "The way Monroe raves about your cooking, Beulah, he'd probably take you up on your offer—"

"Almost!" Ruby teased, elbowing her older sister. "I

think you have first dibs, Christine. Go for it—and then tell us all the juicy details when you get back!"

"My ears are burning already," Beulah put in as she carried a blue enamel roaster to the worktable. "Must be something about this place that turns on the romance. Mattie's married Amos, and Rosetta's found Truman, and now you're catching Monroe's eye—not even two weeks after he came."

As Beulah opened the roaster, fragrant steam filled the kitchen with the aroma of another venison roast cooked with onions and vegetables. "You sisters should advertise Promise Lodge as a place for folks who're looking to get hitched," she added with a chuckle.

"Speak for yourself, sister," Ruby teased. She smoothed the white apron that covered her magenta and pink floral-patterned dress. "At my age, I don't have time to train a man. And what would I do with a husband if I had one?"

"I don't want to know," Beulah shot back. "If you'll bring in that big platter on the serving table, I'll put out this roast. The first one disappeared before I had a chance to eat any of it. These folks are tucking away a lot of food!"

Christine squeezed Beulah's shoulder as she passed through the kitchen. "*Denki* for such a wonderful meal, ladies. It made Amos and Mattie's day even more special."

She hurried through the lodge's lobby before anyone else could stop her to talk. When she opened the front door, Monroe was smiling at her from the sleigh he'd pulled up to the porch stairs. Queenie, Noah's Border collie, yipped and whirled in a circle a few feet away— until the bishop silenced her by pointing his finger. "Sorry, girl, this isn't your date," he said.

The black-and-white dog sat down in the snow, alertly watching the bishop and his huge horse.

Christine was impressed that Monroe had so quickly— and kindly—put Noah's dog in her place. The last thing she wanted was for Queenie to chase after the sleigh barking and calling attention to them. She inhaled the crisp January air. The early-afternoon sun made the snow-covered lawn sparkle—but it was nothing compared to the expression on the handsome bishop's face.

"Going my way?" he asked as he stepped over to help her down the stairs. "Amos was a real sport, letting me borrow this fine old sleigh. Never met a lady yet who didn't enjoy cuddling under the blankets and gliding over the snow."

Christine hoped her response would be rational. The way Monroe held her hand between his was wreaking havoc on her mind. She felt sixteen again, bedazzled by the chance to ride beside such a fetching man. "*Jah*, as I recall, Truman has given Rosetta a nice ride—and Roman Schwartz has driven Mary Kate Lehman around the grounds in it, as well."

When she'd settled on the cushioned seat and Monroe got in beside her, he held her gaze for a long moment. "Only one rule about this ride, Christine," he murmured. "What happens in the sleigh stays in the sleigh, all right?"

Her eyes widened. What on earth did he intend to do, if it had to remain such a secret?

Monroe tucked a couple of old quilts around them. "Geddap, Clyde," he said. The sleigh lurched, and then the enormous Clydesdale settled into an easy trot, making the harness bells jingle merrily as they turned onto the main road.

When he looked at Christine, his eyebrows rose. "Did I say something wrong? Or did I cross the line with my teasing?" he asked softly. "Truth be told, I'm feeling like a clueless kid taking his first girl home from a Singing."

Christine laughed—and relaxed. "I—I'm feeling the same way. I wasn't sure what you meant by—"

"Everyone at Promise Lodge doesn't have to know

every little thing you and I do or say, that's all." When he sighed, the white vapor of his breath flew back in the breeze. "We have your girls to consider, after all. I don't want to embarrass them, or make them think we're doing anything improper or—"

Christine laughed. "You've obviously never had daughters," she said. "Laura and Phoebe are polite enough not to let on, but I suspect they sometimes feel embarrassed by what their mother says and does just because younger generations do that. No matter what you and I do, they'll have their opinions. All of the young people—and even the kids—already have their ideas about us, Monroe."

"True enough. A bishop has a house like everybody else, but he really lives in a fishbowl."

Christine gazed out over the white lawns of Noah and Roman Schwartz's new homes. Beyond them, Rainbow Lake and the orchard looked especially pretty in the bright sunshine. She wondered what else she should say about Phoebe, who was twenty, and Laura, who was seventeen—but she wouldn't let on that her daughters already quizzed her and teased her about her very fast, very obvious relationship with Monroe.

"And speaking of bishops and young girls," Monroe said as they started up the hill, "what's the story about Mary Kate Lehman? I don't know Floyd well. He's surely different from when he was a healthy man, but I'm surprised he allowed his unmarried daughter to keep her baby."

Christine smiled as she recalled the day Floyd and Frances Lehman had come to Promise Lodge. "Floyd proclaimed himself our bishop the moment he arrived," she recounted. "My sisters and I were concerned that he would be no more considerate of women than our bishop in Coldstream had been—until Frances confided that he'd come to Promise Lodge so Mary Kate could have her baby without all the hullaballoo his church members out

East would raise. She was . . . overpowered by an English man who left her in the ditch down the road from their home."

"Oh, my," Monroe murmured. "She seems like a sweet girl. And she's a very attentive mother to baby David."

"Don't be surprised when Roman speaks to you about marrying the two of them. Gloria Lehman was in hot pursuit of him, but he only had eyes for Mary Kate—and he even helped her when she was birthing the baby."

Monroe's eyebrows shot up as he looked at Christine. "And Floyd allowed that? Was he somewhere else when this was going on?"

Christine smiled. She didn't feel nearly as shy while talking about other people's dramas. "He was home, but very disoriented from his fall. Frances and Minerva Kurtz, our midwife, saw the benefit of having Roman present while Mary Kate was struggling with her long labor," she explained. "As you can see, we're more liberal than a lot of Plain settlements. But we insist on propriety and we follow our bishop and preachers as we live lives that honor God."

Monroe considered her response as Clyde pulled them past Floyd and Lester Lehman's tall white houses. When he'd driven them beyond Preacher Marlin's home and barrel factory, he slowed the Clydesdale to a halt. "I've had some time to think this week while I've been staying at Lester's place," he murmured. "Amos showed me a map of the Promise Lodge property and pretty much told me I had to build on this end of the settlement. Any idea why he's being so distant with me? When he's around other folks, Amos seems easygoing and very personable."

Although her sisters had hinted about Amos's reservations concerning Monroe's unannounced arrival on Christmas Eve, Christine didn't want to ruin this wonderful moment talking about something she wasn't sure about— or anything potentially unpleasant. "You'll have to ask

Amos about that," she hedged. "Most of the property near the entrance to Promise Lodge has already been purchased, and now that the Helmuths will be building their nursery and greenhouses on plots along the county highway, this end of our settlement is all that's open."

Monroe's smile told Christine he sensed she wasn't telling him everything. "What if I wanted some property beyond the orchard and the lake—behind the Peterscheim place where Preacher Eli has built his forge?"

"Ah. The Peterscheim property butts up against Truman Wickey's land," she replied. "And the pasture behind the dairy barn is mine, where my Holsteins graze."

"Such a woman of means, you are, Christine," he said lightly. "To me, this is the most amazing thing about Promise Lodge—how you and your sisters purchased the abandoned church camp and started up your own businesses. Where I come from, Amish women don't do that!"

"Welcome to Promise Lodge," Christine teased. "It was an advantage we had as two widows and a *maidel*, who had no men remaining in our family to take us in—not that we wanted to be under a man's roof or rule, anyway. So Mattie operates a produce stand, Rosetta runs the lodge and rents apartments to other unattached Plain women, and I moved my dairy herd here. Roman manages it for me, so I don't do the milking or the mucking out anymore."

Monroe was gazing at her, following her every word. "Maybe you want no part of my attentions, then," he speculated—not that he sounded worried. "Seems to me you three sisters believe you can run your businesses—and your lives—without any male involvement. Makes me wonder what'll happen to Mattie's produce business now that she's married Preacher Amos."

Christine laughed. "Amos knew when he came here that we women intended to pursue our own paths and support ourselves. Constructing new houses and his sons-in-laws' greenhouses will keep him very busy this spring, while Mattie will be planting her crops. I predict their marriage will be more of an equal partnership than most Amish couples share."

"Meaning that Amos won't have the upper hand and make all the decisions?"

Christine shook her head, holding his gaze. "Consider yourself warned, Monroe," she said lightly, although she meant every word. "Don't think that as our new bishop, you can force us independent women to revert to the subservience most Old Order churches believe is the role women are born to. And we do *not* tolerate spousal abuse. Just saying."

Monroe's laughter filled the crisp air around them. He slipped his arm around Christine's shoulders and hugged her. "I don't think you could make your point any clearer, dear—although in most Amish colonies, you'd get a stern lecture from the bishop for saying such a thing. But tell me this." He paused, pondering his next words carefully. "If—*if*—you and I were to marry, would you become a stay-at-home wife and mother when our children started arriving?"

Christine inhaled sharply, easing out of his embrace so she could study his face. "I—I don't have an answer for that," she murmured, suddenly nervous. What if she said the wrong thing and Monroe wanted nothing more to do with her? "I believe we'd have to work that out between us. But tell *me* something, Bishop."

She sat up taller, willing herself not to flinch or burst into tears if he didn't say what she wanted to hear. It was awfully soon to be discussing such personal matters, but maybe it was better to have his answer now, before their hearts and lives became further entangled.

After several moments of silence, Monroe lowered his face until their noses nearly touched. "What's your question, Christine?" he whispered.

Christine swallowed hard. "What . . . what if there are
no babies? Maybe you should know that because of complications when Laura was born, I—I'm unable to have
any more children. So if you'd rather take up with someone else—"

"Christine. Christine," he murmured as he drew her into
his embrace. "I'm sorry. I didn't mean to embarrass—"

"I thought you should know now rather than later."

"I appreciate your honesty." With a sigh, Monroe
thumbed a tear from her cheek. "You've bared your soul,
so it's my turn. My wife, Linda, Lord bless her, wasn't able
to carry a baby to term," he said in a voice that had a hitch
in it. "When she passed, she was almost six months along
with our fourth child—we had such hope for a healthy
baby—but complications developed. She . . . she was so
determined not to lose the baby that she didn't tell me she
was bleeding. I didn't know I should've called the midwife
or rushed her to the hospital until it was too late."

Christine's heart shriveled. She knew how this story
ended, but it didn't make it any easier to hear. "I'm so
sorry, Monroe," she whispered.

He shook his head, as though to release the memories
that still plagued him. "When I got home from a meeting
with my preachers, Linda was unconscious on the kitchen
floor," he continued with a sigh. "She'd lost too much
blood. The paramedics—and the emergency room doctor—
couldn't save her. The chord was tight around the baby's
neck, so we lost her, as well."

Christine wound her arms around him and rested her
head on his shoulder. For several moments they sat in
silence, allowing Monroe's grief to subside. She felt bad
for him, but she still had to wonder if he would prefer to
court a woman who could give him the family he longed
for. It was a question she couldn't bear to ask.

With a sigh, Monroe placed his hand over hers and then

gently kissed her cheek. Christine shivered with a jolt of awareness. She wanted to continue this new relationship— did she dare call it *love* already?—but she didn't want to get her hopes up until he answered her question.

Monroe cleared his throat, resting his forehead against hers. "Maybe we should get out and walk around," he said hoarsely. "I had some other matters to discuss before we wandered into the topic of making babies—and on that note, I need to put some space between us before things get entirely out of hand. Even though I'd like that," he added with a chuckle. "Know what I'm saying?"

Christine's face prickled with heat, yet she felt like a desirable woman—the opposite of a lonely widow. "*Jah*, I think I do," she replied as she eased out of his arms to get out on her side of the sleigh. "You were talking about where you were going to buy your land and build your home and barns, as I recall—unless you've changed your mind about staying here as our bishop, knowing what an unruly bunch we Bender sisters are."

Monroe's laughter rang through the evergreens on this part of the property. He got out of the sleigh and gazed around. "Maybe Amos was doing me a favor, telling me to settle on this end," he murmured, shading his eyes with his hand. "What a view! If I put my house on this hill, I could see the lodge and the lake and everyone's homes—and my horses wouldn't be disturbed by incoming traffic."

Christine smiled. "You could be king of the hill," she teased. Then she turned to look at the woods behind them. "I've not been up here before, but I recall Mattie saying the county highway's on the other side of these woods. It forms the boundary of the property."

"And look over this way," Monroe said as he walked several feet to their right. "The trees are a natural barrier between the road and this valley below us. I'd have to do a lot of seeding and fencing to turn it into a good pasture—

but then, I might have to do that wherever I choose to buy land," he mused aloud.

Christine walked over to stand beside him, her eyes widening. "Oh my, I had no idea what this part of the property looked like. I bet it'll be beautiful this spring when all the trees get their leaves," she said, pointing ahead of them. "Can't you just imagine your Clydesdales grazing on this ground over here—with your barns on this side, and your house right here on this rise?"

"I can see everything just as you're describing it, sweetheart," he whispered as he slipped his arm around her shoulders. "It's the picture of horse farm heaven—and I'm hoping you'll be my angel in residence."

Christine's mouth dropped open. "Are you sure you want—even if we'll have no children to—"

Monroe punctuated her sentence with a soft kiss. "I want," he replied. His face was shaded by his wide-brimmed black hat, but his eyes shone warmly as he gazed at her.

When he pulled her close for a kiss that lingered on and on, Christine felt the world spinning around her—but rather than feeling disoriented or rushed, she had the sense that her life was coming together again. She hadn't kissed a man since her Willis had died when their barn burned down. She was suddenly aware of the void she'd been living in—and that Monroe was putting the past two years of emotional isolation behind her. When Christine slipped her arms around his neck, she reveled in how tall and sturdy and strong Monroe was, a fitting man to train the huge horses with which he made his living.

A man who knows me, yet wants me anyway.

With a sigh, she relaxed in his embrace and accepted delectable kisses as soft as butterfly wings.

"Two little lovebirds sitting in a tree," a familiar female voice called out behind them.

"K-I-S-S-I-N-G!" her male companion joined in.

With a sigh, Monroe straightened to his full height and allowed Christine to ease away from him. She knew her face was flushed and she probably appeared guilty—but at least it was Rosetta and Truman who had caught them kissing, instead of some of the kids. "Don't you two have anything better to do than follow us around?" she demanded playfully.

Truman chuckled. He was clasping Rosetta's gloved hand, appearing every bit as happy as Christine felt. "Sorry we interrupted you," he began, "but we have a pressing question to ask Bishop Monroe—"

"And Mattie's wedding seemed like a fitting time to discuss our situation, now that Monroe's been at Promise Lodge long enough to understand what he's getting into," Rosetta put in breezily.

"*Jah*, I understand that the women here are determined to do things their way," Monroe remarked. "But I'm happy to answer your question—and happy to be here. Christine and I have just decided where I'll build my house and the barns."

"Congratulations," Truman said, extending his hand. As Monroe shook with him, Christine said a quick prayer on behalf of her sister and the man she loved so much.

"Rosetta and I would like to get married," Truman began, "but my being Mennonite and her being a member of the Old Order Amish church has presented a problem, because her previous bishops haven't allowed intermarriage. How do you feel about that issue, Monroe?"

Monroe clasped his hands behind his back, considering his response. "The district I've come from in Illinois— near Macomb—is fairly conservative. If we were there, my answer would be an immediate, unquestionable no," he replied. He gazed from Rosetta to Truman. "Why do you feel compelled to defy the Amish religion and thereby place Rosetta's soul at risk, possibly denying her the eternal life God has promised to those who have come to Him through our Lord Jesus?"

Truman didn't blink. "Rosetta and I have discussed this often and prayed over it ever since we met. I believe the God you and I worship is bigger than any one religion," he replied firmly. "If I felt I'd be compromising Rosetta's soul by marrying her, I wouldn't be here with her now. I've offered to join your faith, if that's the only way we can marry."

"As for me," Rosetta said, "I can't believe that the God who created me in His image—with His love—would cast me into the fires of hell because I'm defying man-made rules about the way we should worship and believe in Him."

Monroe nodded. "Even though your response is awfully progressive for the Old Order, you've obviously considered your situation carefully. How do you and Mattie and the others feel about them getting married, Christine?" he asked, turning to her. "Do you anticipate a separation of your family if Rosetta marries a Mennonite? In my former district—and most districts I know of—there would be weeping, wailing, and gnashing of teeth, and the person who married outside the Old Order would be cast away as a lost soul."

Christine held his gaze. "If you think Mattie and I will refuse to associate with Rosetta because she marries Truman, you don't know us very well, Bishop."

After what seemed like an endless silence, Monroe cleared his throat. "Many things about Promise Lodge differ greatly from the faith I've practiced since I was young," he began, "but I came here for a fresh start like everyone else. If you two were young, clueless kids, I wouldn't marry you. But I believe your hearts are sincere in your love for God and for each other, so I'll be happy to officiate at your wedding—"

Christine's heart danced as Rosetta threw herself into Truman's arms and he held her tight.

"—but that's not to say we can allow people to come to Promise Lodge just because we'll let folks of different Plain faiths get married," Monroe continued firmly. "I also insist that the three preachers agree to let me perform your ceremony. If Amos, Eli, or Marlin disapprove, I won't override their objections."

"*Jah*, we understand that," Rosetta said as she swiped tears from her face. She hurried over to give Monroe a big hug. "But at least we're discussing the possibility of change. I appreciate the way you've listened to us instead of shutting us down."

"I'm a grateful, happy man," Truman put in as he shook Monroe's hand again. "We'll leave you two to take up where you left off."

When Monroe laughed, his dimples came out to play. "You know, all this decision making has me wondering if there's any pie left in the dining room. How about if you two hop in the backseat of the sleigh and we'll head over to the lodge to find out."

Rosetta smiled impishly at the bishop. "Matter of fact, Christine and I made sure you'd have a selection of desserts when you returned, Bishop Monroe," she said. "Seems to me we have something else to celebrate now, with pie and chocolate cake—"

"And maybe wedding cake, if Mattie and Amos have decided it's time to cut it," Christine said. She tucked her hand in the crook of Monroe's elbow. "We need to celebrate every *gut* and perfect gift God's brought our way lately. If we put our pasts behind us and focus forward, He'll show us the way He wants us to go."

"Couldn't have said that better myself," Monroe remarked as he helped her into the front seat. "Next thing

I know, the women here will be preaching sermons and reading Scripture in church, demanding to become preachers and deacons—or the bishop."

The four of them laughed loudly as Clyde made a wide turn and started down the snow-covered hill. "Nope," Christine said. "I'm happy to leave the leadership of this district to you and the preachers, Monroe."

"Glad to hear it."

Chapter Four

Monroe felt years younger as he pulled the sleigh up to the lodge to let Rosetta, Truman, and Christine go inside. It had taken something out of him to recount the details of Linda's passing, because only his closest friends in Macomb knew what had happened.

But now he felt free. His budding relationship with Christine wouldn't change what had happened in his past—and he would never forget Linda, just as Willis Hershberger would always be a part of Christine's life. But her empathy had unlocked a dark room in his heart so the sadness could drift away on the wings of angels.

As Monroe returned the sleigh to Amos's barn, he whistled under his breath. When he realized how light-hearted "You Are My Sunshine" made him feel, he thanked God for the wonderful hilltop experience he'd shared with Christine. The memory of her kiss warmed him all over again. Monroe had other important aspects of his life in Macomb to share with her, but they could wait. And he knew she would understand.

He jogged across the lawn and up the lodge stairs to the porch, energized by the crisp winter air and the dazzling beauty of the sunlit snow. When Monroe went inside, he stood in awe of the two-story lobby with its huge chandelier made of antlers and the stone fireplace that crackled with a cheerful fire. The dining room was still filled with guests who were talking and laughing, intending to spend the remainder of the day celebrating Amos and Mattie's wedding.

Monroe hung his long black coat on a crammed rack near the wall and placed his broad-brimmed black Stetson on top of the rack. He stood in the doorway for a moment, taking in the sound of friendly voices telling stories he would probably hear again as he became close to the folks in this district. Monroe looked forward to the day when he would be settled into his new home and established here as the shepherd of this lively, unpredictable flock.

When he spotted Amos and Mattie, he made his way between the crowded tables, smiling as folks greeted him and shook his hand. Rosetta was bringing out a tray of desserts and setting it on the *eck* table while Christine poured coffee into four mugs. The slices of pie and cake she'd chosen enticed him, but he had business he wanted to settle before he ate dessert.

"Decided you liked our company after all?" Amos teased him with a raised eyebrow. The preacher was a sturdy, compactly built fellow of fifty, with a trimmed beard that sported some silver. "Mattie and I wondered where you made off to—until we realized that the rest of the wedding party had disappeared, as well."

Monroe smiled. He still detected an edge to Preacher Amos's voice, so he put his best words forward. "I went to investigate the other end of the property—the section you told me was available," he clarified, smiling at Mattie. "And I have to thank you for saving the best parcel of land for me, Amos. Whenever you're ready, let's figure the boundaries and the acreage and I'll pay you in cash, so we're settled up."

Mattie's brow furrowed. "We still have several parcels of

land open, Monroe," she murmured with a questioning glance at her new husband. "Which area have you chosen?"

Amos shifted, holding Monroe's gaze. "I merely pointed him toward property at the far end of our holdings—"

"Land that would be harder for folks to build homes on because of the hills and valleys and woods," Truman pointed out as he and Rosetta joined the conversation. "But it would do for pastureland for his Clydesdales, after he puts down some fertilizer and seed. I'll conduct some soil tests so you'll know where you'll need to apply some lime, Monroe, and I'll be happy to do the seeding, as well," he added. "It's the least I can do for your consideration of our upcoming marriage."

Mattie's eyes widened. "Does this mean you're allowing them to marry, Bishop?" she asked excitedly.

"*Jah*, I am, if our preachers agree to it," Monroe replied, smiling at Truman and Rosetta. "After discussing their situation and their firm faith in God, I've agreed to perform their ceremony. But I don't believe interfaith marriage is right for every couple—especially for younger folks who might just be looking to jump the fence. We should establish our official policy about this when we meet next, don't you think, Amos?"

"We will," the preacher agreed. "And it would be a *gut* idea to get a clearer picture of *you* when we meet, as well, Bishop."

Monroe noticed Mattie, Rosetta, and Truman's puzzled expressions, and his gut tightened in anticipation. He'd figured on approaching this subject with Eli, Marlin, and Amos when they met, but he sensed Amos was pushing for answers now. "What would you like to know?" he asked.

The preacher stood straighter, as though he'd been

waiting for this opportunity. "You've been here more than a week, yet we've heard nothing of the community you were leading before you showed up here out of the blue on Christmas Eve."

Monroe heard more than one question embedded in Amos's remark, but he stuck with the most obvious. "I was the bishop in a district near Macomb, Illinois. We were outgrowing ourselves, far as how many families a bishop and two preachers can serve—and I'd reached a point where I felt a fresh start would be beneficial, after mourning my wife for nearly a year."

"So you up and left?" Amos asked with a frown. "If your district was splitting into two, those folks would be needing an additional bishop rather than wanting to let one go."

Monroe nodded, treading carefully. "We ordained our two preachers as new bishops," he explained. "Each district ordained two new preachers, with the understanding—their blessing—that I was moving on. It was all very amicable."

Mattie looked puzzled again. "Amos, are you having doubts about Monroe?" she asked quietly. "If that's the case, you should've asked your questions before—"

"Before Bishop Floyd proclaimed him our new leader?" Amos countered. He was speaking quietly, but the folks around them stopped talking to follow the conversation. "Everyone else seemed overjoyed that Burkholder showed up when he did, as though God had moved him into place just when we needed him. And *jah*, I'm glad he could marry us while Allen and my girls are here," he added, shrugging. "It just seems odd that he appeared without contacting us first—and on Christmas Eve, the holiest night of the year, when *most* folks are surrounded by family and friends to celebrate our Lord's birth."

Amos's suspicion whispered like the steps of a spider

spotting a fly in its web. Monroe had been astounded that he'd unknowingly arrived after Bishop Floyd had become incapacitated—and he'd expected a lot more questions from the folks at Promise Lodge. Troyer was apparently the only one who'd noticed the lack of details Monroe had offered, perhaps because he'd arrived while everyone was enjoying dessert after the scholars' Christmas Eve program.

"This looks like quite a serious discussion, considering we're at a wedding celebration. Our coffee and desserts are ready," Christine said as she joined their circle.

Monroe smiled at her, for she'd probably been another reason no one had asked him a lot of questions. The moment he'd set foot in the Promise Lodge lobby, Christine and her sisters had welcomed him and introduced him to everyone, obviously delighted that he'd come—and his flare of attraction to Christine had felt mutual.

"I'd intended to arrive a few days earlier," he said, returning his focus to Amos, "but I got waylaid by a buggy repair near Kirksville, and the snow slowed me down. Truth be told, I wasn't eager to spend another Christmas alone, because with my uncle and aunt and wife all gone—"

"You could've celebrated with members of your church," Amos interrupted.

Monroe prayed for patience. Troyer was splitting hairs now. "*Jah*, and I had several invitations," he said, "but everyone knew why I was leaving. They'd read the ads for Promise Lodge in the *Budget*, and we'd prayed over it, and they wished me well as I came to Missouri to see if this place would be a *gut* fit for me and my horse business." He paused, wondering what would convince Amos that he was sincere. "If it would make you feel better, you can contact Ralph Byler or Marion Yoder—the bishops who're leading the Macomb districts now. I'll give you their phone numbers—"

"No need for that, Bishop Monroe," Mattie said emphatically. She tucked her arm through Amos's. "This is a day for celebrating the wonderful-*gut* gifts God has bestowed upon us, and you are one of them. We're pleased you've chosen your home place—another reason to celebrate," she added as her sisters nodded their agreement. "You've got coffee and dessert waiting for you, and I see the Peterscheim boys eyeing your pie!"

Monroe pointed a teasing finger at Lavern and Johnny, laughing along with everyone—except for Amos, who merely gazed at Mattie. Monroe was more grateful to Mattie than she would ever know for bringing the discussion about his past and his motives to an end. For now.

If Amos called Ralph or Marion, they might mention another compelling reason that Monroe had left Macomb—which would inspire an even tougher inquisition from Amos.

Monroe decided to cross that bridge if he came to it. Christine's green eyes implored him to spend time with her, and Rosetta's smile beckoned him to join her and Truman for the dessert they'd delayed. There was a time and a place for everything, and he was ready to enjoy pie and the company of folks who accepted him for who he was.

"Wow, how am I supposed to choose from all these different kinds of pie? And chocolate cake, too?" he asked as he held out a chair for Christine. He was glad when Truman pulled chairs over to the other side of the table so he and Rosetta would be facing them.

"Pick what you'd like, and then I'll choose," Christine

suggested. "I suspect Truman and my sister have already had their dessert—"

"Not that I won't take another slice of pie," Truman said with a laugh. "I can tell you that Ruby's chocolate cake is fabulous. And you can't find a bad piece of any pie Beulah makes—and Rosetta made the lemon meringue, the apple, and the rhubarb pies."

Monroe folded his hands on the table. "You choose first, Christine," he murmured. "I suspect you made some of these pies, as well."

Her cheeks turned a delicate shade of pink as she took the slice of rhubarb pie and a piece of chocolate cake. "I made the pecan, the raisin, and the cherry pies. Rosetta and I were ecstatic that Amos and Mattie wanted their wedding so quickly, so we've been busy bees in the kitchen these past few days."

Monroe chose a slice of raisin pie and a slice of lemon meringue. "Doesn't get any better than this," he said as he picked up a fork. "I appreciate you ladies thinking to save back my favorite kinds." He smiled as Roman Schwartz and Mary Kate Lehman approached the table with baby David in a basket between them. "You kids can join us for pie, as well. Plenty here for everyone."

Roman was a tall, slender blond in his mid-twenties, Monroe was guessing. The tight expression on Mary Kate's pretty face told him they were interested in something more serious than dessert.

"We—we were hoping you'd agree to perform our wedding in a few weeks, Bishop Monroe," Roman said a little nervously. "Preacher Eli and Preacher Amos have already begun our premarriage counseling sessions—"

"I'll be delighted to marry you," Monroe said as he stood to shake Roman's hand. "When I heard the details of David's conception, I was pleased that the two of you have found each other and plan to become a family. Do you have a date in mind?"

Mary Kate looked up at Roman with a shy smile. "We were thinking about Thursday the twenty-sixth, but we've not done the traditional thing and had our wedding published at church, so maybe you'd rather we waited until—"

Monroe squeezed her shoulder and caressed David's plump cheek as he wiggled in his basket. "We can take care of that little detail right here and now," he said. He clanged a knife handle against a water glass until everyone in the room got quiet and turned expectantly toward their table.

"Folks, I have the pleasure of announcing that Roman Schwartz and Mary Kate Lehman will be married three weeks from today," Monroe said loudly. "I'm proud that this colony has provided a haven for Mary Kate and a place for her son to become a welcome member of the Promise Lodge community of faith."

Applause filled the dining room. As folks congratulated the young couple, Frances Lehman made her way through the crowd to stand beside Monroe. Tears made her soft brown eyes shine as she took his hand. "Oh, this is the best news, Bishop Monroe," she said with a hitch in her voice. "We're all so glad that Floyd immediately recognized you as the bishop Promise Lodge needed. I'm grateful to God that Mary Kate has found Roman and has a nice new house to share with him as they raise David together. He's a fine young man—"

"And my son couldn't have found a sweeter, more loving wife than your Mary Kate," Mattie insisted as she slipped her arm around Frances's shoulders. "It's all *gut*, Monroe. See what wondrous things God hath wrought by bringing you to us?"

As Monroe gazed at the mothers' smiles, and at the

young couple accepting congratulations, and at Rosetta and Truman—and Christine—he believed with all his heart that God had led him to Promise Lodge for a lot of wonderful reasons. He'd come here from Macomb to pursue his future, not just to leave his past behind, and it felt good to bask in the glow on these people's faces.

Chapter Five

Rosetta hugged Bernice and her twin, Barbara, as they all stood in the lobby of the lodge on Monday morning. "I'm so glad you and your hubbies and Allen came to visit your *dat*, and then stayed for his wedding," she said, smiling at Sam and Simon Helmuth. "Have a safe trip home. We'll look forward to seeing your houses and your nursery buildings being built when the weather's warmer."

Redheaded Sam—or was it Simon?—nodded happily as he put on his hat. "This worked out unbelievably well, Rosetta. When we called to tell my parents we were moving to Missouri, they were sad—"

"But in the next breath," his twin put in, "Dat said he'd provide a bunch of starter stock for our new nursery. He'll be putting a couple of our younger brothers in charge of the garden center we're leaving behind, so—truth be told—we've opened the door for those fellows to earn better livings."

Rosetta turned to Allen Troyer then. He appeared a little doubtful, but she hugged him anyway. "Your *dat* is so pleased that you'll be living here, too, Allen," she insisted. "*Gut* luck taking your licensing exams."

Allen buttoned his coat, smiling at his sisters. "We'll have lots of time during the ride home for the girls to play teacher," he remarked wryly. "Buddies from my plumbing and electricity classes mailed me some sample tests, so Barbara and Bernice will be sure all that information's drilled into my head. Nice to know I'll have work when I get here, too."

Christine came out of the kitchen and hugged the five young people, as well. "You'll all be able to stay in cabins while your homes are built," she reminded them. "If it's still chilly, we'll have space heaters for you."

Allen nodded. "I might be bunking in a cabin for quite a while, as I don't see the need for a house just yet."

Rosetta and her sister exchanged a knowing smile. "Something tells me Gloria Lehman would like to give you reason to build one," she teased.

With a roll of his eyes, Allen headed for the door. "Do *not* encourage that girl," he insisted. "I've told her again and again that I'm broke and in no hurry to join the church, but she doesn't seem to hear that."

Rosetta chuckled as the five young people went out onto the porch. She waved at the English lady driver who'd pulled her van up beside the lodge, and then she closed the door. "From what I could see during Amos and Mattie's wedding, Gloria's got her heart set on Allen," she said as Christine walked to the kitchen with her.

"Why wouldn't she?" Christine asked. "Allen's a handsome young man, and I suspect his rebellious attitude attracts the attention of a lot of girls."

"Now that Mary Kate's marrying Roman, I'm guessing Gloria feels like a hopeless *maidel* because she's five years older than her sister," Rosetta said as she opened the refrigerator.

"She's what—twenty-two?" Christine began pulling baking pans from the cupboard.

"*Jah*, or twenty-three," Rosetta mused aloud. "As I recall, you were married and had two little girls by the time you were that age. And Mattie had both of her boys in her early twenties. Gloria feels the clock ticking—and we don't have all that many eligible fellows here."

Christine placed a fist on her hip. "Only takes one man—the right man—and a certain gal I know didn't meet her perfect mate until she was thirty-seven," she pointed out. "So Gloria's not out of time yet—and congratulations again, Rosetta. I'm so glad Monroe has agreed that you and Truman can marry."

Rosetta raised her eyebrows as she opened a carton of eggs. "Why do I have a feeling I'm not the only Bender sister who might be tying the knot soon? You and Monroe seem pretty chummy. Downright kissy."

"Puh! I've seen you and Truman kissing plenty of times," Christine shot back. "Our parents would've been lecturing us about such public displays," she added with a wry smile, "but I have to admit that it feels *gut* to have a man hold me again. A lot of bishops would be sterner—more inclined to follow the old conservative ways that favor the men—but Monroe has an open mind. I like that about him."

Rosetta laughed. "You like a lot of things about him, sister. What did you two talk about up there on the hill?"

Christine poured a bag of cranberries into a saucepan and added a box of chopped dates and water. "None of your beeswax," she teased. "But I'm looking forward to seeing big red barns and Clydesdales grazing in Monroe's pastures. Amos might not realize it, but from up on that hill, the bishop will be able to watch over almost our whole community. I still don't understand why Amos has such a chip on his shoulder about Monroe."

"Me, neither. I'm guessing Mattie will set him straight pretty soon, or tell him to settle things with Monroe."

Rosetta measured brown sugar and shortening into a mixing bowl and began creaming them with her hand-cranked mixer. "Feels kind of odd when I walk past Mattie's empty apartment upstairs."

"*Jah*, it sure does." Christine stirred her fruit mixture until it was thick, then took her pan off the stove. "Have you figured out what'll happen with the apartments after you marry Truman? I'm assuming you'll move into his house then."

Butterflies fluttered in Rosetta's stomach as she added more ingredients to her cookie dough. "We'll be discussing that soon," she replied softly. "And although I like Truman's *mamm* just fine, it'll feel strange to live in Irene's house. When I took her home from our picnic last fall, I got the impression that she's crammed a lot of furniture into the house. And sharing a room with a man—now *that* will take some getting used to!"

"All the more reason for you to stay here at the lodge!" Beulah called out as she came down the back stairway. "Why, if you and Christine get hitched and move out, Ruby and I will be rolling around this place like two peas in a shoe box."

"Whatcha cookin'?" Ruby chimed in as she took her apron from a wall peg.

Rosetta smiled at the two Kuhn sisters. Beulah was wearing a red plaid dress, and Ruby's dress of bright pink and green stripes made her look younger than the age to which she admitted. "Would you believe we've gone through all those bars and goodies we baked for Mattie's wedding?" she remarked. "I'm mixing up a double batch of chocolate chip cookies—"

"And I'm making cranberry-date bars," Christine added. "With all the fruit and oatmeal in them, we can almost call them health food."

Beulah peered into the bowl as Christine drizzled

melted butter over the ingredients for the bars' crust. "Sure glad to see that butter going into them," she teased. "At my age, I've decided to go for the *gut* stuff."

"*Jah*," Ruby agreed as she pulled more mixing bowls from the cabinet. "Beulah and I have a pact to die happy rather than skinny. Life's short, so we prefer to eat dessert first!"

"We've got Roman and Mary Kate tying the knot later this month, so I'm all for baking the bars and pies for their wedding dinner now. That way we can focus on the main meal a few days before the ceremony." Beulah surveyed the baking staples in the pantry and then opened the main freezer. "Might be a *gut* idea to make a trip to town after lunch," she remarked. "We can stock up on chicken and all the fixings for that wedding meal—just in case a snow-storm keeps us from shopping later in the week."

Rosetta began to spoon dollops of dough onto a cookie sheet. "We should ask Mary Kate and Roman if they have any favorite dishes they want for their wedding dinner. And while we're shopping, we could load up on baking supplies and canned goods—and even meat—as a nice wedding gift for them."

"Or here's another thought," Christine said, spreading the cranberry date filling over its crust. "We could stop at the butcher shop in Forest Grove and order a quarter of beef and half a hog for their freezer."

"That's a better idea! Count me in on that, and we'll ask Mattie about it, too," said Rosetta. She put two sheets of cookies into the oven, smiling as the Kuhn sisters began gathering ingredients so they could start baking, as well.

"Ruby and I will give them a certificate *gut* for a year's supply of cheese from our factory," Beulah said as she measured flour into a large bowl.

"And honey, too," Ruby added happily. "I'll set a few big jars back for them—a gift from my little bees, even though they're wintering in their hives now. Come spring, I bet they'll be glad to have so many apple trees to pollinate—thanks to your Truman, for the way he cleared out the underbrush and pruned the trees."

Rosetta's cheeks prickled with warmth. She wasn't yet used to folks considering him *her* Truman, but it had a nice ring to it. "And what would we have done without his help and heavy equipment, taking down dead trees and laying out the road after we moved here?"

"I knew from the first moment we met you and Truman—that night last summer when we arrived with our suitcases," Ruby recalled with a smile, "that you two were meant for each other. I'm so glad your new bishop has agreed to marry the two of you—"

"And happy that Monroe's taken such a shine to Christine, too!" Beulah put in. "It's a lot more fun to plan these parties for you lovebird couples than to think about getting hitched myself. I'd rather make a dozen pies before breakfast every morning than pick up after a man and tolerate his rules and moods."

"Amen, sister!" Ruby chimed in. "But it's *gut* that so many folks are pairing up and having families, or Promise Lodge would turn into an old folks' home."

Rosetta and Christine laughed. Soon Christine's daughters joined them and the kitchen smelled like warm chocolate and cherries. Phoebe and Laura prepared fruit fillings for the piecrusts Beulah was rolling out, and by noon eight warm pies were cooling on the counter, and Ruby had baked the heart-shaped layers for Roman and Mary Kate's tiered wedding cake, as well.

Rosetta smiled at the results of their morning's work as she plucked a chocolate chip cookie from the plate they shared with some of Christine's cranberry-date bars. "Many hands make light work, ladies," she said as she passed the plate around. "I'm ready for a quick sandwich and a trip to Forest Grove."

"*Jah*, let's do it!" Beulah closed her eyes over the rich sweetness of cranberry-date filling and oatmeal crust, her face creased with thought. "But if the six of us crowd into a big buggy, where will we put our groceries?"

"I want to get some yarn at Nina's Fabrics," Laura said eagerly.

"And I'll buy some material to make a quilt for Roman and Mary Kate's wedding present," Phoebe put in. "We can all work on it these next couple of weeks."

Christine's face lit up. "Monroe's big rig has a hitch on the back—"

"And we've got your wagon in the barn," Rosetta put in. "I say we feed the bishop and ask him to drive us into town. He can help us load our supplies into the wagon and then carry them in for us, too. How can he resist a shopping trip with six charming women like us?"

When Monroe clucked at Clyde, the buggy and wagon rolled along the snow-packed road toward the county highway. Although he'd been jotting plans for moving his Clydesdales and equipment from Illinois and hadn't planned on leaving the house, he was happy to drive Christine and the other ladies into town. The afternoon sunshine made the snow-covered hills and trees sparkle, and the laughter in his double-sized rig lifted his spirits. Christine's girls and the Kuhns were seated in the back, discussing plans for their crochet club and Roman Schwartz's upcoming wedding. With Rosetta and Christine sharing the front seat, the tight fit meant that Christine was seated slightly forward to allow room for everyone's shoulders, with her hip pressed firmly against his thigh.

Even in her heavy black coat and matching bonnet, she

enticed him. To keep his thoughts from wandering into dangerously delectable territory, Monroe glanced at Rosetta. "Do you suppose Truman would be willing to help me transport my Clydesdales here after my barns are built?" he asked. "I know where I can get some big stock trailers, but my friends in Illinois don't drive trucks."

Rosetta's face lit up at the mention of her fiancé's name. "Truman's got three big trucks he uses for his landscaping business," she replied. "If you can move your Clydesdales before spring, when his crew goes back to full-time work, he could probably supply two other drivers to help you, as well."

Monroe's eyes widened. If he had that many drivers, he could probably get his horses, equipment, and household furnishings moved in one trip. "What do his employees do during the winter? I can't imagine Truman paying men for the months they're not able to do any landscaping."

"Ah, but they have snow removal work for the businesses in Forest Grove and a couple other towns," Christine said. "Those big trucks have blades on them now. It didn't take Truman but an hour to clear our road and the paths to our barns after that last big snowstorm."

Monroe nodded. The more he heard about Truman Wickey, the happier he was to have the Mennonite living next door to Promise Lodge. "I'll have a chat with him. If he'd be willing to help with my move, my plans to relocate would be a lot simpler than hiring English drivers."

After he parked beside the Forest Grove Mercantile, he helped all the women from the buggy. They agreed to complete their shopping in about an hour and a half, and then hurried across the street toward the grocery store and the fabric shop. Monroe chuckled at the way they nattered about what they were going to buy. In their winter wraps, they reminded him of a flock of chattering crows—but he knew better than to tell them that.

Monroe ambled across the parking lot toward the mercantile's lumber store to discuss the building materials he'd need for his barns, his house, and his pasture fence. Last week he'd called the Illinois carpenter who'd constructed his uncle's barns, and he'd received the basic drawings and dimensions in the mail, along with a list of supplies so Amos, Marlin, and the other men could duplicate those facilities for him here. He'd studied the house he was renting until Floyd Lehman's brother, Lester, returned to Promise Lodge, and he was impressed with its solid construction and craftsmanship.

As he imagined two large red barns in the pasture, set off by a white plank fence, and the pretty brunette with whom he hoped to share his new home, he felt warm all over. His decision to move to Missouri had been made on impulse, yet it was clear that God had given him the go-ahead to move to Promise Lodge when he'd read Rosetta's ad in the *Budget*.

After Monroe ordered lumber for the house and pasture fence, metal roofing for his barns, and the other supplies he would soon need, he drove the wagon across the street. The women were checking out of the grocery store, with Laura and Phoebe to help wheel their loaded carts out to the curb. Their fifty-pound bags of flour, boxes of other baking staples, canned goods, and sewing supplies filled half of the wagon, and they all thanked Monroe repeatedly for his help.

He smiled at Christine as the other women climbed into the buggy. "Do I dare hope to be invited in for a piece of one of those pies I saw at lunch?" he asked. "They should be cool enough to eat by now, right?"

Her smile did crazy things to his insides. "You'll have to ask Beulah," she teased. "She's freezing those pies to serve at Roman and Mary Kate's wedding. But even if she says no, I'd be happy if you'd come for supper—nothing fancy, understand, but we'll concoct something you won't mind eating."

Monroe laughed at her understatement. Sitting across the supper table from Christine—even with the other ladies present—promised to be a fulfilling end to his day . . . a foretaste of the contentment and joy he hoped would be his for years to come.

Chapter Six

The day before Roman and Mary Kate's wedding, Christine, Rosetta, and Mattie were making bread while the Kuhn sisters prepared a large bin of the calico slaw the bride had requested. In the dining room, Laura and Phoebe were draping long white cloths over the tables, getting ready to set out the plates and silverware, while in the meeting room, Preacher Amos, Bishop Monroe, and Truman set up the new pew benches Amos and Eli had built the previous week. The aroma of seasoned chicken and warm yeast filled the large kitchen—and made Christine's stomach rumble loudly.

Rosetta chuckled as she placed dough into six bread pans that were held together by a metal plank. "Time for a snack?" she teased her sister. "With all the *gut* smells surrounding us, it's a wonder all of our tummies aren't grumbling."

Christine pinched the seam on the bottom of the honey whole wheat loaf she'd shaped. "The egg muffins I ate this morning are gone," she remarked. "But I hope you make those again, Mattie. They were really cheesy and *gut*."

Mattie smiled at her two younger sisters. "I like that recipe because you can make a dozen or two at once, ahead of time, and warm them the next day," she said. "They must've been a hit with Amos and Monroe, too, considering how they're all gone."

"And because we've got chickens to supply our eggs, and cheese from the Kuhns' factory," Christine pointed out as she filled another pan with dough, "they don't cost us much to make."

Beulah took a big pot of boiled chicken off the stove. "After lunch, let's cut our day-old bread into cubes for stuffing. The meal will be a lot easier to finish tomorrow morning if we have the chicken and stuffing already mixed in the pans. I really appreciate you sisters giving us so much help."

"And it's *gut* to have you with us today, Mattie," Christine said as she placed her bread pans in the hot oven. "We've missed having you around since you hitched up with Amos."

"But we can't help enjoying that rosy-cheeked happiness that's lit up your face," Rosetta remarked. "Marriage agrees with you, I think."

Mattie's face turned pinker. "Well, it's *different*, cooking three meals a day and keeping up the house without all of you ladies to help," she admitted softly. "But compared to what I endured while Marvin was going downhill with his diabetes, living with Amos is heaven on earth. He's gentle and kind—"

"And he's crazy about you," Rosetta added happily. She was pleased to have her eldest sister put memories of Marvin's abuse behind her, knowing Mattie was much better off in her second marriage.

"*Jah*, it's a real pleasure to see Amos all healed from his accident, hale and hearty—and happy—again," Christine said. "You two are an inspiration to us all, Mrs. Troyer. Examples of how God's love and a fresh start can totally change lives."

"Hello?" someone called from the lobby. "Okay if I come in?"

"Hi, there!" Phoebe replied from the dining room. "We're so busy getting ready for a wedding, we didn't hear you come in."

Christine brushed her floury hands on her apron as she passed between the tables in the dining room. She smiled at the attractive young blonde who was removing her black bonnet. "How can we help you?" she asked. "I'm Christine Hershberger—and these are my girls, Phoebe and Laura. If you're looking to rent an apartment here, my sister Rosetta's in charge of that."

The young woman gazed around the large dining room at the tables draped in white tablecloths. "Wow," she murmured. "Looks like you're having quite a party. Do—do you need dinner rolls or pies, by any chance?" she asked as she picked up the covered basket she'd set on the floor.

Christine smiled, waving her toward the kitchen. "We've been baking our breads this morning, and our pies are all made, *denki*. But do come in! Let me hang your coat so we don't get flour on it."

As she draped the young woman's heavy black wrap over a peg near the kitchen door, Christine figured their visitor was about Phoebe's age, and Mennonite. She wore a calf-length cape dress of blue tweed, and her circular white *kapp* covered only the bun she wore high on her crown. She was slim and very pretty, with big blue eyes that sparkled in a flawless face.

"These are the gals who're making the lodge smell so wonderful-*gut*," Christine began, gesturing to each woman in turn. "Beulah and Ruby Kuhn rent apartments upstairs, and these are my sisters, Rosetta and Mattie."

"I'm Maria Zehr, from Cloverdale—a few miles up the road that runs past your entry," their guest said. She set her basket on the worktable as she looked around. "Now *this* is a kitchen!"

"Promise Lodge used to be a church camp, so dozens of kids at a time were fed here," Rosetta explained. "We've converted several of the rooms upstairs into apartments. If you're interested, I'll take you up to look around."

Maria's smile expressed excitement mingled with hesitation. "*Jah*, I recall when this place was hopping with all manner of campers, back when I was a kid," she murmured. "I'm glad you've brought the place to life again, and—and I'm wondering if I can relocate my bakery to Promise Lodge and live here. I think my business would be a lot more profitable here, because of all the businesses you Plain folks have started up."

"A bakery?" Rosetta murmured, her eyes alight with interest. "We have a cheese factory, a dairy, a barrel factory, and a produce stand—and we'll soon have a nursery and a garden center and stables of Clydesdales," she added. "I'll have to say, however, that our menfolk will be building three houses and the garden center and barns before they'll have time to construct a bakery building—"

"Oh, I have a small building," Maria interrupted excitedly, "and it sits on a concrete slab. I've talked with guys who can load it onto a big flatbed, so all the walls and the roof will remain sturdy while they drive it down the road and place it on a new slab."

"Oh my, that'll be something to see," Mattie said as she wiped her hands on a towel. "So you're probably just wanting to buy enough property for your bakery building? And you'll live in an apartment?"

"Well . . ." Maria's face clouded over. "Once I pay to move the building, I'm not sure I'll be able to afford any property—but I'd pay rent for some," she added. "Maybe we could roll my apartment and property rents into one payment each month?"

Christine exchanged glances with her two sisters. "That's probably a workable idea. We'll have to figure out where to put your building and what to charge for—"

"Can I put it next to that little building by the barn?" Maria pointed out the kitchen window. "Seems to me that folks coming to that place will quite likely shop at mine, as well."

"That's our cheese factory," Ruby said. "Business is really slow now that winter's set in, but this spring—when the produce stand opens—we'll have more customers."

The sound of male voices came from the dining room. "Say, what's a man got to do to get something to eat around here?" Monroe teased.

"Smells like there ought to be chicken and fresh bread we could stuff into our faces," Amos joined in. "Nothing like setting up pew benches to work up an appetite."

Christine turned as the men entered the kitchen. "*Gut* news," she said. "This is Maria Zehr, and she wants to move here with her bakery—and she's already got a building. Maria, this is our bishop, Monroe Burkholder, and one of our preachers, Amos Troyer—"

"And what a nice surprise to see *you*, Maria," Truman said as he came in behind Amos. "So you think your bakery will do better at Promise Lodge? From what I've seen these past several months, that might be an accurate assessment—but it'll take a while to build up your business here," he pointed out. "I doubt folks from Cloverdale will come so far to buy your doughnuts and Danish."

He slipped his arm around Maria's shoulders and gave her a loose hug. "Maria goes to our Mennonite church in Cloverdale," he explained to everyone. "She's a hard worker. Supports herself and her younger sister on what she earns in her bakery."

Maria hugged Truman's waist with an enthusiastic smile. "You probably haven't heard that Lizzie's going to live with our older sister Malinda and her family—to help look after the kids and tend the housework," she added with a sigh. "Malinda's multiple sclerosis is getting worse."

"I'm sorry to hear that," Truman murmured. "So what'll happen to your house? You've lived there since you were born."

Maria nodded. "A family from our church—the Slabaughs—are interested in renting it. I'm hoping their monthly check will float me until I reopen my bakery."

"So the rest of your family—and your parents—are gone?" Bishop Monroe was looking Maria over, smiling his encouragement.

"I'm the youngest of seventeen," Maria explained proudly. "My folks passed a few years ago, and my older siblings are all married—most of them scattered around Missouri and Iowa. It's just been Lizzie and me for the past couple of years."

Amos nodded. "I can see why you'd want to live where you wouldn't be by yourself all the time," he said. "You'd be in *gut* company with Christine and her girls, and Rosetta and the Kuhns. Promise Lodge is all about making a fresh start."

Maria's smile widened. She slipped out from under Truman's arm and unfolded the tea towel in her basket before offering it to Monroe. "Speaking of fresh," she said, "I brought some of the pastries I made early this morning. Try an apple fritter, or a—"

"The jelly doughnut's mine!" the bishop exclaimed, grabbing it.

"And I see a cream cheese Danish," Amos said as he stuck his hand into the basket.

Truman peered eagerly at the selection. "Oh, here's a glazed chocolate cake doughnut with my name on it." He handed the basket to Christine. "Maria provides the goodies for coffee fellowship after our church services, so I've probably tried everything she bakes. Haven't found one yet that I didn't like."

Christine chose the apple fritter. "It's a real treat to eat goodies somebody else made," she said as she passed the basket to Rosetta.

"Maria, you've got my vote," Monroe said after he licked jelly and frosting from his fingers. "Say the word, and we'll help you get settled in—get us the measurements and we'll pour the concrete slab for your bakery as soon as we get a warm spell."

"I can get those dimensions for you," Truman said, "and I'll include the placements for the gas, water, and electricity, too."

"You've got my vote, too," Amos said with a satisfied smile. "Why not go upstairs with Rosetta and choose your rooms? If you want some walls painted, or any sort of renovation to join the rooms into one apartment, we can get that done for you now, because it's inside work."

Maria's eyes sparkled. "What a wonderful welcome," she said. "I'd love to have a look around upstairs."

Rosetta had crossed the kitchen and was opening one of the ovens. "Mattie, how about you or Christine showing her around? We've got bread that needs watching."

"Come with me, Maria," Mattie said, gesturing toward the dining room. "There's a back staircase, but I'll give you the tour of the lodge on our way upstairs. Maybe you'll want the apartment I just moved out of. I married Amos and moved into his house, you see."

As Mattie and Maria left the kitchen, each of the men took another pastry and followed them out. Ruby and Beulah began lifting cooked chicken pieces from the big pot with slotted spoons. "Wouldn't that be something, to have a bakery here?" Ruby said. "I really like to bake, but I've never been one to fuss over doughnuts."

"I think Maria will do pretty well, come spring—and

we have some girls who might want to work for her, too,"
Beulah speculated. "But we'd probably run up quite a bill
for baked goods, considering we'd have to pay her for what
we ate."

"Hmm. Maybe Monroe and Amos will ask Rosetta to
work out an arrangement that might go toward Maria's rent
payment," Ruby teased.

Christine chuckled at this suggestion as she began
mixing the ingredients for another batch of bread. When
she realized her younger sister was no longer checking the
ovens, she walked over to look into the mudroom. She
watched Rosetta turning the bars of goat's milk soap she'd
made the day before so they would dry properly. Rosetta
was blinking rapidly, and her expression could've curdled
milk.

"Hey, there," Christine murmured as she joined her
sister at the small table. "You look like you bit into a lemon,
sweetie. What's wrong?"

Rosetta looked away, angrily wiping her face with her
apron. "You didn't see how *chummy* Maria and Truman
were?" she demanded in a quavering voice. "For all we
know, she's really moving to Promise Lodge to be closer to
him—now that she's *all alone*. And he looked more than
happy to see her."

Christine's eyes widened as she slipped an arm around
her sister's shoulders. "That's not the impression I got," she
remarked. "Truman was merely being friendly, encouraging someone from his church, the way I saw it. And besides
that, why would he be interested in Maria when he's so
crazy in love with you?"

Rosetta inhaled deeply to settle herself. "Is he?" she
whispered. "Did you see the way Amos and Monroe prac-
tically fell all over themselves to make her welcome? And
the way Maria batted her lashes and widened those baby
blues at them?"

Christine considered this. During the years Rosetta had
lived at the home place, she'd never hinted at any regrets
or let on about how she'd sacrificed courting and marrying
while she'd cared for their aging parents. She hadn't
appeared angry or depressed when her friends had introduced their beaus and fiancés, either. Yet in a matter of
minutes and the passing of a basket, Maria Zehr had stirred
up a major case of envy—and Rosetta was conjuring up a
worst-case scenario simply because Truman had hugged
their pretty young visitor. "Is that why you didn't take
Maria upstairs?"

Rosetta arranged the bars of cream-colored soap in precise rows on the drying screen, her movements stiff and
exaggerated. "I might've scratched her eyes out," she
replied brusquely. "I have a feeling our apple cart's about
to be upended here at the lodge apartments. I can't imagine what it'll be like to have beautiful blond Maria living
upstairs with us, Christine. But I obviously have no say
about it, because Amos and the bishop have already
declared her welcome."

Christine sighed. What could she say to console
Rosetta, to soothe her frayed nerves and convince her that
her assumptions about young Maria were unfounded?

*Probably nothing. Rosetta's so upset right now she can't
see straight, let alone see reason.*

"Tell you what," Christine said softly. "I'll pay special
attention to Maria's comings and goings once she moves
upstairs with us—and Ruby and Beulah will be watching
and listening, as well. But meanwhile, she'll be going back
to Cloverdale and you'll have a chance to talk things out
with Truman," she reasoned. "I bet he has no idea how he
and Maria have upset you. He *loves* you, Rosetta. He's
made no secret of that since the moment he met you."

Rosetta appeared doubtful, but at least she stopped
crying. "He's a guy. He's known her for years. He'll deny

he has any feelings for her," she said with a sigh. "And if he knows I've been crying, he'll think I'm a big baby. Please don't tell him."

"My lips are sealed, and I'm on your side, little sister," Christine murmured. "But please talk with him—sooner rather than later. This is the sort of molehill that can grow into a mountain and get blown way out of proportion, unless you deal with your feelings right away."

Rosetta nodded and finished lining up her bars of soap.

Christine returned to the kitchen, sensing her sisterly advice had gone in one of Rosetta's vulnerable ears and out the other. Perhaps she should talk to Truman herself, or to Monroe, if Rosetta continued to fret about the presence of their new renter.

Or maybe it's best if I leave this situation in Your hands, dear Lord, she prayed as she resumed her bread making. *Only You know what's in our hearts and minds—and whether our problems are real or imagined.*

Chapter Seven

As Christine sat on one of the new pew benches between Mattie and Rosetta Thursday morning, her heart over-flowed with happiness. Mattie's son Roman stood in front of Bishop Monroe, appearing uncharacteristically nervous and solemn as he waited to exchange wedding vows with Mary Kate Lehman. Mary Kate was trembling, yet she held steadfastly to Roman's elbow, determined to say and do everything just right on her wedding day.

Christine recalled how her own knees had shaken as she'd stood before the bishop with Willis Hershberger half her lifetime ago. It occurred to her how very *young* she'd been, at twenty—and how blissfully unaware of the challenges, fears, and disappointments that would come after she'd pledged to be his wife until death parted them. Although she still had the occasional night-mare about the burning barn collapsing on Willis, Christine had felt great hope when she and her sisters had bought the Promise Lodge property. Who could've guessed how their lives would improve as they'd witnessed first Noah's wedding to Deborah Peterscheim, and then Mattie marry-ing Amos at long last, and now Roman's ceremony?

Beside Christine, Mattie dabbed her eyes. She looked

radiant, crying happy tears for her son—and perhaps recalling her own wedding to Amos three weeks ago. Christine squeezed her hand, relishing Mattie's squeeze in return. She slipped her arms around both of her sisters, rejoicing in the life they now shared because they'd had the gumption to make a major change. They were surrounded by the women in the Peterscheim, Kurtz, and Lehman families, along with Ruby and Beulah Kuhn and the friends who'd come from Coldstream to mark this special occasion. Who could ask for more?

Butterflies fluttered in Christine's stomach as Bishop Monroe continued his stirring remarks.

"I'm particularly pleased to be marrying these two fine young people," he said in a resonant voice that filled the large meeting room. "Roman and Mary Kate stand as an example to us all of the true meaning of love, as the apostle Paul described it in his letter to the Corinthians. They personify patience and kindness. Their relationship is strong enough to bear and believe all things, to hope and endure all things that come along as they raise little David and expand their family. I believe God has wonderful blessings in store for them."

Christine's heart fluttered as Monroe gazed briefly at her before continuing. How blessed they were that this stalwart man of faith had appeared just when they'd been losing Bishop Floyd to complications following his stroke. Monroe had paid for his property in full now, and he would transport his Clydesdales from Illinois as soon as his barns were ready for them. He was such an inspiration, so upbeat and positive about their faith and their future at Promise Lodge. Christine smiled, eagerly anticipating the day when she and Monroe would be saying their own wedding vows.

Outside the lodge, on the far side of the building, Queenie barked. Noah's Border collie was an energetic watchdog—but she might be barking at Christine's dairy cows or at Rosetta's goats, or just because she was tired of being by herself while everyone was inside. Christine shifted on the pew bench, focusing again on Monroe's remarks as he prepared to lead Roman and Mary Kate in their vows.

"I commend Roman for the way he's been helping the Lehman family with outdoor chores, and for his ability to see beyond Mary Kate's circumstances and love little David as his own son," the bishop said earnestly. "And I greatly admire the Lehmans for coming here to Promise Lodge rather than expecting Mary Kate to give up her baby for adoption. I predict a healthy, positive future for— for—"

Christine sat up straighter. Monroe had choked on his words and turned pale, his expression registering shock and something else she couldn't define as he gaped toward the back of the meeting room. The men were peering toward the doorway, too. Christine turned with the other women to see what had made the bishop falter as though a ghost had grabbed him by the throat.

A young woman Christine had never seen stood at the back of the room on the women's side. She had obviously come inside despite Queenie's barking, and had hung up her wraps in the lobby without anyone hearing her. In her brown cape dress, with her brown hair pulled up under her *kapp*, she resembled scores of girls who lived in every Old Order community Christine had ever visited.

But this girl was gazing at Monroe with great love— and possessive triumph—shining in her eyes. She seemed oblivious to the fact that she'd interrupted a sacred ceremony. For several more moments she stood, holding the bishop's attention until he cleared his throat and focused on the bride and groom again.

"And now, Roman and Mary Kate," Monroe continued, "you shall repeat these vows after me. I, Mary Kate—"

"I, Mary Kate," the bride said as she gazed at Roman.

Christine glanced back at their unexpected guest, who'd taken a seat a few rows behind the other women. Who was she? Why had she shown up without calling or writing first? And why had her presence unnerved Monroe so much? He was leading Mary Kate and Roman in vows that had remained the same for decades and generations, but his voice had lost the exultant ring Christine admired whenever he was preaching. For the first time since she'd met Monroe, he seemed to be struggling.

Mattie nudged Christine with her elbow, frowning. "Who is that girl?" she whispered.

Christine shrugged, shaking her head.

With an impatient sigh, Mattie turned her attention back to her son and his bride. The women around them shifted, their aprons whispering against their dresses, all of them surely wondering the same thing. The men across the room were still stealing glances at the newcomer. On the preachers' bench behind Monroe, Amos, Eli, and Marlin appeared puzzled, too. They didn't whisper among themselves, but their bearded faces expressed a doubt that went far beyond curiosity.

Monroe had barely finished pronouncing Roman and Mary Kate husband and wife before a compelling female voice filled the room.

"I'm here to make you an honest man, Monroe Burkholder," the stranger announced boldly.

Gasps filled the room as Christine and the others stood up for a better look at their visitor. What could she mean?

"While you were still married, counseling me as I prepared to be baptized into the Old Order, you *ruined* me so that nobody else will have me—and no one else will satisfy me. You can run, but you can't hide anymore."

In the awkward silence that followed, Roman and Mary Kate stood staring from the front of the room, where they'd been prepared to accept congratulations—except this outspoken young woman had stolen their thunder.

Monroe froze, pressing his lips into a tight line as he considered his response. "My friends, this is Leola Duff, and she comes from my former community of Macomb, Illinois," he finally said. "I believe dinner will soon be served, so please go in and enjoy yourselves as we celebrate Mary Kate and Roman's big day."

Mattie scowled. "This is unthinkable. Just plain rude," she muttered. "What on earth does Leola think she's doing, accusing Monroe of ruining her? Why, she can't be half his age!"

"I have no idea, but I suspect we'll hear more than we care to by day's end," Christine said. Her insides tightened as Leola made her way toward the bishop, beaming at him. Christine had the overpowering urge to eavesdrop on the conversation between Monroe and his unexpected guest.

As the bride and groom hurried toward the heavenly aromas drifting from the dining room, the other folks followed them, murmuring as they glanced suspiciously at Leola. Amos stepped up to accompany Mattie as she, Christine, and Rosetta reached the aisle.

"Well, we all knew Burkholder had something to hide, arriving unannounced and not fully answering our questions," the preacher said ominously. "And here she is."

As Christine followed the others to the dining room, she glanced behind her in time to see Leola standing on tiptoe to kiss Monroe's cheek. Monroe appeared flummoxed as he took the young woman by the arm to steer her to a private place, away from prying eyes.

What if they do a lot more than talk? Christine's thoughts whirled like a funnel cloud. *What if Monroe really did take advantage of Leola—and while he was still married to Linda? A handsome man like him—a man with charisma and power in his community—surely attracts the attention of all the women . . .*

Monroe fought for control as he entered the short hallway behind the meeting room. This area of the lodge was mostly for storage. Wheeled racks holding metal folding chairs, podiums, and other furnishings from the days when campers worshipped here sat in the largest storeroom—but he decided against entering a room with a closed door. Leola had already shattered his reputation by announcing that he had ruined hers, so he wanted no hint of secrecy or indecency to further cloud the opinions of his new flock at Promise Lodge.

He turned to face Leola, crossing his arms. He intended to hear her out, and then send her back to Macomb—right after he called her parents. "Why are you here, Leola?"

Her shoulders slumped and her expression fell. "Don't be mean to me, Monroe," she whimpered. "I *love* you. I missed you so bad, I had to come—"

"How'd you get here?" he asked, careful to keep his frustration out of his voice. If Leola started weeping, everyone in the dining room would assume he was mistreating her. He knew she got noisy when she was upset.

Leola hiccupped. "I hired a driver," she replied. "I—I remembered you saying something about Promise Lodge before you left us, and he had a gizmo in his car that told him how to get here."

Monroe closed his eyes, wondering how to proceed. "It's a long drive from Illinois. Probably four hours in a car," he mused aloud. "Where'd you get the money for gas and the driver?"

Leola looked down at her clasped hands, sniffling. "Mama's egg money. She keeps it in a teapot in the pantry."

He wanted to march her into the kitchen and call her

parents immediately, but the Kuhn sisters and the other women would be taking pans of food from the oven within earshot of the strained conversation—and the Duffs had a phone shanty, so he'd only be able to leave a message, anyway. As he'd done dozens of times, Monroe wondered why this vulnerable young woman had become so attached to him, so infatuated. Why did she repeatedly announce that he should marry her because he'd *ruined* her? He winced as he recalled the expressions on the men's faces a few minutes ago.

"And your driver has already left?" he asked.

She nodded. "Oh, *jah*. He carried my suitcases to the porch, because I told him I'd be staying. Forever."

Monroe swallowed a groan. It would remain a mystery, why God had created Leola with such a pretty face yet so challenged in other areas . . . but it did him no good to wonder about God's motives. He had to focus on the fact that somehow Leola had left home without her parents' knowledge, and on figuring out what to do with her until they came for the runaway. He prayed quickly that Christine, her sisters and daughters, and the Kuhns would help keep an eye on Leola—

Christine. Monroe sighed. She surely must think the worst, after the way Leola had spoken out. He had no doubt that Amos, Eli, and Marlin would demand an explanation—and even though Monroe hesitated to talk in front of Leola, he knew they had a right to hear about his relationship with her. It was her word against his, and he already knew how she would gaze at the preachers with her sparkling eyes and dewy complexion and unwittingly condemn him with every loving word she said about him.

Monroe stepped away from her open arms. "Tell you what," he said as he started toward the dining room. "We'll eat some dinner and get you settled into a room upstairs," he suggested as Leola caught up with him. "And then I'll call your parents—"

"They're not home!" she said gleefully. "It's just you and me, Monroe. Just like it ought to be."

His heart sank as he saw some of the folks in the dining room turn to follow their conversation. Despite their pleasant chatter—and their speculation about him and Leola, no doubt—her strident voice had carried clearly.

Monroe put on the best smile he could manage, gesturing toward the buffet tables along the wall. "Shall we eat?" he said gently. "Wedding food is always the best, isn't it?"

Leola gazed up at him adoringly. "*Dirt* would taste *gut* if I was eating it with you, Monroe."

Chapter Eight

Rosetta savored a mouthful of flavorful "roast" made of chicken, stuffing, and gravy. All around her, folks were eating their meal and speculating about the young woman who'd shown up and said such shocking things to—and about—Monroe. The bishop had guided Leola Duff to one end of the only unoccupied table in the room, and as he ate his dinner, he seemed at a loss for conversation while his unexpected guest gazed adoringly at him.

Christine, who sat across the table from Rosetta, scowled as she drew her fork through her food without eating it. The lines in her forehead aged her, and Rosetta felt as saddened and perturbed as her sister looked. Their day of celebration for their nephew Roman had spiraled out of control, and no one knew how to recapture the joy they'd all felt earlier, during the service. Beulah and Ruby had cooked a fabulous feast, yet because she felt so concerned for Christine, the food didn't taste nearly as special as it had at Mattie and Amos's wedding.

"I can't believe things between Monroe and Leola are the way she described them," Truman remarked as he glanced in their direction. "Something's going on that we haven't figured out yet. But my money's still on Monroe. He's a *gut* man."

Rosetta sighed. She was extremely relieved that Maria Zehr had returned to Cloverdale and hadn't come to the wedding—but she had no idea how to discuss her qualms about the pretty blonde with the man who sat beside her. In a way, Leola's mysterious appearance had provided a diversion from the serious conversation she needed to have with Truman. "Even the best of men fall prey to temptation," she said softly.

Truman didn't seem to notice that her statement might apply to him. "The same could be said for women. I suspect that a fine-looking fellow like Monroe has had plenty of attention from the ladies all his life," he said. "Stands to reason that at some time or another, one of them might behave in an inappropriate manner—without Monroe doing anything to encourage her. Makes me glad I'm just an average-looking fellow. No spectacular features that call attention to me."

Rosetta's brows rose. With his light brown collar-length hair and hazel eyes, Truman Wickey was extremely attractive, to her way of thinking . . . and it was no secret that Maria Zehr thought so, too. Rosetta set aside her bitter thoughts to concentrate on her sister, who was looking more miserable by the minute.

"Christine, I'm sorry this situation has hit you where it hurts," Rosetta murmured. "When we saw Monroe kissing you on the hill after Mattie's wedding, I was sure he intended to marry you sooner rather than later."

"Me, too," Christine muttered. She set her utensils across the top of her plate, apparently finished with the meal she hadn't eaten. "Seems he still has *entanglements* in Illinois, however. I was dreaming of marrying Monroe on my birthday, but I don't see that wish coming true now. Sorry I'm such bad company. I'm going upstairs." She picked up her dirty dishes and stood, walking off before anyone could stop her.

Rosetta felt compelled to follow Christine to the kitchen, but she didn't know what to say to make her feel better. Her sister's February twenty-fifth birthday allowed only a month to clarify or forgive Monroe's apparent detour down the primrose path—if indeed he'd done anything wrong. She watched Mattie rise from her chair, apparently with the same thought, so Rosetta allowed her eldest sister to console Christine.

Now that she was already in a bad mood—and she was alone with Truman—it seemed like a good time to tell him exactly how she felt about Maria Zehr taking up residence at Promise Lodge. Rosetta gathered her courage, hoping her words came out in a way that Truman would understand her concerns, but he, too, stood up.

"The pie table's calling my name," he said, smiling at her. "What kind shall I bring for you, honey-girl?"

Honey-girl. The endearment clutched at her heart, yet Truman seemed unaware of her distress. Rosetta gazed toward the dessert table, where several folks were choosing plates of pie, along with the bars and cookies she and Christine had baked. "How about cherry? Or lemon?" she murmured. She might as well have a reason to appear puckered, considering the sour mood she was in.

No sooner had Truman made his way across the crowded room than Monroe approached Rosetta, with Leola tagging along like a love-struck puppy. The bishop's smile looked strained. "Rosetta, this is Leola Duff, and she'll be needing a place to stay for a while," he said in a low voice. He held her gaze as though he hoped she would read between his lines. "Would you mind taking her upstairs so she can choose from the empty rooms? I have some business to attend to."

Rosetta hadn't thought about Leola sticking around for

any length of time. It was too cold for her to stay out in one of the unheated cabins behind the lodge—and who would invite Leola to stay in their home?—so a room upstairs was the only practical answer.

Rosetta stood up, managing a smile. "Do you have luggage, Leola?"

The young woman's face brightened. "*Jah*, I left my suitcases out front—packed nearly every dress I have, considering how I'll be here the rest of my life."

Catching Monroe's grimace from the corner of her eye, Rosetta figured it was time to get Leola out of the dining room so he could gather his thoughts. "Let's take them upstairs," she suggested, gesturing toward the doorway that led to the lobby. "We'll go up the main stairway."

Truman was returning to the table with both kinds of pie she'd asked for, as well as his own, but Rosetta smiled ruefully at him. "Don't wait to enjoy your dessert," she murmured. "I'm taking Leola upstairs to choose a room."

"Ah. Take your time," he said. "I'll visit with other folks for a while so we can share our pie when you get back."

Nodding, Rosetta led the way into the lobby. The three suitcases sitting beside the stone fireplace looked the worse for wear, but Leola rushed toward them as though she was embarking upon a great adventure. "This place is really *something*," she said. She gazed up at the huge chandelier made of antlers and then at the curving double stairway, which was polished to a gloss. "I've never known Amish folks to live in a place like this—like a grand hotel!" she gushed. "I'm really going to like it here! But I'll be living with Monroe, soon as we get hitched."

Rosetta grabbed the handle of one of the suitcases, studying Leola while she took hold of the other two bags. She looked about the same age as Christine's daughter, Phoebe, who was almost twenty-one, yet something about her seemed almost adolescent. Leola's peaches and cream complexion ripened to a deep pink when she realized Rosetta was looking at her.

"*What?*" she demanded. Her brown eyes narrowed in suspicion. "Not polite to stare, you know."

Rosetta started for the nearest stairway, cringing. "I wasn't really staring," she insisted as she lugged the heavy old suitcase. "This is the first chance I've had to really look at you close-up, Leola. You, um, *surprised* us all when you came in during the wedding. We didn't hear you knock."

"How was I to know about a wedding?" Leola shot back as she started up the stairway with her luggage. "I ducked inside real fast before that black-and-white dog could bite me."

Rosetta paused at the top of the stairs. "Oh, Queenie would never bite anybody," she insisted kindly. "She just greets people who come onto the Promise Lodge property— even the folks she knows."

"I hate dogs."

Rosetta's eyebrows rose. "Well, if you're to live here, Leola, you'll have to make your peace with Queenie. Once you pat her and give her time to sniff you, she'll be fine."

Leola topped the stairs, looking doubtful. "Doesn't matter, really. I'll be with Monroe, in his house, and he won't let that dog bother me. He *loves* me, so he'll protect me."

Rosetta blinked. Monroe apparently hadn't informed Leola that he was staying in Lester Lehman's house until his own home could be built—when it was warm enough to pour the foundation. She decided to take the girl down the hallway where no one else had selected rooms yet, opposite where she, Maria, and Christine had their apartments.

"Let's leave your bags here until you decide which room you'd like," she suggested. All the doors were open to keep the rooms from smelling musty, so she gestured toward the nearest one. "If you think you'll be staying awhile—"

"Forever," Leola insisted happily.

Rosetta sighed to herself. Monroe would have an even bigger problem on his hands if Leola decided she was going to stay with him at the Lehman place—an unthinkable arrangement for folks who weren't married. From what she'd seen so far, however, this unexpected guest didn't seem to bother with following the rules. "What I mean is that we can paint your room if you'd like," she went on in a firm voice. "These rooms haven't been spoken for yet, so we haven't fixed them up."

"Who lives here?"

Leola's blunt question took Rosetta by surprise. "I do, and my sister Christine—my other sister, Mattie, just moved out because she married Preacher Amos," she explained as patiently as she could. "The two older ladies in flowery dresses—they were refilling the pans on the buffet table downstairs—rent apartments from me."

Leola appeared puzzled. "This lodge is yours?"

"*Jah.* I own the lodge and the cabins behind it, and single Plain ladies can come here to live." Rosetta entered the nearest room, which had a simple bed and spare dresser in it. "How's this look to you? It's close to the stairs—"

"People pay you money to live here?" she asked abruptly.

Rosetta smiled kindly. "*Jah.* That's how we have money to cook for our residents, and to pay for gas and such to keep the furnace and the stoves going."

As she turned away, Leola's worried grimace suggested that she had no money. She looked around, seeming a bit frantic. "Maybe I better take the very smallest room then," she murmured, shaking her head. "Or I'll just have to stay with Monroe until—"

"That wouldn't be proper," Rosetta said sternly. "Don't worry if you can't pay any rent. We'll figure something out."

Leola's face brightened like the afternoon sun. "Can I see your room?"

Rosetta's eyes widened. She didn't really want to give Leola ideas about living in the same hallway she and Christine shared, so she hoped to convince Monroe's guest to live on this side of the U-shaped floor. "How about if we pick out your room first, Leola?" she asked gently. "You must be tired from your trip, so spending some time hanging up your clothes—or taking a nap—might be just the—"

"Babies nap," Leola snapped. "I'm no baby, so stop treating me like one."

Rosetta blinked, willing herself to remain patient. "I'm sorry. It wasn't my intention to make you feel like a baby," she said carefully. "We have seven open rooms along this hallway for you to choose from. We can move a different bed and dresser, and an armchair, and rugs into your room, and we have some pretty quilts you can choose from."

Clasping her hands tightly at her waist, Leola gazed at the open doorways, where afternoon sunlight spilled into the hallway from the rooms' windows. "Nope, I can't stay here—don't wanna be all by myself. I wanna be close to *your* room."

Rosetta was at a loss for an answer. Leola seemed to change moods as easily as most folks breathed in and out. In the opposite hallway, the Kuhn sisters lived in the back corner apartments, and the rooms adjoining theirs were empty. On the other side of the empty rooms was Christine's apartment, which was next to Mattie's former place, where Maria would soon be living. Rosetta's rooms were on the front corner—and she didn't have the heart to place Leola next to Christine's apartment, so this hallway and the short end of the U, next to Beulah, were the only logical spots to consider.

As she met Leola's eager gaze, however, Rosetta sensed that there would be nothing logical about this young woman's behavior.

Christine stood at her apartment windows, oblivious to the beautiful day and the bright sunshine that made the snow sparkle on the ground below. Just on the other side of the wooded area behind the lodge, the hilltop where she and Monroe had kissed—the land where he would build his house and barns—taunted her. Until today she had enjoyed gazing at what she'd assumed would be her future home, but that joy was forgotten as she replayed Leola's entrance in her mind again and again.

Was Amos right all along? Is Monroe Burkholder too good to be true—a bishop with a tarnished reputation who's tried to escape an inexcusable relationship?

In her mind, for the umpteenth time, she watched Leola stand on tiptoe to kiss Monroe and heard again the telltale remarks she'd made.

"Stop it!" Christine muttered, pivoting on her heel. She couldn't recall the last time she'd felt so angry and frustrated. Or stupid. Ordinarily, she could pray about situations that upset her and gradually become more peaceful, but praying was the furthest thing from her mind. She wanted to throw something heavy and breakable against the wall for the satisfaction of the *crash*—a sure sign that she wasn't her normal, rational self.

It's almost scary, how easily Monroe sucked you in . . . how quickly you surrendered to his allure. Silly goose.

The solid knock on her door startled her. With bitter tears streaming down her face and nothing good to say, she was in no mood for company—and her sisters would've tapped lightly before letting themselves in.

So help me, if it's Leola, I'm going to—

"Christine? It's Monroe. Please, may I have a word?"

The sound of his urgent, silken voice made her feel hopeful, yet irritated. Why would she want to talk to Monroe, or hear his dubious explanations? Christine stared at the door. If he dared open it without her inviting him in, she would have proof of his impropriety, wouldn't she?

"Please, sweetheart? I know you're probably upset—and with good reason—"

"You have *no idea*!" Christine shot back.

After a pause, Monroe tried again. "I don't have much time while Rosetta is with Leola," he pleaded. "If you don't let me explain, neither one of us will recover—and we'll not return to the way we were as a couple."

The way we were as a couple. Christine sighed. He was right, but she wasn't ready to fall for his persuasion, his charm, so soon after her illusions had been shattered. It occurred to her that if she didn't let Monroe in, she'd have no chance to tell him exactly how disappointed and furious and exasperated she was without an audience following their every word.

She strode to the door and threw it open. "You!" she spat, as though the sight of him made her ill.

Monroe sighed. "At least you're speaking to me."

"You have no idea what I want to say to you, *Bishop*. There aren't enough hours in the day to tell you how—how crushed and betrayed and—"

"Maybe I'd better step in, *jah*? So everybody downstairs won't be in on our conversation?"

Once again Monroe was right, and that irritated Christine even more. How dare he gaze at her like a desperate puppy as she shut the door, glaring at him? Couldn't he see she was beyond politeness and logic? "Sure, why not? It's not like any hanky-panky's going to happen."

Monroe knew better than to respond with his usual flirtatious banter. "Christine, I am so sorry," he began tentatively. "I had no idea Leola would run away from home—follow me here—"

"Is it true, what she said? That you ruined her?" Christine crossed her arms hard and turned away from him. "If so, you're despicable and I have nothing more to say to you."

Monroe's breath escaped in a hiss. "Well, then, it's a *gut* thing I've never had any sort of physical relations with her," he said softly. "But if you can't believe my word against hers, then I might as well leave." He remained behind her, where she'd left him. "I understand why you feel hurt and betrayed, Christine, after what you witnessed this morning. Until you can listen with an open mind, however, I'll save my breath."

Christine's heart thudded in her chest. She closed her eyes against a fresh burst of tears. She wanted to believe Monroe was a man of integrity and truth—a servant of God who rose above ordinary standards of behavior. She had to admit that many other bishops she'd known would be ordering her to her knees to beg forgiveness because she'd spoken in such accusatory anger . . . had jumped headfirst into a red pool of fury, despite the Old Order's teachings that insisted upon peace and forbearance.

She released the tension in her shoulders. Her head dropped forward and she mopped her face with the hem of her apron. "You're right. I'm not being fair," she mumbled. "I heard Leola's words and watched her kiss you, and jumped to all sorts of hasty conclusions."

"You and everyone else," he said with a humorless laugh. "She didn't leave a lot to the imagination—but Leola sees the world through a different lens than most of us do. I'll call her parents as soon as Rosetta has her settled into a room, so we can get to the bottom of this."

Monroe's sigh sent goose bumps up her spine, even though he remained halfway across the room. Christine longed for the comfort of his embrace and a shoulder where she could rest her head, confident that the future she'd envisioned with this man would be restored—and that Leola would go home, never to return. But it didn't seem like the appropriate time or place to open her arms to him—and she didn't want Monroe to think she would give in to his pleas and his physical attraction so quickly.

Christine turned to look at him, sorry that her face was such a mess from crying. But if they were to become a couple, Monroe would see her tears many times over the years, so perhaps his reaction would set the tone for their future disagreements. If he tried to gloss over her emotions, or chide her for expressing her hurt and disappointment, then she would know this handsome bishop wasn't good husband material—for her, anyway.

Monroe gazed sadly at her. "Do you believe what I've said? That I've not made inappropriate advances toward Leola?" He paused, his green eyes widening when she didn't answer immediately. "Shall I explain the situation further? If *you* don't believe in me, Christine, no one else will."

She pressed her lips together. She badly wanted to hear the details of Monroe's relationship with Leola—wanted him to expand upon his statement about the different lens through which the young woman saw the world. "Maybe we should sit down," she suggested, gesturing toward her sofa. "I'm sorry I can't offer you coffee or—"

"We can share some dessert downstairs, if there's any pie left—and if you'll come with me," Monroe said. He exhaled a little nervously. "And maybe, for propriety's sake, I'll stay standing. Even though you're a widow and I'm a widower, some folks downstairs might not think it's proper for me to be in your apartment. In fact, I'll just open the door—"

Christine's confidence in him was somewhat restored by his actions. With her relief came weariness, so she sat in the armchair and left the sofa for Monroe. When he opened the door, however, she heard Rosetta's urgent plea in the hallway.

"No, Leola! That apartment belongs to my sister—"

Monroe's breath left him in a rush as Leola threw herself against him. "Monroe! I've been looking all over for—why are you in this lady's room?"

Christine's heart sank like a rock. Even if the wedding guests downstairs hadn't overheard Leola's outburst, she sensed the young woman would have no qualms about mentioning the fact that she'd found the bishop in Christine's apartment. As she stood up, she saw Rosetta peering in from behind Monroe, aghast at what had happened.

"Shall we all come in and talk?" Christine asked. She hugged herself hard, as though holding her body and soul together. It wasn't as though anything improper had gone on, yet she sensed that—as Monroe had stated—their guest did indeed see things differently.

Leola pulled away from Monroe to study Christine closely. "All right, I'm gonna stay in the room next door," she stated, looking at Rosetta and then gazing up at the bishop. "But where do you live, Monroe? I could be with you—"

"No, you may not," Monroe interrupted sternly. "Your parents taught you better than that, Leola. Do they know where you are?"

Leola burst into tears, crying out so loudly that anyone within earshot might think she was being beaten. "No!" she wailed, curling in on herself as she turned toward the open door. "They wouldn't bring me here to see you, so after Dat dumped me off at Aunt Polly's, I—I came by myself."

Monroe appeared stricken by Leola's loud crying, but he carefully stepped away from her. "Where did your folks go, Leola?" he asked gently.

"I don't know!"

Rosetta slipped her arm around the young woman. "Maybe you're more tired than you thought," she suggested. "Shall we go to your new room and unpack your suit-cases?"

"No!" Leola jerked away from Rosetta. She glared accusingly at Christine and her sister before wiping her tear-streaked face on her sleeve. "I wanna be with you, Monroe. I *want* you. Nobody else loves me the way you do."

Monroe appeared at a total loss about what to do next. Christine realized that he'd somehow caught Leola's fancy despite his attempts to dissuade her affection for him. He placed his hands on the young woman's slender shoulders, keeping her at arm's length as he held her gaze.

"Leola, you're upset. You're not thinking clearly," he said gently. "Is it time for your pills?"

Leola looked away from him, shaking her head.

"I want you to go to your new room with Rosetta, all right?" he continued. "You can unpack your clothes later. Right now I want you to lie down and rest, and I want you to say your prayers. Don't come out of your room until at least four o'clock, understand me?"

Leola blinked repeatedly. "How will I know what time it is?"

"I've got just the clock for your room, Leola," Rosetta said, smiling at the girl. "We'll hang it on your wall where you can see it. It has a battery, so you'll never have to wind it."

When Leola looked at Monroe again, he nodded his encouragement.

Her shoulders slumped and she looked like a whipped pup, but she left the room. Rosetta smiled sadly at Christine before she followed Leola down the hallway.

Monroe let out a long sigh. He appeared so downhearted that Christine longed to wrap her arms around him and assure him they'd get through this difficult situation somehow, yet it felt right to refrain. For all they knew, Leola would find a reason to come bursting into her apartment again.

"You're a *gut* man, Monroe," she murmured. "I'm sorry Leola's coming here will muddy the waters, far as what folks will think about you."

He smiled gratefully. "*Denki* for your understanding, Christine. It means a lot."

She pondered their situation for a moment. "Give me a minute to splash some water on my face, and then let's go downstairs, all right?" she suggested. "If the pie's all gone, and Roman and Mary Kate haven't cut their cake yet, I know where to find some cookies to go with our coffee— something to sweeten this day a bit."

"Count me in. I'll wait right here."

Chapter Nine

As Monroe sat at the end of a long table with Christine, Rosetta, and Truman, eating a slice of the best lemon pie he'd ever tasted, he felt relieved. The wedding guests' chatter filled the room as longtime friends talked among themselves or congratulated the newlyweds, so he had a few moments to collect his thoughts. Leola's arrival had struck him like a thunderbolt. Christine's acceptance of the situation boded well, for if she believed in him—believed he'd done nothing to encourage Leola's infatuation—then he stood a chance of regaining the confidence of the rest of his flock.

"Mighty fine pie," Truman remarked as he rubbed his fork over the final crumbs on his plate. "As always, you sisters and the Kuhns put on a fine feed. Hardly any leftovers—and not a slice of pie remains, either."

Although Rosetta and Christine still seemed a little taken aback by the conversation upstairs, they managed smiles. "It's *gut* to see so many of our friends from Coldstream came, considering they were just here three weeks ago for Mattie and Amos's wedding," Christine said. "Beulah and Ruby seemed a little frazzled as they pulled the last pans of food from the ovens, thinking they hadn't cooked enough."

"Nobody went hungry," Truman insisted. "And it's a better meal than most of them would've eaten at home, because even the best of wives doesn't put out such a spread on your ordinary Thursday." He smiled boyishly at Rosetta. "Except maybe you, honey-girl. You're the finest cook I know."

Rosetta's cheeks turned pink, yet she didn't seem completely thrilled with Truman's compliment. Monroe sensed it wasn't the time to ask questions—or to tease Rosetta into her usual sunny mood. He was well aware of what she'd endured while showing Leola the rooms upstairs.

He ate his final bite of pie and glanced at the large clock on the dining room wall. Three thirty. There was no telling how much longer Leola would stay in her room. He touched Christine's hand. "Hate to eat and run," he murmured, "but I've got some calls to make concerning Leola's parents and—"

"Say there, Bishop," a familiar male voice said from behind him. "What's happened to your girlfriend?"

Trying not to wince, Monroe turned to face Amos. "Rosetta helped her choose a room upstairs. I hope she's napping."

"*Jah*, I bet you do," the preacher murmured. He pulled an empty chair from the table behind him, placed it next to Monroe, and sat down with an expectant expression on his bearded face. "Care to explain what's going on?"

Monroe knew an open-ended question—and a trap— when he heard one. "What would you like to know?" he asked carefully. "Leola Duff is a member of the church in the Macomb district—"

"We know all that," Amos interrupted brusquely. "So why is she crying out for all to hear that you ruined her? Any truth to that?"

The rapid tattoo of thick heels on the wooden floor made Monroe look up.

"Amos Troyer, this is not the time or the place for this discussion," Mattie declared as she clapped a hand on the preacher's shoulder. "Roman and Mary Kate are ready to cut their cake, and I want no contentious talk to spoil the rest of their day. Let's join them at the *eck*, shall we?"

Amos seemed ready to put his new wife in her place, as a lot of Amish men would, yet he thought better of it. He shot Monroe a purposeful glance as he stood up. "Plenty of time to get the details. How long's she staying?"

Monroe shook his head. "I have no idea."

Amos's bushy eyebrows rose. "All of us in the ministry get tested now and again, Bishop. Seems it's your turn."

Monroe sighed as the preacher followed his wife to where folks were gathering in front of the *eck*. Mary Kate and Roman stood behind it, flanking the tall white cake on its pedestal platter. The joy on their young faces took him back to when he and Linda had been sharing the first slice of their wedding cake . . . when he'd been young and in love and filled with all manner of dreams. He'd had no idea about the trials and tribulations that came with maturation.

As Rosetta and Christine stood up to join the others, Monroe saw his chance to slip out. "See you all later," he murmured. "If anything happens with Leola, come and get me—and thanks again for looking after her."

Christine and her sister nodded, and Truman clapped him on the shoulder. Monroe headed for the lobby, where his black coat hung among dozens of others that resembled it. He fumbled with collars, looking for the distinctive green tag sewn inside that bore his initials. A few moments later he stepped out onto the lodge porch and placed his black Stetson on his head.

Queenie came around the corner of the building and yipped her greeting.

"Hey, there, girl," Monroe murmured as he scratched between her black ears. "If I was any sort of friend, I would've brought you a little scrap of something, *jah*? Sorry about that."

The Border collie ran circles around him, dipping her nose into the snow and flinging it into the air, delighted to accompany him. Monroe strode to the road and passed Noah's house, and then Roman's. He inhaled the cold air to collect his thoughts, walking quickly past the Troyer place and up the first hill to where the two Lehman homes stood. Frances had told him that Floyd and his brother, Lester, were in the siding and window business, which explained why all the new houses sported off-white siding. The phone shanties at the roadside did, as well.

Monroe opened the door of the shanty he shared with the former bishop's family and sat down on the chair. Closing the door against the brisk breeze, he took a handwritten list from the drawer of the small table where an old push-button phone sat. Most folks had newer equipment, but it didn't matter. As he dialed Polly Duff's number and heard it ring, he was just grateful to be able to communicate with folks he'd left behind in Illinois.

When her machine prompted him, Monroe spoke. "Polly, it's Monroe Burkholder, and I hope you're feeling *gut* and doing well," he began. "Leola showed up here in Missouri, where I live now. She says Chester and Edna left her with you, but couldn't tell me where they went. I have a feeling she's not taking her medications. Give me a call when you can, all right?"

Monroe said the phone number slowly, twice, and hung up. Then he dialed Chester Duff's place. "Chester— Monroe Burkholder here. I suspect you're away on a serious type of trip if you left Leola with your sister, and I wanted you and Edna to know that she's safe and she's here with me. Hope all's well, and hope to hear from you soon."

After he repeated the phone number and hung up, he sat for a moment. He couldn't think of anyone else in Macomb who might be able to help him, so it was a matter of waiting until Polly checked her machine—which, because winter weather bothered her arthritis, might be a few days. He would simply have to rely upon Rosetta, Christine, and the Kuhn sisters to help him keep an eye on Leola until somebody could come for her, or until he knew her parents were home. Most girls of twenty-one could look after themselves, but Leola wasn't like most girls.

A movement outside the shanty's window brought Monroe out of his thoughts. Queenie was bouncing up and down like a pogo stick, yipping to get his attention. He laughed and stepped outside. "*Jah*, what do *you* want?" he teased as he stopped to gather snow between his gloved hands.

He lobbed the snowball several yards in front of them, and Queenie shot out after it. When she picked up the snowball, it fell apart in her mouth and she shook her head excitedly. As Monroe made his way up the hill, he continued packing and tossing snowballs, laughing as the black-and-white dog had so much fun with them. He came to the top of the rise . . . the place where he'd first kissed Christine. Looking out over the hills and valleys he'd just purchased, he had more questions than answers.

Christine seemed tolerant of his situation with Leola, but how long would she remain that way? If Chester had been the one to leave Leola with his sister, did that mean something was terribly wrong with Edna? What if Edna had passed on? Monroe sensed that Chester wouldn't be able to care for his daughter alone for long, so what would happen to Leola? What if Chester asked him to become the girl's guardian?

Monroe exhaled forcefully to rid himself of these troubling thoughts. He sensed he should be at the lodge when Leola woke up, or she might raise a ruckus in the dining room among so many strangers. Who could tell what she might say or do if she panicked and couldn't find him?

We sure do need your help, God, he thought as he started down the hill. *And if it's not too much to ask, I'd like some answers to this dilemma sooner rather than later.*

Rosetta laid her hand carefully on Leola's shoulder, aware of how thin the young woman was—and fragile, in more ways than one. "I think you'll sleep better now that you've had some supper," she murmured. "Tomorrow you'll be rested, and we'll fix up your room, all right?"

Leola was eyeing her warily. "I want blue," she said. "Blue walls and curtains and a blue comforter, like at home."

Rosetta glanced inside the room Leola had chosen. Phoebe and Laura had painted the walls a pale yellow to freshen them, but had done no more because no one had chosen to live in this room or the one that adjoined it. She wondered if it was worth buying paint if Leola wasn't going to be here long, but she sensed that agreeing to her color choice might keep the girl from having another hissy fit.

Or not. Hard to tell what she might do.

"We'll figure it all out tomorrow," Rosetta assured the young woman. "Sleep tight, Leola."

Her thin face lit up. "Don't let the bedbugs bite!" she said quickly. Then her brow furrowed. "Monroe went home, but he'll be here tomorrow, *jah*?"

"He will," Rosetta assured her.

Leola nodded absently. She went to the bed to pick up the nightgown Rosetta had helped her unpack.

Rosetta closed the door and descended the narrow back staircase. The aroma of grilled cheese sandwiches lingered in the air—Leola's choice for supper, which Rosetta, Christine and her girls, and the Kuhns had all eaten, as well, because they had no wedding leftovers. The ladies were still at the table, talking softly among themselves as they nibbled cookies with their tea and hot chocolate.

Ruby looked up when Rosetta poured hot water from the teakettle into a mug. "She's going to bed? It's not even nine o'clock."

Rosetta sat down. "I suspect she's more tired than she wants to admit—like a child who's worn out but doesn't want to miss anything. And who knows how long she'll stay asleep?"

"If we hear her moving around in the night, we should probably check on her," Phoebe suggested. "She's in strange surroundings, and we don't want her falling down the stairs if she's sleepwalking."

"Don't want her prowling around in our rooms, either," Laura murmured. "Is it me, or is Leola a little creepy, the way she clings to Bishop Monroe and says he ruined her? My word, he's old enough to be her *dat*," she added with a disgusted frown.

Rosetta nodded, along with the other women at the table. Until Leola became familiar with the lodge and the women who lived there, she fully anticipated some emotional confrontations with the newcomer—in the night, or whenever Monroe wasn't around to talk her down with his gentle patience.

"Monroe mentioned some medications," Christine put in. "Did you find any when you helped her unpack?"

"Nope. And it's anybody's guess what she's supposed to be taking." Rosetta took her seat at the small table in the kitchen. "One minute she seems about ten years old, and the next thing you know she's declaring that Monroe should marry her."

"Just my guess," Beulah murmured as she reached for a cookie, "but there's something not quite right about Leola. She looks perfectly normal, yet—"

The phone on the back wall rang, so Rosetta rose to answer it. Who would be calling? Nearly everyone they knew had been here for the wedding, and the Coldstream folks, who'd left a couple of hours ago, wouldn't be home yet. The newlyweds and other Promise Lodge residents had left, as well—and she hoped the ringing of the phone wouldn't bring Leola out of her room. Their guest was fascinated by the fact that the bishop allowed them to have a phone in the lodge rather than a shanty at the roadside, because so many lodge residents and businesses shared it.

"*Jah*, hello?" she said, thinking it might be a potential renter. "This is Promise Lodge and I'm Rosetta. How can I help you?"

"Hi, it's Maria Zehr! I've decided I'd like to live in that apartment one of your sisters just left," she replied excitedly. "What will the rent for that one be?"

Rosetta swallowed hard. Mattie's apartment was between hers and Christine's, which meant Truman's special friend would be living right next door to her. Because this situation would require extreme patience and goodwill on her part, Rosetta decided to be more businesslike with her new renter. "I charge two hundred a month. For you to move in, I require the first and last month's rent as well as one month's rent as a security deposit."

"Oh." There was a pause before Maria continued. "What's the deposit for? Most folks I know don't require one."

Rosetta knew better, because she'd read an article in the Forest Grove paper about covering unexpected expenses or damages a renter might incur. "Well, for one thing, it'll go toward some food—because we lodge ladies all chip in on our meals," she replied. "And it will go toward any painting and fixing up you might want done, as well as any furnishings you might need. When you move out and the apartment is left clean and in *gut* repair, you'll get some of that deposit back."

"Ah. Maybe I should get a deposit from the folks who'll be renting my house," Maria mused aloud. She cleared her throat. "I'll be bringing my own bedding and some furniture, but since your bishop and Preacher Amos said they would do any painting and changes I'd like right away—and I'm sure Truman will help—I thought I'd give you my list. Got a pencil and paper?"

Rosetta's eyebrows rose as she grabbed the scratch pad on which they kept their grocery list. Would Maria expect everyone to jump through hoops when she moved to Promise Lodge? Or was Rosetta just irritated because Maria assumed Truman would be at her beck and call, as well? "*Jah*, I'm ready," she muttered, her pencil poised.

Ready to set you straight, blondie, she thought before she could catch her uncharitable thoughts.

"I'd like the bedroom painted delphinium blue—even the ceiling," Maria began, "and I want fluffy white clouds painted on the ceiling and the upper parts of the walls, so I'll feel like I'm surrounded by blue sky and sunshine—or up in Heaven!" she added dreamily. "Let's paint the bathroom petal pink and the sitting room a deeper pink—like raspberry—on the lower walls and have the color gradually lighten to petal pink and then white on the ceiling."

Rosetta bit back a retort as she scribbled these instructions. She was glad she'd asked for a deposit, because it seemed only fair that Amos and Monroe should be paid for the additional work Maria was requesting. "Anything else?" she asked with great restraint. "The furniture you saw belongs to my sister Mattie, but she's willing to let our residents use it. We can put it in our unoccupied rooms if you have your own furnishings."

"Put it somewhere else," Maria said. "I'm making a fresh start with my bakery, so I'm going to splurge on a new couch and a rug and some upholstered chairs. Just have Truman and the guys shift everything out before they paint."

Truman and the guys? You're lucky you're talking to me instead of to our men, missy.

Rosetta cleared her throat, reminding herself to remain patient. "Anything else?"

"That about does it—I'll call if I think of anything," Maria replied breezily.

"When do you figure to move in? I'd like to give Amos and Monroe a heads-up—"

"Oh, I forgot to say! My renters want my house cleared out so they can fix it up a bit and move in by February first," she said with a little laugh, "so I'll be at Promise Lodge Monday. Okay?"

A gasp escaped her as she glanced at the calendar on the wall beside the phone. "This coming Monday?" Rosetta demanded. "With tomorrow being Friday—and Sunday being a preaching service—that only leaves two days for moving furniture and buying the paint and then doing the special work you've asked for. Maybe you should figure on painting those clouds and the mixed shades of pink yourself."

"But—but I'll be working in my bakery tomorrow and Saturday," Maria protested. "From the way Amos and Monroe talked, I thought they wanted to work on my apartment right away."

Rosetta placed her hand over the receiver, meeting the curious gazes of the ladies at the kitchen table. "Oh, but I've got a story for you when I hang up," she said softly. She collected her thoughts and made a quick decision. "Tell you what, Maria, I'm going to leave the painting schedule up to Amos and Monroe. If they don't get finished before Saturday night, you'll have to move in and either finish it yourself, or keep your furniture in the middle of the rooms until they have a chance to do it."

Maria's sigh sounded like a whine. "So does this mean they won't help me move in on Sunday? It's the only day off I've got."

Rosetta's eyes widened. "I guarantee you that even if they weren't preaching, they wouldn't be doing that sort of work on the Sabbath," she replied firmly. Where were Maria's priorities? From what she knew of Truman's Mennonite fellowship, they didn't condone such work on Sunday, either. "We hold our church service in the lodge, so we won't want you and your friends tromping in and out with your furniture that day, either. Maybe you need to take a day away from your bakery, Maria. Or maybe you need to stay in your house as long as you need to, instead of letting your renters set your schedule."

Maria sighed again. "I'll ask Truman to help me. He's got those big trucks . . ."

Rosetta knew better than to speak for Truman. This move was apparently between him and Maria—which suddenly made her ready to be finished with this conversation. "Figure it all out and we'll see you when you get here," she said. Then something struck her. "By the way, how will you be getting back and forth from Promise Lodge to your bakery until you've moved your building?"

"Oh, I have a car," Maria replied matter-of-factly. "I'll be looking for some barn space to park it in, too, so I don't have to scrape the windshields when it snows. I'll have to leave for work before three each morning, you see."

"You'll have to work that out with folks who have barns," Rosetta said quickly. "See you when you get here."

As she hung up, Rosetta didn't know whether to laugh or cry. She returned to the table with her tablet so she could repeat Maria's demands—but first she took a big sip of her cocoa. Even though it had gotten cold, the rich chocolate soothed her.

Beulah and Ruby Kuhn leaned toward her, their eyes

wide. "You're going to tell us what-all she said, *jah*?" Ruby asked.

"You're not looking any too happy—even though you told her she'd be paying you six hundred bucks up front," Beulah remarked. "What made you decide you needed a deposit, Rosetta? You said no such thing to us when we came here."

Rosetta smiled as she reached for Beulah and Ruby's hands. "You weren't making demands and expecting to be treated like queens, either," she replied with a chuckle. She recounted Maria's painting instructions, and then told them about her proposed moving schedule.

"Well, now," Ruby murmured, raising her eyebrows at her sister. "Why didn't *we* think to ask for blue ceilings with fluffy white clouds painted on them?"

Beulah and the rest of the women laughed. "Because I like to think my feet are firmly planted on God's *gut* earth, so my head's not floating around up in the clouds," she replied. "Think of the sunburn you'd get, on top of being considered an airhead."

Rosetta helped herself to a cookie, finding a smile. "*Jah*, that says it all, Beulah. Remind me not to get my nose out of joint when Queen Maria shows up with her furniture, will you? Getting her and Leola settled might make for more excitement than we're used to."

Chapter Ten

Monday afternoon, Monroe sat down in the phone shanty and sighed tiredly. He'd spent all day Friday and Saturday alongside Amos, Truman, and Marlin, painting Mattie's former apartment the way Maria wanted it—as well as painting Leola's room the same shade of deep blue with puffy white clouds. Thanks to the way the four of them had worked together—and used some imagination while painting ceiling clouds and pink walls that got lighter as they approached the ceiling—the rooms were ready. Truman and a couple of his employees were going to load Maria's belongings this afternoon. Everyone seemed excited that she would soon be opening her bakery at Promise Lodge, even though her choice of paint—and the fact that she drove a car—were making folks curious about what sort of resident she'd be.

Monroe was pleased that he'd made it through the Sunday service and the common meal afterward without any questions from folks about Leola. He'd managed to peel her away when she'd wanted to cling to him, and he'd quieted a couple of her outbursts before they escalated into shouting matches. He owed Rosetta, Christine, and the Kuhn sisters a huge debt of gratitude for looking after

Leola and giving her tasks to keep her busy. He'd also been pleased to see the red light blinking on the message machine this morning. Polly Duff had said she'd be waiting for his call at three o'clock.

As he collected his thoughts, Monroe dialed Polly's number. He hoped Chester's elderly sister could answer all the questions that had been bothering him since Leola had appeared.

"Hullo? Is this you, Bishop?"

Monroe smiled. Even though Polly Duff was way past eighty, she still got straight to the point. "It is, and it's *gut* to hear your voice, Polly. How are you?"

"Well, I was fat and sassy until Chester got into a big fix last week," she said with a rueful laugh. "He came here all a-fluster, sayin' I had to keep Leola because they took Edna to a big hospital in Chicago—in a *helicopter*. Can you imagine? And here I am without so much as a phone number to get ahold of him."

"Oh my, that's not *gut*," Monroe murmured as he found paper and a pencil in the drawer of the table. "What happened to Edna? And I assume Chester was going to go to the hospital to be with her?"

"*Jah*, he hired a driver. Week ago today, it was," Polly said. "They might be there for a long while, as Edna's ticker was so out of whack she all but died. They got her revved up again, but Chester thought she'd been dead for several minutes before the paramedics got to their place to revive her. To my way of thinkin', the *Gut* Lord called Edna home and those medical folks shouldn't have been tinkering with her."

"I agree," Monroe murmured. "And I can imagine Leola was in quite an agitated state while all this was going on with her *mamm*, and when her *dat* brought her to your place."

"*Agitated* doesn't cover it by half," Polly blurted. "That girl was goin' from room to room mutterin' to herself and cryin' as though she'd never been to my place. And then when I told her to take her pills, durned if she didn't dump them all down the toilet."

Monroe sighed. "I was afraid of that. Do you still have the bottles—or have any idea what she's supposed to be taking?"

"Nope, she'd already ripped off the labels and wadded them up. I couldn't get them unstuck enough to read them. And I can't tell you the names of her doctors because Leola either doesn't know or she won't tell me." Polly let out a frustrated sigh. "I was sure glad you called to say she'd found you, but truth be told I'm not sorry she ran off. That poor girl's a holy terror, and I just can't keep up with her. I'm grateful to God that Chester and Edna didn't have any more."

Monroe chuckled to himself. Polly Duff was a *maidel* with an opinion about everything, and she'd never been overly fond of children or men who expected their women to wait on them. "I left a message on Chester's answering machine, but it sounds like he might be in Chicago for a while," he murmured. "At least here, Leola has her own room in the lodge and several ladies to keep an eye on her when I'm not around. Sounds like she might be here longer than I thought. Who knows how long Edna will be in the hospital—or in a rehab facility?"

"Leola's in a lodge? And you are, too?" Polly asked. "What sort of setup is *that*?"

Monroe explained about the three Bender sisters who'd bought the abandoned church camp, and told about painting Leola's room a deep blue with clouds on the ceiling— which really got Polly going. He chatted for a few moments more and then remained in the phone shanty after he hung up.

You haven't made this easy for me, eh, God? He opened the door to the brisk winter wind. It wasn't as simple as hiring a driver and escorting Leola back to Illinois—not until Chet and Edna were home and able to keep track of her. As he walked down the road to the lodge, he was happy to toss more snowballs for Queenie, who'd followed him once again.

"Looks like we're in for some snow, girl," he said as he gazed up at clouds the color of elephants.

The dog yipped, gazing eagerly at him until he threw another snowball. Monroe went up the lodge steps and into the lobby. He was glad to see Rosetta restocking her display of goat's milk soap and showing Leola the different kinds of bars that she stored in the drawers of the antique dresser.

When Leola saw Monroe, she rushed over to grab him. "Monroe, I missed you!" she cried. "I helped Rosetta wrap soap, and it smells so pretty—and she gave me a bar to use in my bathroom!"

As he gently pried her arms from around his waist, Monroe smiled gratefully at Rosetta. "We're very blessed that Rosetta and your other new friends are taking such *gut* care of you, Leola," he said. "I just talked to your Aunt Polly—"

"Oh!" Leola screwed up her face. "She's so mean. And grumpy."

Monroe wondered if he should continue, but he needed to give Rosetta a chance to better understand Leola's situation. "Polly's old, and her arthritis bothers her," he explained softly. "She told me you tossed your pills down the toilet and wadded up the labels. How are you supposed to stay well if we don't know what medications to get for you, Leola?"

Her pale face crumpled and she began to cry. "I don't *like* those pills!" she wailed. "They taste yucky. And they make me feel funny."

At the sound of Leola's escalating distress, Christine and Phoebe came through the dining room, wiping their hands on their aprons. "Ah, Monroe, you're back," Christine said beneath the ruckus Leola was raising.

Phoebe walked up to Leola and gently grasped her shoulder. "You know what, Leola? We're making pies and we could really use your help."

"Pies?" Leola hiccupped, considering this information. "What kind?"

"Rhubarb and cherry so far," Phoebe replied. "And we could make a chocolate pie in a graham cracker crust, if you'd like. Does that sound *gut*?"

Leola blotted her tears with her sleeve. "*Jah*, I love chocolate pie," she replied in a shaky voice. "Can we make one now?"

Monroe said a quick prayer of thanks and asked God to bless Phoebe for being so perceptive and kind as she took Leola's hand and led her to the kitchen. He looked from Christine to Rosetta. "Just found out that Leola's *mamm*'s in the hospital in Chicago with serious heart problems. No idea when she'll be able to come home—and Polly didn't know anything about Leola's medications or who prescribed them, because Leola flushed them," he murmured. "I can't thank you ladies enough for looking after her."

Rosetta closed the drawer of the old dresser and joined him and Christine. "It's *gut* we got her room fixed the way she wanted it, then. Sounds like she'll be here awhile."

"She loves the clouds you men painted on her ceiling," Christine added.

Monroe smiled ruefully, wishing he could spend some time alone with the woman he loved—Christine had an irresistible smudge of flour on her nose just begging him to kiss it off. "As odd as I thought those clouds sounded before we painted them, they give the two rooms a summer-time peacefulness I hadn't anticipated." He gazed into her green eyes, happy to see himself reflected there. "Wish I could assure you ladies that those clouds are all we need to keep Leola happy. But God created her as one of His special children. He understands the rhyme and reason of her ways even though we don't."

Late Monday afternoon, Rosetta, Christine, and the Kuhns turned off the burners beneath their pots of meat sauce and spaghetti so they could watch from the dining room—out of the way—as Truman and his foreman, Edgar, hoisted a deep blue sofa between them. As they started up one side of the double staircase, Monroe and Roman entered the lobby carrying upholstered chairs that matched the sofa. Amos and Noah held a rolled-up rug between them.

"You fellows had better wait for this rug to go down before you carry that furniture into Maria's apartment, ain't so?" the preacher called up to them.

"Get it up here, then!" Edgar teased. "And before we carry anything into those rooms, we need Miss Maria to tell us where it goes."

As though she knew she was the subject of their banter, Maria burst into the lobby, her arms around a large laundry basket crammed with clothes. She leaned back against the door to close it, grinning up at her helpers. "I'll be right up. You guys are the best—this is a dream come true!" she gushed.

She wiggled her fingers at Rosetta and the three women who stood with her. "Hi, there! I'll be right back down with my rent and deposit," she said as she started up the stairs. "What with buying my furniture and taking out money for you, my account's cleaned out—but it's all *gut*," she added quickly. "Truman, wait up!"

Rosetta crossed her arms more tightly. "We could probably carry more of her stuff from the trucks, but you know . . . the men seem quite happy to help her."

Christine elbowed her teasingly. "Do I see your brown eyes turning green?"

Rosetta let out a humorless laugh and turned back toward the kitchen. "No green-eyed monster here, sister," she replied. "I'm not envious. I'm just wondering how she'll keep gas in her car and make ends meet, if she's broke. We offered her Mattie's furniture, after all."

"We'll hope she brings you cash," Ruby remarked quietly. "It won't bounce like a check might."

Beulah brought up the rear of their little parade. "Do I need to pour you cats a saucer of milk?" she asked playfully. "I can recall a few times when I was Maria's age and low on cash—mostly because the men in our family didn't allow us to work in restaurants or stores. I squeaked by on egg money and housecleaning jobs. I'm thinking Maria will have more cash in the till tomorrow, after a day in her bakery."

Rosetta peered into the big pot of half-cooked spaghetti. "Her timing's not the best. Our pasta will probably be mushy by the time we sit down to eat."

Christine relit the gas burner. "We'll carry our food to the table when it's ready. If she wants to eat with us, she's old enough to warm up whatever's gotten cold."

As Rosetta went to the refrigerator for the grated Parmesan cheese, she listened to the men talking upstairs as they arranged the furniture the way Maria was directing them. Soon their noisy footsteps and chatter filled the lobby as they descended the stairs and went out to the trucks for another load.

Rosetta peered out the window above the sink, wiping off steam with a tea towel. "Do you suppose that rusted-out red car is Maria's?" she asked quietly.

"Smile when you talk about my Scarlett!" Maria called out as she came down the back stairway. "She's not the prettiest girl on the block, but she gets me where I need to go. Here!" She pulled a wad of paper money out of her jacket pocket before starting through the kitchen. "This should cover the last week of January, all of February, plus those deposits you wanted."

Rosetta clasped her hand around the money so it wouldn't fly all over the kitchen in the wake of Maria's departure. A quick count settled her—at least a little. "Well, she paid an extra fifty on top of the six hundred."

Christine nodded. "Always better to get money than excuses."

Once again they heard Monroe, Amos, and Truman's voices entering the lobby—and then an ear-piercing wail came from the open upstairs hallway where the two stairways met. "Monroe! You left me! I woke up and you were *gone*!"

Rosetta set her money on the counter near the phone. "This could get ugly," she murmured as she started up the back stairway. Leola had been in her room embroidering a dresser scarf, and she'd probably drifted off to sleep and been awakened by the racket the men were making. The young woman was leaning out over the staircase railing, oblivious to the dangerous angle of her slender body as she continued fussing at Monroe.

"Come tuck me in!" Leola pleaded in a little-girl voice. "You know I can't go back to sleep without you."

Rosetta cringed, imagining what Preacher Amos must be thinking—not to mention Edgar and Maria, who didn't know about Leola. She approached Leola quickly and quietly, wondering how best to keep her from toppling over the railing. "Leola! Psst!" Rosetta said. "Let's wait up here, shall we? If you fall over that railing you'll get hurt."

Leola swiveled to look at her. "Did you see all the neat stuff they're bringing in?" she asked loudly. "How come it's not going in *my* room?"

Rosetta reminded herself to remain calm and to consider the consequences of anything she might say. "We have a new renter, Leola. Her name is Maria, and she'll be staying in the apartment between Christine's and mine. Let's get out of the way—"

She took hold of Leola's arm so Monroe and Truman could get past them with a large antique trunk.

"Monroe!" Leola wailed. "I want that!"

The bishop stopped to hold her gaze. "Leola, you're confused," he said gently. "You have furniture in your room. If you want to take another nap, go on back to bed, all right? I'm sorry we woke you up."

Leola blinked rapidly, but tears began streaming down her face. When she tried to follow Monroe down the hallway, Rosetta gripped her arm more tightly.

"Let's go this way," Rosetta suggested. "We can take a peek into Maria's new room on our way to yours."

Amos walked past them carrying a nightstand, doubt creasing his face when he looked at Leola. She appeared fearful, ready to burst into tears again, so Rosetta started down the hallway in the opposite direction. "If we go around this corner—past these empty rooms you looked at," she added as the young woman followed her, "we'll end up at your room. We might peek into Maria's room before the men get there."

Leola seemed caught up in the idea of beating Monroe to Maria's apartment, but they weren't quite fast enough. The bishop and Truman eased the big black trunk through the doorway, and Leola was right behind them. She stopped in the center of the main room, gawking at the blue furniture and the new rug on the floor—and then at Maria.

Rosetta smiled at her new boarder. "Maria, this is Leola Duff, and she's got a room in this hallway for a little while, until—"

"Nuh-uh!" Leola protested, wringing her arm out of Rosetta's grasp. "I'm here forever! I'm gonna marry Monroe!" she crowed. Then she pointed toward the bedroom, with its blue walls and clouds on the ceiling. "But how come you're in *my* room? Those are my blue walls and clouds and—"

Monroe and Truman set the big trunk down with a *whump*. "Leola, you're confused," the bishop repeated. "After you saw how we painted Maria's bedroom, you wanted yours the same. Remember?"

Leola resembled a deer in someone's headlights as she fixed her gaze on Monroe. The tension in the room grew almost unbearable as Preacher Amos stepped in with the nightstand and saw the way she was gazing at the bishop.

"*Jah*, that's how it was, Leola," Amos insisted. "And you'll be going back to your room with Rosetta now, so we can finish carrying Maria's furniture up here."

Leola blinked rapidly, ready to protest until Monroe raised his hand.

"Amos is right. You should go back to your room, Leola," he insisted. "And remember your manners. You're not to come into Maria's room unless she invites you, all right?"

Leola pressed her lips into a tight line and pivoted, stalking out of Maria's raspberry and cream front room.

Was it Rosetta's imagination, or did Maria mutter "Not gonna happen" under her breath? She sensed the relationship between the two young women could be as explosive as tossing a match into a can of kerosene unless she and the other lodge residents were able to convince Leola to keep her distance from Maria—and to stay out of Maria's apartment. It was probably a good thing that Maria would be spending long hours in her bakery six days a week.

"Just leave me alone," Leola pleaded as she entered her room.

Before she could slam the door, Rosetta caught it. How could she make the poor girl feel better—and mind her own business when it came to their new renter? Truth be told, she wasn't wild about having Maria here, either, and she'd followed Leola out of her apartment so she wouldn't have to watch the pretty blonde flirt with Truman. Rosetta spotted the dresser scarf Leola had been embroidering and picked it up off the floor.

"Oh, look at these birds!" she said, amazed by Leola's tiny, precise stitches. "Here's a cardinal and a blue jay— and what's this one going to be?" she asked, pointing at it. "You embroider a lot more neatly than I do, Leola. My stitches always come out choppy-looking, and all different lengths. Yours are nice and even."

Leola cast her a suspicious glance as she thumbed the tears from her cheeks. After a moment, however, she smiled shyly. "I'm gonna make it a goldfinch—dark yellow and black," she replied. "We have lots of goldfinches at our feeders at—at home. But I might not ever get to see them again."

Rosetta carefully hugged Leola's shaking shoulders. "I bet your *mamm*'s feeling a lot better now that she's getting hospital care," she said gently. "You'll be back home before the goldfinches turn yellow this spring—or if you're not, we have goldfinches here, too. We hang bird feeders around the porch, and we see cardinals and blue jays, as well as goldfinches and hummingbirds."

Leola gazed steadily into Rosetta's eyes, swallowing repeatedly to keep from crying. "I like you, Rosetta," she whispered. "You're really nice to me."

Rosetta sent up a quick prayer of thanks. "I hope we can be *gut* friends, Leola. We can keep each other out of trouble, *jah*?"

Leola nodded, glancing absently at the dresser scarf in Rosetta's hands. "I'll get back to my sewing now."

"Or," Rosetta said as she caught the aroma of meat sauce, "we can go downstairs and have spaghetti with Christine and her girls, and the Kuhns. Will you join us for supper? Or would you rather embroider?"

Leola's face lit up. "Sketti? I *love* sketti! Let's go."

As she followed the slender young woman down the back stairs and through the kitchen, Rosetta was pleased that she'd averted another outburst. She was getting used to the fact that, from one moment to the next, Leola might behave as a little girl or as a volatile adolescent—or as the woman determined to marry Monroe Burkholder.

A little later Rosetta and the other ladies were enjoying a chat over their supper at a table in the dining room—and they'd refilled Leola's plate of spaghetti and meat sauce twice—when Maria bounded down the back stairway and past their table, with Truman and Monroe following her.

"I've got a big tin of those cream cheese cake mix cookies—the ones your *mamm* likes so much—in my car, Truman," Maria was saying over her shoulder. "Will you come with me and we'll take them to her?"

Truman waved at the ladies seated around the table, winking at Rosetta. "You don't think I'm going to let Mamm get a head start on those cookies, do you?" he replied with a laugh. "What flavors did you make this time?"

"Lemon with coconut, and chocolate with chocolate chips . . ."

As Maria and Truman passed through the lobby, Rosetta gazed into her plate of spaghetti, no longer hungry. Didn't Truman have a clue about how his flirtation with Maria hurt her? He might as well be sticking a knife in her back.

"Mind if I join you?" Monroe asked as he paused beside the table. "That looks like a mighty fine supper."

"We made plenty for you, *jah*," Christine said as she rose from her chair. "I'll fix you a plate in the kitchen."

"Leola's on her third plateful, so it must be pretty *gut*," Beulah remarked with a smile at the young woman across the table from her.

Leola was too busy gazing up at the bishop to respond. "Sit by me, Monroe!" she insisted, patting the empty chair beside her.

Monroe chose the seat beside Christine, who smiled as she placed his supper in front of him. "You fellows had a lot of stuff to move," she remarked as she sat down. She grabbed the basket sitting in front of Rosetta. "You'll want some of this bread. My girls made it this morning, so it's soft and fresh."

"*Denki*, dear," Monroe murmured as he helped himself. "Maria's pretty well set, I think. That apartment definitely has a different feel from when Mattie was—"

"She's not your *dear*, Monroe. I am."

Everyone got quiet. Leola had placed her fists on her hips and was staring at Monroe and Christine. Spaghetti sauce had splattered onto her chin when she'd sucked up her noodles, but Rosetta knew better than to mention it.

Monroe sat up straighter, resting his fork on his plate. "Leola, we've had this discussion many times," he said, his tone edged with a hint of impatience. "You and I are not a couple. I'm old enough to be—"

"But I *love* you, Monroe!" she blurted. "Stop holding her hand!"

The bishop sighed, but Rosetta was glad—for Christine's sake—that he kept hold of her hand beneath the table. "I love you, as well, Leola—the same way I love your Mamm and your Dat and our friends in Macomb—"

"No! That's not how it is!" Leola's face was growing red

with frustration as she pointed at Christine. "Make her go away! You belong to me!"

Rosetta's heart went out to her sister, who was pressing her lips in a tight line so she wouldn't blurt anything inappropriate. The Kuhns and Christine's two girls watched this drama with wide eyes.

Monroe stood up. In a barely controlled voice, he said, "Leola, you're out of line. I think you'd better go upstairs to your room."

When Leola's face got redder and her mouth opened in protest, Christine stood up beside Monroe. "He's right, Leola," she said firmly. "No matter what you think of me, you're to obey what our bishop tells you."

"I'm not a—a baby!" Leola stood up so fast her chair fell backward and clattered against the floor. She bolted through the kitchen, her anguished cries drifting back to them as the tattoo of her footsteps echoed in the back stairwell.

Monroe sat down again, and so did Christine. His sigh filled the otherwise silent dining room as he looked at the Kuhns, Rosetta, and Christine's daughters. "I'm sorry for the way this is turning out," he murmured, again taking Christine's hand. "I really appreciate the way you all look after Leola, and as soon as I learn her parents have returned home, I'll take her back to Illinois. Meanwhile, I'd welcome your prayers."

"*Jah*, Leola needs our prayers even more than she needs her medications," Ruby murmured. "And you, too, Bishop. We know you didn't ask for this, or encourage her to have such a crush on you."

"It'll all work out," Beulah insisted softly. "God answers our prayers."

Rosetta agreed with her, but deep down she wondered if God would answer their prayers before the situation with Leola spiraled into the dismissal of their new bishop. The women understood that Leola was challenged, but it was only a matter of time before Amos convinced the other two preachers to side with him against Monroe in his quest for the details of the bishop's relationship with Leola.

Why can't Amos see how it is with Leola? Rosetta wondered as she pushed back from the table. Christine rose, as well, and her troubled expression pierced Rosetta's heart. *Why are my sister and I being put to the test where our men are concerned? What have we done that You feel we should be punished for, Lord?*

Chapter Eleven

Over the next three weeks, warmer February temperatures melted the snow and spring fever set in. Mattie ordered the seeds for her produce plots, delighted that she and her sisters would soon be working outdoors again. More local folks were venturing into Promise Lodge to buy Rosetta's goat milk soaps and the Kuhn sisters' cheeses, so they were working more steadily to keep their inventories stocked. Amos's sons-in-law had mailed blueprints for their greenhouse buildings, a barn, and a double-sized home where Bernice, Barbara, Sam, and Simon planned to live and raise their children.

Monroe also had the plans for his barns and the home he wanted, so he'd asked all the men to gather at Noah Schwartz's house with Truman on the twentieth of February to discuss excavating the buildings' foundations. Around eight o'clock that morning they congregated in Noah's dining room, where the building plans were spread out on the extended table. Monroe was pleased to hear the eagerness of the male voices that filled the room with talk of tilling garden plots and expanding the community with homes and businesses. Roman and Noah stood talking with Preacher Eli and Truman, while Preacher Marlin and his son Harley, who farmed and raised sheep, were catching up on the latest news Preacher Amos had of his family.

"Sam tells me the girls are getting rounder by the day, looking forward to June babies," Amos recounted. "We'd best use this *gut* weather to our advantage so their double house and the nursery buildings will be completed before those wee ones arrive. Wouldn't be surprised if we have another burst of winter weather before March is out."

Monroe smiled. It was good to see Amos anticipating the arrival of his grown children and his grandchildren— and it was even better that he'd fully recovered from his fall so he could work on all the structures that would soon be built. Aromas of sugar and spices told him Noah's wife, Deborah, had been busy baking. When she and Christine carried in a big urn of coffee between them and Mary Kate placed a platter of cookies on the sideboard with the coffee, he smiled and called the meeting to order.

"*Gut* morning to all of you," Monroe said above the chatter. "Spring has sprung—and more importantly, the ladies have brought out our goodies. Help yourselves, have a seat, and we'll chat about these building plans."

After he'd put a few cookies on a plate and filled a mug with coffee, Monroe stood at one end of the table where the blueprints and illustrations were displayed. "I'm pleased our friend Truman can be here, and that he's willing for his crew to excavate and help pour concrete for the foundations we'll need."

Truman set his mug on the table and stood near Monroe. "From what I've seen on the TV and online weather stations I follow, these last couple weeks of February look ideal for the excavating and concrete work you folks need," he announced as he held up a sketch he'd done on poster board. "Considering the location the Helmuths have chosen for their nursery, I also suggest a new fork in the road you're using now, which will go from the camp entry over to the nursery parking lot. This will allow shoppers from the nursery to come farther into Promise Lodge and see your other businesses. Here's my sketch of the nursery location and the new road—as well as where the Helmuths' home will be."

As Monroe stepped closer to study Truman's poster, he immediately sensed a ripple of doubt passing through the other men.

"It's all well and *gut* to give folks more access to our businesses," Marlin spoke up, "but that also means we'll have a lot more cars driving through—"

"And if I'm seeing your new road correctly," Amos chimed in, "it'll pass through one of Mattie's biggest produce plots."

"Seems mighty close to the cabins and the lodge, too," Eli Peterscheim pointed out. "I don't believe Rosetta and the other ladies will appreciate the traffic noise—nor do I think the young Helmuths will want another road running so close to their home, because their property is on the county highway."

"Christine's cows won't think much of traffic running near their barn, either," Roman said. "And before we know it, David will be up and running—maybe right into that road, before we can catch him. Thanks for your thoughts, Truman, but I say our businesses—and our families—will be better off without that new road."

Monroe squeezed Roman's shoulder, proud of the young father for speaking up. Rather than appearing put out, Truman was chuckling as he set aside his poster.

"I had a feeling you'd see it that way," he admitted as he picked up a different layout sketch. "One of my crew members thought it would be easy to blade off the roadway while we had the big equipment here—and it would. But I fully understand your reasons for wanting to maintain more privacy with less traffic, so we'll skip the road idea."

The men nodded among themselves and leaned closer to look at the other plan Truman was proposing for the Helmuth place. "Any way we can start preparing the new plots today?" Preacher Eli asked. "It's a little muddy underfoot, but if we get the foundations staked out, you and your crew can dig them whenever you have the time."

"I was hoping we could do that, *jah*," Truman replied eagerly. "We'll have to clear several big trees from the Helmuth land, so if the foundations are marked we'll know which trees should go and which we can preserve."

"Lester Lehman called last night," Monroe put in. "Now that he's sold the siding and window business in Sugarcreek, he plans to move his family here by the middle of March—just a few weeks from now. I'm hoping we can stake out the foundations for my house and barns today, too."

"Sounds like you'll be bunking in one of the cabins once Lester returns," Preacher Marlin remarked. "My family was awfully glad to have those places to stay in while our homes were being built."

"It's a simple lifestyle," his son Harley said with a laugh. "Minerva enjoyed it because she only had one room and the bathroom to clean—and we got to eat our meals with the ladies in the lodge."

Truman smiled. "I have stakes and string in the back of my truck," he said. "If you fellows all hop in the back, we'll head up the hill and mark Monroe's house and barns first. We'll probably be done staking out the Helmuths' four structures by noon, if we hustle."

The men grabbed more cookies before heading to the front room to put on their coats. Monroe was placing their coffee mugs on the sideboard beside the nearly empty cookie tray when Christine came out of the kitchen.

"You fellows made short work of the cookies," she said, reaching for the tray.

Monroe glanced toward the front room, where the other men were heading outside, and turned his broad back toward the kitchen. He lifted Christine's chin with his finger. "Just another little taste of sugar," he murmured before he kissed her. "I hope to have some time alone with you later this week. A little bird told me that Saturday's your birthday."

Her blush—and her response to a second kiss—gratified him. "I'd like that," she murmured. "A lot."

Monroe sighed. "*Denki* for helping with the refreshments over here, as I was concerned that Leola would cause a stir if we met in the lodge," he said softly. "But I don't intend to let her interfere with our lives . . . our courtship."

"I like the sound of that," Christine whispered. "Any word from her folks?"

Monroe shook his head. "Last I heard from Polly, Leola's *mamm* has had some complications. She was in a rehab center, but had to go back to the hospital," he replied.

"Sorry to hear that." Her face, so composed and pretty, turned pink as she met his gaze with her deep green eyes. "I've missed you, Monroe," she whispered. "I understand that you feel responsible for Leola, but I won't wait forever."

Something in his gut twisted at the finality of her statement. "I won't keep you waiting, sweetheart. Let's talk about it Saturday, all right?"

Her smile was the send-off he needed. Monroe grabbed his coat and hurried outside, where the other men waited in the back of Truman's big white pickup.

"One last cookie, Bishop?" Harley teased.

"Something like that," Monroe said as he clambered into the truck. As they rode up the hill to his property, his thoughts whirled. Should he propose to Christine on Saturday? If he didn't, would she really drop him like a hot potato?

Or a cold one, more likely, he mused as they passed the two Lehman homes. Christine's insistent response had taken him by surprise, yet she had reason to be frustrated with him. Keeping his distance from Leola and the lodge these past few weeks hadn't made for a very fulfilling romance for either of them.

When the truck stopped at the crest of the hill, Monroe hopped down from the back along with the other men and grabbed some stakes and string. It felt like a positive step forward to be preparing his property for his three buildings, because it meant he would soon return to Macomb for his furniture and his Clydesdales.

Please, Lord, place Your healing hand on Edna Duff, he prayed. *Leola needs her* mamm *and her meds even more than I need Christine. But Your will be done.*

That afternoon Rosetta turned toward the mudroom door when somebody outside knocked. "*Jah,* who is it?" she called out. "I'm up to my elbows in soap—"

"Engaged in clean living, eh? Maybe I can distract you for a bit, honey-girl."

Rosetta's heart thumped harder as Truman's teasing remark gave her some hopeful ideas. The Kuhns, Phoebe, and Laura were in Christine's apartment with Leola, sewing her some new dresses, and Maria was at her bakery in Cloverdale, so it was a rare time of solitude as she mixed up a batch of goat's milk soap with citrus oils and cornmeal. "Come on in, Truman. It's open."

When he stepped inside and removed his muddy boots, Rosetta couldn't help smiling. "Looks like you men were up to your ankles while you staked out those foundations," she remarked. "*Denki* for not tracking that mud through the lobby."

"I saw you through the window when I drove down the

hill. It's been way too long, Rosetta," he said, wiggling his toes in his socks. "All work and no play is making Truman a dull boy. And lonely, too."

Rosetta finished pouring wet soap into the section of plastic pipe she used as a mold. Truman's smile made her heart flip-flop as he came to stand beside her. "You've been busy, then?" she asked. "What with spring coming, you're probably looking toward landscaping jobs—"

"Looks like I'll have so many jobs I may need to hire more help," he said. "In the past couple of weeks I've been bidding on three new townhome complexes east of Forest Grove—and I got all of those jobs. We'll be planting the bushes and trees, and laying sod around big three- and four-family buildings once their exteriors are finished."

"Wow, congratulations! We're lucky you'll have time to dig foundations for Monroe and Amos's kids." Rosetta held her breath as Truman stepped close to her and slipped his arm around her waist. It seemed like a good time to forget about Maria . . .

"I also landed some decorative metalwork for Noah," he continued in a low voice. "And now that I've figured up what tree removal and four foundations will cost the Helmuth twins, I'm going to call them with my price—and then order as many bushes and young trees as I can for those townhomes. I'm hoping Sam and Simon can bring that nursery stock with them when they come in March."

"That should lower their bill by quite a bit, *jah*?"

Truman nuzzled her nose with his. "It will. But landscaping's on my back burner right now, because the front burner's going full blast," he murmured, his breath tickling her cheek. "If I said you make me feel smokin' hot, would you douse me with cold water?"

Rosetta's eyes widened before he kissed her, which was good reason to close them again. She was still wearing rubber gloves with liquid soap smeared on them, still holding the length of plastic pipe, but she reveled in the feel of Truman's lips pressing hers. "No," she whispered when they came up for air.

Truman eased away, frowning. "That kiss didn't feel like *no* to—"

"I won't throw cold water on you," Rosetta clarified with a giggle. She suddenly felt better than she had for weeks—since before Maria had shown up with her basket of goodies, asking to live at Promise Lodge. Rosetta stood on tiptoe to kiss Truman again.

"Ah. Language." He rested his forehead against hers. "For a moment I forgot my own question. You do that to me, Rosetta," he whispered. "I hope you don't think I've forgotten you lately."

Rosetta placed a plastic cap on the upper end of the pipe, her expression playful. "Well, it's been *different* without you," she said plaintively.

"You've been on my mind night and day," he said, holding her gaze with his warm hazel eyes. "Let's figure on going out Saturday night, *jah*? We can set our wedding date before my calendar fills up with landscaping work. Spring's going to come early and fly by, I suspect."

Rosetta's heart pounded so loudly, she wondered if Truman could hear it. "That's the best idea I've heard for a long while. I don't even care where we go, long as I'm with you."

"That's what I like to hear, honey-girl." Truman kissed her again and then eased away. "I'll leave before I sling you over my shoulder and carry you up to your apartment."

Rosetta laughed and set the pipe on her worktable so the soap would set up. As she washed the soap sludge from her gloves, she had never felt more in love with this dear, affectionate man. "We'd have some ladies peeking in at us as soon as you closed my door," she said, "because they're all on the other side of the wall, in Christine's apartment, sewing dresses for Leola. Some are cutting the fabric, some are pinning pieces together, and Christine's at her machine stitching them up."

"Why am I not surprised they have such an organized system of sewing?" he asked as he walked back toward his muddy boots. "And why am I even less surprised that they're doing Leola such a favor? You ladies have the biggest hearts I've ever seen—which is just one of the reasons I love being around you all . . . and why I've hitched my wagon to your star, Rosetta."

She beamed at him, too overcome with emotion to say anything.

Truman pulled on his second boot and stood up straight, blowing her a kiss. "See you Saturday, sweet Rosetta."

"*Jah*, you will," she murmured. "I can't wait."

Chapter Twelve

As the week of warm weather went by, Christine and the other women watched in amazement as Truman's men felled huge old trees and dug the foundation holes for the nursery buildings, a barn, and the double home where Bernice, Barbara, Sam, and Simon would start their families. On the three days it took to finish their work on the Helmuths' property and at Monroe's place, Truman and his men ate their noon meal in the lodge dining room—along with Monroe and Amos, who were keen to hear about their progress.

"I'm sure glad you fellows didn't take down those evergreens and cedars alongside the road," Christine remarked as she placed a platter of ham steaks on the table. "I think we'd feel really exposed if we could see the state highway—and the folks driving on it could see us."

Truman smiled. "Those trees are still healthy—and a *gut* windbreak for you folks," he said. "We only cleared away trees that were standing where the greenhouses, nursery plots, and the Helmuth house will be."

After everyone was seated, they prayed silently for a moment.

"I think that intersection will be an ideal place for a nursery," Monroe said as he spooned up a helping of hash brown casserole. "Folks driving along the highway and the county road will be able to see all the nursery plots and the greenhouse and pull in from either side."

"And from there, they'll also be able to see the rest of Promise Lodge," Amos pointed out as he stabbed a ham steak. "I'm glad we agreed not to put an extra road through our property, but maybe we could post signs at the nursery directing folks to the produce stand, the cheese factory, and the new bakery—and even to Marlin's barrel factory."

"A slatted sign like the one Noah painted for the entry would work," Mattie said as she passed a bowl of steaming green beans to Truman. "Maybe it could be one big sign with all of our shops listed, pointing down from the intersection."

"This is really exciting," Rosetta said as she smiled at Edgar, Truman, and the other workmen. "We're so glad you fellows are here, accomplishing in days what it would take our men *weeks* to do with hand tools and horse-drawn equipment."

"I'm pleased the Helmuths are starting up a nursery," Truman remarked. "When I called Sam last night to tell him what sort of trees and bushes I'll be wanting for our new townhome projects, he was delighted that he could barter his plants for most of the expense of our excavating and tree removal. And he'll provide us with heat-resistant varieties that'll grow well here in Missouri."

Truman smiled at Preacher Amos. "I think your girls hitched up with some smart businessmen," he said. "I wouldn't be surprised if they eventually latch on to some additional land for other nursery plots to keep up with the demand for their plants. They might also take over the orchard and sell the apples as a part of their business. That would be a good fit with your other enterprises."

Amos chuckled. "I can recall when Allen made fun of Sam and Simon because of their fiery red hair, but he's changed his tune—and he left me a phone message this morning to tell me he's passed all of his licensing exams."

Mattie clapped her hands. "I knew he could do it! So now he's a certified plumber and electrician?"

Amos nodded proudly as he buttered a hot biscuit. "I called him back to congratulate him—and to encourage him to come soon so he can help with these new houses and buildings. He was a pretty fair carpenter even before he went to trade school."

"The apple didn't fall far from the tree, eh?" Truman teased. His eyebrows rose when he saw Ruby and Beulah carrying in casserole pans that filled the room with their sweet, fruity fragrance. "And if my nose is working right, I'm guessing we've got apple crisp for dessert."

Beulah nodded as she set the big glass pan in front of him. "And peach cobbler, too. I know how you fellows like your sweets, and we're happy to bake them for you. Folks who come to the new nursery—and Maria's new bakery—will most likely visit our cheese factory."

"And the nursery will be another great place for my bees to get their nectar," Ruby put in as she placed the cobbler between Monroe and Amos. "I might need to start up another hive or two this summer."

"We've made so much progress," Christine said as she slung her arms around her sisters. "Last year at this time, Mattie and Rosetta and I were just getting up the nerve to buy this abandoned church camp, and look how far we've come."

When the front door banged in the lobby, everyone looked up to see Maria hurrying into the dining room. Her face glowed with happiness as she found Truman among the other men. "Is that staked rectangle in front of the barn where my bakery will be?" she asked eagerly.

Truman nodded as he spooned apple crisp onto his plate. "I measured your building after church last Sunday, and we've dug out enough dirt to pour your slab when the concrete truck comes—which might be tomorrow or Saturday."

"That is so cool!" Maria exclaimed. "I'll be glad when I don't have to drive to Cloverdale so early in the mornings to start my baking."

"Seems like you're back a lot sooner than usual today," Beulah said. "I hope that means you sold every single roll and pastry you made."

"I did. The principal from the school wanted a lot of stuff for a staff meeting, and he cleaned me out." Maria gazed at the bowls and platters of food on the table. "Mind if I fill a plate? I haven't had a real meal today."

"Dig in," Ruby said. "Whatever you eat now won't be leftovers we eat this evening."

Christine laughed along with everyone else, but it was Monroe's secretive wink that made her pulse speed up. After Truman's men had finished eating and Maria had taken her dinner upstairs, she and Mattie and Rosetta began stacking the dirty dishes and carrying the platters and bowls back to the kitchen. She was surprised that Monroe followed them with the breadbasket and the peach cobbler—or what was left of it.

"May I have a word?" he asked as he set down what he'd carried. He looked around tentatively. "Dare I ask what's kept Leola occupied while we've been eating?"

Rosetta began running hot water into the sink. "Phoebe and Laura took her out for dinner and to get some material for more dresses. Nina's Fabrics in Forest Grove has a nice selection—and Leola was wanting some more pieces to embroider, too," she added. "She's really very *gut* at handwork."

Monroe nodded. "I'm glad she's finding projects to

keep her busy," he said, "and I appreciate the way your girls have become her friends, Christine. In Macomb, where folks have known Leola all her life, she doesn't have many gal pals. The girls her age have married, or they have interests that don't include somebody who requires a lot of patience and understanding."

Christine smiled as she scraped the dinner plates. "I'm proud of Phoebe and Laura. They've always taken the side of the underdog and the unfortunate."

Monroe stepped closer to her, under the guise of carrying her scraped plates to the sink. "Still on for Saturday?" he whispered.

She nodded. "Got a plan?"

"My place. Four o'clock."

Christine smiled as she scraped the last plate. "What shall I bring for supper?"

"Just yourself." He nodded at her sisters and stepped away from her. "*Gut* to have you with us today, Mattie. Glad Amos hasn't chained you to the stove at home."

Mattie laughed. "You think I'd let him get away with that?" she teased. "I love being a wife again, but sometimes I miss cooking with my sisters and friends. This kitchen is a lot livelier than mine."

Christine smiled at her elder sister. Someday soon she hoped to be wearing the same expression of married contentment that softened Mattie's face.

On Saturday, Christine, her girls, her sisters, and Leola spent the morning making pies and preparing the dinner that would be served on Sunday after the church service. She couldn't help wondering what secret plans Monroe had for their supper this evening—and she couldn't keep a smile from her face as she and Rosetta mixed up a big batch of sweet and sour bean salad. "It's nice to be serving summery foods in February," she remarked as she stirred oil and vinegar together for the dressing. "We'll no doubt have another flurry or two of snow, but this bean salad will hit the spot alongside the fried chicken Mattie's making."

Rosetta glanced across the big kitchen to where Laura and Leola were taking pies from the oven. She lowered her voice. "Puh! The *thing* you have for the bishop will melt any snow we get, birthday girl."

"I'm not the only one with a date tonight," Christine shot back softly. "I take it you've settled your differences with Truman?"

Rosetta's cheeks turned pink. "He, um, sort of settled them himself. I was wrong to doubt him."

"Glad to hear it. Maria may be young and pretty, but she has nothing on you, little sister."

When they finished the baking and cooking for Sunday, Christine and the rest of them gathered around a dining room table to share slices of the lemon birthday cake Phoebe and Laura had made as a surprise for her. Christine chuckled as her older daughter began lighting the five candles arranged in a circle. "You've done me several favors, not putting forty-one on here," she said.

"She did us all a favor," Mattie teased. "Think how many holes all those candles would've made in our cake!"

"We figured that one for each decade, plus one for the extra year, would be enough," Laura explained when flames danced on the candles. "Make a wish, Mamm! And make it a *gut* one."

Closing her eyes, Christine leaned close enough to her cake to feel the warmth of the burning candles. *I wish . . . I wish Monroe would ask me to marry him—and find a bishop to perform our ceremony—very soon. And I wish the same happiness for Rosetta.*

She inhaled deeply and blew out all the candles with one breath. As everyone clapped, Phoebe plucked out the smoking candles so Laura could cut thick slices of the cake.

"Too bad Ruby and Beulah are making cheese today," Rosetta remarked as she added scoops of lemon sherbet to the plates of cake. "We'll have to save them back some of this luscious cake."

"What'd you wish for, Christine?" Leola asked excitedly.

Christine smiled as she accepted her generous piece of cake with a double scoop of sherbet. She knew better than to admit her wishes about Monroe—especially when Leola appeared as happy as a girl at her own party. "If I tell, my wish won't come true," she replied. "When's your birthday, Leola?"

Leola smiled around a mouthful of yellow cake. "April second!"

Mattie spooned up some ice cream. "We'll have to have a party for you."

"Or maybe you'll be home with your family by then," Rosetta put in, smiling kindly at Leola. "I'm sure your *mamm* hopes to celebrate your birthday with you."

"*Jah*, she says I'm her special girl," Leola replied wistfully. "But then, I'm her only girl. And we've got no boys."

Christine sensed some homesickness in Leola's words, and she prayed that the young woman would indeed be home with her parents to celebrate her birthday. Leola had been at Promise Lodge a little more than a month—a long time to go without her mother and her medications. She appeared to be nearly normal and in control of her emotions today, but they all knew she could change in a heartbeat with the slightest hint of a subject that upset her.

After they'd finished their cake and ice cream, Christine went upstairs with her daughters and Leola to finish the two dresses they'd started earlier in the week. It was gratifying to see the delight on Leola's face when she tried on the royal blue dress and its matching cape.

"I could be a bride!" she said as she turned from side to

side in front of the full-length mirror. "It's really pretty. *Denki* for sewing it for me."

"You're welcome, Leola," Christine said. "We all enjoy new clothes, and it may be a while before your *mamm* can make any for you. Have you heard how she's doing lately?"

Leola pressed her lips together, shaking her head dolefully. "Last time Aunt Polly talked to Monroe, Mamm wasn't quite ready to go home. Maybe soon, though."

"We're keeping her in our prayers," Phoebe put in. "I'm almost finished hemming this green dress so you can try it on one last time."

A short while later, Leola was smiling at her reflection again. "I'm going to wear this to church tomorrow," she said. "It reminds me of green grass in the summer sunshine."

"And it's a nice knit that won't need to be ironed after you wash it," Phoebe said as she began putting away her pins and sewing scissors.

Christine folded the sewing machine down into its cabinet and closed the lid. Once the three girls left her apartment, her thoughts turned to what she'd wear for her date with Monroe . . . perhaps a dress a deeper shade of green than Leola's, because it accentuated her eyes. It was three thirty, so she changed into the fresh dress and slipped a white apron over it.

The mirror confirmed her hopes: in her crisp white *kapp* and clean clothes, she appeared no older than forty-one—and she felt a lot younger, anticipating her evening with Monroe. Had they not both been previously married, going to his house alone would've been considered improper, but she planned to use her unattached state to best advantage. As she wrapped a shawl around her shoulders and slipped down the back stairs unnoticed, she intended not to be a widow for much longer.

Christine's heart danced as she strode up the road to Lester Lehman's house. Farther up the hill, flagged stakes marked the freshly poured foundation of Monroe's new home. *My new home, too—if my wish comes true,* she thought as she went up the walk toward the man she loved.

Chapter Thirteen

Monroe's heart pounded as he stood at the door watching Christine come up the walk. Her smile looked years younger than when he'd met her last Christmas. The spring in her step told him she was as eager to be with him as he was to have her to himself for the evening. In some ways, he was more excited about courting and winning Christine than he'd been when he'd gotten engaged to Linda. This time around, he knew what marriage was all about, and he'd learned how important it was to make his woman feel special.

When Christine knocked, Monroe suppressed a grin as he looked out the door's high window at her. She saw him then, laughing as she held his gaze. When she nipped her lip in anticipation, he could wait no longer. He had to taste those lips, show her how much he loved her. Wanted her.

"Get yourself in here, birthday girl," he teased as he opened the door. He took her in his arms and turned, leaning against the door to close it.

"Where's my present?" she demanded playfully.

Monroe lowered his face toward hers, stalling as long as he was able, gazing into her green eyes. When he kissed Christine, she rose on her tiptoes to return his fervor. The rest of the world ceased to exist for the long moments they shared their affection, until Monroe finally eased away. "Marry me, Christine," he murmured urgently.

She gazed at him for the longest time. "*Jah*, Monroe, I will. I'd be honored to be your wife," she said solemnly. Then she chuckled. "Maybe because something smells awfully *gut*. A husband who cooks is a real catch," she teased. "What's for supper?"

Monroe pulled her close and kissed her again, deeply pleased that she'd agreed to be his, now and forever. "I learned to cook a few easy things out of desperation, after Linda passed," he explained. He took her hand and led her toward the kitchen. "I figured out that hamburger and spaghetti noodles and a big jar of sauce—and shredded cheese—make a casserole that lasts me a few meals. I confess that the salad is out of a bag, and that I had Maria make your cake at her bakery."

When he gestured toward the counter, Christine's eyes got wide. "Roses! The biggest red roses I've ever seen—and so many!" she exclaimed as she rushed toward the huge bouquet. She closed her eyes and sniffed them, sighing ecstatically. Then she looked at him, one eyebrow raised. "And what if I hadn't said *jah*?" she teased.

Monroe laughed. "Actually, I'd planned to propose a little later in our evening, with those roses as an enticement," he admitted. "But the words just popped out. I couldn't wait, Christine. I—I love you so much."

"Oh, Monroe," she said with a sigh. "You make me a happy, blessed woman. I love you, too."

He joined her at the counter as she looked at the round, two-layer cake frosted in white with *Happy Birthday, Dear Christine* in green letters across the top. She picked up the card beside it, appearing absolutely delighted. "Two cakes in one day," she murmured as she broke the envelope's seal with her thumbnail. "I'll be *waddling* back to my apartment—"

"Have I ever told you about my favorite form of exercise?" Monroe teased, wiggling his eyebrows at her. "A hint: it's *not* jogging around a training ring with a Clydesdale. And it's something I hope we'll both enjoy often."

The rising color in her cheeks made him wish he could sweep Christine into his arms and carry her upstairs—but this wasn't the time or the place. He would wait until they were married and his new home was built . . . or at least until the walls were in place.

She leaned into him as she pulled out the birthday card with a bouquet of lilacs and sweet peas on the front. "'To the woman I love,'" she read aloud before opening the card. "'May your birthday bring you sunshine and blessings to last a lifetime. All my love, Monroe.' Oh . . . roses, and a cake, and a pretty card. This is my best birthday ever."

When Christine looked up at him with a tear trailing down each cheek, her face alight with adoration, Monroe knew his life was about to take a major turn for the better. He gently thumbed away her tears. "So now I have to keep making each year even better—and I look forward to doing that for you, sweetheart."

"And your birthday is when?"

"August first. By then we'll be settled into our new home, sitting in the porch swing and looking out over green pastures where my—"

A loud knock at the door made them both jump.

Monroe reluctantly excused himself, wondering who could possibly be at the door. Lester and his family weren't due to return for another couple of weeks—and he'd told no one Christine was coming over, wanting no interruption of the romantic evening he'd—

"Monroe! Look what I made you!"

When the door swung open, he regretted that he hadn't locked it. Leola was beaming at him, holding out a cherry pie with a lattice crust as she hurried toward him. Monroe swallowed his frustration and quickly prayed that Christine wouldn't take this the wrong way—as though Leola made a habit of visiting him. Something in the young woman's furtive smile told him she hadn't chosen this particular arrival time out of coincidence.

He crossed his arms, determined not to get angry—but not to allow this intrusion to end his date with Christine, either. "Leola, why are you here?" he asked firmly. "You know it's not proper to come into my house by yourself."

Leola stopped a few feet in front of him, still holding out the pie. "But I didn't!" she crowed. "I saw Christine come over, so I knew it would be all right to bring you a present."

Monroe crossed his arms tighter, quelling the urge to grab her slender shoulders and escort her out the door. Leola's shining eyes told him she knew exactly what she was interrupting. He wasn't surprised to hear Christine coming from the kitchen, and when she stopped beside him, she appeared even more infuriated than he felt.

"That's one of the pies Rosetta baked for the common meal tomorrow," she stated. "She always makes a lattice crust like that."

Monroe raised an eyebrow. "So you didn't bake the pie for me, Leola. Your parents taught you better than to lie about—"

"Nuh-uh!" she protested with a quivering chin. "Why do you believe Christine instead of me? I want *you* to have it, Monroe! I just wanted us to have a piece of pie together!"

He shook his head slowly, wondering how to avert the crisis that was about to flare like an unattended grease fire.

"Why did you follow me?" Christine asked tersely.

"You have to understand that, unless Monroe invites you, you have no reason to—"

"I love Monroe! And I'm going to marry him—not you!" Leola shrieked. "You leave! Not me."

Monroe stepped forward, but Leola moved faster—and she heaved the cherry pie at Christine. Christine caught it against her snowy white apron, exasperated but managing to keep it in one spot.

"That's it. You're going back to the lodge," Monroe said as he turned Leola toward the door. "You've really made me angry this time—"

"But I *love* you!" Leola cried out as she struggled to keep up with his stride.

Monroe stopped, holding her at arm's length, praying he would say the right thing. He knew he could crush her spirit with harsh words, but somehow he had to get his message across. "Leola," he began, curbing the tone and volume of his voice, "when you love somebody, you don't throw a pie at his friend—or at his fiancée. And you don't come to his house when you know he has company—or when he hasn't invited you. I know you understand this."

Leola gawked at him as though he'd sprouted a second head. Then she burst into tears. "No!" she wailed. "I love you and *I'm* going to marry you."

"No, you're not, Leola. Please get that through your head." Monroe didn't dare look behind him to see how Christine was reacting to this awkward scene. Would she think less of him because of the way he was treating a mentally and socially disadvantaged young woman? "I'm old enough to be your *dat*—"

"No! Dat is way older than you, Monroe."

She was right. And he wondered how he kept talking himself into a maze of words that had no exit. "Never mind that. We are *not* getting married," he insisted as he steered her toward the door again. "But we *are* getting you to a doctor this week."

He maneuvered Leola through the doorway, pausing to glance back at Christine. Where she had removed the pie from her midsection, her white apron had rows and columns of little red patches. She was nipping her lip in frustration.

"Please stay," he pleaded softly. "But I can sure understand why you wouldn't want to."

For a moment she looked ready to cry, but then she glanced at the pie in her hands. "I'll come with you," she said hoarsely. "This pie's a little the worse for wear, but we can still eat it tomorrow. I'll turn off your oven."

Monroe thanked God for Christine's understanding, her practical outlook on life. As he accompanied Leola down the stairs and along the walk, he vowed to take up where he'd left off with the wonderful woman who'd agreed to be his wife.

Rosetta smoothed her cream-colored apron over her brick red dress, pleased that she looked fresh and relaxed after a day in the kitchen. She'd showered and rewound her bun and put on a fresh *kapp*, even though Truman would be happy to see her even if she wore the old gray dress she gardened in. She grabbed a shawl and started down the back stairway, figuring to take her time walking out to the road and up the hill to the Wickey place. She hoped to get better acquainted with Truman's *mamm*, Irene, meanwhile picturing herself a married woman living in her mother-in-law's home. It would be an adjustment, but Rosetta believed with all her heart that she could make a happy marriage with Truman in the house where he'd grown up.

As Rosetta reached the kitchen, a commotion in the

lobby made her hurry in that direction. The last thing she'd expected to see was Bishop Monroe guiding a wailing Leola inside, followed by Christine—who was carrying a crushed yet familiar-looking pie.

Rosetta's eyes widened. "What happened?" she whispered to her sister as Monroe started up the big staircase, gently steering Leola ahead of him. "And what's that on your apron?"

Christine shook her head ruefully. "You won't believe it. Leola saw me going to Monroe's, and she followed me with this pie. She claimed she'd baked it for him, but when he refused to accept it—or her pleas that I should leave and she should stay," she added, "Leola threw the pie at me."

"Oh, no. I was hoping it would be a wonderful evening—"

"And Monroe had planned one of those," Christine put in as they headed for the kitchen, "but the date came to a halt when our, um, visitor, let herself into the house."

As her sister set the crushed cherry pie on the counter, Rosetta shook her head. "This can't continue," she murmured. "Surely somebody back where Leola and Monroe came from could take responsibility for her. Surely her parents will be home soon."

"Monroe's taking her to a doctor first thing next week, to figure out what sort of medications she's supposed to be taking." Christine sighed. "I'd better go upstairs to help him. I have no idea what we'll do if she refuses to stay in her room."

Rosetta sighed. "Well, I hope you can still spend some time with him tonight."

"Me, too. Monroe made dinner, and had a cake and a card—and the biggest bouquet of roses I've ever seen—waiting for me," Christine added wistfully. Then she grabbed Rosetta's hand, her face alight with a smile. "He asked me. And I said *jah*."

"Oh, Christine!" Rosetta hugged her hard. "That's the best news ever. I'm so happy for you!"

Christine eased away to gaze at her. "I'll be praying that your evening with Truman is just as romantic—without any surprise visitors."

Rosetta nodded happily. Maria usually worked late on Saturday, preparing some of her dough and frostings so they'd be ready when she went to work early on Monday morning. Rosetta watched Christine climb the back stairway, sending up a prayer for a peaceful conclusion to this unsettling episode with Leola.

When she stepped out to the lodge's porch, a siren and flashing blue and red lights made her frown and jog toward the road. An ambulance was rushing up Truman's driveway! Rosetta ran faster, watching as the paramedics wheeled a stretcher into the Wickeys' front door. Was Truman ill, or was it his mother who needed emergency help?

Rosetta reached the county road and jogged to her left just as a familiar red car topped the hill coming toward her—and then swerved into the Wickeys' driveway. *How did Maria know just when to show up?*

By the time Rosetta reached Truman's place, the paramedics were coming out of the house with Irene on the stretcher and Truman in their wake. Maria rushed from her car and grabbed Truman in a hug, babbling something about going with them—and then she followed the stretcher into the ambulance. Truman ran toward his garage, oblivious to Rosetta's presence. When the ambulance raced down the driveway, Rosetta could only step back out of the way, gawking in disbelief.

A few moments later, a big white pickup sped out the driveway, throwing gravel—until Truman saw her and stopped. "Mamm passed out and I couldn't bring her around," he explained. "I'll keep you posted when I get back."

Nodding, Rosetta watched his truck race the rest of the way down the driveway. When his tires squealed on the county road, she prayed earnestly. *Keep him and his mother safe, Lord, and guide the folks who are caring for Irene.*

Sighing, Rosetta started home. She felt bad that their date had been canceled by such an emergency, and she understood why Truman had probably forgotten all about it.

But why had Maria rushed into the ambulance, as though she were family—as though she and Irene were close? Had Truman called Maria after he'd phoned 911? The timing of her arrival was too perfect to be a mere coincidence—wasn't it? It wasn't as though he'd told Maria to return to her car—and he hadn't given a single thought to asking Rosetta to go with him.

Rosetta took her time walking home. As she passed beneath the curved metal Promise Lodge entry sign, it still seemed strange to gaze past the garden plots to where so many large trees had been cleared. The concrete foundations had been poured for a greenhouse and a large nursery building, and—across what would soon be a parking lot— the basement for the Helmuths' double house and the slab for their barn rose up from the mud. Ahead of her on the road, Monroe and Christine walked hand in hand toward Lester Lehman's house to continue their date.

At least those two will have a nice time tonight, she thought.

Rosetta entered the lodge through the mudroom and was glad to see Ruby and Beulah in the kitchen. "Got enough leftovers for me, too?" she asked.

The gray-haired sisters turned, their eyebrows rising. "Thought you had a date," Beulah said. "We just got your sister and the bishop squared away. What can we do for you, sweetie?"

"We're glad you can join us, understand," Ruby put in gently. "But we're sorry about whatever happened with Truman."

Their kindness almost made Rosetta cry. "Who's watching Leola?"

Beulah shook her head as though the situation with their guest was beyond her comprehension. "Phoebe and Laura are crocheting in her room while Leola embroiders, and—"

"We took them up a big tray of sandwiches, cookies, and milk," Ruby added. "That young lady's getting more confused by the day, and she's making it look bad for your bishop, too."

Rosetta nodded. "I'll be back after I change out of this dress. *Denki* for looking after us all, ladies."

Chapter Fourteen

Christine sat between her sisters on a pew bench Sunday morning, following Monroe's flowing voice as he brought the second, longer sermon to a close. It was no coincidence that he had spoken at length about the way Jesus had accepted men and women from every walk of life. He had eaten with tax collectors and healed people simply because they—or their friends—believed He could perform a miracle for them.

"Jesus is our example," Monroe said, meeting the gazes of folks in the congregation. "He healed a Roman centurion's servant from afar with just a word—even though Rome had occupied Jerusalem for decades—because for Jesus, the centurion's faith overrode the day's political difficulties. He loved little children, he respected women—which wasn't common in Bible times," he continued earnestly, "and he took pity on lepers and those who were possessed by demons. Today we don't think of people being possessed, but I'd like to suggest that diseases such as cancer, Alzheimer's, and mental illness qualify as demons."

Christine held her breath when Monroe smiled at her before he continued preaching. He had a way of holding everyone's attention, applying lessons from the Bible to their everyday lives—just as he constantly let her know she was loved and cherished. The supper, conversation, and cake they'd shared yesterday evening had made her believe even more fully that Monroe was a man of God—and the man with whom God intended her to spend the rest of her life.

"What a wonder it would be if Jesus returned in our lifetime and wiped out those demon diseases," Monroe continued with awe in his voice. "Until He does return for us to take us into His kingdom, however, we must watch and pray. We must care for those who are ill and can't help themselves."

Mattie was nodding, no doubt recalling the demon of diabetes that had tortured her first husband and wreaked havoc on their marriage. Frances Lehman sat with her hands clasped in her lap, most likely worried because Floyd hadn't felt strong enough to come to church this morning. Christine sent up a prayer for Irene Wickey, hoping she would soon be well enough to come home, and she prayed for Leola and her parents, as well. It would indeed be a blessing if Jesus could cast out the demon of Leola's mental challenges . . .

They sang a final hymn, filling the meeting room with the men's resonant baritone voices and the women's sweet harmonies. As the familiar song ended, Bishop Monroe closed his hymnal and smiled at all the folks around him. "Do we have announcements or concerns to share before we eat?" he asked.

Rosetta sat straighter on the bench beside Christine. "Truman's mother was rushed away in an ambulance last night, unconscious," she said.

As folks were murmuring about that, Frances Lehman spoke up. "Floyd complained of feeling weak and very tired this morning," she said in a tight voice. "If you'd care to visit him later in the day, it might perk him up."

After another moment passed, Monroe suggested they go to the dining room—but he was interrupted.

"Monroe, I wore my new blue wedding dress today!" Leola proclaimed proudly. "Now we can get married, just like you said!"

Christine turned, pleased to see that Phoebe and Laura were trying to get Leola to hush and sit down, but the awkward subject of her relationship with Monroe had already made folks gaze at the bishop with questions in their eyes.

"Leola, I've told you time and again why that won't happen," Monroe said patiently.

"But you *ruined* me!" she cried out ecstatically, hurrying to the end of the row to rush toward him. "Now you've gotta marry me, coz I love you so much, Monroe!"

Christine's stomach tied itself in a knot when Preacher Amos rose from the preacher's bench to stand beside Monroe, who was doing his best to hold Leola at arm's length.

"What's going on, Bishop?" Amos asked loudly enough for everyone to hear him. "This isn't the first time Miss Duff has claimed that you ruined her—and I saw her walking up the road to your place with a pie and a big smile last night," he continued tersely. "I insist you give us a full, valid explanation of your relationship with her."

Monroe stood head and shoulders taller than Amos. In an attempt to settle Leola, he allowed her to wrap her arms around his waist as he put an arm around her shoulders. "We're taking her to the doctor as soon as we can get an appointment—hopefully tomorrow," Monroe said. "She's been off her medications since she left home, so I'm hoping we can get prescriptions for—"

"The question I asked you has nothing to do with medications, Burkholder," Amos snapped. "She's been chasing after you—all the way from Illinois—and she obviously has reason to believe you've behaved inappropriately. Did that happen again last night?"

"This isn't what it seems," Christine blurted out, popping up from the pew bench. "I was at the Lehman place with Monroe when Leola arrived, and I can assure you that nothing inappropriate happened. Leola is confused—"

"Nuh-uh!" Leola cried out. "Monroe has to marry me, coz I love him."

Christine paused, praying for patience and for Amos's open mind. "I love him, too, Leola," she said, "so that means we have to *help* Monroe instead of getting him in more trouble. Please be quiet."

Leola frowned, not fully understanding. At least she complied as she leaned against Monroe.

Christine looked at Amos, who'd suffered a brief physical disability—and with it depression serious enough that he'd broken his engagement to Mattie. "Remember how you lost your senses last winter when you were confined to a wheelchair? And how taking antidepressants brought you back to the land of the living?" she asked him gently. "Leola was upset when her mother was taken away to a distant hospital, and she came here without her medications—"

"When you make excuses for Leola, you don't relieve my suspicions about Monroe's relationship with her," Preacher Amos interrupted. He looked over at the men's side, as though asking for their agreement. "Our bishop still hasn't given us a straight answer about coming here to Promise Lodge, or about this young woman who followed him, or—"

"Here's *my* answer," Christine cut in. It was rude and improper to challenge a leader of the church, but Amos was just *wrong* to be stirring a pot of misinformation and suspicion. "Monroe asked me to marry him last night, and I've agreed—we're engaged," she continued boldly. "I can assure you I saw no signs of inappropriate behavior as he tried to explain to Leola that she shouldn't have come to his house alone or uninvited. If I had, I would've walked away from our engagement," she stated, gazing steadily at Amos. "Apparently you saw Leola walking up the hill, but you didn't see the three of us returning to the lodge about ten minutes later."

When Amos remained silent, Christine sat down. Rosetta and Mattie took her hands, nodding their support.

"Leola looks perfectly normal to me," Preacher Eli said as he rose from the preacher's bench with Marlin.

"*Jah*, but appearances can be deceiving," Phoebe put in as she stood up, extending her hand toward Leola. "How about you and I go to the kitchen, Leola? We can start putting out the food while these folks finish talking. You can help me cut that chocolate pie."

Leola brightened. When she looked up at Monroe and he nodded his encouragement, she followed Phoebe out of the meeting room.

"Amos, I believe we've settled the matter for now," Mattie said, standing up to make her point. "After what Christine went through when her first marriage ended with a barn fire, I can assure you she'd not be sticking up for Monroe if she didn't believe he was a decent, respectable man. We should keep Leola and her parents in our prayers, asking God to bring them all home and back to their normal lives."

Preacher Amos's expression hardened, and he appeared ready to put Mattie in her place. Christine figured she might be in for a lecture, as well. Preacher Marlin came up beside Amos, however, and said what was probably on a lot of people's minds as most of the women went to the kitchen to help set out the food.

"It's a puzzlement, Amos, because Leola doesn't look like folks who have Down syndrome or other obvious disabilities," he said quietly. "But the more I hear what she says, over and over, the more I suspect she has difficulty functioning both socially and mentally."

"Still doesn't feel right to me that Monroe sticks up for her, yet he won't give me a straight answer about what he has or hasn't done to her," Amos muttered. "*Somebody* has to hold him accountable, because he's had the women wrapped around his little finger since the moment he arrived. He's the bishop, for Pete's sake—our model of Christ's behavior."

Knowing nothing she could say would change Amos's harsh opinion, Christine let him and Marlin pass ahead of her, headed for the dining room. She waited at the end of the pew bench for Monroe, who was chatting with Frances and Gloria Lehman about Floyd's deteriorating condition. After those two ladies thanked him, they congratulated him and Christine and proceeded toward the meal that awaited them.

Monroe approached her and took her hand. They were the only ones who'd remained in the meeting room, and he gazed at her for a long moment. "I wish you didn't have to defend me," he murmured, "but I appreciate it. I just feel really uncomfortable talking about Leola's condition as though she's not in the room—and Amos always puts me on the spot when she and everyone else can witness it. Countless hours he and I worked together on the new foundations this past week, yet he never asked me about my relationship with Leola."

Christine smiled sadly. "Amos is a strong leader—a man whose heart is in the right place," she said softly. "We couldn't have come nearly so far with our businesses had he not come to Promise Lodge with us. But for some reason he believes everything Leola says."

She paused, holding Monroe's green-eyed gaze. "Why has she latched on to you so fiercely, Monroe? What makes her think you'll marry her?"

He shook his head, sighing loudly. "I wish I knew. Even if I understood what's going through her mind when she says I ruined her, I doubt she'd stop saying it. She behaved this way back in Macomb every now and again—but she's gotten a lot worse since she's been off her medication."

"I'll pray that the doctor you see understands Leola's condition and prescribes whatever will bring her back into balance."

Monroe licked his lips. "I was hoping you'd go with me, Christine. It doesn't look so good for an unrelated male to take her to the clinic—and who knows what she might say about me to the doctor?"

Christine had no trouble imagining what Leola might say or do if she got upset in the doctor's office—and folks all over the clinic would hear her piercing voice and her unflattering accusations. "*Jah*, I'll go," she agreed. "Just being in the waiting room with English folks and the doctor might be enough to set her off. Between the two of us, we'll have a better chance of getting her in and out of the clinic than if you take her by yourself."

"You're an angel and I love you," Monroe whispered. He tucked her hand into the crook of his elbow, his dimples winking at her when he smiled. "Shall we join the others? If there's chocolate pie, I want to grab a piece before it's all gone."

Christine chuckled, feeling young and desirable—and needed—as they entered the dining room. Later she would be praying for strength and patience to face their trip to the clinic, but for now she wanted to enjoy the company of the man she loved.

Our situation is in God's hands, she reminded herself as she took a plate from the table where the food was arranged. *He'll reveal everything in His own gut time.*

Chapter Fifteen

Christine's temples began to pound, and by the time the doctor came into the exam room, she had a full-blown headache. Monroe had called the clinic as soon as it opened Monday morning and explained their situation, but the only doctor who saw Plain patients without insurance didn't have an opening until Wednesday, unless another patient canceled. The lady on the phone had told him he could take his chances and show up, and perhaps the doctor would squeeze them in—so they'd left Promise Lodge at eight in the morning.

It was now three thirty. Monroe had gone to a deli across the street and brought them sandwiches at noon, but Leola had been antsy all day and barely picked at her food. She'd sucked down her cola, so Monroe had returned to the deli for another one, which she'd spilled all over the waiting room floor. *Frenzied* didn't begin to describe Leola, and Christine was beginning to feel frazzled, as well. She marveled that Monroe remained so calm and patient, but the deepening lines around his eyes told of his weariness. At long last the receptionist told them a cancellation had opened up a time slot, so they were escorted to an exam room.

"What can I do for you folks today? I'm Dr. Todd." The slender doctor shook hands with Monroe and Christine as he entered the room, but he got a wary look from Leola, who refused to offer her hand. He appeared to be around Monroe's age, although his thinning hair was a contrast to the bishop's thick, wavy mop.

Monroe responded. "This is Leola Duff. When she came here from Illinois, she didn't bring her medications—"

"I flushed them down the toilet and crumpled up the labels," Leola announced proudly. "Aunt Polly got really mad at me, so I left."

Dr. Todd's eyebrows rose. He skimmed the information form Monroe had filled out earlier in the day. "What medications is she on?" he asked. "What conditions are being treated?"

Monroe glanced at Christine, as though to gather strength. "Leola doesn't see the world the way the rest of us do," he began cautiously. "She . . . she's socially and mentally disadvantaged—"

"Monroe, you know that's not true," Leola interrupted matter-of-factly. "I'm just fine, now that I'm here with you."

Dr. Todd was following the conversation attentively. "And what was she taking?" he asked again.

Monroe shrugged wearily. "I have no idea. Leola's parents were called away to Chicago on a medical emergency involving her mother, and the aunt they entrusted her to doesn't know her doctor's name—or what medications she was taking. I'm really hoping you can help us out, Dr. Todd," he added with a sigh. "Leola says things to other folks to make them believe that I—I—"

"You ruined me, Monroe," Leola said with a dreamy-eyed gaze. "But I love you anyway."

Christine flinched. The doctor appeared to be getting the same negative ideas that Preacher Amos had about

Monroe's relationship with Leola. Once again he studied the information sheet on his clipboard.

"I see you're no relation to Leola," Dr. Todd stated. "And even if you were, I can't prescribe medications without giving her a physical exam—and then a mental health practitioner would need to run a thorough battery of tests so we know what she's being treated for."

"Please go ahead and give her an exam, because you're the only doctor we could find who sees Plain patients without insurance," Monroe insisted. "If you can set us up with that mental health doctor—"

"I don't *want* any more pills," Leola blurted. "And you can't make me take them!"

Dr. Todd focused on the young woman and then glanced at her sheet. "How old are you, Leola?"

Smiling, she held up two fingers on each hand.

When the doctor's eyebrows rose, Monroe gently took hold of Leola's shoulder. "Say your age, sweetheart. You are not four."

"I'm twenty-two," she protested. "You know that, Monroe."

Dr. Todd was studying Leola closely. "Yes, that's what your form says, too. Do you want to see another doctor—take those tests you probably took at home—"

"No!" she snapped. "I don't like all those questions. They make me feel stupid."

"May I call your parents and get their permission to test you—or better yet, ask them what you've been taking?"

"They're not home! They dumped me off at Aunt Polly's," Leola said, her voice rising with her frustration. She rose and began pacing around the small exam room.

"And you don't want to be back on your medications so you'll feel better?" the doctor asked.

"No!" she cried out. "They taste awful. And they make me feel weird."

Dr. Todd laid aside his clipboard, apparently reaching his conclusion. "Because Leola is of age, and because you folks aren't related to her," he said to Monroe, "I don't have the authority to override her refusal to be treated. I'm sorry."

Christine patted Monroe's arm. Without putting it into words, Dr. Todd had conveyed his concern about Leola as well as his empathy for Monroe's dilemma. Leola was still walking a tight circle around the room, like a wild animal pacing in a cage. With each passing moment she displayed more evidence that she needed treatment.

Monroe thanked the doctor, steered Leola out of the exam room, and paid the bill at the reception desk. The ride home in the buggy was quiet, because Leola immediately dozed off in the backseat—and because Christine didn't know what to say, and didn't want to wake her. As she studied her fiancé's profile, Christine knew he was more than just a handsome, persuasive man caught in a difficult situation. Though he'd spent his entire day trying to remedy Leola's unpredictable moods and words and had come away from the clinic without answers, Monroe had shown nothing but patience for the young woman whose incriminating remarks were getting him in hot water with Preacher Amos.

When they arrived at the lodge, Monroe parked the buggy near the steps. He turned to look at Leola, who was still snoozing in the backseat. "Leola, we're back," he said loudly. "You need to wake up so you can go to your room and finish your nap."

"No nap!" she blurted as she quickly sat up. Leola blinked and looked out the buggy window, getting her bearings. "I'm still tired," she murmured. "Maybe you could carry me upstairs—"

"Nope. You're too old for that and you know it." Monroe turned in the seat so he could focus on her more directly. "You have to understand, Leola, that if you won't take your medications—and you keep telling these people I have to marry you—I'll be in big trouble," he said sternly. "I'm sorry you said no to the doctor today, but I'm not finished. I'm calling your Dat again to see if he can send me your prescriptions."

Leola stared at him, her chin trembling. "But I don't want to—"

"We all have to do things we don't want, Leola. It's part of being a grown-up—and you are a grown-up." Monroe's voice filled the buggy. He wasn't yelling, but his tone left no doubt that he'd reached the end of his emotional rope. "We'll go in and see if there's something around for supper, and then you're going to your room. No arguments. No crying or causing a fuss."

Leola's eyes had widened, but she nodded meekly. "Are . . . are you mad at me, Monroe?" she whimpered.

"I'm not happy. I want you to be well, but you've refused my help." He sighed and opened the door. "Let's go in. We're all tired and hungry."

Christine headed quickly into the kitchen, where the Kuhns and Rosetta were clearing the small table after having eaten their supper.

"Ah, there you are!" Ruby said. "We kept the rest of the stew warm for you, and biscuits, too. Nothing fancy, but it's *gut* and it's filling."

"*Denki*," Christine murmured as she hung her wraps on a peg in the mudroom. "After the long day we've had, I'm grateful that you cooked supper."

"How'd it go?" Rosetta asked softly. She smiled at Monroe and Leola as they entered the kitchen.

Christine sighed. "Not so *gut*. The doctor can't prescribe any medications because Leola's of age and she refused them—and because we're not related to her."

"However," Monroe said as he headed for the phone on the back wall, "because Polly hasn't called me with a

number for the hospital in Chicago, I'm going to try again
to reach Leola's *dat* at home. If he and her *mamm* are there,
I'll be taking Leola back to Illinois tomorrow. Won't take
but a minute to leave another message—I know the number
by heart now," he added as he began to dial. "If you've got
something I can share for supper, I'll be eternally grateful."

Christine nodded and took three bowls from the cabinet. Leola had already taken her seat at the table, looking
very subdued and forlorn. She was listening to Monroe,
apparently aware that he meant business and wouldn't tolerate any more of her outbursts.

"Chester, it's Monroe again," he was saying into the
phone. "We've hit a snag trying to get Leola's medications,
so as soon as you're home, give me a call, all right? She's
safe and she's doing okay, but we really need to get her
back home as soon as Edna can handle it. Hope you're
both well. Hope to hear from you soon."

As Christine ladled stew into their three bowls, she stole
a glance at Leola. The young woman appeared tired and
very sad, but what was anyone to do for her? Leola studied the bowl of stew and the biscuits Christine set in front
of her as though she didn't recognize any of her food.

"Not hungry," Leola murmured, propping her head on
her hand.

"You should eat some of that," Monroe suggested.
"You'll feel better. We want you to be well, Leola."

Christine sat down beside Monroe and bowed her head.
*We're grateful for Your presence today, Lord, and for
getting to see the doctor. Hold Leola and Monroe in
Your hands as we try to follow Your will during this difficult time.*

When she opened her eyes, Monroe was still deep in
prayer, his forehead resting on his clasped hands. Christine

waited patiently for him. At this point, she didn't know what else to do.

After Monroe went home, Rosetta waited for the Kuhns, Leola, and Christine to go upstairs. She'd tried to remain positive—tried to pretend it hadn't bothered her that Maria had slipped out with a suitcase Sunday just as the women were setting out the meal after church. From her apartment window, she'd also seen Maria's car parked up at the Wickey place, and she'd seen her renter park beside Truman's barn again this afternoon after she'd finished at her bakery.

Rosetta sighed. What was she supposed to think about these situations?

She was tired of all the suggestive scenarios that had been whirling in her head since yesterday morning, so she worked up the nerve to go to the phone. Rosetta dialed Truman's number quickly—almost hung up—but gripped the receiver with her eyes closed, wondering who would answer. What would she say if it was Maria? After three rings, someone picked up.

"Hello? You've reached the Wickey residence."

Rosetta swallowed hard as Maria's cheerful voice filled her with regret—and the worst assumptions. "Hi, Maria, it's Rosetta," she managed in a weak voice. "Everything all right up there?"

There was a pause. Was Maria making up a story? Covering the receiver with her hand, talking to Truman?

"Irene got home last night," the young woman replied. "I've been helping with the housework and cooking, as she's not supposed to overdo it for a few days. Truman's, uh, not able to come to the phone right now. Shall I have him call you back?"

Images of what might be keeping Truman away from the phone only made Rosetta more uncomfortable. "No, that's all right," she insisted. "Glad to hear his *mamm* got home. Give everyone my best."

Rosetta hung up, her heart sinking like a rock. Irene surely knew that she and Truman were engaged. Did she wonder why Maria had come over but Rosetta hadn't?

Nobody—namely Truman—told you she was home, after all.

It was too late to pay a visit, because Irene was probably in bed—not that Rosetta had any inclination to walk over, at this point. With a heavy sigh, she trudged up the back stairway to her apartment.

Just how chummy are Truman and Maria becoming, anyway? Why is she staying there when it's a two-minute drive from Promise Lodge to the Wickey place?

Rosetta went to bed, but sleep eluded her for several hours.

Chapter Sixteen

March came in like a lion, with heavy, wet snow and wind—but that didn't stop the Helmuth twins and Allen Troyer from arriving on the afternoon of the eighth. Christine was taking a pan of chocolate beet bread from the oven when she saw a large moving van and a stock truck trundling into Promise Lodge from the county highway.

"We've got company!" she said, motioning Rosetta and the Kuhns to the window. "With two big vehicles like those, it surely must be Amos's kids."

"*Jah*, they'd be moving two households of furnishings plus their horses and buggies," Rosetta said eagerly, "not to mention Allen's stuff."

"You girls go on out to meet them, and I'll put on some coffee," Beulah suggested.

"*Gut* thing we baked some bars and coffee cake this morning," Ruby put in as she went toward the containers on the counter. "Those Helmuth fellows and Allen can really pack away the sweets—and they'll have drivers who're hungry, too."

"This calls for a big supper tonight, with everybody here at the lodge," Christine suggested as she put on her heavy coat and boots. "We'll all want to catch up with

Barbara and Bernice and then get the five of them settled into cabins before tonight."

"Ruby and I can handle the meal while you folks tend to your company," Beulah offered. "We already have a couple of chickens in the fridge, so we'll take some pork chops out of the deep freeze and go from there."

"You ladies are a marvel," Rosetta said as she, too, put on her wraps. "Soon as Christine and I welcome our new residents, we'll let Amos know they're here—and we'll get the word out about tonight's supper. It's a big day for Promise Lodge!"

Christine slung her arm around Rosetta's shoulders as the two of them stepped out through the mudroom door. She'd sensed her younger sister had been stewing about something she didn't care to share for the past several days, so it was good to hear the excitement in Rosetta's voice. "We'll have to fetch the space heaters from the back storage room," she said, "but otherwise, we've freshened the sheets, and the three largest cabins are ready. Have we forgotten anything?"

"We'll figure it out after the Helmuths and Allen come in." Rosetta waved her arm high in the air as they approached the big trucks that were stopping in the road. "We'll need to make a grocery run soon, because Allen, the girls, and their husbands will be joining us for meals until they can move into their new home."

"Hullo, you Bender sisters!" one of Amos's twin daughters cried out as she climbed down from the extended cab of the moving van. "Trouble has arrived at Promise Lodge! And we brought a couple of cousins with us, too!"

"*Jah*, you won't believe how much stuff we had to haul out here," her sister added with a laugh. "We're packed so full, we nearly had to tie Allen to the top of the stock truck!"

Christine and Rosetta laughed and broke into a jog. By the time they were hugging Barbara and Bernice, Sam,

Simon, and Allen were emerging from the extended cab of the stock truck with two other young men, who were eagerly looking at the lodge and the property around it.

"Christine and Rosetta," one of the Helmuth twins said, "these dark-haired rascals are our cousins Jonathan Helmuth and his younger brother Cyrus. When we told them about Promise Lodge, they decided they were up for the adventure of helping us run the nursery."

Jonathan appeared to be around twenty-three, and Christine was guessing his brother was closer to twenty—and they were cute enough that her girls would probably be very glad to meet them. "We're so glad you came along!" she said, then pointed to the area behind the lodge. "We've fixed up those cabins you can see from here. You fellows can bunk in one of them until you figure out what you'd like for a more permanent place to live."

"Bet all of you are ready to be off the road," Rosetta remarked as she hugged the Helmuth brothers. "And we're glad you came along to join us, Cyrus and Jonathan. Promise Lodge has room to grow!"

"We've got coffee perking and goodies in the kitchen," Christine said as she reached for Allen.

Allen hugged her and then Rosetta, seeming very happy to be back at Promise Lodge. "I'll never turn down anything you and the Kuhn sisters whip up," he said jovially. Then he pointed across the snow-covered produce plots. "It was a big surprise to see that the double house and the barn are up and have their roofs on—"

"And the nursery buildings are almost enclosed, too!" one of the redheaded Helmuth twins said excitedly. "Dat will be sending a couple more trucks this way with our nursery stock—and the trees and shrubs Truman ordered—in a few weeks. He wanted us to get settled—"

"And maybe by then the snow will be gone," his freckled brother put in with a grin. He gazed toward the buildings that rose up near the state highway, his face alight with joy. "Wow, you folks have made a lot of progress since we left. Can't thank you enough."

Christine gestured toward the Troyer place. "Allen, if you'll go invite your *dat* and Mattie over for coffee, we'll get caught up with all of you," she suggested. She smiled at Sam and Simon, still unable to tell them apart. "Amos, Bishop Monroe, and our other two preachers, Marlin and Eli, worked most of this past week getting the buildings framed in and the shingles put on."

"With a big assist from Noah, Roman, and Marlin's son Harley," Rosetta added. "Lester Lehman and his family are to be here in a few days, so the siding and windows will be installed soon after that. We're really excited about you kids joining us with your nursery business."

After the driver-side doors of the trucks opened, a couple of burly fellows came up to join their circle. "This is our *gut* friend Tyler and his buddy Jeff," one of the Helmuth twins said as he pointed to each man in turn. "They drive for us back home when we have major deliveries."

Christine and Rosetta nodded at the two men, who wore plaid flannel shirts beneath their leather jackets. "You fellows are welcome to stay as long as you like," Christine invited. "We've got more beds in those cabins—"

"And space heaters for you, too," Rosetta put in. "Why don't we all go inside? You can warm up with some coffee and cocoa and goodies before you start emptying those trucks—"

"And we can talk about where-all to store our furniture and stable the horses," the other Helmuth twin said as they started toward the lodge.

Christine chuckled. "I'm thinking we might have to put name tags on you twin brothers until we figure out who's Sam and who's Simon," she teased as she walked between the two redheads. "I've known your wives since they were born, and we've seen enough little differences to know Barbara from Bernice—"

"Maybe we'll just keep you guessing," the man on her left said with a laugh.

"That way, when one of us does something that irritates you, he can blame it on the other one!" his brother put in. "It's a system that's served us well all our lives."

"Not that anyone ever finds fault with us," the other twin joked.

As they went inside and showed their guests where to hang their wraps, Barbara and Bernice, both looking plump with upcoming motherhood, took Rosetta and Christine aside. "Here's our secret," Barbara whispered. "Sam's name sort of rhymes with *tan*, so I sew his clothes mostly in tan and brown."

"And because Simon's name is more like *lime*," Bernice said, "my husband is usually dressed in shades of green. We sisters decided to dress them this way because when they were courting us, Sam and Simon loved to fool us."

Christine glanced at the slender redheaded men as they removed their coats. "So, unless they exchange clothes, we know that the one nearest the door is Simon—"

"And Sam is heading for the dining room," Rosetta finished.

"They never miss a chance to eat—and how they stay so skinny, I'll never know," Bernice said, placing her hands on her rounded abdomen.

"They've been talking about the food you and the Kuhn sisters cooked ever since we left," Barbara said with a chuckle. "It's a real blessing, knowing you ladies can keep us all fed until we move into our house."

Christine slung her arms around the two young women as they passed through the dining room toward the kitchen. "It's a big move for you kids, coming all the way from

Ohio to start up your nursery here with us. Takes a lot of bravery and faith, even if you'll be close to your *dat* now."

"It'll be *gut* to see him and Mattie—and everyone else," Bernice added as she smiled at the Kuhns. "We already have a bunch of friends here, like a big family to welcome us, and that makes everything easier. We're really glad to be at Promise Lodge."

"And we're all happy to have you—even if I see a few extra fellows in the dining room we didn't know about!" Beulah teased as she turned from the stove. "Not a problem. You young folks keep the rest of us from getting old."

"Speak for yourself, sister," Ruby said with a twinkle in her eye. "I'm barely out of my twenties—in my mind, at least!"

Christine and the twins laughed as they began carrying the coffee urn and plates of goodies to the dining room. Nothing was better than children returning to live near their parent—unless it was the excitement of awaiting Barbara and Bernice's babies.

That evening at supper, Monroe enjoyed watching the folks around the two extra-long tables where all the residents of Promise Lodge—except for Maria and Truman—were talking and laughing as they ate. With the Helmuths' drivers, he counted thirty-six adults and kids, plus little David, who gurgled in his basket on the floor between Mary Kate and Roman. The four Peterschiem kids sat at one end of a table with Fanny and Lowell Kurtz, fast friends already. Poor Floyd sat at the other end of that table in his wheelchair, with Frances and Gloria on either side of him, coaxing him to eat. It was good to see Amos and Mattie catching up with the two sets of Helmuth twins—

So maybe he'll be happier now. Not as inclined to interrogate me about Leola.

With a quick prayer for forgiveness, because Amos's attitude vexed him so, Monroe rose to get some dessert from the side table. "What can I bring you, sweetheart?" he asked.

Christine smiled from the chair next to his. "You can't go wrong, Monroe. Choose two or three different ones and we can share them."

His heart thumped as he anticipated sharing much more than cake and pie with the beautiful woman who held his gaze. He had an idea about who would serve as the officiating bishop at their wedding, but he wanted the house to be finished before they married—and of course, he had to return Leola to Macomb, as well. Leola was seated between Rosetta and Phoebe, and he was grateful that those two had befriended her.

At the dessert table, Monroe chose a piece of custard pie, lifted a large square of apple slab pie from its cookie sheet, and then gave in to a slice of dark chocolate layer cake with walnuts pressed into the mocha frosting. When he was happy, chocolate called his name.

"Eating for three, Bishop?" Lavern Peterscheim teased him.

"Say, I hope you saved enough for us newcomers," Allen said as he looked at the array of sweets. "A fellow could just waste away here, from what I've seen."

Monroe laughed. "Not a chance," he said. "But you're right—we're blessed with a lot of women who know their way around the kitchen."

Gloria Lehman sidled up to the dessert table, widening her brown eyes at Amos's son. "*Jah*, I love to cook," she murmured. "What's your favorite, Allen? I've been baking treats for the men while they work on the new houses, so I'd be happy to make what you really, really like."

Monroe bit back a smile as he returned to his seat with his desserts. It was obvious that Allen wasn't nearly as smitten with Gloria as she was with him, so things might get interesting when she brought her baked goods to their work breaks—especially if Allen preferred what Phoebe brought, or if he took a liking to Maria. Monroe looked down the table from where Christine awaited him, just in time to see Jonathan and Cyrus sneaking glances across the table at her daughters.

"Well, dear," he murmured as he set the three small plates on the table, "Phoebe and Laura have some fellows checking them out. With the Helmuth cousins joining us, that brings the count to four young ladies—if we include Maria—and three young men of an age to marry."

Christine's eyes widened before she glanced at her girls. "Don't even think such a thing," she muttered. "Laura's not yet eighteen, and Phoebe won't be twenty-one for a couple months yet."

Monroe smiled at her protective tone of voice. "If my math is correct, you were about Phoebe's age when you hitched up with Willis," he said as he cut off the tip of the custard pie. "I was about that age myself when—"

"This has nothing to do with math," Christine insisted as she grabbed the plate of chocolate cake. "Laura's been to Singings but never on a date, and Phoebe's only been out with a couple of boys from Coldstream who were so tongue-tied she lost all interest in them."

"That's because she's pretty and capable, like her mother, so she intimidated them," Monroe murmured. As his fiancée attacked the chocolate cake he'd craved, he inched his fork toward it to claim a big bite. "Like it or not, my dear, your chicks will leave the nest—maybe sooner than later. At least they won't go far, what with Jonathan and Cyrus coming here to help run the new nursery."

Christine leveled her green-eyed gaze at him. "How about if you keep track of your Clydesdales and I'll manage my girls?"

Monroe held her gaze, aiming his fork at the chocolate cake again. The smile teasing at Christine's lips told him she wasn't really irritated with him—she was just a conscientious single parent with two attractive daughters.

Without shifting her eyes, she clamped down on his wrist. "Get your own cake, too," she teased him in a whisper. "Better hurry, before Sam and Simon inhale what's left of it."

Monroe placed his hand on top of hers. "You said we were going to share," he reminded her. "I had plans for some of this chocolate—"

"I'm a woman. I just changed your plans."

Monroe adored Christine's spunk, yet he sensed it was time to draw a line. Someday they'd be sparring over issues more serious than chocolate cake. "And I'm a man," he said firmly. "Sometimes I get to be right."

Christine cleared her throat. She glanced away, fighting a smile. "*Jah*, you're quite a man and I'm lucky to have you—lucky you'll have me," she murmured. "Why don't you bring us another piece of Ruby's fabulous chocolate cake, and we'll practice this sharing thing? After all, we'll be sharing everything someday soon."

Monroe wondered if the four Helmuth cousins could hear his heart banging against his rib cage as he joined them at the dessert table. No matter what sort of mood Christine was in, she enticed him. "Dibs on the last of this cake," he said as he picked up the entire cake plate. "You men know how it is when your woman has to have what she wants."

Sam and Simon laughed out loud. "You've got that right," one of them said.

"*Jah*, now that they're carrying," his brother put in, "nothing in the kitchen's safe if they get a craving for it. We've seen Barb and Bernice hold a half-gallon container of ice cream between them and polish it off without even offering us any."

"But they're happy and healthy, and that's what counts," Monroe said. For just a moment he mourned Linda and the babies she hadn't been able to carry to term. Then he gazed at Christine, relishing the way her face lit up when she saw him carrying the cake platter to their table.

This is what counts, he thought as he returned her smile. *Making Christine happy.*

Chapter Seventeen

On Thursday morning, Rosetta threw herself into helping the Helmuths and Allen get the rest of their belongings unloaded. By the time Jeff and Tyler pulled their big empty trucks onto the county highway, returning to Ohio, Barbara and Sam were settled into the cabin nearest the lodge and Bernice and Simon had made their temporary home in the one next to their siblings'. Jonathan and Cyrus were sharing the third cabin. Rosetta wasn't surprised that Allen had chosen a small cabin farther down the line rather than bunking in the spare bedroom at Amos and Mattie's place. He'd lived alone ever since he'd left his home in Coldstream, and it didn't bother him a bit that he only had the minimal furnishings Rosetta and her sisters provided for him.

"As long as I don't have to use an outdoor toilet and I eat home-cooked meals, I'm a happy man," Allen said as he walked to the lodge with her. "I'll pay you whatever rent you want. I just hope Gloria leaves me alone, you know? She's pretty, but sheesh—she's pretty obvious, too."

Rosetta laughed and let him open the mudroom door for her. "I suspect she's a little more anxious to find a man now that her younger sister's married," she mused aloud.

"And it can't be much fun seeing her *dat* in a wheelchair, so quiet and slumped over. Floyd certainly wasn't that way when he came here."

Allen nodded as he looked around the mudroom shelves, where bars of goat's milk soap were drying. "Wow, do you make this stuff? And the Kuhn sisters are making cheese, and we'll soon have Maria's bakery open," he said. "This place is really hopping."

Rosetta hung up her coat and then reached for some bars of soap. "Take these square bars to your sisters when you go back. You and the other fellows might like this citrus soap with the cornmeal in it for scrubbing up after a day's work."

Allen inhaled the aroma of the round bars she gave him. He was such a handsome young man, and Rosetta suspected that Amos had looked the same when he was Allen's age. "This'll be great, Rosetta. I figure to start installing some plumbing at the twins' house today—"

The ringing of the phone made Allen jump. "I'm still amazed that you've got an indoor phone," he said with a laugh. "Even though all you ladies in the lodge use it for your businesses, most bishops would tell you to have a phone shanty." He preceded Rosetta into the kitchen, eyeing the coffee cake on the worktable.

"We're a persuasive bunch, when it comes to getting things the way we want them," Rosetta teased as she lifted the receiver. "Hello? You've reached Promise Lodge, and this is Rosetta. How can I help you?"

The caller sighed heavily. "Rosetta, it's Lester. I've got *gut* news . . . and not-so-*gut* news."

Rosetta's eyes widened. Lester Lehman sounded as though he'd aged fifty years since she'd last talked to him. "Uh-oh," she said softly. "What's happened, Lester?"

"Well, my two girls got hitched last week," he replied in a more cheerful voice. "So, even though I was hoping they'd come to Missouri with me, at least they've found husbands to take care of them. They married a couple of brothers, like Amos's girls did."

"Well, congratulations!" Rosetta said, although Lester didn't sound convinced that his new sons-in-law met his expectations. "It'll just be you and your wife and your son coming to live here then?"

Lester cleared his throat. "My boy . . . well, the day after the double wedding, he was driving Delores into Sugarcreek. A truck popped over the hill while it was passing a car, and it came straight at their rig—"

"Oh no," Rosetta whispered.

"—and, um, there wasn't a whole lot of them left to bury," Lester finished with a sob.

Rosetta leaned against the wall, covering her eyes with her hand. She hadn't met the members of Lester's immediate family, but she'd come to know them while talking with him and Floyd and Frances. "Lester, I'm so sorry," she mumbled, aware of how inadequate her words sounded. "What can I do to help you? Have you called Frances yet?"

Lester blew his nose loudly. "Should've done that right after the accident, but I couldn't bring myself to leave such a message on their machine," he said softly. "Delores and Frances were close friends, and with Floyd being incapacitated, I hated to burden her with this news—knowing she'd probably not be able to come anyway."

"Don't worry about a thing, Lester. I'll take care of it for you," Rosetta suggested.

"I appreciate it. You sisters are so *gut* at looking after everyone, I just know my family would've felt right at home there," he continued in a weary voice. "The girls are telling me I should stay in Sugarcreek, near them, but— well, I had my hopes set on running the siding and window business we've set up in Missouri. Especially since Floyd's unable to carry on with it."

Rosetta sighed. This wasn't the time to tell Lester that his brother appeared weaker by the day. "Maybe you need some time to figure out what you'll do next," she suggested. She glanced up the back stairway as Christine and her girls were coming down to the kitchen. "You'll be pleased to know that Amos's kids have just arrived, and that their nursery buildings, barn, and house are enclosed now—along with Bishop Monroe's buildings. They'll all understand if you need to take more time before you come here . . . or if you decide not to."

Christine's eyes widened. "Who is that?" she whispered.

Rosetta covered the receiver with her hand. "Lester's in a bad way," she replied quickly.

"Glad to hear everything's going well there," Lester continued. "You might tell Roman and Noah to go ahead and finish those new places, because they helped me enough last fall that they know how to install the siding and the windows just fine. And they know who to order supplies from."

"I'll pass that along," she assured him. "Amos's son and Harley Kurtz can probably help, as well."

Lester was silent for a moment. He chuckled ruefully. "You know, just hearing you talk about the progress that's been made lately has convinced me that Promise Lodge is where I need to be," he said softly. "I've got a nice house there, I've got Floyd and Frances, who could use my help— and I'll be surrounded by folks who look forward instead of dwelling in the past. There's no sense in me hanging around here, being a burden to my girls—especially because I've sold the siding business here in Ohio. I'll see you in a week or two."

Rosetta brightened. "You've got it right," she said. "We'll all be glad to have you here again. Everyone who visits remarks about how Promise Lodge looks so nicely put together—and that's because of your siding and windows,

Lester. Travel safely. We'll keep you in our prayers—and I'll go speak with Frances right now."

"God bless you, Rosetta," he murmured. "You're a *gut* woman."

She hung up and looked at Christine, her nieces, and Allen. "Lester's wife and son were killed in a bad buggy accident last week," she said sadly. "His two daughters got married the day before, and they want him to stay in Sugarcreek—but he's decided to come here and be a part of our progress. I suspect he figures hard work amongst *gut* friends will get him through his grief."

"That's the way Lester would see it, *jah*," Christine remarked. She wrapped her arms around Laura and Phoebe, hugging them hard. "We should take this as a reminder that family is everything—and that everyone is family. Let's go get Mattie and the bishop, and we'll all be there to share Lester's message with Frances and her family."

"Let's take one of those coffee cakes Ruby baked this morning," Rosetta suggested as she reached for her coat. "We can see how Floyd's doing while we're there, too."

"We'll go with you," Phoebe put in as she started upstairs with Laura. "Gloria could use a friend after losing her aunt and cousin. It'll just take a second to get our coats."

When Rosetta noticed the wonderment on Allen's face, she smiled at him. "You could go along to visit with Gloria, as well," she teased. "The more the merrier."

"You know my answer to that—but you've also reaffirmed the rightness of my coming to live here," Allen said. "I'm happy to be surrounded by folks who care about what happens to me, and who believe in me. That wasn't happening when I was living single in Indiana."

Rosetta squeezed his shoulder, and she and Christine tied on their black bonnets. When they stepped outside with Phoebe and Laura behind them, the day reminded her more of May than March: the sky was blue and bright with promise, and her five goats were peering at them through the barnyard fence, with chickens walking around them. In the distance she heard the bleating of Harvey Kurtz's sheep, followed by Queenie's authoritative bark. Everything seemed so peaceful. So pleasant.

"It's going to be hard to pass along Lester's sad news," she remarked to her sister and her nieces, "but when Allen talked about Promise Lodge being a place where he felt welcome and appreciated, I felt a big surge of happiness and faith. He was always a bit of a loner—"

"*Jah,* Allen rebelled at every little thing when he lived in Coldstream," Phoebe put in.

"Maybe because his *dat* was a strict preacher," Laura speculated. "Preacher Amos has changed, though. He's mellowed."

Christine was nodding. "We've *all* changed, don't you think? Buying this property was a huge risk for three Amish women, but—with Amos's help—we've made it work," she said proudly. "Every one of us has stepped up to meet new challenges, and we're stronger for it."

"Folks are taking us seriously," Rosetta added. "If Allen feels welcome here—and if Lester's returning alone—then we've done what God asks of us. We've loved our neighbors as ourselves. We've let our light shine so folks can see our *gut* works, and they'll glorify the Lord because of it."

She gazed at Christine and her daughters, sighing contentedly. "We are so blessed, girls," she murmured.

Monroe opened the door and immediately knew something was wrong. Although it was a joy to see Christine, her daughters, and her sisters on the front porch, looking at him with expectation in their bright eyes, their expressions warned him of a challenge.

"To what do I owe the pleasure of your company?" he

asked as he set aside his tool belt and stepped outside with them. He noticed that Phoebe was holding a coffee cake, but he sensed it wasn't for him.

Mattie spoke first. "We just received word from Lester that his wife and son were killed in a bad accident last week—"

"Sounded like they didn't stand a chance when a big truck hit their buggy," Rosetta added sadly.

Monroe's heart thudded in his chest. He knew all about the fog of pain and mental anguish a man suffered following the loss of his wife. "That's terrible," he said in a low voice. "Let's raise Lester and his family up in prayer for a moment. He has a couple of daughters, *jah*?"

"They got hitched a day before the accident," Christine replied. "He said they were insisting that he should stay in Sugarcreek so they could look after him—"

"But when I told him about your house and barns going up, along with the Helmuths' buildings," Rosetta continued, "Lester knew he wanted to be here with us, looking forward instead of back. He didn't have the heart to break the news about his wife and son to Frances by leaving a message on the answering machine."

Monroe nodded, and then bowed his head. After a few moments of silence, he said, "Lord of all being, we believe that in life and in death we belong to You, and we ask Your presence with Lester and his girls. Bless him with Your comfort and keep him safe as he returns to us. Make us aware of his needs and feelings and help us to provide him a new life and new vision as we welcome him. We ask it in Your name. Amen."

"Amen," the ladies murmured. As they opened their eyes, they looked to him for guidance. Monroe felt grateful that they'd included him in this solemn errand when they could have comforted Frances, Floyd, and Gloria without him.

"I'll grab my coat and hat and we'll be on our way," he said.

A few minutes later, Monroe and the ladies walked down the hill to the off-white house on the next plot of ground. He considered what he'd say and was glad that these women were with him to comfort Frances in ways he couldn't. They all stepped up onto the front porch.

As Monroe knocked, he glanced through the glass in the door. Soon Gloria came out of the kitchen, followed by her mother.

"Bishop Monroe, we were just thinking we should come and get you," Gloria said as she let them in. "We . . . we can't get any response from Dat."

"Oh, you're an answer to our prayers," Frances said with a hitch in her voice. "I—I couldn't convince Floyd to get out of bed this morning and now . . . I just don't know what to do. Please come in, all of you."

Monroe had a sinking feeling about what he'd find when he went upstairs to check on the previous bishop. He was relieved when Mattie slung her arm around Frances's shoulders, and he suspected the ladies might delay telling Frances about Lester's situation so they could deal with her concerns first.

"I suspect the *Gut* Lord was steering us up here because He knew we could be helpful," Mattie assured her friend.

"And we brought a coffee cake," Phoebe said, handing it to Gloria.

Gloria took hold of the gift by clasping Phoebe's hands around the glass pan. She looked very fragile as she focused on catching her breath so she wouldn't cry. "Let's all go in the kitchen while the bishop heads upstairs," she suggested.

Frances clasped her hands in front of her. "I haven't

made any coffee or—not a very *gut* hostess, I'm afraid," she fretted.

"Leave it to us," Christine said as she and the others removed their bonnets. "We'll brew a nice big pot of tea, and you can sit at the table while we wait on you."

A tremulous smile flickered over Frances's features. "What would we do without our friends?" she asked softly. She looked up at Monroe. "Bishop, why don't you and I go upstairs now. Maybe you can help us decide if Floyd needs to go to the hospital—"

"But you know what Dat would say about that," Gloria insisted ruefully.

Monroe draped his coat over the sofa and placed his hat on top of it. He did know what Floyd would say, because he'd heard the stories about how the bishop had tried to catch Amos as he fell from the roof of the shed—and about how Floyd had declared that God was his doctor, so he needed no earthly physician. As Monroe gestured for Frances to precede him up the stairs, he prayed for wisdom and understanding.

When he entered the shadowy bedroom, Monroe sensed that Floyd's soul had already left his emaciated body. The curtains were drawn. The stillness was absolute. A sense of peace surrounded the bed. Floyd lay utterly still beneath the quilts with his head lolled to one side and his mouth hanging open. Monroe's instincts were confirmed when he felt how cool Floyd's cheek was. He detected no pulse when he pressed his hand to the vein in Floyd's neck.

With a little gasp, Frances placed her arms on her husband's shoulders. "Floyd!" she whispered, and then she began to weep. "Floyd, have you really left me? Oh, dear Lord, what am I to do now?"

When Monroe opened his arms, Frances flung herself against him, quaking with sobs. He held her, keeping his silence, knowing that her mind and soul would fill soon enough with desperation and grief that mere words could not relieve. "He's at peace now, Frances," he murmured. "I didn't know Floyd when he was healthy, but I can tell you he's been relieved of the pain and the weakness that plagued him these past months. He's gone to his reward, and to be with his Lord."

Frances nodded, easing out of his embrace. "*Denki* for being here with me, Bishop Monroe," she whispered. "At least now I can stop checking him every few minutes, wondering if he's breathing, or hurting, or beyond hearing what I've tried to tell him. And now Gloria can relax, too," she added sadly. "Poor girl hasn't faced death before, and it's bothered her to see her *dat* in such a state, out of his head and saying such crazy, cantankerous things to her."

"Do you want me to bring her up here?"

Frances shook her head, gazing at Floyd's slack features. "I'd like some time alone with him. But you might let Mary Kate and Roman know what's happened. He's finished the milking by now."

"I'll do that." Monroe pulled a nearby chair closer to the bed for her. "Take all the time you need, Frances. We're all here for you."

As he descended the stairs, Monroe ached for the Lehman family. He wasn't one to question God or His will, yet he had to wonder why Floyd and Lester's wife and son had been called away mere days apart. It seemed a harsh blow for folks who had left family and friends in Ohio to come here for a fresh start—mostly so Mary Kate could raise her baby without censure. It was no time to burden these folks with his questions, however.

Monroe entered the kitchen. He placed his hands on Gloria's shoulders as she sat with the other ladies at the table, sipping tea.

"I'm sorry, Gloria," he murmured. "Your *dat* has gone home to be with Jesus."

Her hand flew to her mouth, and her brown eyes filled with tears. When Phoebe and Laura scooted closer to her, she slumped and accepted their condolences, their embraces. Mattie, Christine, and Rosetta gazed at him sadly.

"How's Frances?" Christine asked.

"She's spending some time with him. I think she'll be okay." The apple coffee cake they'd cut enticed him, but he had more important matters to attend. "I'll go talk with Mary Kate and Roman, and then I'll confer with Amos, Marlin, and Eli. We'll figure out where our cemetery should be and contact a funeral home that understands about Plain burials."

"You have a lot on your mind, Bishop Monroe," Mattie said. "If you'd like, I can break this news to Mary Kate. I think Roman's probably working at the Helmuth place."

Monroe nodded gratefully. "We're blessed with young men who work hard with one another," he remarked. "I'd really appreciate it if you'd do that, Mattie."

"We'll stay here with Frances and Gloria for a while," Rosetta said softly. "Then we'll make plans for the funeral meal—"

"And Gloria, we'll go into town and buy the white fabric for your *dat*'s burial clothing, so your *mamm* won't have to worry about that," Christine put in. "We're so sorry you've lost your father. Never forget that you're not in this alone. We're here for you, and God never leaves us."

Gloria nodded miserably.

Monroe took his leave, relieved that the women would be spreading their consolation while he attended to other details. The sound of hammers, a generator, air-driven drills, and nail guns came from farther up the hill as he strode toward the two-story house where he would soon be living . . . with Christine. That thought—and Queenie bringing him a big stick—cheered him as he waved at the men who were shingling his roof.

Monroe lobbed the stick down the hill, delighting in the Border collie's excitement as she fetched it. "When you reach a *gut* place to stop, come on down," he called up to the men. "We have some urgent business to discuss."

Preacher Marlin immediately set aside his nail gun. Within minutes, he and Preacher Amos, Harley, and Preacher Eli were clambering down the scaffolding and the ladders. They approached him with cautious faces.

"First of all, *denki* for starting work without me," Monroe said. "I got waylaid by the ladies, telling me that Lester's wife and son have died in a buggy accident—and when we got to the Lehman place to share this news with Frances, we discovered that Floyd has also passed away."

The men sighed sadly, shaking their heads. "Lester's got a hard row to hoe," Marlin murmured.

"Guess Floyd had to pass sometime, but it seems too soon to be losing one of our new friends," Amos said, shaking his head. "And I can't forget that if Floyd hadn't been trying to break my fall, he would've remained perfectly healthy. Building his coffin is the least I can do."

"We've got a plot that's fairly level on the back side of the orchard," Marlin suggested, pointing in that direction. "It's smaller than most families would want to settle on, far as putting stock out to pasture, so maybe that's a *gut* place for a cemetery."

"I've heard Truman mention the funeral home in Cloverdale—the one his Mennonite church uses," Harley put in. At Queenie's nudging, he took the dog's stick and tossed it down the hill. "I'm guessing they'll know about Plain customs and won't insist on embalming Floyd. Want me to check it out?"

Monroe nodded. "Let's see if they can have his body ready for visitation on Sunday night and the funeral on

Monday, to give Lester and other folks from Ohio a chance to get here." He sighed, feeling the weight of all the sadness that had descended upon them today. "This news might prompt Lester to find a driver who can haul his household belongings a little sooner than he'd anticipated. His girls were insisting he should stay in Sugarcreek with them, but he told Rosetta he'd still be coming to live here."

Preacher Amos nodded. "I'll give Lester a call right now about Floyd's passing and service, and then I'll go visit with Frances and her girls. The Lehman family's in for some tough times, dealing with so much loss."

Amos returned to the roof to gather his tools, and Harley headed for the phone shanty he shared with his *dat*.

"Shall we stake out the boundaries of our cemetery?" Monroe asked Marlin and Eli. "I still have the sticks and string we used to mark my foundation stashed in Lester's barn."

As they started down the hill to fetch these items, Queenie ran circles around them. Preacher Eli said, "Once we get the cemetery marked, I'll measure the perimeter. Noah and I can make a nice wrought iron fence so folks will know it's hallowed ground rather than just a patch of pasture. If we get right on it, we might even have it finished in time for Floyd's burial."

"That's a fine idea," Monroe said. As he considered all that had to be accomplished before the funeral next week, he was grateful for the way the folks at Promise Lodge looked after each other—and him.

Chapter Eighteen

Tuesday morning, Christine stood shivering as the three preachers and Bishop Monroe spoke final words at Floyd's graveside. Seven inches of snow had walloped the area on Sunday, delaying Lester and the other folks coming from Sugarcreek, so they'd postponed the funeral by a day. A large rented motor coach carrying fifty folks had arrived Monday afternoon, followed by the moving van that carried Lester and his belongings, so nearly eighty people had filled the meeting room for Floyd's funeral service. Except for Leola, who'd stayed in her room with a bad cold—and Maria, who'd gone to her bakery—everyone at Promise Lodge stood reverently as the six pallbearers lowered the plain wooden casket into the open grave with ropes.

"Ashes to ashes and dust to dust," Monroe intoned, "we commend the spirit of our brother Floyd into Your keeping, Lord. We ask Your comfort and peace for his family in this difficult time."

After a few moments of sad silence, Noah, Roman, and the four pallbearers from Sugarcreek shoveled dirt into the grave. Folks in the crowd began to pay their respects to the Lehman family. Lester and Frances appeared haggard, their pale faces a stark contrast to her black bonnet and his broad-brimmed black hat. Mary Kate and Gloria clung to each other, struggling with the finality of their father's passing. Several folks from Sugarcreek lingered around them, so when Christine saw Ruby and Beulah start toward the lodge, she and her sisters followed. The tables were set and the pans of food were staying warm in the ovens, but serving dinner for eighty people would take some additional last-minute effort.

Christine walked quickly between Mattie and Rosetta along the wide path Truman had so kindly plowed for them after the snow had stopped. He had also cleared the area around Floyd's grave site, and he had offered to dig the grave with his backhoe. But in keeping with Amish tradition—and grateful that a March thaw had softened the ground—Lester and Roman had dug it by hand.

"Preacher Eli and Noah made us a very nice wrought iron fence—and managed to install it before the snow came, too," Christine remarked as they approached the gate. "The top border of oak leaves and acorns took a lot of work."

"They worked in the forge all day Friday and Saturday. Noah had already made the ornamental pieces for one of Truman's landscaping clients, but they scaled back on the project, so he kept them," Mattie explained. "At first he was concerned that the design was too fancy for a Plain cemetery fence, but Bishop Monroe insisted that because oak trees are God's creation—and we have a lot of them here—the ornamental work was appropriate."

"And oaks are a symbol of strength," Rosetta remarked. "Everyone who's lost a loved one needs that."

As they were passing in front of Amos's house, a loud racket pierced the silence. Christine scowled. "What on earth—?"

"Sounds like a chain saw—or two of them," Mattie put in beneath the noise. Queenie had been waiting outside the wrought iron fence during the graveside service, but she ran toward the strange noise, barking frantically.

"Look—on the road," Rosetta said, pointing. "There's a big truck pulling a building on a trailer. And Maria's car is behind it."

"Must be her bakery," Christine mused aloud, shielding her eyes with her hand. "But what are they cutting—"

A loud *whump* filled the air. A large area of sky suddenly became visible above the entry to Promise Lodge. On one side of the road a huge old lilac bush was missing, and on the other side a maple tree had been felled—and it was one of the trees that had shaded Mattie's produce stand.

At the same time, Truman jogged past them, followed by Allen, the redheaded Helmuth twins, and their cousins. Roman and Noah were close behind them. "Hey! Hold on there!" Truman hollered as he ran. The other folks who'd been at the grave were coming down the plowed path now, curious about what was causing the ruckus. Monroe, Amos, and Marlin jogged quickly around the crowd in an effort to catch up to the younger fellows—just as the loud buzz of a saw started up again.

"I'm not liking this one bit," Mattie muttered as she took off. "I'm going to make sure my produce stand is all right—"

"Wait!" Christine cried, grabbing the sleeve of her sister's black coat. "Truman's reached the road, and Amos and Monroe will be sure nothing else goes wrong. It's probably better if we stay out of their way—"

"And we should be in the kitchen helping Beulah and Ruby set out the food," Rosetta pointed out. "Now that folks are leaving the cemetery, they'll be going inside to eat."

Mattie sighed, still frowning doubtfully. "*Jah*, you're right," she admitted. "It's a *gut* thing those chainsaws didn't disrupt Floyd's funeral service. Who knows what might've gone down had our men been inside preaching."

The three of them hurried toward the lodge and entered through the mudroom door. The aromas of turkey and seasoned stuffing filled the air. As they hung their coats on wall pegs, Christine called into the kitchen. "The meal smells wonderful-*gut*, ladies."

Beulah opened one of the oven doors. "I'm mighty glad we cooked everything yesterday and put it all in the oven to warm before the funeral," she said as she lifted the lid from a roaster. "I thought folks would stay longer to speak with Frances and the girls—"

"Would you look at this!" Ruby huffed as she approached them with a pie. "I just checked to be sure the desserts were all out, and here's what I found."

Rosetta joined Ruby and groaned. "Who would eat the middle of a cherry pie—with a spoon—instead of cutting a piece? My word, all that's left is a couple of inches along the outer crust!"

Mattie surveyed the damage and pointed silently up the back stairway. "Leola was the only one who stayed here this morning, *jah*?" she asked softly.

"This seems like something Leola might do." Ruby exhaled in frustration. "That's eight slices of pie we've lost."

Christine gathered her thoughts quickly. "No sense in crying over spilled milk or a ruined pie," she reminded them. "Seem to be a lot of strange things happening right now, but we still need to put the Lehman family first. They've lost a whole lot more than a pie—"

"And a lilac bush, and a tree, and maybe a produce stand," Mattie added sadly. "*Jah*, we can replace what we've lost, while Frances and Lester can't. After we hear what's been going on at the road, we'll figure out what to do. We sisters haven't come this far by whining and wringing our hands."

Ruby managed a smile. "You've got that right, Mattie. We'll have everything set out on the buffet table in due time, and folks'll be able to relax and enjoy their meal. Even with this many guests, we probably have more than enough dessert to go around."

Beulah started back toward the oven and then gawked out the window. "My word, would you look at that!" she said. "Here comes a big truck pulling a building behind it. And Maria's little red car just whipped around it. Somebody better grab Queenie before she gets hit."

Christine and her sisters crowded around the sink to peer outside with the Kuhns just as Maria hopped from her car. Truman, Amos, and Monroe had jogged alongside the truck and were speaking to the driver and the other English fellow who'd been watching the bakery building as it rolled toward its new concrete slab. Noah took hold of his dog's collar and placed his legs on either side of her as she sat down. When Monroe said something, beckoning toward the crowd that had gathered, a bunch of the men stepped forward.

"What are they going to do?" Rosetta whispered. "Surely they don't intend to move the building from the dollies it's riding on by—"

"My stars, look at those fellows!" Beulah interrupted. "They're standing shoulder to shoulder, grabbing hold of the building at the bottom—"

"And it's rolling off the dollies—and up off the support beams—and they're surrounding it to carry it over to the slab," Ruby whispered excitedly. *"Wow!"*

Christine chuckled, relieved that enough men were helping with the small building—and that they'd only had to move it a few yards with their gloved hands. "Those fellows are so strong from doing construction work, they could even move that bakery in their church clothes," she said with a chuckle.

When the men carefully lowered the building onto the slab and released it, the crowd broke into applause. Christine and the other ladies began clapping, as well. The truck's engine roared, and as the second English fellow hopped into the cab, the other folks began walking toward the lodge.

Christine started filling big pitchers with water. "Here come my girls and Amos's twins and Minerva," she said. "We'll have everything set out in no time."

"And maybe we'll get the rest of the story about what went on with those saws before Truman got to the road," Mattie said as she grabbed two filled pitchers. "Even if my produce stand is all right, Maria owes us an explanation for that maple tree and the lilac bush coming down."

"The arched metal sign must be down, as well," Rosetta added. "The bakery building was probably too wide to get through it."

Christine was grateful that her daughters, along with Barbara, Bernice, and Minerva Kurtz, had arrived so quickly and were removing their wraps. They began pushing wheeled carts holding large platters of sliced turkey and big bowls of mashed potatoes, stuffing, and gravy into the dining room. The guests from Ohio were ushering the Lehmans inside, and after the rest of the folks hung their wraps on racks in the lobby, Monroe and the preachers appeared.

"Let's all find seats in the dining room and we'll have our prayer before the Lehmans lead us through the buffet line," Monroe said above the chatter. He entered the kitchen then, just as Mattie and Christine were loading other wheeled carts with baskets of bread.

"Let's wait until after the meal to quiz Maria about what happened out at the road," he suggested in a low voice. "No reason to let our guests hear all the details, because she has some pretty tall explaining to do."

Mattie's eyes widened. "Is my produce stand all right?"

Monroe squeezed her shoulder. "Amos already has a plan for fixing it. Truman and the Helmuth twins have agreed to cut up that maple tree and get it out of the ditch," he continued. "And Noah sees this incident as a *gut* reason to make us a taller, wider metal sign arching over our entry. We'll see how much of this damage Maria intends to pay for when we talk with her later."

"But no matter what she does or doesn't pay," Christine said, "we can be grateful that once again our men have pulled together to make everything right."

"*Jah*, thanks for watching over things out there, Bishop," Beulah said. She carried a large bowl of cranberry salad in the crook of each arm. "Ruby and I are figuring to make a big batch of cheese tomorrow, so we're glad that truck driver didn't hit our little building with Maria's."

Monroe's smile hinted that he knew things he wasn't telling. "Happy to help, ladies. *Denki* once again for preparing a wonderful meal. The turkey and sides remind us of Thanksgiving—and that we're thankful the Lehmans are staying, despite the loss of their loved ones."

That evening after a simple supper, the folks who'd come from Sugarcreek retired to their cabins, the rooms upstairs in the lodge, and the homes some of them were visiting so they'd be ready to leave in their motor coach before dawn. Rosetta checked to see that her guests had plenty of towels and soap and was gratified by their appreciation for the simply furnished cabins and rooms. "We'll have biscuit sandwiches and muffins ready for your breakfast," she told them. "It was so kind of you to come all this way for Floyd's funeral."

After she said good night to the guests in her cabins, Rosetta made her way around the U-shaped upstairs hallway of the lodge. When she reached Leola's room, she tapped lightly on the door. After a few moments, she peeked inside to see the young woman sprawled in her armchair looking miserable. Crumpled tissues littered the floor and a plate of food sat untouched on the end table.

"Leola, are you all right?" Rosetta asked warily. "You look like you feel worse than you did this morning."

Leola groaned and hugged her middle. "Got a bad stomach now. Maybe I'm getting the flu."

Rosetta bit back a remark about how much cherry pie Leola had eaten. "Would you like some ginger ale?"

The young woman rose from the chair, shaking her head. "Gonna go to bed. Don't let anybody wake me up."

Rosetta closed Leola's door and headed down the hall to the back stairway. She had a hunch that Monroe and Amos were ready to discuss the day's damage with Maria, and she didn't want to miss a word. When she reached the kitchen, Christine's girls were helping Beulah and Ruby bake muffins and biscuits. Phoebe pressed a finger to her lips, nodding toward the dining room, where folks were talking.

"It was awfully nice of you men to position my bakery on its slab today," Maria said in a lilting voice. "What a sight, when you all lifted the building off that big dolly as though it didn't weigh anything! And after the funeral meal, Truman sealed the edge where my building meets the concrete and Allen hooked up my water and electricity. I can be baking early tomorrow morning!"

Rosetta slipped into the nearest empty chair at the long table where Bishop Monroe and the three preachers sat, along with Maria, Mattie, and Christine. Truman was there, too . . . and although Rosetta wondered why he hadn't said anything to her during the funeral meal about helping with Maria's building, she returned his quick smile.

"Maria, we're wondering why the fellows who moved

your building took down a tree and a big lilac bush—as well as sawing off the posts of our metal Promise Lodge sign," Bishop Monroe said. He sat back against his chair, apparently relaxed, but his tone of voice made it clear that he wasn't happy.

Maria's eyes widened. "Well—because the bakery wouldn't go through the opening—"

"What we're really saying is that you or your drivers should've spoken to us first," Amos interrupted sternly. "I'm amazed the tree didn't fall on the power line along the road—but it did take off one side of Mattie's produce stand."

Maria sighed. "Yeah, Bobby Ray should've been more careful."

Mattie frowned, but before she could speak up, Preacher Marlin responded.

"*Careful* doesn't cover it," he put in, gazing earnestly at the blonde across the table from him. "Moving a building is a huge undertaking that involves getting permissions all along the route beforehand, to be sure landowners understand what has to be moved out of the way," he explained. "Not only did we lose a tree and a bush, our sign was also ruined, and Mattie's building was damaged—and nobody offered to pay for those things or replace them. Had we been properly informed, we would've taken care of those obstacles ourselves."

The room got so quiet that Rosetta heard the gentle click of muffin tins going into the oven. She chided herself for enjoying the way Maria shifted nervously in her chair. *You know how scary it feels when you've been wrong and folks are holding you responsible for your mistakes.*

The men were right, though: the responsibility for damage fell on the men who'd moved the building. Maria probably hadn't thought a thing about trees and signs having to come down—but her movers were long gone, so the consequences were hers to bear.

"I—I'm sorry," Maria whispered, looking to Truman for help. "I didn't know about this stuff. I hired Bobby Ray and Darrell, figuring they'd do everything right."

Truman cleared his throat. "They surely carry insurance for incidents like these," he suggested. "You should check their contract—their customer care agreement—to see what they might cover."

Maria's face was turning bright pink. "I don't have a contract. I've known those guys for years," she murmured—and then she sat up straighter. "But how would you figure what an old tree and an old lilac bush would be worth, anyway?" she challenged. "And the metal sign could be put up again—and it needs paint, so what's the big deal?"

Rosetta's eyebrows rose at Maria's attitude. Before she and Mattie could object, Monroe jumped in.

"No, Maria, the sign's posts were sawed off at the ground, so there's not enough post left to put it up again," he said. "If you or your movers had told us ahead of time about these objects being in the way—even if they'd asked us right before they did their cutting—we would've helped them remove these obstacles. As it stands, our property was damaged and we're left to clear away the mess and make repairs."

Once again Maria sighed forlornly. "They tried wiggling the sign so they could pull it out, but they couldn't move it. And if you folks are expecting me to pay for the damages, well . . . I don't have the money," she whimpered. "Bobby Ray charged me more than he originally said, because they had to take down the stuff you've mentioned. I wrote him a check that cleaned out my account."

Rosetta felt a little sorry that Maria's friends had handled this move so unprofessionally. Plenty of times she'd hired Plain folks with just a nod of her head and a handshake, but they'd always followed a code of honor and made good on their promises. She now realized that her newest renter might not be very smart about money.

"We learn some hard lessons as we establish ourselves," Christine said softly. She glanced at Rosetta as she kept talking to Maria. "If you ever realize you're going to be short come time to pay your rent, you should say something to Rosetta rather than writing a bad check—or thinking you can let it slide. Do you understand why?"

Maria looked away, still upset. "Sure, that's only fair," she mumbled. "After all, my customers pay me the moment they've chosen their bread and doughnuts. I only hope I sell enough stuff here to . . . to pay my bills."

"You'll do fine, Maria," Truman assured her. "Come spring and summer, you'll have all the customers who come to Mattie's produce stand and the Kuhns' cheese factory. You made the right move."

Rosetta considered what Truman had said. Was he trying to restore Maria's confidence? Or did he figure to float her a loan whenever she ran short—or perhaps buy all the goodies she baked? Once again a worm of suspicion squirmed in her stomach, and Rosetta wished this conversation would come to an end. How many times, in how many ways, did they have to point out to Maria that she and her mover friends hadn't accepted their responsibilities? She hadn't heard Maria offer any reparations, either.

"It's been a long day and we have a very early morning, feeding our guests before they return to Sugarcreek," Rosetta said as she rose from her chair. She nodded at Maria. "In case you leave before we're up, have a *gut* first day in your new location."

Maria looked imploringly at Rosetta, and then at the others around the table. "I'll make *gut* on all the damage that was done today," she said in a quavering voice. "Please give me a chance! If nothing else, I'll do all your baking to make up for any shortfall in my rent."

Mattie and Christine stood up and pushed their chairs under the table. "We'll cross that bridge if we come to it," Christine said kindly. "As I recall, you paid your rent on March first, so you're *gut* for another week and half, until April. You'll sell a lot of rolls and doughnuts by then."

Maria's face brightened. "I appreciate you ladies' positive thinking. You're making me feel as if anything's possible here at Promise Lodge."

Rosetta was making her way through the kitchen, and as she stopped to admire the tins of blueberry and banana muffins cooling on the counter, she heard giggling behind her. When she turned, Phoebe was planting herself against a counter, pulling Laura over beside her—as though to keep Rosetta from seeing something. Ruby and Beulah were trying to act as though they knew nothing, but their girlish grins gave them away.

Mattie and Christine shared a loaded look. "Isn't it nice that we have such dedicated ladies in our kitchen?" Mattie asked purposefully. "*Denki* for the fine funeral lunch today, and for baking such wonderful-*gut* muffins and, um, *other* goodies for us to enjoy."

"Our pleasure," Beulah said. "You sisters make our lives so much fun, we're happy to cook for you. We *have* been awfully busy in this kitchen lately."

"All for a *gut* cause," Ruby put in. She smiled brightly at Rosetta. "Get your rest tonight, dearie. Tomorrow promises to be another big day."

As she climbed the back stairs to her apartment, Rosetta smiled in spite of the troubles they'd been discussing and the fact that they'd buried Floyd today. Could it be that her nieces and the Kuhns were preparing a surprise for her March twenty-second birthday? She lit her lamp, donned her nightgown, and pulled out her hairpins. As she stood at the window brushing the long brown hair that hung below her hips, she gazed out into the clear night.

Moonlight glistened on the snow that blanketed the lawns and the orchard . . . and the Wickeys' lawn up the hill. The glow in Truman's bedroom window made Rosetta sigh. When he'd eaten with her after the funeral, he'd remained very quiet. Was it because of the somber occasion, or was he losing interest in her? Truman seemed to be at pretty Maria's beck and call—always encouraging her. Was it because he had special feelings for her?

Or are my sisters right, saying that Truman's infatuation with Maria is a big overblown figment of my imagination?

Rosetta climbed into bed. She would be thirty-eight tomorrow, and more than anything she hoped she wasn't destined to grow dry and crusty . . . like a stale, unclaimed loaf of bread on Maria's bakery shelf.

Chapter Nineteen

". . . Happy birthday, Rosetta, happy birthday to youuuu!"

Rosetta blinked in disbelief. She stopped in the kitchen doorway with the pan of cinnamon rolls she'd taken from the oven, gazing into the crowded dining room. How had her friends from Promise Lodge arrived so early and so quietly without her hearing them?

She'd already greeted their guests from Sugarcreek as they'd come for their early breakfast, and her sisters and the Kuhns had been helping in the kitchen—but she hadn't expected her neighbors to gather in the dining room at the unthinkable hour of four thirty to celebrate her birthday. The aromas of coffee, cinnamon, and warm eggs filled the air. The buffet table was covered with the muffins, biscuit sandwiches, and fruit salad she'd helped prepare for the Lehmans' visitors—but the tiered cake in the center stole the show.

Rosetta set down her pan of rolls to look at it. It was three two-layer tiers supported by white pillars—like a wedding cake—and covered with luscious dark chocolate frosting. The upper two tiers were decorated with rainbow sprinkles and fancy pink rosette borders, and more candles than she wanted to count covered the top. Pink writing on the large bottom layer said *Happy Birthday to Our Dear Rosetta.*

This explains why Mattie was keeping me busy at the oven while everyone else put the food on the table, she realized with a smile.

Phoebe came up to her, smiling impishly. "Happy birthday, Aunt Rosetta. It's not often we take you by surprise, ain't so?" With a match, she lit a candle on the edge and used it to light the colorful forest of candles on the top tier. A few folks began calling out.

"Make a wish, Rosetta!"

"*Jah,* shoot for the moon—make it a *gut* one!"

"You can't be as old as all those candles say you are," Mattie chimed in as she and the other ladies came out of the kitchen.

"Nope, you were born yesterday!" Christine teased, slinging her arm around Rosetta's shoulders. "But our family wouldn't have been the same without you, little sister. Now blow out those candles so we can get our chocolate fix from that cake."

"We made enough for everybody to have a big piece," Beulah said with a chuckle.

"Because birthday cake is everybody's favorite breakfast—but mostly because we didn't think we could keep it hidden until dinnertime," Ruby added happily.

Gazing at the smiling faces that filled the dining room, Rosetta stepped closer to the table. *See there? Nobody here believes thirty-eight is the end of the line,* she thought as she inhaled deeply. *I wish . . . I* believe *Truman and I can start again and live happily ever after.*

Blowing with all her might, Rosetta extinguished all of the colorful candles with one breath. Loud applause filled the dining room, and Mattie handed her a long serrated knife.

"Cut yourself a big slice of joy, little sister," she murmured.

"Nobody deserves it as much as you do—you and this handsome man behind you."

Rosetta spun around to find Truman gazing warmly at her, a wrapped box beneath his arm. He'd come here to join her celebration—at this early hour, when it was still dark! She set the knife on the table and reached for him, exhilarated when he pulled her into his arms and kissed her exuberantly.

"More where that came from, honey-girl," he whispered as he eased away. "I'm hoping you and I can spend the day together. It's been too long."

Rosetta's eyes misted over. Truman was taking the entire day off work to be with her. "*Jah*, it has," she murmured. "Let's—let's make some plans for happiness today."

Truman's face glowed. "It all starts with coffee and chocolate cake. Who knows how it'll end?"

Overjoyed, Rosetta grasped the knife again. Her heart was pounding. Amazing, hopeful thoughts whirled in her head. *And Maria's out working in her bakery,* she noted after another glance at the crowd. Monroe, Amos, and the Kurtz family stood nearby, as did Leola, the Helmuth bunch, and the Peterscheims—including the kids, who appeared sleepy but eager for cake. Even Frances had joined them, with Gloria, Roman, Mary Kate, and baby David. Deborah and Noah stood beside Lester, smiling at her.

Ruby was removing the top two cake tiers, along with the white plastic pillars. "There—we can start with the bottom, because it's the biggest," she said. "Cut what you want, Birthday Girl, and then we'll serve everyone else."

Rosetta drew the knife through the double-layered cake and then paused. "If you and the girls baked this last night, when did you decorate it?" she asked softly. "My word, you were busy with the funeral meal and then the biscuits and muffins for today's breakfast, and yet you also made this huge cake?" She sighed, overwhelmed. "*Denki*, Beulah and Ruby. With all my heart, I appreciate this."

Beulah shrugged, blinking rapidly. "The older we get, the less sleep we need," she explained quickly. "For you, Rosetta, we were happy to fuss over this cake. You gave us a chance at a whole new adventure—at our age!—and we love you for it."

"*Jah*, you set us free from a lifetime of herding our unruly nieces and nephews—in a house with just one bathroom," Ruby put in gratefully. "Making you a cake is the least we can do, Rosetta. You go, girl!"

You go, girl. What other advice—or affirmation—do you need?

Rosetta cut a very large piece of the cake for Truman, and then helped herself to one that was only slightly smaller . . . probably five inches around the round outer edge.

Laura came to the table then, carrying gallon containers of strawberry and Butter Brickle ice cream. "Wouldn't be right to have birthday cake without ice cream. Happy birthday, Aunt Rosetta," she said cheerfully. She set the ice cream on the table and pulled two scoops from her apron pocket. "Take *big* scoops. When will you ever eat ice cream for breakfast again?"

Rosetta laughed and placed a large scoop of each flavor on her plate and Truman's. She felt indulgent and pampered, and when Truman met her with two steaming mugs of coffee, they made their way to a table in the back corner. The white tablecloths from the funeral meal had been shaken and put back on, and bowls of colorful hard candies had been placed in their centers, along with birthday napkins, sugar bowls, and small pitchers of cream.

"This is quite a treat," Truman said, pulling out a chair for her. "Well worth coming over before dawn."

Rosetta sat down, feeling like a young girl—a guest of

honor. "I'm sorry your *mamm* didn't come. It's been a long while since I've seen her."

Truman forked up a big bite of chocolate cake. "She sends her birthday wishes and hopes you'll understand about her staying in her warm bed to sleep." He closed his mouth over the cake and let out a groan. "Oh . . . wow. Now *this* is chocolate cake."

Rosetta was also savoring the exquisite richness of a bite of cake with its creamy mocha frosting. "Mmm. The Kuhns outdid themselves." She glanced at Truman. "I hope your mother's recovered from her trip to the hospital?"

"*Jah*, she's up and around. I suspect she's being more careful than she needs to be, but better safe than sorry."

Rosetta felt awkward asking, but it was the only way to find out. "So, what exactly was wrong? I—I was going to go see her, but when Maria answered the phone, I figured—"

"Don't think for a minute that something's going on between me and Maria." Truman gazed intently at her, leaning closer. "I love *you*, Rosetta. Sometimes Maria gets a little carried away, but her heart's in the right place."

When he took her hand between his, Rosetta felt stupid for assuming that pretty, blond Maria had wormed her way into Truman's heart. She nodded, unable to speak.

"Mamm had an episode with her heart, and she was also coming down with a bad case of the flu," he explained. "She'd love to see you anytime—matter of fact, when I told her Monroe was going to marry us, Mamm was ecstatic. I've never seen her happier."

Rosetta held her breath. Her shoulders relaxed and the resentment she'd harbored for Maria dissipated like the steam coming from her coffee mug. "Let's visit with her sometime today, all right?"

"We can do that." He reached for the gift he'd set on the table. "She sent you this for your birthday, and I have a little something for you later. Go ahead—open it."

Rosetta pushed back her plate. The box was about the size of a shirt box but a little deeper, and as she ripped off the rainbow-striped paper, butterflies fluttered in her stomach. When she lifted the lid, her eyes widened. "What's this?" she whispered as she lifted something made of delicate white organdy. "An apron! With beautiful white roses stitched across it." She gazed at Truman. "This is way too beautiful for working in the kitchen—"

"So wear it on our wedding day," he said softly. "Mamm made the apron and did the embroidery just for you, Rosetta."

Rosetta gaped as she held it up. "Here, take it so I don't get cake on it," she said in a tiny voice. In the bottom of the box was a length of blue fabric that made her think of the Blue Willow dishes her mother had kept for special occasions.

"For your wedding dress," Truman explained. "Mamm wasn't sure about your size, but she knows you or your sisters can make it to fit the way it's supposed to. I chose the color, thinking the deeper blue would suit your pretty complexion better than a pale shade."

"It's beautiful," she whispered. "Oh, Truman. *Denki* from the bottom of my heart."

He gently folded the organdy apron and laid it back in the box on top of the blue fabric. When he leaned forward to take her hands, the expression on his handsome face took Rosetta's breath away. "I don't think your heart *has* a bottom, sweetheart," he whispered. "From what I can tell, you have an infinite capacity for love and understanding. I'm a lucky man to have you for a bride."

Rosetta swallowed hard. Why had she ever doubted Truman's intentions? "When?"

Truman stroked her hands with his thumbs. "A week from today? That'll be March twenty-ninth."

Rosetta's thoughts raced, yet when she realized that they were still surrounded by guests, family, and friends—and the evidence of the Kuhns' time in the kitchen—she made a quick decision. "How about in two weeks? That will give us time to catch our breath from having so much company. You know Ruby and Beulah will want to go all out with the cake and the meal."

Truman did some mental calculating. "April fifth, then. Let's do it!"

"*Jah*, let's do it," Rosetta repeated. Her voice sounded high and tight with excitement, but it didn't seem to matter to Truman.

He stood up, still clasping her hand. "Let's get ourselves on the bishop's calendar right now. That way, everybody will know to save the date."

Rosetta followed him between the tables, returning the smiles of everyone around her as they approached Monroe. He was seated with Christine and the Lehman family, talking quietly with them as they ate their cake and ice cream. He turned when Truman grasped his shoulder.

"Truman and his birthday girl," Monroe said with a knowing smile. "And what can I do for you two?"

"April fifth," Truman declared.

Rosetta nodded ecstatically, gazing around the crowded dining room. "It's official!" she blurted out. "We're getting married two weeks from today, and of course you're all invited!"

Applause filled the dining room, and people stood up to congratulate them. Christine and Mattie rushed to Rosetta's side to hug her hard.

"See there?" Christine whispered. "I knew Truman was still your man."

"*Jah*, and he's a keeper, too," Mattie said, blinking back tears. "Oh, but I wish Mamm and Dat were here to celebrate with us. We'll do it up right, though. Only the best for you, Rosetta, after you've waited so long."

Rosetta blinked back tears of joy. It wasn't yet five in the morning, and she'd already celebrated the best birthday of her life.

A half hour later the guests from Sugarcreek were boarding their big bus for the ten-hour ride back to Ohio. As the vehicle pulled down the road toward the county highway, Lester let out a sigh. "Might be the last time I see those folks," he murmured. "But moving on—moving here—is the right thing for me. Guess it's time to unload that truck that's parked alongside my barn."

Rosetta slipped an arm around Lester's shoulders. He looked so droopy and sad, and she knew better than to try to cheer him up while his wife, son, and brother's funerals still felt so fresh to him. "How about if a bunch of us women give your place a *gut* cleaning?" she asked.

"I second that suggestion, because I wasn't the tidiest housekeeper while you were away," Monroe said, smiling at Lester. "Then the men can help you carry your furniture inside. I really appreciate you letting me bunk at your place, Lester."

Lester managed a smile. "I was glad somebody could make use of that nice new house. By the looks of your place up the hill, Bishop, it won't be long before you can move in."

"That's the plan. When my barns are ready, I'll be heading back to Illinois for my Clydesdales," Monroe said. "I've kept awfully busy helping build my place and the buildings that belong to Amos's kids, but I'm looking forward to working my horses again."

Truman came over and shook Lester's hand. Then he smiled at Rosetta. "If a lot of us help clean and carry furniture for Lester, you and I can still have the rest of the day to ourselves—if that suits you," he added.

Rosetta nodded. "Your plan trumps any I had. I think we women will all welcome the work at Lester's place as something different from cooking for so many people."

"You've got that right!" Ruby said. "Beulah and I will help you this morning—because many hands make light work—and we'll catch up on our cheese making this afternoon."

Lester nodded. "Can't thank you folks enough for all your help," he said quietly. "It'll feel *gut* to be putting siding on your new houses and installing your windows—and building up the business again. You friends are my reason to keep putting one foot in front of the other."

In a couple of hours the women were hanging fresh towels in Lester's bathrooms and saying how nice the place looked after they'd scrubbed and dusted. The men made short work of carrying furniture to the upstairs bedrooms and arranging another sofa and some chairs in the sparsely furnished front room. They waved good-bye to the English man who'd driven the moving van, and then they loaded Christine's old kitchen set into a wagon, along with the bedroom furniture Lester had borrowed from Mattie when he'd first come to Promise Lodge.

Lester looked around, seeming reluctant for everyone to leave. "This'll take some getting used to, seeing all the furniture Delores picked out in this house she's never going to live in," he said with a ragged sigh. "But I'll make it work somehow."

"Come over anytime you like—eat your meals with us," Frances insisted, smiling sadly. "Gloria and I will welcome the company."

"It'll give us a reason to eat something besides sandwiches," Gloria put in. "We've had a lot of grilled cheese since Dat passed."

Rosetta and the others wished Lester well, and they all
dispersed to their own homes and pursuits—which meant
the Kuhns and Christine were returning to the lodge. Some
of the men headed to the Helmuth property to finish roofing
the house, while the younger fellows planned to cut up the
maple tree and the lilac bush that lay at the roadside.
Queenie was keeping pace, her tongue lolling as she ran
loops around everyone.

When a familiar hand enfolded hers as the crowd walked
along, Rosetta smiled at Truman. "I'm glad we all helped
Lester get settled," she said. "It's got to be tough, living
alone in the home he'd planned to share with his wife and
three kids."

"I've got some leads on siding and window jobs for
him," Truman said quietly. "When I mentioned the Lehmans'
business to the manager who's building those townhomes
I'm landscaping, he seemed very interested in having an
additional fellow to do that sort of work—especially since
Lester's Amish. You folks are known for your careful
craftsmanship."

"We appreciate that, Truman," Amos said from behind
them. "We haven't heard from any folks lately who want
to come here, so once my kids' buildings and Monroe's are
finished, Lester will welcome the work."

"I'll give him a ride, too," Truman said, "because I'll
soon be heading that direction myself, to start my landscaping jobs. Before you know it, this snow will be gone
and we'll be planting our gardens."

Rosetta inhaled deeply. They'd almost reached the
lodge—and Maria's bakery—where rich aromas of spice,
sugar, and pastry hung in the air. "Why is it that even after
I ate that huge piece of chocolate cake, the smell of somebody else's baking is making me hungry?" she murmured.

Allen Troyer broke away from the crowd, along with

Cyrus and Jonathan Helmuth. "Let's give Maria some business before we cut up that tree," he said to his pals. "After I hooked up her water and electricity, she said she'd pay me with goodies."

Cyrus let out a laugh. "You sure we won't be interrupting anything, Troyer?"

"*Jah*, the way you're talking, those *goodies* could include a lot more than doughnuts," Jonathan teased.

Allen waved off his companions as they strode toward the bakery. "Suit yourselves. But Maria did mention that she's really into guys wearing boots and tool belts."

Cyrus elbowed his brother. "We can wear our tools next time. Might as well check her out to see if she's worth our attention."

Truman laughed, still clasping Rosetta's hand. "It'll do Maria *gut* to have some eager young fellows paying attention to her," he remarked. "In Cloverdale she was so busy looking after her sister and keeping her bakery going, she didn't have much time to socialize."

"I suspect Gloria will give Maria some competition," Rosetta said. "She may be mourning her *dat*, but she's had her eye on Allen from the moment she met him."

"It was the same the first time I saw you," he said in a husky voice. He held her gaze for a long, lovely moment. "Shall we visit with Mamm for a bit, maybe have lunch with her before we leave? You've got some shopping to do."

Intrigued, Rosetta nodded. As they reached the roadside, she noticed the damage Maria's movers had done. The large maple tree and the lilac bush rested in the ditch on either side of the entry to the lodge property. One side of Mattie's U-shaped produce stand had been crushed, and the arched metal sign rested against it. Rosetta was pleased to see that the wooden welcome sign and the slatted produce sign that Noah had painted were still intact.

"Maybe it wasn't such a bad thing that our opening at the road got widened," she murmured. "If we get a lot of traffic this summer, we might be glad to have room for two lanes of cars—one coming in and one leaving at the same time."

"Spoken like the optimist I know you to be, honey-girl," said Truman. "Before Noah gets started on a new arched metal sign, I'll see if Monroe wants me to do any roadwork or new plantings at your entry. I think you're wise to anticipate more traffic this summer."

"I think I'm wise to be marrying you, Truman." The words flew from her mouth before she even thought about them, yet Rosetta felt giddy—positive that this sandy-haired man with the hazel eyes was indeed the man with whom God intended her to make a new life.

Truman stopped at the edge of the road and pulled her close for a lingering kiss. "I need to do this a lot more often," he murmured as he eased away from her. "Once we're on the road this afternoon, I might be pulling over every now and then to show you just how much I love you, Rosetta."

Late that evening, Rosetta quietly entered the mudroom and hung up her wraps. She smelled cocoa, and she wasn't surprised to see lamps lit where Leola, the Kuhns, and Christine and her girls sat around one of the tables in the dining room. Leola was embroidering while the other ladies crocheted, and they all looked up as she came through the kitchen.

"So how was your big day with Truman?" Phoebe quizzed her.

"You were gone a really long time," Leola remarked.

"I hope it was the perfect end to a wonderful-*gut* birthday for you, dearie," Ruby said with a smile. "We saved you some cocoa and cookies—"

"Because we want to hear every little detail about what-all you and Truman did," Beulah finished.

Christine flashed Rosetta a knowing smile. "We understand, however, that at thirty-eight, you're entitled to keep a few things to yourself."

Rosetta sat down in a chair and poured some cocoa from the carafe. "First we ate lunch with Irene—"

"And she's doing better, I hope?" Christine asked. "I've really missed seeing her at our recent gatherings."

Rosetta nodded. "Her medications have stabilized her heartbeat and she seems fine now. I suppose you saw the apron she made for me, and the fabric for my wedding dress?"

"*Jah*, we put them up on your bed so they'd stay clean," Laura replied. "It's so exciting that in two weeks you'll be marrying Truman—at long last."

"But we digress," Ruby teased. "What'd you do after your lunch at your future home?"

Rosetta smiled. Maybe all the kissing stops during their truck ride were details she would keep to herself. "Truman took me to three different shops that sell furniture, over in Willow Ridge," she murmured. "For my wedding gift, he wanted me to pick out a bedroom set—to replace the one he's had since he was a kid—as well as a larger table for their dining room. He and Irene want enough chairs and table leaves for occasions when my family and friends come over."

"What a lovely idea," Christine said. "And what did you choose?"

"We went to all three stores before I could make up my mind," Rosetta replied. "I chose a refurbished walnut bedroom set at Detweiler Furniture Works, and I got the table and chairs in a shop called Simple Gifts. Oh my," she whispered, "I could've come away with *several* items from that store! But Truman was already paying so much for the furniture that my heart nearly stopped when I did the math."

"Might as well let him spoil you," Beulah said, quickly working her hook and yarn into another row of the striped afghan she was making. "I suspect he didn't blink an eye at what he was paying. He impresses me as a saver and a *gut* businessman."

"Probably paid cash," Ruby murmured, concentrating on the square she was crocheting. "And he bought quality furniture to last you a lifetime, instead of cheap stuff."

Rosetta's heart thudded. "He unrolled a big wad of bills and settled up at both stores. Everything's to be delivered the weekend before the wedding."

"That's so romantic, having new furniture to start your new life," Phoebe said with a dreamy-eyed sigh.

"And exciting, too!" Laura put in. "You'll no more than get your wedding dress made than it'll be time for the ceremony!"

Beulah turned her afghan to start a new row, meeting Rosetta's gaze. "And what's Truman's opinion of you keeping the lodge and being our landlady?" she asked quietly. "Not worried about being kicked out. Just wondering about the management."

Rosetta nodded. "We talked about that today on our trip," she replied. "I'll be living at the Wickey place, of course, but Truman has no objection to me owning and operating the lodge and the cabins. I'll keep selling my goat's milk soap, as well."

"Glad to hear that!" Ruby exclaimed. "With you and Christine moving out soon, that'll leave just the two of us sisters and Maria here—and Leola," she added when she saw the young woman's head snap up. "We'll look forward to seeing you when you come over, Rosetta. It'll be quieter, but it'll still be our home."

"My home, too—until I marry Monroe," Leola added with a confident nod.

The room got quiet for a moment. Phoebe placed her hand on Leola's shoulder. "You're confused, sweetie," she said quietly. "It's my *mamm* who's marrying Monroe. He's taking you back to Illinois as soon as your parents come home."

Leola's scowl warned of an impending outburst as she glared across the table at Christine. Phoebe got up and massaged her slender shoulders until she exhaled and focused again on the pillowcase she was embroidering. "Maybe," Leola muttered. "Maybe not."

Rosetta slipped her hand under the table to grasp Christine's. Her sister's wedding was on hold until Monroe's house was finished—and until they found a bishop to perform the ceremony. Unless Leola returned home soon, the topic of Christine's marriage would continue to be a tense one.

Christine squeezed Rosetta's hand. "Meanwhile, we have your wedding meal to plan, little sister—"

"And it'll be a feast!" Ruby exclaimed. "You and Truman let us know what sort of food you want, and we'll do it up right."

Rosetta's pulse pounded with pleasure. "I vote for another chocolate cake like you made for my birthday, with the mocha frosting," she said immediately. "Compared to that one, white cake takes a backseat."

"I agree with you there," Beulah said. "I suspect we'll have several guests from Coldstream and from Truman's church, so we might as well make two cakes—and if you want them both to be chocolate, why not? Your wedding, your rules."

Rosetta sighed happily as she glanced at this circle of

dear women and basked in their excitement. It had been one of the most fabulous days of her life. At long last, she and Truman were tying the knot—and thanks to her sisters' love and Bishop Monroe's progressive attitude, she could marry outside the Old Order Amish faith and still remain close to her family and friends. Her dreams were indeed coming true . . . and they tasted like mocha frosting and Truman's kisses.

Chapter Twenty

On Saturday morning, Christine and Rosetta were delighted to visit the Troyer place to see the cold frames Amos had built for Mattie in the sunny yard behind the house. It was March twenty-fifth, and—as often happened in Missouri—the recent snow had disappeared as quickly as it had come. The warmer temperature was a sign that spring was definitely on its way.

"Amos is tickled with himself for making these cold frames out of lumber scraps from the houses he and the other men have built," Mattie said as she lifted the lid of the largest frame. "And he used glass sections Floyd and Lester let him have after they'd made everyone's windows, too."

Mattie beamed as she propped the lid open on the simple wooden braces her husband had built in. The top and sides of the cold frame were mostly glass, with heavily varnished wooden edges. "He's been too nice to say so, but he'll be glad to have my trays of seedlings away from the southern windows. I had them arranged on spare doors, supported by sawhorses, so the house has been a little more cluttered than he likes."

"But look at these sturdy little broccoli plants—and bell peppers, too," Christine said as she gazed at a couple of the high-sided trays in which Mattie had planted her seeds. "This takes me back to when we were kids and Mamm always started her tomatoes, peppers, and cabbage in old roasters and glass pans filled with potting soil."

"*Jah*, the whole back side of the house, upstairs and down, had a table at every window with those pans on them," Rosetta recalled with a smile. "It looks like you've already got a nice blend of garden soil and compost in your cold frames, Mattie. Where would you like us to plant each of your vegetables? The three of us can transplant these seedlings in two shakes of Queenie's tail."

As though the Border collie had heard her name, she came loping over from her sunny spot on Roman's front porch. Rosetta scratched behind her shaggy black ears and then pointed toward the open yard. "You stay out of our way and out of Mattie's cold frames," she instructed firmly. "These seedlings don't stand a chance if you step on them."

With a forlorn expression, Queenie trotted away. As she plopped down in the grass to supervise, Christine and her sisters pulled old serving spoons from the pockets of their barn coats and arranged the pans of seedlings so the same vegetables would be planted together. The cold frames were in a row along one edge of the Troyer property, so they chatted as they worked. With their spoons, they carefully separated single plants with a spoonful of soil each and placed them in neat rows inside the cold frames. The glass would magnify the sun's warmth so the plants would grow strong and stay moist, and they'd be protected from any cold spring weather.

"Your garden plots will have a head start this year, what with these seedlings and the several months' worth of compost Noah worked into the soil when he plowed," Rosetta remarked. "Last year when we arrived, it was too late to plant some of these vegetables."

Mattie's smile held a secret. "And about that time last

spring, Deborah showed up and upset Noah's apple cart, wanting him to forgive her and court her again," she recalled fondly. "This year, it's a different story entirely. They're not saying anything yet, but Deborah's feeling queasy a lot lately, which makes me think—"

"A baby, maybe! Oh, that's *gut* news," Christine said excitedly.

"But you didn't hear that from me," Mattie insisted as she placed more cabbage seedlings in her cold frame. "I suspect Deborah's confiding in her own *mamm* instead of in me, but that's natural. Alma will most likely whisper to me about it, and when Noah and Deborah are ready, they'll announce they're starting their family."

For a moment, Christine felt envious of younger women who were able to conceive and bear children—but she quickly set aside her glum thoughts. She'd been blessed with two wonderful daughters who were the joy of her life—and Monroe had insisted that her inability to have his children didn't matter.

The whacking of hammers carried from the roadside, where Amos and Monroe were repairing Mattie's produce stand. From the opposite direction, the whine of air-driven screws announced that Preachers Marlin and Eli, with Harley and Roman's help, were attaching the sections of black metal roofing to one of Monroe's horse barns. A whiff of sugar and cinnamon hinted that Maria's baking was in full swing. Young male laughter came from the Helmuth place, where Sam, Simon, and their two cousins were constructing the glass walls of the greenhouse. So much progress was being made!

After all the seedlings had been transferred, Mattie shut and hooked the tops of the cold frames. Christine smiled when her elder sister went to the nearest shed and rolled out a rotary cultivator. Mattie also grabbed a plastic sack full of seed packets, which she handed to Rosetta and Christine so they could sort them on the grass.

"This is just like old times, when we girls were in charge of planting the garden back home," Rosetta remarked wistfully. "Mamm's back was in no shape for so much stooping over, and Dat's patience with gardening only lasted as long as it took him to get the soil turned each spring."

"Noah's already tilled a couple of the plots, so we might as well plant some lettuce, peas, spinach, and radishes today," Mattie suggested. "I'll have to go into Forest Grove to get my onion sets soon. Depending on how warm the weather stays, we might be opening the produce stand with salad greens in a month or so."

"I think folks will be glad to see us at the roadside again," Christine said. "And I know Laura and Phoebe are figuring to have Lily Peterscheim and Fannie Kurtz help them sell produce this year, too."

"Do you suppose Deborah plans to sell her baked goods at the stand again?" Rosetta asked as she wheeled the cultivator toward the nearest garden plot. "Maria might not be too happy to have that kind of competition. Have you seen any cars pulling in at the bakery?"

"Nope, not a one," Mattie murmured. "She might have to deliver her goodies to Cloverdale to keep her customers there. Unless they call her for special orders, I can't see folks driving down this way just to pick up a few doughnuts."

"If Deborah's in the family way, she might not want to do any extra baking," Christine said. "She's got that double oven, though."

"We'll see what they decide," Mattie said with a shrug. "Thanks to Truman, Noah's making a steady living with his welding and metalwork now, so they'll be okay for money even if Deborah doesn't bake."

Rosetta positioned the cultivator at the end of the plot,

along the edge where Noah and his horse had plowed. She lowered the heavy metal rotary blade and grabbed the long wooden handles, walking behind it to smooth and level the soil. After she got a good start, Christine followed her with a hoe, angling it to cut a row in the loosened soil. Mattie opened a packet of leaf lettuce seed, pinched some between her fingers, and walked slowly along the groove Christine had made, sprinkling her seeds in it.

By the time they'd worked an hour, trading off on the cultivating, hoeing, and planting, they had a sizeable section of the plot planted with salad greens and radishes. "We're off to a really *gut* start," Mattie said, holding her back, "and I for one need to let my poor old muscles rest for the remainder of the day."

Christine laughed as they gathered the empty seed packets from the ground. "Poor old muscles?" she teased. "Are you feeling your grand old age of forty-six, sister?"

"I can just picture you propping your feet up on the couch for the rest of the day, Mattie," Rosetta said breezily as she rolled the cultivator into the shed. "You could be a true lady of leisure."

Mattie rolled her eyes. "Like that will ever happen. What I mean is that a different form of exertion will stretch my muscles so they don't get stiff and sore," she explained. "You sweet young things just wait. When you're as *mature* as I am now, I'll remember to rub it in about how ancient and creaky you feel."

Christine chuckled. As they approached the lodge, she saw Monroe and Amos coming up the road with their tools. Now that the bishop was living in one of the cabins, he ate his meals with them—as did the Helmuths and Allen Troyer—and she looked forward to the day's progress report on Mattie's produce stand and the other construction sites. "I think we're smart to hook up with husbands who're a bit older than we are, Mattie," she said. "That way we'll always feel younger and nimbler—"

"And no matter how we feel, we'll have each other to commiserate with," Mattie said, slinging her arms around Christine and Rosetta. "That's the best part of having you girls for sisters. In sunshine and in shadow, we're moving through life together and we'll never be alone. I wouldn't admit this to Amos, but the bond I feel for you two will always be as strong as what I share with him in marriage— different, but just as deep."

Christine's heart swelled as she and her sisters paused in a huddle, hugging. "*Jah*, you've got that right," she murmured. "Willis was a fine, loving husband, but my love for him was never the same as what I've felt for you sisters all my life."

"I totally understand that, even if Truman's younger," Rosetta said as they eased apart. "No matter how deeply in love I am with him, my roots with you two go back to the day I was born. He'll never be able to catch up on that sort of connection."

"We can't lose!" Mattie exclaimed as they opened the door to the mudroom.

As Christine followed her sisters inside, she caught Monroe's eye. He waved from the road and hollered that he'd be there for dinner in a few minutes, but she could tell he was curious about what she, Rosetta, and Mattie had been discussing in their huddle.

If he asked, Christine wouldn't even try to explain it. Some kinds of love were just too marvelous and mysterious to fully comprehend.

Rosetta carried the last bowls of haystack fixings into the dining room and set them on the table where the Helmuth twins, their two cousins, Allen, and Monroe were taking their seats for the noon meal. The room quickly filled with talk about the progress they were making on their projects.

"I'll be starting the plumbing at your place this afternoon, Bishop," Allen said as he spooned a layer of hash browns onto his plate. "If you haven't bought faucets for your kitchen, bathrooms, and mudroom, you might want to get them this afternoon so I can install them tomorrow. Toilets and sinks and your bathtub, too."

Monroe's green eyes glimmered with excitement. "This makes it sound like my house is nearly finished," he said as he arranged a layer of seasoned hamburger on his hash browns. He glanced across the table at Christine. "You should go to Forest Grove with me and pick out what you want, dear. I have no idea what sort of faucet and sink you'd like in your kitchen."

"The mercantile has a good selection," Allen put in. His haystack had grown tall with meat, cooked onions, stewed tomatoes, and bell peppers, and he was ladling cheese sauce over the entire mound. "When I went there earlier this week, I found all the stuff I'll need for the places at Promise Lodge and for wherever else I find work."

Rosetta spooned stewed tomatoes onto her haystack, considering what Allen had said. He'd be looking for work shortly, because he'd already done the plumbing for the Helmuths' home and nursery buildings. "You might talk to Truman," she suggested. "He's contracted for some extensive landscaping jobs at three new townhome communities. They'll surely need plumbing and electrical work."

"Truman's taking Lester with him to install windows and siding, starting next week," Monroe said. "Couldn't hurt to ask him. He certainly got Noah hooked up with a number of contractors."

Allen's face lit up. "That would be fabulous! I'll give

Wickey a call when I've finished eating—which might be a while, considering how much stuff I've piled on my plate!"

Rosetta laughed along with Ruby and Beulah. It amazed her how much Allen, Jonathan, and Cyrus ate at a meal, so she was glad the Kuhn sisters were preparing more of everything they cooked these days. Although they were very slender, Sam and Simon kept up with burly Monroe plateful for plateful, so it wasn't long before all of the men were passing the bowls of vegetables and ground beef to build their second haystacks. Conversation was lively, and the topic evolved to what colors Barbara and Bernice wanted their walls painted.

"Tell you what," said Monroe. He stepped into the kitchen for a pen and pad of paper. "While Christine and I are in town, we'll pick up the paint for your place and mine—"

"And I bet my girls, along with Lily and Fannie, will be willing to do that painting for you," Christine said. "They've painted nearly every house we've built, so they're quick— and they're tidy about it. They turn it into a frolic."

"It's always more fun to work in somebody else's house than your own," Beulah said with a chuckle. She smiled at Amos's twin daughters, who were looking rosy-cheeked and round. "If you let the girls paint, you ladies-in-waiting won't be tempted to climb ladders or wear yourselves to a frazzle."

"You don't have to ask us twice," Barbara teased.

Bernice nodded in agreement. "We've never been keen on painting, so we're happy to let the girls do it. I've always been partial to butter yellow, pale blue, and white."

"*Jah*, those colors go with all the furniture we've brought," Barbara said.

"Duly noted," Monroe said as he jotted his shopping list. He glanced at the Kuhn sisters. "Do you ladies need baking supplies or—"

When the lodge's front door slammed, everyone turned toward the lobby. A young woman was carrying large, white bakery boxes stacked so high they couldn't see her face—until Maria carefully set them on the nearest table. She appeared flustered, downright overwhelmed, as she looked at everyone who was seated.

"Okay, so I've baked my normal amount of stuff for the past three days," she said in a rush. "I even took boxes of doughnuts and muffins to Cloverdale yesterday, but I didn't sell them all—and nobody's coming here to buy anything. I can't go on this way! I'm flat-out broke."

When Maria burst into tears, Allen and the two Helmuth cousins eyed the stack of white boxes. When Allen scooted his chair back from the table, Cyrus and Jonathan followed him over to see what sorts of goodies Maria had brought. They opened all the boxes, inhaling the aroma of yeast and sugar and spices.

"So what're you charging for this stuff?" Cyrus asked.

Maria sniffled loudly. "If—if I get a dollar apiece, I'll break even."

Rosetta's eyes widened. She shared a glance with Ruby and Beulah, who also realized that Maria's ingredients hadn't cost her nearly that much, because she bought them in bulk. Although the young men might be willing to pay that price, Rosetta and the Kuhns wouldn't make a habit of supporting Maria's bakery, because they baked goodies that would feed more people for less money.

Dollar bills were landing on the table as the three younger men chose what they wanted. When Christine went to the kitchen to fetch plates for them, Monroe, Sam, and Simon also purchased a few pastries apiece. After the men had finished buying, Maria rearranged the pieces that remained. She smiled hopefully at Rosetta, Christine, and the Kuhns.

"I still have three boxes of apple fritters, doughnuts, Danish, and muffins," she entreated. "You wouldn't have to bake dessert or breakfast for *days*."

Rosetta clenched her jaw so she wouldn't say things she might regret about Maria's business practices.

Beulah rose from her chair to look at the three boxes of pastries. She counted them silently with her finger. "You've got about six dozen pieces here," she said, "but why would I pay seventy-two dollars for them, when for the same money I could make enough coffee cakes, muffins, and cinnamon rolls to cover two or three of these dining room tables?"

Ruby nodded in agreement. "*Jah*, I could see paying you *half* that amount, and freezing your goodies to serve with breakfast when folks come for Rosetta and Truman's wedding," she said in a businesslike tone. "But we can't be your everyday customers, Maria. Rosetta would have to raise our rent to cover the increase in our food budget. Even with the profit we make at our cheese factory, we can't afford that."

"Well, we could afford it, but we don't want to," Beulah clarified.

The dining room got very quiet. Maria's face turned pink while everyone waited for her response. "Rosetta and Truman are getting married?" she murmured. "Um, maybe I could make their wedding cake—"

"I've already got the layers baked and in the freezer, waiting for April fifth!" Ruby said.

Rosetta told herself she shouldn't feel so gratified by Maria's baffled expression. Was the blonde really surprised to hear about the wedding? Or was Maria upset because the Kuhns had refused to bankroll her bakery?

After some hesitation, Maria sighed. "Okay, I'll sell it all to you for thirty dollars—fifty percent," she said with a shake of her head. "But—but how am I supposed to stay in business? I paid all that money to get my building moved, and—"

Monroe gave her an encouraging smile. "Have you advertised? Put any signs up in Cloverdale, inviting folks to visit you at your new location?" he asked. "You could also post cards on the bulletin boards in the Forest Grove stores, like Mattie did last year for her produce stand."

"I'd be willing to build you a sign for the roadside," Allen offered. "We could put it alongside the sign for Mattie's produce stand, pointing through the entryway to your bakery."

"That's a *gut* idea," Maria said. "But it'll be a while before her stand is open—"

"Probably late April," Christine put in. "Our first salad vegetables should be ready by then."

Maria's forlorn sigh filled the dining room. Rosetta wondered if she was making a play for more pity from the men—and then reminded herself that such an uncharitable attitude didn't sit well with God. *I'm sorry, Lord. Forgive me for thinking ill of Maria when she's having financial difficulties.*

Beulah said, "I'll go fetch some money from my coffee can, and I'll pay you the thirty-*six* dollars we agreed to. The first rule of running a business is not to cheat yourself by taking less than folks offer you."

As Ruby followed her sister into the kitchen, Rosetta again kept her remarks to herself. Maria's expression suggested that she hadn't taken the time to note that half of seventy-two dollars was thirty-six, rather than thirty. Considering how moving her bakery had been a lot more expensive than Maria had figured on—and how she'd apparently believed that her customers would follow her to Promise Lodge—Rosetta was even more convinced that Miss Zehr was a much better baker than she was a businesswoman.

What if Maria didn't earn enough to pay her rent by the first of April, only a week away? What if the young men got tired of buying goodies because they felt sorry for her? It wouldn't be easy or pleasant to ask Maria to leave Promise Lodge for being habitually delinquent with her rent— because her building was here now—but it wasn't fair of Maria to expect folks to bail her out every couple of days, either. She needed to realize that baking less might be a good idea until business picked up.

Help us figure it out, Lord, she prayed as she rose from the table to bring out Ruby's rhubarb crisp. *And help me not to be so quick to pass judgment when Maria doesn't measure up.*

Chapter Twenty-One

"Whoa, Clyde," Monroe called out to his Clydesdale as he pulled the wagon up to the lodge that afternoon. It was a beautiful spring Saturday, and he was looking forward to spending time with Christine as she chose the sinks, faucets, and paint for their new home. The completion of the house made him eager to return to Illinois next week for the Clydesdales he bred and trained, along with his furnishings—but he was hoping to take Leola home to her parents on that same trip, and he hadn't heard from Polly or Chester Duff lately. It was time to call them again.

And the following week, on April fifth, Monroe was officiating at Truman and Rosetta's wedding. Truman had agreed that he and a couple of his men would drive their large trucks to haul his horses and belongings, but he'd need to be patient if Wickey took time off to be with his new bride. He also had to line up a bishop to conduct his own wedding . . .

Christine's smile waylaid Monroe's hectic thoughts. She was tying the strings of her black bonnet, gazing at him as though she was as eager as he was to get away from the lodge for a while. "I updated our shopping list with a few things Beulah wants from the grocery store," she called out as she nimbly descended the porch stairs. "It's a *gut* thing we're taking a big wagon today!"

Monroe stepped down to lift Christine up to the bench seat, delighting in the closeness of her body . . . craving a kiss—except someone in the lodge might be watching through the window. "I love you," he whispered.

Christine's face lit up. "I love you, too, Monroe," she said softly. "And I'm so excited about choosing the kitchen and bathroom fixtures—"

"Wait for me! I'm coming, too!"

Monroe closed his eyes at the sound of Leola's voice. Christine stiffened as he boosted her up to the seat. He turned, reminding himself to remain patient. "Leola, we'll be spending a lot of time at the mercantile getting plumbing and paint," he said sternly. "There's nothing there that will interest you. And we didn't invite you to come along."

Leola bounded down the stairs with her coat and bonnet flapping under her arm. She stopped in front of him, grinning like a kid in a candy store. "But I gotta get more things to embroider! And more embroidery floss," she announced happily.

"Did you bring any money?" Christine called down from the bench.

Leola's expression wavered, and then brightened again. "No, but you can get me what I want and it'll be for my birthday!" she exclaimed, gazing raptly at Monroe. She slipped her arms into her coat sleeves, fully expecting to go to town.

Monroe's thoughts were whirling. He didn't want Leola tagging along—

"When's your birthday?" Christine asked. "I could pick you out some new iron-on patterns and floss, and we'll wrap them up so they'll be a surprise to go with your birthday cake."

Christine's idea was excellent, and Monroe hoped it

would convince Leola to stay—but he should've known better. Her face was turning red and she was breathing faster as she crammed her black bonnet over her head.

"You *know* my birthday is April second, Monroe," Leola blurted shrilly. "Tell Christine to stay home so you can take *me*! Just us two—because I *love* you."

Monroe glanced toward the Helmuth place, where Lester and the three preachers were installing windows. If he allowed this scene to escalate, Amos would be following the conversation—and so would everyone else at Promise Lodge, because Leola's strident voice would attract their attention. He wanted to grasp the girl's shoulders and steer her back inside, but if Leola latched on to him, she wouldn't let go—and Amos would be watching that with great interest.

"Leola, settle down," he muttered. "I'm not taking you anywhere if you're going to yell at me. Understand?"

Leola burst into tears. She covered her mouth to keep from wailing, but she showed no sign of going inside.

Monroe sighed. He'd planned to spend the afternoon shopping with Christine and then treating her to dinner at the café in Forest Grove, taking the long way home . . . but those private, tender moments were popping like soap bubbles.

"I'm sorry, Monroe. I promise I'll be quiet," Leola whimpered.

He turned to gaze apologetically at Christine, who wore a closed, resigned expression. When Monroe faced Leola again, he tried to think of a convincing idea that would keep her at the lodge—but once she intended to do something, Leola was like a dog who wouldn't release a bone.

"*If* I take you," Monroe began, "you will *not* fuss at me or at Christine, and you will *not* hang on to me—"

Leola's eyes widened. "But I love—"

"Stop!" Monroe interrupted sharply. "I'm telling you

that you have to behave yourself or you're not going. And I'm going to call your *dat* again after we return from town. You belong at home, and you need to be on your medications."

Leola bowed her head forlornly. "Don't be mean to me, Monroe."

Monroe crossed his arms. "Are you going to obey my rules, Leola? Or are you staying here? Christine and I didn't invite you to come along, and you're being very rude, carrying on like a spoiled child."

He regretted his words as soon as he said them, because Leola would never mature beyond the point she'd reached—socially, she would remain about ten years old, and that wasn't her fault. She was sniffling, clutching at her coat, trying very hard to understand why he'd reprimanded her—yet Monroe sensed that Leola knew exactly what she was doing whenever she wedged herself between him and Christine. For a moment, hope flared within him when she turned to look at the door of the lodge.

Leola let out a quavering sigh. "All right. I'll be quiet. I promise not to be a bother."

Monroe closed his eyes, praying again for patience. He wasn't about to let Leola sit between him and Christine. "Let's go around to the other side. You'll have to sit close to Christine, because the bench isn't very wide."

When Leola realized that she wouldn't be riding next to him, she balked. "I'll sit in the wagon."

Monroe's eyebrows rose. Although young folks often rode in wagons, Leola didn't realize what she'd be enduring. "You'll get tired of the bumps. There's a tarp you can sit on, but you'd be more comfortable on the bench—"

"No. In the wagon."

Monroe walked to the end of the wagon, which had a wooden back behind the seat and slatted sides of the same height. When he helped Leola into it, she quickly settled against the back—which meant she'd be listening to every word he and Christine said. When he finally climbed into the seat and took the lines, he felt as if he'd already spent the entire afternoon dealing with Leola rather than enjoying Christine's company.

"I'm sorry," he mouthed, clapping the leather lines lightly on Clyde's back.

Christine shrugged, appearing as disappointed as he felt.

It was a quiet twenty-minute ride to Forest Grove. As he drove, Monroe considered ways to occupy Leola so she wouldn't be tagging along like a puppy, expressing her opinion of every faucet and sink and can of paint they looked at. He slipped his hand around Christine's. "Where's the best place to find the embroidery stuff she wants?" he murmured.

"Nina's Fabrics!" Leola replied excitedly.

Christine nodded. "I have a plan," she whispered.

Monroe nodded, sensing he should leave Leola's shopping to Christine . . . hoping her idea would give the two of them some time alone. When they arrived in Forest Grove, the main street was lined with angle-parked cars until they reached the mercantile's big parking lot. Clyde knew to head for the long hitching rail on the side of the building, where a few other horses waited with buggies and wagons.

"Leola, let's you and I go to Nina's," Christine suggested as Monroe hitched his horse to the rail. "Monroe can start shopping for paint and toilets, because he won't want to go into a girly fabric store with us."

Monroe smiled as he lifted Christine from the wagon. "*Denki*," he mouthed. "I'll make this up to you, sweetheart."

She winked at him. "We'll find you in the mercantile," she whispered. "And we'll find somebody a chair, too."

As Monroe handed Leola down from the back of the wagon, she frowned. "But you're supposed to be getting my birthday present, Monroe," she protested.

"And you're supposed to be quiet and follow my rules, remember?" he countered. "Pick out what you want with Christine. I don't want to hear that you gave her any trouble, either. Understand?"

With a long sigh, Leola nodded. As she followed Christine across the parking lot, hanging her head, she resembled someone who'd just been put under the *bann*.

Monroe entered the mercantile and found one of the large flatbed carts he'd need for his bulky purchases. Most men would choose all the fixtures and be done with it, but he wanted Christine to have a say about how their new home would look—even if she chose sinks and faucets that were a little fancier than most Plain women had.

But a toilet's a toilet, Monroe thought as he maneuvered the cart down the wide aisle. The mercantile was busy, so it took a few minutes to reach the bathroom fixtures. He was surprised at how many styles basic white sinks, stools, and tubs came in. As he was comparing prices, a wiry guy wearing a vest with a store logo approached him. His black beard made him appear Plain—except he had a bushy mustache.

"You're just in time for our tub sale!" he said cheerfully. He stuck out his hand. "I'm Bert, and I'm here to help."

Monroe introduced himself and gestured along the large display of bathroom fixtures. "I'd like to stay pretty basic in my new house, but I could use some help getting a tub onto this cart—and a couple of toilets and some sinks, as well."

Bert smiled. "You live within twenty miles of here? We can deliver all your stuff tomorrow and you won't have to lift a finger."

Monroe liked this guy already. "That would be a big help. We're about three miles away, at Promise Lodge."

"Ah—you one of the Plain folks that's settled at the old church camp?" Bert asked as he pulled an order pad from his vest pocket. "Sounds like you'll easily meet our two hundred dollar amount to qualify for free delivery, so where shall we start?"

Monroe appreciated the way Bert talked him through the features of the various toilets, sinks, and tubs. By the time Christine found him, he was ready for her to choose between the three styles he thought would be appropriate for an Amish bishop.

"This is my fiancée, Christine," Monroe said as he took her arm. "Bert has been very helpful. We're getting everything delivered tomorrow—"

He stopped talking and looked around. "Where's Leola?"

Christine flashed him a smile. "I bought her a new embroidery hoop, scissors, floss—the works—so she's sitting in the patio display, starting on a new project."

Monroe realized yet again how many ways he loved and respected the beautiful woman who stood beside him. With her usual efficiency, Christine chose all the bathroom fixtures in the style that appealed to her, and then chose sinks for the kitchen and the mudroom, along with faucets and hardware. Bert wrote stock numbers down as she pointed to what she wanted.

"Wow," he murmured as he finished. "This is the fastest I've *ever* seen a woman make up her mind about so many fixtures. Good job!"

Monroe chuckled. "Christine's not one to waste anybody's time or money," he said proudly. "If you can mix some paint for us, Bert, we'll be all set."

"Let's go to the service counter and I'll have an associate enter your delivery information and your purchases from this department into the computer," Bert said as he escorted them down the aisle. "Meanwhile, I'll have a guy in the paint department waiting to help you, and your paint will go on the same order."

"You've been a tremendous help, Bert. I appreciate it."

At the service counter, Monroe watched in amazement. The sales associate was a young woman whose fingers flew over the keyboard as he gave his address. In a few minutes she had all the information she needed, and she began entering the items from Bert's order sheet.

"Ready to pick your paint colors?" Monroe asked Christine as they headed down the aisle.

"I'm fine with the same colors Barbara and Bernice asked for," she said, tucking her arm through his. "Let's slip over this way to check on Leola. I hope she hasn't wandered off."

Monroe didn't even want to think about the chaos Leola would cause if she started looking for him and couldn't find him. As they approached the display of picnic tables, big umbrellas, and gas grills, he spotted her immediately and stopped walking. In her calf-length cape dress and white *kapp*, Leola looked out of place embroidering in a glider while English folks passed by with their shopping carts and kids—*Lost in her own little world,* he realized. She was so focused on her project she didn't notice anyone else, however.

"You're a genius," he murmured to Christine. "Let's get our paint before she spots us."

Monroe took off toward the overhead sign for the paint department, thrumming with an ulterior motive. The mercantile was busy on this springtime Saturday afternoon, yet when he spotted an aisle where there weren't any shoppers, he walked faster.

Christine kept up with him, looking around at the bins of bolts and nails on either side of the aisle they'd entered. "Do you men need more of this stuff to finish—"

"No, I need this." Monroe felt like a kid with his first girlfriend as he framed Christine's face with his hands and kissed her. Her low giggle, her eager response, made him wish they were alone in the wagon on the way home—so he kissed her for as long as he dared before releasing her.

"Well now, Bishop," Christine murmured as she demurely straightened her *kapp*. "I've never been kissed in a store."

"Glad to hear it." Monroe's pulse roared in his ears as he walked her toward the paint department. *If I had my way, I'd marry you right this minute, sweetheart—or elope, as I've heard some English folks do.*

Truth be told, however, he wanted Christine to enjoy the traditional ceremony and the company of her friends and family as they began their life together. And without a bishop to lead them in their vows, their marriage wouldn't be valid in the eyes of the Old Order, so Monroe set aside his fantasies of a quick, immediate wedding.

"Is our kiss something we'll need to confess at a church meeting?" Christine teased.

Monroe laughed. "I won't tell if you won't. Couples are entitled to keep a few things to themselves, don't you think?"

Once again he delighted in Christine's ability to choose her paint colors without hemming and hawing. She plucked a couple of paint sample cards from the long display of colors on the wall rack and handed them to him.

"This pale yellow, this off-white, and this light blue," she said, pointing to the small colored squares. "You get to figure how many gallons we'll need. Yellow for the kitchens, white for the front rooms and hallways—and ceilings—and the blue for some of the bedrooms. We'll paint the remaining rooms with whatever colors we have left."

"Sounds like a plan." The gray-haired man at the paint counter wore a store vest with *Stan* on the name tag, and he was smiling at them. "Depending on how many gallons you want, we have these three colors in stock—and ceiling paint comes in five-gallon buckets. I can tint five-gallon buckets of your wall colors, too, if you'd like."

"Hmm. That might be easier than dealing with so many cans," Monroe said.

"And you can reuse the buckets for a lot of things," Stan pointed out.

Monroe pulled a notepad and pencil from his pocket and estimated the square footage of the walls and ceilings in the two large homes. He rounded up by quite a bit and ordered ten gallons of each color and ten gallons of ceiling paint. "We'll have other folks building homes in the future, so leftover paint won't go to waste," he explained to Christine.

"The Helmuths might want some of it for their store, too," she said. "Let's get new roller covers and foam brushes while we're here. That's what the girls like to use."

"And if we take the ceiling paint with us, they can start first thing Monday morning, if they want to," Monroe said.

"They probably will. Those girls have such a *gut* time spreading paint," Christine said with a chuckle. "It gets them out of helping in the kitchen or with the laundry, but nobody minds. Minerva considers their painting a service project—and Lily and Fannie are ahead in their lessons— so she gives them time away from the classroom."

Christine held Monroe's gaze, her lips twitching with a smile. "We older girls don't enjoy climbing ladders all day—and that's the last thing Bernice and Barbara should be doing. We're blessed to have such industrious daughters amongst us."

Monroe pictured the female Helmuth twins, for a brief moment wishing that he would someday see Christine looking so round with his child—but he set aside that useless thought. She was everything he wanted in a wife . . .

and if he had no children of his own, he could pay more attention to the members of his congregation and their kids.

While the clerk located the ceiling paint on the shelf, Monroe and Christine selected large packages of roller covers and a couple sizes of foam brushes for painting the edges and the trim. After Monroe paid for all of his merchandise, the clerk grabbed a low, flat cart for them. Monroe placed the two five-gallon drums of white ceiling paint on it while Christine set the painting supplies alongside them.

"Thanks for doing business with us, folks," he said. "The delivery driver will call you when he's within fifteen minutes of your place."

Monroe started down the central aisle with the cart, Christine at his side. "Maybe you could fetch Leola while I take this outside—"

"Monroe! Here I am!" a familiar voice called to them. "Don't forget *me*!"

He stopped the cart, relieved to see that Leola was smiling from ear to ear as she hurried toward them with a bulging plastic sack from Nina's Fabrics. "We were just coming to get you," he said. "I hear you've been busy sewing."

Leola's forehead creased as she tried to figure out how Monroe had known what she was doing. Her concern vanished, however, when she spotted the cart. She hopped onto it and sat on one of the five-gallon paint buckets, as delighted as a little child. "Push me!" she said, oblivious to the customers who were watching her. "Give me a birthday ride."

As he steered the cart toward the exit doors, Monroe almost envied Leola's childlike view of the world—the simple things that excited her. After he loaded the paint and supplies into the wagon, he drove across the road to the bulk store and bought the fifty-pound bags of flour and other baking staples Beulah had requested. Leola had always been fascinated by the small bags and plastic containers of candies and cookie sprinkles displayed in Plain bulk stores, so Monroe wasn't surprised that she joined him and Christine in the checkout line with an armful of treats.

"Gummy worms!" Leola whispered ecstatically. "And chocolate-covered raisins! And cinnamon disks and root beer barrels and peach rings!"

Monroe held Leola's gaze as the Mennonite girl at the cash register rang up their purchases. "Promise me you won't eat all this stuff before we get back to the lodge," he insisted. "You know how sick you get when you eat too much sugary stuff."

Leola's expression waxed angelic. "I wouldn't do any such thing, Monroe."

When they returned to the wagon, Leola made no fuss about sitting in the back with the paint and the groceries. She immediately pulled out her embroidery. As Monroe drove, he occasionally peered behind him, pleased that she was too occupied with her stitching to open any of her sweets. He held the lines in one hand and Christine's hand in the other, grateful to God that their shopping expedition had gone much more smoothly than he'd anticipated.

When they arrived at the lodge, Leola grabbed her treats and treasures and bolted upstairs to her room. Monroe hefted a sack of flour over his shoulder, gazing into Christine's green eyes. "You are such a gift," he murmured. "Do you suppose you could slip out after supper? Spend some time in the cabin with me? Or if that seems too cozy—"

"I'll be there," Christine whispered.

Monroe's heart thumped rapidly. "I'll repay you for

what you spent in the fabric shop, and we can catch up with each other."

"I like the sound of that."

After they'd unloaded Beulah's groceries, Monroe drove to the Helmuth place to drop off the paint. Both sets of twins were delighted that the girls could start painting their ceilings on Monday—and they insisted that Monroe could make his call from their new phone shanty.

He settled into the small structure, which sat near the road between the house and the nursery buildings. A basic touch-tone phone sat on the built-in table, and Monroe dialed Polly Duff's number from memory. He was expecting to leave another message, but she picked up after the third ring.

"*Jah*, who's this?" she demanded. She still used an old phone that didn't have caller ID.

Monroe chuckled. "It's Monroe, Polly. Did I catch you when you were making a call?"

"Bishop! *Gut* to hear your voice," she said. "I can guess what you're calling about, and there's *gut* news and bad news. Edna finally made it home from the hospital, couple of days ago—"

Monroe's heart pounded with rising hope.

"—but yesterday, Chester took a fall while tending his livestock. Had to get checked out at the emergency room to be sure he didn't have a concussion," Polly went on. "If it weren't for bad luck, those folks would have no luck at all."

A frustrated sigh escaped him. "So he's in no shape for me to bring Leola home?"

"He's got to lay low for a week or so, to be sure his head's on straight," Polly replied, laughing at her own joke. "I'm taking supper over to them tonight, so I'll let them know you called again." She paused. "Dare I ask how

Leola's doing? I feel mighty bad about her being at your place for so long without her medications."

"Some days she's fine, and other times she pitches a fit or cries for no particular reason." Monroe chatted for a few more minutes before hanging up. Polly seemed fascinated that he was living at a converted campground, and she was pleased that his house was nearly finished.

"So you'll soon be marrying that lucky lady you told me about?" she asked. "I'm so pleased that you've found somebody to spend the rest of your days with, Bishop. I wish you all the best—and I hope I'll get to meet her someday."

"You'll like Christine," Monroe assured her. "We'll make a point of coming to see you after we get settled—and I hope to see you when I come for my horses and household belongings, too."

"I'm counting on it. You're in my prayers every day, Bishop Monroe," she said wistfully. "Just isn't the same around here without you."

Monroe hung up and sat for a moment, gazing at the dense woods across the highway from the Helmuth place. At least the Duffs were home from Chicago and Edna was improving. He needed to be patient for another couple of weeks . . . give Chester a chance to recover from his fall. The sight of bright green buds on some of the trees gave him hope: just as spring would soon come to Promise Lodge, his own dreams would eventually bud and blossom if he kept believing in them.

Chapter Twenty-Two

For Rosetta, the following week passed quickly and joyfully. She made her wedding dress from the beautiful blue fabric Truman's *mamm* had given her and then took it over to the Wickey place to show it off. She and Irene visited for a long time while Truman was away at the townhomes he was landscaping—and she was pleased that her future mother-in-law had asked Truman and his men to clear out the dining room and his bedroom. The new furniture would arrive on Saturday, and Irene was eager to see what Rosetta had chosen.

Rosetta and Christine helped Mattie plant more of her garden plots, and—despite their objections—Rosetta also helped the Kuhn sisters bake pies and bars to freeze for her and Truman's wedding. After the girls had finished painting at the Helmuth house on Monday and Tuesday and Allen had installed their plumbing, Rosetta, her sisters, and the men helped Sam and Simon move their furnishings into their new home on Wednesday. It was exciting to walk through the huge two-story house, where each couple had bedrooms on either side of the big kitchen and front room they would share.

"It's clear the Helmuths plan to fill all those bedrooms

with kids," Rosetta remarked to her sisters as they walked back to the lodge. "That's the biggest house I've ever seen!"

Christine slipped her arm around Rosetta's shoulders. "Unless I miss my guess, you and Truman will be starting your own family soon—and I can't wait!"

"I'm looking forward to having wee ones in the family again," Mattie agreed. "Truman will make a wonderful *dat*. He's always got a kind word, and he's as patient as the day is long."

How do I know I'll be able to conceive? Rosetta wondered. *And what if the child's impaired because I'm too old to be having a first baby?*

She focused on the budding trees and the blue sky spotted with fluffy white clouds. Whatever happened, she and Truman would handle it—with God's help—so fretting was a waste of her time. Rosetta set aside her worries to join in her sisters' conversation, because their excitement was contagious.

"I can't wait to see how Ruby decorates your two chocolate wedding cakes," Christine said. "But no matter what she does for trim, that mocha frosting will have everyone going back for seconds."

"*Jah*, it's *gut* that Ruby's doubling the usual amount of cake," Mattie joined in. "I suspect that even if guests from Coldstream or on Truman's side didn't come, we Promise Lodge folks could polish off both of them."

As they entered the lodge, they saw Laura, Phoebe, Lily, and Fannie gathered around the worktable in the kitchen, snacking on brownies and milk. Their old work dresses and kerchiefs were splotched with blue, yellow, and off-white paint. "We needed a little energy boost," Phoebe explained as her sister and friends nodded. "We've painted all the ceilings at Bishop Monroe's house—"

"And we've done the front room and the kitchen," Lily

chimed in. "My legs are telling me I've been going up and down ladders for three days now."

Christine snatched a brownie from the open pan. "I'd be delighted to paint the lower half of the walls if you girls would do the high parts," she said.

Rosetta smiled as she took a brownie. "I'll put on my painting dress and come along, too. Many hands make light work."

"You're on! We'll see you up there in a few!" Fannie challenged, gazing at her friends. "We could get the upper walls of the upstairs hallway done before Rosetta and Christine show up and stay ahead of them—and out of their way."

"Sounds like a plan," Phoebe said, grabbing another brownie. She looked at the pan, which had four brownies left in it. "Let's take these to Allen. Installing toilets and sinks is hard work, too—and he's been nice enough to open our paint buckets for us."

Rosetta chuckled as she headed upstairs. Phoebe was an old hand at opening paint buckets, so perhaps she was flirting with Allen. Rosetta quickly slipped into her old paint-splotched dress and replaced her *kapp* with a brown kerchief and then joined Christine in the hallway.

"Do you suppose Allen and Phoebe are checking each other out?" Rosetta speculated. "They grew up together in Coldstream, after all, and he's just a few years older than she is."

"I suspect I'll be the last to know," Christine said, shaking her head. They descended the back stairs and grabbed their jackets in the mudroom. "My girls and I have always been close, but they're of an age to keep their secrets when it comes to boys—not that Allen's a boy anymore."

"*Jah*, he probably looks a lot like Amos did at that age. Easy on the eyes—and an all-around nice guy, too,"

Rosetta remarked as they started up the hill toward Monroe's house. "We're lucky he came back with his sisters. I'm guessing he had the attention of several young gals in Indiana."

"We'll probably never know. I suspect he's another one who keeps his social life to himself." Christine saw movement in the pasture and pointed. "Look! That's Roman and Noah and the four Helmuth fellows constructing a board fence around the pasture."

"That's quite a job—and quite an expense, I'd think," Rosetta remarked, shading her eyes with her hand. "Think of how pretty that fence will look when it's painted white."

"Monroe doesn't do anything halfway. He told me that his Clydesdales have to have a substantial fence, because a wire one won't hold them." Christine gazed at the tall, white house ahead of them, sighing contentedly. "I have to say, this is the prettiest house I've ever lived in. Monroe has put everything together just right, and he wants me to have what makes me happy."

As they approached the front door, Rosetta slipped her arm around her sister's shoulders. "We're blessed to have wonderful-*gut* men in our lives now," she said softly. "I'll miss being with you all the time, once we're each married and I live up at the Wickey place. We don't see nearly as much of Mattie now that she's Mrs. Troyer."

"Once we get settled in with our new husbands, I suspect the three of us will still work together in Mattie's garden plots and cook big dinners together," Christine said in a hopeful tone. "I'm really happy that Truman's all right with you remaining the landlady of the lodge. Do you think you'll still come to church with us?"

Rosetta opened the door and was immediately greeted by the smell of paint. "We still have to figure that out," she replied. "I, of course, want to keep coming here for services, but I suspect Irene wants us to go to their Mennonite church in Cloverdale."

"Oh, look at the pretty front room!" Christine's face lit up as she gazed around the large, open area. "Monroe is partial to green, so we asked the girls to stir some of the blue paint into the yellow."

"It's refreshing, like mint and celery. And look at these beautiful floors," Rosetta said as she stooped to run her hand over the glossy wood. "I like the wider planks. They look more modern than what's in the lodge—and what we had back home."

"The wider planks were Monroe's idea, too. He really enjoyed planning the details—"

A loud *whump* above them, followed by a scream, made Rosetta and Christine race up the stairs. "Girls, are you all right?" Christine called out.

"What a mess! And on these brand new floors," Phoebe exclaimed. "Quick! Get some more rags and towels."

Rosetta raced along the upstairs hallway, peering into the rooms she passed until they reached the largest bedroom at the back of the house—probably the one Christine and Monroe would share. Fannie, Lily, and Laura were scurrying with their rollers to keep a large puddle of pale green paint from spreading on the floor while Phoebe was using a big foam brush to push paint into a metal paint tray.

"Gloria? I suggested that you should use a drop cloth, right? And that you shouldn't fill your paint tray so full?" Allen asked tersely as he came out of the master bathroom. He held a squeegee and a wad of paper towels as he hurried toward the girls who were cleaning up the paint spill.

Gloria, who stood forlornly beside a ladder, burst into tears. "I—I was just trying to help—"

"You came here mostly to gawk at me," Allen retorted as he squatted beside Phoebe. He deftly directed the paint toward her tray with the squeegee, a scowl darkening his handsome face. "If you don't want to find a damp mop and a bucket of warm water, just go on home, all right? Matter of fact, we'll finish up here. Bye, Gloria."

"I know where there's a bucket and mop," Christine said. As she hurried from the room, Gloria sobbed louder.

"Why do you have to be so—so *mean*, Allen?" she demanded as she mopped her face with her sleeve. "I was only trying to—"

Allen stood to face her, clearly annoyed. "How many times do I have to say it?" he entreated in a loud whisper. "I don't want to go out with you, Gloria. Don't waste your time on me, all right? I hadn't intended to embarrass you in front of your friends, but you went against their advice—and mine—about painting. So here we are."

Rosetta sighed. Her heart went out to Gloria, who'd had her heart set on Allen since she'd met him, yet she understood Allen's frustration. When Gloria ran out of the room, her crying echoed in the hallway and stairwell.

The front door slammed below them. Allen sighed and continued using the squeegee on the shrinking puddle of paint. "Sorry," he murmured, glancing at the girls and Rosetta. "Every day Gloria finds a new way to pester me—and ignores me when I remind her I'm not interested. I should probably apologize to her—"

"But then she'll think you want to kiss and make up," Laura pointed out.

"If it makes you feel any better, she was acting just as silly when she was chasing after Roman," Phoebe said. "It bothered her a *lot* when he married her younger sister."

"Here we go—warm water and a sponge mop," Christine said as she breezed back into the room. "The nice thing about latex paint is that it cleans up with water."

"We're sorry Gloria made such a mess on your beautiful new floors," Fannie said with a sigh. "We really did tell her to use a drop cloth."

"Looks like she dribbled paint on the baseboard, too," Lily said. She dipped a clean rag into the water and squeezed it out. "I suspect she's never painted before. One of us should've stayed in the room to coach her."

"No use crying over spilled paint," Christine quipped. She began mopping the green spot from the floor with vigorous strokes while Rosetta came behind her and wiped up the water with a clean towel. As she scrubbed, she was relieved to see all traces of the green paint disappearing from the glossy hardwood.

Allen wiped his squeegee with a rag and stepped out of the way. "*Denki* for your help, ladies. I'll put the faucets on the sink and shower, and then I'll finish the plumbing in the downstairs bathroom. I have to say, this house and the Helmuth place are the nicest ones I've ever worked in."

Christine smiled at him as she rinsed her mop in the bucket. "We've been blessed with more than our share of *gut* carpenters—like your *dat*—and with Lester's windows and siding, and now a certified plumber," she said. "Promise Lodge has come together as a community in ways my sisters and I couldn't have imagined."

Allen smiled a little self-consciously and headed back into the bathroom.

"You girls are doing a really nice job, too," Rosetta said. "By the time Christine and I paint the lower walls in the hallway, you'll probably have all the bedrooms finished."

Lily smiled, draping her arms around Fannie's shoulders and Laura's waist. "We're a team," she stated emphatically. "And Phoebe's our leader. Let's go, girls. There's no stopping us now!"

As the four of them headed back to the room they'd been working on, Rosetta couldn't help smiling. "We're a team," she repeated softly. "Lily and Fannie might not be your girls' sisters, but they're close in all the right ways."

Christine nodded. "They're like a new generation of Benders," she agreed. "The names are different, but the sisterhood lives on."

Chapter Twenty-Three

Monroe gazed out over the Sunday morning crowd in the lodge's meeting room as he brought his sermon to a close. He felt blessed to see the four Helmuths and Allen on the men's side, and he smiled at Barbara and Bernice, who sat among the women. The aromas of the pot roast and scalloped potatoes the Kuhns had put in the oven were wafting in from the kitchen, and he was ready to devour his share as he sat with Christine.

"I had the pleasure and privilege of visiting Harley this past week as he welcomed some new lambs," Monroe said with a smile. "Most of them tottered around in the pen on their wobbly legs and got acquainted with their mothers, but one little fellow sprawled in the hay as though he didn't have the energy to stand up—or even to survive. Sometimes we forget what a struggle it is to be born into this world."

Clasping his hands before him, Monroe lowered his voice to make his final point. "As I witnessed the way Harley gently massaged that lamb, encouraging him to keep breathing," he said earnestly, "I couldn't help but think about how God cares for each of us from the time of our conception. He provides us parents and families, food

and drink and shelter. He leads us in paths of righteousness
for His name's sake—just as the Twenty-Third Psalm tells
us—and He restores our souls. I got goose bumps when
Harley finally helped that little lamb to its feet, and I
almost cried when it let out a bleat and went to its mother
to suckle."

Monroe paused, basking in the glow of the faces around
him. "We are blessed when our Lord lifts us up, as Harley
assisted his lamb—and we should give thanks when God
guides us in the way He wants us to go . . . sort of like
Queenie herds the sheep into Harley's barn when she feels
a storm coming on."

Folks chuckled. At one time or another, Queenie had
herded them and their livestock, too.

"Go in peace this week, my friends," Monroe intoned.
"Abide in His many blessings and share them with others."

As they sang a final hymn, Monroe joined in with
gusto. Now that Amos's four married kids, along with
Cyrus, Jonathan, and Allen, had come to Promise Lodge,
the music rang more loudly. He pronounced the benedic-
tion and then smiled at all who'd gathered, his heart full to
overflowing with the way they had accepted him as their
bishop.

"We look forward with great joy to Wednesday, April
fifth, when Rosetta and Truman will unite in holy matri-
mony," Monroe announced, smiling at the bride- and
groom-to-be. "Amos, Marlin, and Eli have discussed the
matter of interfaith marriages with me, and we have agreed
that under the circumstances—because Rosetta and Truman
are solid in the faiths into which they were baptized long
ago—we will allow our Amish sister to take a Mennonite
husband."

"And you can marry *me*, Monroe!" Leola gushed as she
popped up from her seat on the women's side. "Today's my

birthday, and I'm wearing my blue wedding dress! We're all set!"

Monroe sighed inwardly, reminding himself to remain calm. "Leola, we've discussed this time and again—"

"But you *have* to marry me, Monroe!" she cried, rushing toward the center of the room where he stood. "You ruined me! And I love you for it!"

He held out his arms to catch Leola by her shoulders, but she dodged them, launching herself at his midsection so forcefully that they both teetered. Monroe tried to peel away the slender arms that were wrapped around his waist, but Leola was stronger than she appeared. "Leola," he implored. "You have to let me go. This is not the time or the place—"

"This is indeed the time and the place," Preacher Amos insisted as he rose from the preachers' bench to stand alongside Monroe. His face was contorted with a scowl. "I insist that you explain your relationship with this young woman right here, right now, so all of us can understand it."

"I love Monroe and he loves me!" Leola blurted ecstatically. "And we're gonna get married!"

Monroe's stomach rolled as he again tried to free himself from Leola's incriminating embrace. He could feel the curious stares coming from the men's side and from the two preachers behind him. Preacher Amos planted his fists on his hips, awaiting Monroe's answer. In his black trousers and vest, with his silver-shot beard framing his swarthy face, Amos resembled an Old Testament judge . . . or an executioner.

"Leola, be quiet," Phoebe pleaded as she stood up. "You're confused, sweetie."

"Come sit down," Christine cajoled as she, too, rose and opened her arms. "You need to be here with us so Monroe can speak to Preacher Amos."

Gratitude welled up in Monroe's heart, even though the pleas of his fiancée and her daughter weren't convincing Leola to sit down.

"This is not what you think, Amos," Rosetta said as she started toward Leola. "We women who live in the lodge have witnessed plenty of evidence that—"

"You women have *always* favored Monroe," Preacher Amos retorted. "Since the moment he showed up unannounced in that Christmas Eve snowstorm, you've fawned over him and given him the benefit of every doubt." Amos turned to gaze at the crowd. "Nobody's leaving until the bishop speaks for himself and gives us the answers I'm demanding—answers any upstanding church leader should've provided months ago."

Monroe's throat got so dry he couldn't swallow. Again he tried to loosen Leola's arms, yet when Rosetta came up behind her to grasp her shoulders, Leola only whimpered and buried her face in his vest. He knew how improper this appeared—especially to Amos and the other men—but he also knew they'd have a major meltdown on their hands if he pushed Leola away from him.

"Have you no shame?" Preacher Amos demanded, his scowl deepening. "Why do you think we'll let our bishop get by with behavior that disgusts our Lord? Leola's half your age! God does *not* condone what you've been trying to hide, Burkholder."

"I have nothing to hide," Monroe protested, but Amos was already warmed up to deliver a scathing sermon.

"If you can't make me believe your relationship with Leola is normal and honorable—if you can't get down on your knees right now and confess to us all," the preacher said in a rising voice, "we'll not only put you under the *bann*, but you'll also be leaving Promise Lodge. We'll buy back your home and property so you can return to Illinois before you establish your Clydesdale business here."

Mattie stood up quickly, appearing frightened and appalled. "Amos, listen to yourself! You're taking this way too far," she protested. "You've had since Christmas to ask Monroe about his background and his—"

"You're out of line, Mattie. Sit down," Amos snapped.

A gasp went up from the women's side, but it didn't make Monroe feel any better. Leola's arms seemed to be squeezing the breath from him . . . stifling his future. The room was whirling slowly around him, and he had dark visions of being forced to leave Promise Lodge and Christine behind—all because Amos perceived illicit behavior and motives where there were none.

"Amos, the ladies are right," Monroe pleaded hoarsely. "As a rule, I refuse to discuss Leola's limitations when she's present, because it's extremely rude—and surely you can understand how it would upset her. Please believe that the Kuhns and Rosetta and her sisters have all seen how Leola struggles to keep her emotions in check—how childlike she is—"

"Don't you talk to my Monroe that way!" Leola cried out, glaring at Amos. She sniffled loudly and swiped at her eyes. "He loves me! And he takes *gut* care of me—"

"—but if everyone believes I should confess," Monroe continued doggedly, "then of course I will—even though the conclusions you're jumping to about my relationship with Leola are totally unfounded and—"

"Leola Mae! Come to your paw-paw, punkin!" a man said loudly from the back of the room.

Thank you, Lord! Monroe prayed when Leola turned toward the familiar voice. Chester Duff opened his arms, entreating his daughter. He appeared pale and slightly stooped, his deeply lined face revealing how his wife's extended illness had aged him these past couple of months.

"Paw-Paw!" Leola's face lit up with joy as she rushed

to him. "Where's Mama? Did you bring her to see me and Monroe get married?"

As Monroe took a deep breath, the folks around him turned to see who'd spoken. Chester was hugging his ecstatic daughter, gazing over her shoulder at Monroe with an apology in his eyes. When Leola had settled down, Chester grasped her arms firmly and eased her away so he could look into her eyes.

"Your mama's resting at home, Leola," he said gently. "She's been very, very sick—we almost lost her. But she'll feel a whole lot better once you come home with me."

Leola's expression wavered. "But—but I'm gonna marry—"

"No, you're not," Chester said firmly. He steered her to the end of a pew bench on the women's side, where Christine's daughters scooted over to make room for her. "You're gonna sit right here, Leola," he insisted, pressing down on her shoulders until she sat. "I want you to stay still and be quiet, understand me? From what I overheard just now, you've gotten Bishop Monroe in a whole lot of trouble."

Leola sighed, fighting tears. "But I *love* Monroe! He ruined me so I'll never love anyone else!"

"That's enough of that foolish talk!" Chester said, pointing his finger at her. "It's time for you to be quiet while I try to explain what you've been saying and doing." He looked at Monroe. "Do you mind if I stand there with you, Bishop, so I can talk to these folks face-to-face?"

Once again Monroe thanked God for Chester's timely appearance, hoping he could put Preacher Amos's accusations to rest. "Of course you may," he replied as he looked out over the crowd. "Folks, this is Chester Duff, from Macomb, Illinois. As you might know, his wife Edna was rushed to the hospital in Chicago way back in

January, and she's been struggling to regain her health so she could return home."

"And I can't thank you enough for looking after Leola, Bishop Monroe," Chester put in as he shuffled up the aisle toward the center of the room. When he reached Monroe, he stuck out his hand. "Mighty *gut* to see you again, Bishop, despite the circumstances."

When Monroe clasped Chester's hand, he was aware of how weak his old friend's grasp felt. Before he could say anything, Chester turned and extended his hand to Amos. "Couldn't help overhearing your . . . insinuations as I came inside, Preacher," he said as their hands clasped. "Sounds like I'm more than a day late and a dollar short, far as getting here in time to prevent the doubts that cloud your mind. If you—and you fellows," he said, turning toward Eli and Marlin, "will sit with the others, I can talk without my back to you."

The room was absolutely still as the three preachers took places on the men's side. Monroe let out the breath he'd been holding. "Want me to sit down, too, Chester?"

Leola's father linked his arm through Monroe's. "Bishop, you've been my rock for more years than I can recall," he replied earnestly. "I might need to lean on you a bit. It's not my way to tell preachers where to go—or to think I'm worthy of standing here beside you."

The men chuckled and relaxed. The women leaned forward, smiling again as they prepared to listen to Chester.

Monroe nodded at the short man who was hanging on to him. The Duff family was quietly humble and faithful—and he was grateful that his old friend Chester had made the trip to fetch Leola and was setting aside his customary shyness to speak in his behalf.

"Like Bishop Monroe told you, I've had my hands full keeping my wife alive for the past several weeks," Chester began softly. "When we finally got home this past week, I was astounded at the number of phone messages he'd left—and all the times he'd called my sister Polly after Leola had run away from her place to find Bishop Monroe. My girl has a knack for figuring things out when she has to," he added with a shake of his head. "When I learned that she'd flushed her medications down the toilet, I knew I'd better hire a driver and come after her soon as I could. I'm sorry I wasn't here weeks ago."

"You're Leola's father," Preacher Amos protested. "You saw the way she was clinging to Monroe, and several times she's said he *ruined* her. That can only mean *one thing*. How can you condone his behavior?"

Chester tensed, frowning. "Surely by now you realize that Leola is one of God's special children," he stated protectively. He sighed as he glanced back at his daughter. "For reasons He alone knows, He created her with a body that became a woman's while her mind has remained a child's."

The room rang with a strained silence. Monroe saw Phoebe reach for Leola's hand, murmuring something in her ear when the young woman's expression crumpled.

Chester let out a resigned sigh. "I know it looks improper, the way Leola throws herself at Bishop Monroe," he admitted. "It started on the day she was baptized and accepted Jesus Christ as her savior. We were gathered on the bank of the creek, and the three other young folks had already been immersed. Leola's deathly afraid of moving water, but she had faith in the bishop and in the Lord, so she grabbed Monroe's hand and walked out waist-deep into the creek with him."

The women were nodding their encouragement as the men followed Chester's words with earnest attention. In his mind, Monroe was reliving Leola's baptism as her *dat* recounted it. Would Chester's explanation convince Doubting Amos that his intentions, his relationship with Leola, had remained above reproach? His whole future was hanging on whether Leola's father could win over the preacher who harbored such serious doubts about him.

"Monroe was gentle, talking softly to Leola and telling her he'd have ahold of her as he immersed her," Chester continued. "But once she went underwater, she floundered and flailed—sucked in water and was choking something awful. When Monroe brought her up, he held her and patted her back . . . kept telling her she was God's own child, safe in the arms of Jesus, who would always love her. Leola gradually settled down and got quiet. Her face was radiant. It . . . it was a holy moment," he whispered. He smiled at Leola then, his face alight with love.

"You've probably heard about how newly born ducklings bond with the first creature they see," Chester went on in a stronger voice. "That's how it was when Leola stopped choking and gazed up at Bishop Monroe. She loved him to pieces because, to her way of thinking, he'd saved her from drowning—and from sin. Not long after that, Leola heard a song playing in a café where the singer said she was ruined, and she loved it. But you must understand," he insisted, gazing at Amos, "that Leola has no idea about men and women getting physical in the marriage bed. She just says those words because the song stuck in her head and they make her happy."

Amos crossed his arms as he held Monroe's gaze. "This still doesn't explain why you showed up on Christmas Eve—the holiest night of our faith—out of the blue, without writing first or letting us know you were coming," he said tersely. "You told me your family was all gone, but I've never been convinced you were telling the whole story. Seemed to me you were running away from something—that you'd set your sights on being our bishop no matter what we had to say about it."

"Amos Troyer, you've crossed the line," Mattie muttered.

Preacher Marlin stood up beside Amos. "I believe Monroe is innocent of the sordid stuff you're accusing him of, Amos," he said fervently.

"And I believe God called Monroe to be our bishop because He knew Floyd's health was failing," Preacher Eli said as he, too, stood up. "And now that I've heard Chester's story—and watched Monroe care for a member of God's flock who can't look after herself—I feel we've been blessed beyond belief. I stand with Bishop Monroe."

Monroe's heart pounded as, one by one, every person in the room rose from the pew benches, their faces alight with love and loyalty—everyone except Amos. Even so, he felt exonerated; free from the burden of proving himself to the people who'd welcomed him and helped him build a home. When he met Christine's loving gaze, Monroe knew she would stand by him no matter what—even if he'd been forced to return to Macomb.

Chester crossed his arms, imitating Amos. "You want to know why Bishop Monroe came here all of a sudden?" he challenged. After a moment, he regained control of his emotions and went to stand in front of the doubtful preacher. "Monroe left our district with everyone's blessing, because they understood that after losing his wife, he needed to start fresh in a place where Leola's affection wouldn't interfere with his finding another woman to marry. In late December he showed us the ad for your new colony in the *Budget*, and after we prayed over it, we sent him off toward a new future with our Christmas blessings."

Monroe smiled at Christine. "Your prayers have been answered, Chester, as I have indeed fallen in love again," he said reverently. "Our new home is nearly complete, and I'll marry Christine as soon as I find a bishop to perform the ceremony."

Chester turned to smile at him. "I'm so pleased to hear that, Bishop. You deserve your happiness." He turned again to Preacher Amos, sighing loudly. "You appear unmoved and still hard of heart, my friend. Earlier you asked how I as a father could condone Bishop Monroe's relationship with my daughter, so I'll repeat that I owe him a debt of gratitude I can never repay. Despite the way she ran off from her Aunt Polly's, and flushed her medications, and has apparently caused you a great deal of turmoil and doubt, Bishop Monroe looked after Leola when her mother and I could not," Chester insisted. "Please accept my apology for Leola's unseemly behavior. She truly can't help herself."

Amos blinked. Everyone else in the room remained standing, entreating him with their gazes, yet he didn't reply to Chester.

Chester cleared his throat. "My English driver's waiting, so I'll be taking Leola home as soon as she can pack her clothes," he said softly. "Preacher Amos, I hope you'll find it in your heart to rethink your opinion of Bishop Monroe once we've gone back to—"

"But Dat, I can't leave!" Leola wailed. "I love Monroe and I'm going to marry him!"

With weary determination etched on his face, Chester approached his daughter and took her hand. "If somebody'll show us where to get a glass of water," he said, "Leola can take her pills and then we'll pack her suitcase."

"Please stay and eat dinner with us—your driver, too," Rosetta insisted as she stepped from the pew to escort the Duffs to the kitchen. "We've got more than enough pot roast and sides to go around."

"You're very kind," Chester said above his daughter's blubbering, "but it's best if I get Leola back home. I don't want to leave Edna alone overnight—and you folks are due for some peace and quiet."

The men began to murmur among themselves, their voices optimistic. The women started for the kitchen to set out the food—except for Christine, who hurried forward to embrace Monroe.

"I knew we'd see this situation to an honorable solution," she said, gazing at him with deep green eyes. "I've never doubted you for a moment, Monroe."

Monroe longed to kiss her, but knew better than to make such a public display of his love for her. "I couldn't have gotten through this without your patience and understanding, Christine," he murmured. "You're a special woman, and I love you."

Their romantic mood was interrupted by Mattie's voice behind them. "Amos, you owe our bishop a huge apology," she said tersely. "You can only hope Monroe will forgive you and not believe *you* are the one who's unfit to lead us." The tattoo of her footsteps rang on the hardwood floor as she left the room, followed by most of the men.

Monroe nodded at Amos, who remained on the front pew bench, and then headed for the dining room with Christine. He was grateful to Phoebe and Laura for going upstairs to help Chester pack Leola's belongings, because Leola was too upset to do it herself. His heart overflowed as Rosetta, Frances, Amos's twin daughters, and the Kuhn sisters hugged him, and he eagerly gripped the hands of the men as they stated their confidence in him.

Within half an hour, he'd escorted Leola and her *dat* to the car where their driver awaited them and Leola had bid him a tearful, subdued good-bye. She was so quiet that Monroe knew her sedative was already at work, and he prayed she would regain control of her emotions and be content to remain at home with her parents. It saddened him that a pretty, sweet girl like Leola would be challenged to find a mate and that her parents would probably need to find her a guardian as they approached the end of their lives. But God knew what He was doing, and His plan would suffice.

When the car had turned onto the county highway, Monroe strode back to the lodge to enjoy the dinner his friends had postponed until the Duffs' departure. The spring sunshine warmed his face, and he felt happier, more peaceful, than he had since Leola's unexpected arrival. He was reaching for the doorknob when the door swung open.

Preacher Amos blocked his entry. His expression was somber, yet his lips twitched with the hint of a smile. "Burkholder, it seems I've been unreasonable—as stubborn as a Missouri mule—and I'm sorry," he said with a sigh. "I hope you can forgive my unfounded accusations about Leola . . . all the trouble I've caused you. Now I understand that when you showed up out of the blue on Christmas Eve, you were being spontaneous and open to change. And those are qualities we folks at Promise Lodge have always valued."

Monroe gazed at Amos's face. The preacher's skin was weathered, and lines scored his forehead and bracketed his lips. Even if his black hair and beard hadn't been shot with strands of silver, he would've exuded a sense of wisdom that came with age and experience—and a healthy sense of doubt when newcomers seemed to challenge the Old Order ways. When Amos extended his hand, Monroe clasped it.

"Apology accepted," said Monroe. "We all make mistakes—and I wasn't exactly forthcoming about the details of my departure from Illinois. Given the circumstances, you were right to question me. You were watching out for the folks who've come here and placed their trust in us."

Preacher Amos squeezed his hand and released it before standing aside to let Monroe enter. "I should've listened to what Mattie and her sisters were saying all along about

Leola's mental state," he said softly. "My wife will never let me forget that, either."

Monroe loved the way Amos's laughter blended with his to fill the front lobby with mirth. "Women are *gut* at reminding us of our shortcomings," he agreed as they entered the dining room together. "They keep us honest and humble—whether we need it or not."

Chapter Twenty-Four

As the Monday morning sunrise shimmered with glorious streaks of peach, yellow, and lavender, Rosetta paused outside the barn to count her blessings. She'd just finished milking her five goats, and the two large buckets of milk she held would make a lot of fresh soap to replenish her display in the lodge's lobby. In two more days she'd be marrying Truman at long last, and she'd never felt happier. Her wedding dress was sewn, hanging with the beautiful apron Irene had made—and Ruby was going to frost and decorate the two chocolate wedding cakes today, to be ready for all the friends who'd be coming from Coldstream and from the Wickeys' Mennonite church in Cloverdale early Wednesday morning.

Rosetta held her face up to the rising sun, unable to stop smiling. Who could've imagined, last year at this time, that she and Mattie and Christine would all be engaged or married by now? Just last spring they'd discovered this property—an abandoned church camp—and they'd quickly sold their farms to purchase the place and start fresh.

From where she stood, near the barn that housed Christine's dairy herd and the Kuhns' little cheese factory, she could see the houses that belonged to Noah and Roman

Schwartz, the Peterscheims, Preacher Amos and Mattie, the two Lehman places, and Bishop Monroe's new home atop the hill near Preacher Marlin's house and barrel factory. Directly ahead of her, the new Helmuth double house rose above their nursery buildings and barn, and rows of salad greens were peeking out of the earth in Mattie's garden plots. The lodge still needed a new roof, but she'd heard the men talking about tackling that job in another week or so. The cabins stood in a tidy line beneath the large old trees that shaded them. So much progress . . . so many new friends who'd come to join them here.

When Rosetta inhaled, the aromas of yeast, pastry, and sugar made her stomach rumble. She gazed at Maria's bakery building and decided it was time to mend some fences. The pretty blonde had been working long hours, baking and delivering her doughnuts, breads, and other goodies to Cloverdale and to the grocery store in Forest Grove, so she hadn't been around much lately. Maria was doing her best to earn a living all by herself—and she'd paid her April rent on time. Wasn't that the kind of work ethic and mission that Rosetta and her sisters had embraced when they'd come to Promise Lodge?

Rosetta set her pails of goat milk in the grass, wiping her hands on her apron as she approached the bakery's door. The Kuhns still had the goodies they'd purchased earlier from Maria to serve for breakfast when her wedding guests arrived, but what would it hurt to buy some fresh doughnuts and pastries to enjoy with their breakfast this morning? She could pay Maria later, from the teapot of money where she kept what she earned from her soaps.

Rosetta smiled as she opened the door, again inhaling the heady aromas of fresh bread and sweets. "Maria, it smells so wonderful-*gut* in here—"

Rosetta gasped, pressing her hands to her heart. Behind the glass display cases, between the stove and the worktable,

Maria and Truman stood in a close embrace. Their arms were wrapped around each other—and by the time Maria caught sight of her in the doorway, Rosetta had seen enough.

"Oh!" she cried out, hoarse with disgust and dismay. "Truman, I—I can't marry you if you keep—the wedding's off!"

Rosetta's heart was pounding so loudly she couldn't understand his reply—and she didn't care. She rushed outside, racing past her buckets of milk, blinded by tears and Truman's betrayal. Why hadn't he left for his landscaping job at the townhomes? What had been going on between him and Maria behind her back? What if Maria had been gone so much because she'd been with Truman instead of delivering her pastries?

"Rosetta, wait!" Truman hollered behind her.

She slipped on a clump of damp grass but somehow kept from falling. She made it to the lodge steps before he caught up to her.

"Please listen," Truman pleaded breathlessly. "It's not what you're thinking."

"I know what I saw!" Rosetta countered, wrenching her wrist from his grasp. She glared bitterly at him. "She's had your attention ever since she moved here."

"*You* are the woman I love, Rosetta," he declared. His hazel eyes held hers doggedly as they both struggled to catch their breath. "All I did was—"

"I don't *care* what you did! She was holding you—standing with her body close against yours, as though she does that every chance she gets," Rosetta retorted. She burst into tears and then mopped her face with the sleeve of her barn coat before continuing up the stairs.

Beulah opened the door, a kitchen towel over her shoulder as she gazed outside. "I heard you two squabbling and wondered what on earth—"

"The wedding's off!" Rosetta sobbed as she pushed past

her friend to go inside. "I've had enough of catching him and Maria together."

"Maria was only hugging me because I found her another store that wants to sell her pastries," Truman protested. "Please let me come in so we can talk this out."

"Too late for talk!" Rosetta called over her shoulder. "Actions speak louder than words."

When she arrived in the kitchen, she stopped in her tracks. Bacon and scrambled eggs were being kept warm on the stove. Christine and her girls were putting pies into the oven—pies to serve Wednesday at the wedding meal— while Ruby stood at the worktable lavishing mocha frosting on the large bottom layer of a chocolate wedding cake. The four of them looked at her in stunned silence until Christine set down the pie she was holding.

"Rosetta, what happened?" she asked as she crossed the kitchen. "I've never heard you speak in such a tone, much less yell at Truman."

Rosetta fell into her sister's arms, blubbering desperately against her shoulder. She felt so overwhelmed by the memory of Maria and Truman's embrace replaying continuously in her mind, she couldn't respond to Christine for a long while. She felt Phoebe and Laura hugging her from either side, and she sensed the presence of Beulah and Ruby, who looked on in puzzled silence. The kitchen rang with her sobs until she finally ran out of steam and had to gulp air.

When she was able to release Christine, Rosetta eased away, managing a tearful smile for her nieces. "I'm sorry," she rasped. "I'd appreciate it if you'd tell Monroe that Truman and I are—are not getting married, and if you'd call our friends in Coldstream so they won't—"

"Hold on, dearie," Ruby interrupted softly. She crossed her arms, holding a spatula coated with chocolate frosting in one hand. "What could possibly have happened to separate you and Truman? Beulah and I had just set foot at Promise Lodge last summer, and you two were the first folks we met—"

"And the moment we laid eyes on you," Beulah continued, "we knew you and Truman were meant for each other. Maria's just a girl—and a clueless one, at that. Surely you're not going to let her come between you."

Rosetta sniffled loudly. "I didn't *let* her do anything," she muttered. "Ever since she's moved to Promise Lodge, she and Truman have been way too cozy. I was going into the bakery to—to compliment Maria on working so hard lately, and what did I see? That sneaky little blonde and Truman were hanging on to each other—crushed so close that if I'd arrived a few minutes later, I might have caught them . . . well, you know."

The Kuhns' eyes widened. Christine stepped back, studying Rosetta's face. "I heard Truman say he's found Maria another place to sell her baked goods," she recalled softly. "And I can imagine she was excited and grateful to him—"

"*Jah*, Maria gets pretty excited whenever Truman's around," Phoebe murmured.

"—because they've been friends for a long while," Christine continued earnestly. "Are you sure you're not overreacting, Rosetta? Truman is deeply in love with you. He's committed to your future together. Ready to welcome you into his home."

Rosetta scowled. "It was one thing for Leola to grab Monroe and say she was going to marry him," she retorted, "but it's another thing altogether when Maria hugs Truman—mainly because Truman hugs her back. They were sharing quite a clinch in the bakery. I know what I saw."

Ruby sighed. "Maybe you should eat some breakfast and give yourself time to cool down, to think about what you're doing," she suggested. "Breaking an engagement—calling off your wedding so suddenly—is serious business, Rosetta."

Rosetta let out a shuddering sigh. "I'm sorry you've all gone to so much trouble already, baking and planning, but—but my heart shattered into a million pieces when I walked in on my fiancé clinging to another woman," she explained with a hitch in her voice. "And I'm even sorrier that I let Maria come here with her bakery. If I can't trust Truman to keep his hands off her, I'll forever live in doubt about the two of them. That's no way to start a marriage."

The sadness filling the kitchen nearly suffocated her. Rosetta returned the sorrowful gazes of her family and friends, clasping her hands tightly. "I'm going upstairs to sort out my thoughts about . . . what comes next," she whispered. "I'd appreciate it if somebody brought in the buckets of goat milk I left outside the barn."

"I'm on it," Laura said resolutely. She started toward the mudroom door, but turned to smile at Rosetta. "No matter what, we'll always love you, Aunt Rosetta," she promised.

"And we'll always be here for you," Phoebe stated. "Anything you need, you just let us know."

Rosetta nodded numbly, grateful for her nieces' show of loyalty. She headed toward the back stairway, glancing at the six unbaked pies on the countertop beside the oven. Her body felt heavy and sluggish as she climbed the steps. In the upstairs hallway, she sighed. Her apartment was her haven, but it adjoined Maria's rooms, so there would be no way to avoid her pretty young renter.

Avoid her—really? Rosetta's thoughts challenged. *Whose lodge is this? Maria's the one who needs to relocate.*

She passed her apartment to stand in front of Maria's door. She knew she had no business snooping in her tenant's rooms—*But you're the owner, so you have a right to look around, right?*

Rosetta opened the door and entered the main room, allowing her gaze to travel up the deep raspberry walls that faded to cream at the ceiling. The furniture was nothing fancy, but she recalled how Maria had admitted to overspending . . . said she'd underestimated the cost of moving her bakery building.

You underestimated a lot of things, girlie. Including me.

Rosetta blinked, unaccustomed to thoughts that felt so spiteful. When she stepped into the bedroom with its delphinium blue walls and ceilings, she rolled her eyes at the white clouds. Monroe and the preachers had so eagerly bowed to Maria's whims and painted these rooms on short notice.

You men fell at her feet after just one taste of her goodies, she thought with a loud sigh. *And Truman? Who knows how many times he's sampled what she's offering?*

Rosetta knew she was going overboard with her unspoken accusations, yet in her current frame of mind, Maria's unmade bed and the clothes scattered on the floor seemed overtly suggestive. She left the apartment, slamming the door behind her. What she needed was peace and quiet. Time to think . . . to consider her next move, now that she was to remain a *maidel*.

She thought sadly of the beautiful table and chairs that filled the Wickey dining room and recalled the joy she'd felt while selecting the bedroom set she and Truman were to share. *It's only stuff—pricey stuff,* she reminded herself as she entered her apartment. *Serves Truman right that he'll have to look at all that shiny new furniture and explain to his mother why I won't be living there, using it.*

Rosetta drew all the curtains to shut out the bright morning sunshine before plopping down on her bed. Bowing her head, she asked God to forgive her nasty thoughts about Truman and Maria and to forgive her for breaking the most important promise she'd ever made—except for her vow to belong to Jesus and the Old Order Amish church.

"And I almost broke that promise, too," she said sadly. "Is this canceled wedding—this coming face-to-face with Maria and Truman—my punishment for wanting to marry a Mennonite? Have I been listening to my own desires rather than to Your voice, Lord?"

The silence held no answers.

Around noon, Christine knocked on Rosetta's door and listened for a response. "She surely isn't snoozing," she murmured to Mattie, who held a plate of hot roast beef with potatoes and gravy. "Rosetta's not one to nap—or to skip breakfast, for that matter."

"I'm surprised she's been holed up in her apartment all morning," Mattie remarked with a frown. "And I'm *really* surprised that she's broken up with Truman. I thought they'd ironed out their differences about Maria and—"

The door opened and Rosetta peered out at them. Her eyes were rimmed with red, her hair was mussed beneath her rumpled *kapp*, and she looked twenty years older. "*Jah*? Hi," she mumbled.

"We brought you some lunch," Christine said as she entered Rosetta's main room. "Truman came by before he went to work to see if you'd talk to him. But we said you were busy."

"I was really sorry to hear about this blowup, sweetie," Mattie added as she handed Rosetta her plate of food. "Are you *sure* you won't talk to him? Sometimes men do things—stupid things—that appear a lot more serious to us women than they really are."

"Maybe it's Maria you should be quizzing," Christine

suggested. "If her story matches Truman's about having a new outlet for her baked goods, you could just tell her to keep her hands to herself."

Rosetta gazed gratefully at the roast beef dinner, sighing. "I prayed about this and cried myself to sleep," she admitted, "but my heart still feels heavy. If there was a way to move Maria and her bakery someplace else, I would. She's so much younger and prettier than I'll ever be. It's no wonder Truman finds her desirable. That *thing* between them won't go away, you know."

Christine slipped into one of the two upholstered chairs, observing Rosetta as she sat on the couch so she could put her plate on the coffee table. It was so unlike Rosetta to harden herself against anyone—especially because she'd always been so crazy about Truman. It wasn't Rosetta's way to be so critical of herself, either. Christine was relieved to see her younger sister take a big forkful of mashed potatoes and gravy. "Monroe is concerned about both you and Truman," she said. "Will you talk with him? I'll be there, if you'd like me to."

Rosetta chewed her food, considering this request. "I don't know what the bishop could say that would change my mind. But thank him for his concern."

Christine shared a glance with Mattie, who sat in the recliner. "We don't have to tell you that Monroe and Amos and the other preachers will strongly encourage you to forgive Maria and Truman . . . which implies that you'll again be willing to marry him."

Rosetta's eyes widened. "Why is that? *Jah*, I'll need to forgive him, but taking up where we left off isn't a requirement of the Ordnung. When a woman sees irreconcilable differences—traits she didn't notice in her man before he proposed to her—then she should walk away from the relationship before she marries him and can't get out of it. Isn't that what the engagement period is all about?"

Christine couldn't argue with that, but she'd wanted to try one more time. Rosetta's words saddened her, because she felt her sister was giving up on a chance at lifelong happiness with a wonderful man.

Mattie sat forward, gazing intently at their younger sister. "When Bishop Monroe visited with us a little while ago, he said that if you were absolutely sure the wedding is off, he would have Truman and two of his men drive their big trucks to Illinois to fetch his Clydesdales and furnishings."

"*Gut!*" Rosetta said defiantly. "That means he and Christine can marry sooner. And it means Truman won't be over here pestering me to talk to him."

Mattie sighed loudly. "I'm sorry to hear about this misunderstanding, Rosetta. I hope you won't live to regret this," she said softly. "Do you want us to stay while you eat, or leave you to your thoughts?"

"You probably have better things to do than watch me pout," Rosetta replied quickly. "Tell Monroe he should go to Illinois. I'm sure he's eager to settle all his business there and get his horses moved. *Denki* for thinking of me."

Christine rose from the chair, squeezing Rosetta's shoulder before leaving her apartment. Mattie followed her down the back stairway to the kitchen, where Monroe was finishing a piece of peach pie as he chatted with the Kuhn sisters.

"What did you think?" Christine asked her sister. "In my opinion, Rosetta's not handling this well at all. I'm worried about her."

"Me, too," Mattie said as they approached the table. "I think she's making a huge mistake, not letting Truman explain his situation with Maria."

Monroe looked up at them. "She's really canceling the wedding, then? No last-minute reconciliation?"

"Nope. She was very clear about that," Christine replied.

"She wants you to go ahead and fetch your horses and household belongings," Mattie confirmed. "Maybe it's best that you and Truman aren't here on Wednesday so she can move on past the canceled wedding. And maybe you'll hear Truman's side of this story and figure out what to do next. I can't believe he'll accept this canceled wedding as an end to their relationship."

Nodding, Monroe rose from his chair. "I'll give him a call so he can plan to be gone for a few days. *Denki* for the pie, ladies," he added, smiling at the Kuhns.

"You're always welcome, Bishop," Beulah said. "It was one we'd baked for Rosetta's wedding."

"*Jah*, if you're interested, I know where there's a whole lot of chocolate cake," Ruby put in sadly. "We can freeze it—along with the rest of our pies and the beef roasts and the chickens we won't be cooking tomorrow. But I sure don't like doing that."

"When Maria breezes through here on the way to her room, I have a mind to sit her down for a stiff talking-to," Beulah said gruffly. "I don't care *how* excited she was about having another place to sell her baked goods. She needs to keep her hands off another woman's man. I'm not sure I would've tolerated seeing her in Truman's arms any more than Rosetta did. But what do I know?" she added as she rose from the table. "I'm just a crotchety old biddy who's set in her ways."

"You're Rosetta's friend, too," Christine pointed out. "She could use any advice and company you care to share with her."

"We'll fetch her plate a little later. See how she's doing," Ruby said. "If we find something to keep her busy—maybe remind her she's got milk to make more soap—she'll be better off."

"I'm sure you'll all do your best with her," Monroe said. "We'll compare notes when I get back from Illinois."

Christine placed her hand on his arm, entreating him to stay a moment longer. "You know, Rosetta made a good point to us. Had Leola been in her right mind, aware of what she was doing and saying, I would've become very upset about the way she clung to you, Monroe," she said softly. "When Rosetta saw Maria in Truman's arms, she lost all confidence in herself. She thinks that because Maria is younger and—supposedly—prettier, Truman surely must find her more attractive."

Monroe's forehead furrowed as he considered this. "I don't understand that," he remarked. "Rosetta is much more mature and better suited to Truman than—"

"But it's that maturity issue that's bothering her," Mattie put in gently. "Rosetta's thirty-eight now, and she's feeling past her prime—a lot older than most gals when they marry the first time. It's not that she envies Maria's youth or looks—she *fears* them. She believes Truman must be attracted to Maria, or he wouldn't be putting his arms around her when they're alone in the bakery."

"And there's no denying how you and Amos and the other men fell all over yourselves when Maria showed up with that basket of goodies," Beulah pointed out.

"You fellows went out of your way to get Maria's apartment painted in short order, too," Mattie added. "I suspect you'd have felt differently if she didn't have blond hair and sparkly blue eyes when she batted her lashes at you."

Monroe stifled a smile. "Well, you might be right about that part," he admitted. "I'll discuss Maria with Truman during our four-hour ride to Illinois. *Denki* for pointing out these details. It'll help if he sees this situation from Rosetta's viewpoint."

Chapter Twenty-Five

By eight o'clock Tuesday morning, Monroe was sitting in the cab of Truman's big white truck, heading onto the highway that ran past Promise Lodge. Two more trucks with large trailers, driven by Truman's employees, Edgar and Harvey, followed them as they headed for Illinois. The sunrise made the buds on the trees shine neon green, as though they emitted their own light, and the glass windows of the Helmuths' new greenhouse sparkled. Monroe opened the window and waved to Sam and Simon, who were coming from their barn.

"Have a *gut* trip!" one of the slender redheads hollered.

"See ya when you get back, Bishop!" his brother added with an exuberant wave.

Truman shifted the truck into a higher gear, glancing out at the Helmuth place. "Those fellows should be receiving their shipment of new plants any time now," he said. "I've asked them to join me at one of the townhome communities I'm landscaping, to be sure the plants I've suggested will be suitable for the soil and the sunny areas where they'll be planted. The developer took out all the big trees, so it'll be a few years before those yards have any shade to speak of."

"Seems a shame to get rid of trees," Monroe remarked, raising his window. "But I suppose those contractors want a certain variety of trees, arranged just so, instead of where Mother Nature put them."

"That's how it is—and some of the trees there weren't going to live much longer, anyway," Truman said. "Because we were allowed to take them down and run them through our big chippers, we made a huge amount of mulch we can use next year after it decomposes a bit. The developer was pleased that in exchange, I'll use my seasoned mulch for their landscaped areas instead of the store-bought kind. Saved them a pile of money."

Monroe nodded. He had plenty of time to quiz Truman about his relationship with Maria, so he didn't push that subject. "I appreciate you rearranging your schedule for these next few days during your busy season," he said. "I called some of my friends in Macomb. They'll help with the loading, so it shouldn't take long to get the horses and my stuff on the road again."

Truman's lips formed a thin line. "Just as well I'm going to be gone for a few days," he said with a sigh. "There's no living with Mamm now that the wedding's been canceled. And frankly, I'm wondering if I want to keep that new furniture I bought, because . . . well, it'll remind me every day that Rosetta was to be sharing it with me."

Regret edged Truman's words, and he stared through the windshield as though he was seeing a lot more than the blacktop. Since he'd mentioned the subject, Monroe decided to ease into it, as well.

"The way I understand it, you've asked to speak with Rosetta and she's refused to talk to you," he began.

"*Jah*, that came as a real slap in the face," Truman muttered. "There's been nobody else for me since the moment I met her last spring—and I thought she understood that.

She might as well have cut out my heart with a butcher knife."

Truman's raw pain filled the cab of the truck, and Monroe hoped they could talk without upsetting the poor fellow so badly that it affected his driving. "Rosetta didn't take up my offer to talk, either," he said, "but her sisters gave me some insight into why she canceled the wedding. Maybe between the two of us, we can figure out a way to change her mind."

"I'm all for that." Truman raked his sandy hair back with his hand.

After a few moments of silence, Monroe continued his subtle interrogation. "A lot of this concerns your relationship with Maria—and how Rosetta perceives your feelings for her."

"Maria? She's just a kid!" Truman protested. "I've known her since she was ten, if I remember correctly. Mamm and I have been friends with her family since they joined our church—and we've been keeping closer tabs on Maria and her sister now that their parents have passed on and the older kids have moved away."

Monroe detected a trace of defensiveness, but nothing out of line. "There's no getting around the fact that Maria's awfully pretty. And she seems to throw her arms around you at the least provocation."

Truman's eyebrows shot up. "She does that when she's happy. I hug her, too, but that doesn't mean I'm romantically attracted to her."

"Well, the way I understand it, the two of you were alone in the bakery when Rosetta walked in," Monroe replied. "Rosetta saw you hugging her—or her hugging you, if that's how it was—and assumed you'd taken the opportunity to be alone with Maria for a little . . . hanky-panky before you left for work."

"Hanky-panky?" Truman blurted. "Maria's like a kid

sister to me. I—I had just told her about another place that wants to carry her pastries and pies, and she got so excited—"

"And what was Rosetta supposed to think when she walked in on that?" Monroe interrupted gently.

Truman sighed impatiently. "I've told her again and again that Maria's just a friend. Rosetta needs to get over—"

"Rosetta won't be completely at peace until Maria is no longer in the picture." Monroe observed the way Truman's eyes widened in disbelief. "Now that she's seen you two in a clinch in the bakery, she'll have a hard time trusting either one of you," he said. "According to her sisters, Rosetta feels a little too old to be a first-time bride, and her confidence got shot down when she saw you hanging on to a younger, prettier woman."

"Maria doesn't hold a candle to Rosetta!"

Monroe reached across the cab to rest his hand on Truman's shoulder. "Easy now, friend," he murmured. "I'm not trying to send you into the ditch while you're driving. I'm just saying that your best bet for winning Rosetta back might be to find Maria someplace else to go. You've found her other places to sell her baked goods, after all."

Truman focused on the road, at a loss for a response.

"How do you think she feels, having Maria's apartment right next to hers? And seeing the bakery every time she milks her goats or stands at the kitchen sink and looks out the window?" Monroe asked softly. "It's not much different from you having to deal with all that new furniture she helped you pick out, now that she's refused to marry you."

"But Maria's finally selling her pastries and pies to enough stores to be making a go of it again," he said with a sigh. "I can't think she'll be happy to leave Promise Lodge before she's even recouped the cost of moving her building. She's only been there a couple of months."

Monroe smiled to himself. "I have a feeling that the faster Maria moves away, the faster you'll be marrying Rosetta. Just saying."

Thursday afternoon, Monroe rode in the backseat of Truman's extended cab with his old friend Ralph Byler, who'd been a preacher in the Macomb district and had taken Monroe's place as one of the new bishops. His body was tired from loading the trucks all day Wednesday, and his legs were a little cramped in the space behind Truman's seat, but he thrummed with the anticipation of returning to Christine within fifteen minutes—with a bishop in tow.

"I was amazed at how quickly we got all your stuff loaded," Ralph said as he gazed at the greening Missouri countryside. "Nearly every fellow in the district turned out to help. It was a tribute to your time with us as our bishop, Monroe. It's not the same without you amongst us—but I'm glad you've found the new home you needed."

Monroe pointed out the window on his side. "If this section of woods was gone, you'd be able to see my new house, Ralph," he said, excitement creeping into his voice. "And two big red horse barns are nestled into the hillside of a valley that'll make great grazing land for the Clydesdales this summer—thanks to Truman, who's seeded and fertilized it for me."

Truman glanced at them in the rearview mirror. "Happy to help, Monroe. You've got the prettiest place in Promise Lodge—and a wonderful woman to share your new home with."

"Can't wait to meet her," Ralph said. "It's a real honor to be the one who'll conduct your wedding ceremony, Bishop Monroe."

As the truck slowed in front of the Helmuth place to turn onto the county road, Monroe's thoughts were racing. "Let's pull up by the lodge and stop a minute so I can introduce Christine to Ralph," he said to Truman. "Then we'll go on to my place and unload the horses. They'll be ready for some water and exercise."

"Will do." Truman shifted gears and drove slowly along the blacktop so he could make a wide turn into the Promise Lodge entry. "Look at this! Noah and Preacher Eli have put up your new metal sign. Looks great."

Monroe opened his window and stuck out his head, grinning. The new sign sported ornamental metalwork of sunflowers and wheat sheaves, and it arched higher and wider over the road than the previous one. "They did a bang-up job on it, too," he remarked, loving the way the white metal shone in the sunshine.

The new sign seemed as bright and shiny and sturdy as his dreams. Monroe's heart was beating eagerly, and he realized that it was because he'd come *home*. Truman drove on, and he'd barely stopped the truck before Monroe was clambering down from the cab and jogging toward the lodge. He took the steps two at a time, stopping suddenly when the door swung open.

"You're home!" Christine said as she stepped outside. Her green eyes shone as she gazed at him. Then she glanced at the other trucks that were lumbering toward the lodge.

"Yes, I am," Monroe murmured, drinking in the sight of her. He'd only been gone a couple of days, but he didn't ever intend to leave Christine behind again. "I'd like you to meet my old friend Ralph Byler. *Bishop* Ralph Byler. Ralph, this is Christine Hershberger—the woman I'm going to marry. *Soon.*"

Christine's face lit up with excited comprehension as

she shook hands with Ralph. "I'm so glad you could come, Bishop Ralph. Welcome to Promise Lodge!"

"*Jah*, we're all glad you're here," said Beulah as she and Ruby came outside. Rosetta joined them, as well, appearing calm—but Monroe noticed how she kept her eyes on this circle of friends rather than looking over toward Truman's trucks.

"Mighty happy to meet you folks," Ralph said. "I have to confess, though, that this'll be the first wedding I've conducted, so it might not go as smooth as it does when Bishop Monroe performs the ceremony."

Monroe slipped his arm around Christine's shoulders. He'd been waiting to spring this surprise for a while, and he could tell the Kuhn sisters were excited enough to go along with whatever he suggested. The joy on Christine's face was a sight he'd remember always. "I know how much work you ladies put into wedding meals," Monroe said, holding Ruby and Beulah's happy gazes, "so it's up to you—and Christine, of course—when we schedule the wedding."

Beulah clapped her hands, gazing at Rosetta and Christine. "Would it hurt you ladies' feelings if we thawed the pies and the meat we'd intended for yesterday's wedding to serve for this one?"

Rosetta shook her head. "Of course not! I'm tickled that Monroe brought Bishop Ralph along—and we shouldn't keep him waiting, ain't so?"

"We all know that food will be wonderful," Christine added happily. "It's not like we'll be serving leftovers."

Ruby smiled at Christine and Monroe. "What would you folks think of a chocolate wedding cake?" she asked. "I know it's not the traditional flavor—"

"But we also know how fabulous your chocolate cake

is," Monroe pointed out. "If it's all right with my bride, it's fine by me."

Christine tightened her arm around his waist. She looked absolutely delighted by the way these plans were coming together. "This is Thursday afternoon," she said, thinking aloud. "So if we took the food out of the freezer now, we could make our side dishes and have everything ready to serve by—"

"This Saturday noon, on April eighth!" Beulah put in excitedly. "Does that suit everybody?"

"I'm in!" Christine replied as the other women nodded their agreement.

Bishop Ralph shook his head. "You gals didn't blink an eye about having all the arrangements made in two days," he marveled. "Out our way, it takes weeks to prepare for a wedding."

"We've had a lot of practice," Beulah said with a wink. "If you fellows will excuse us, we've got things to do."

"And I have Clydesdales to pasture," Monroe said. "*Denki*, ladies. You're the best. And you, Christine, are the *very* best," he said as he hugged her again.

"No, *you* are, Monroe," she whispered. "This is the nicest surprise ever."

His lips burned with the need to kiss her, but he managed to release his beloved and descend the porch steps with Bishop Ralph. "I owe you big-time," he said. "I think I just scored several points with Christine for—"

"Bishop Monroe! Hey, can we come help with your horses?" an eager boy called out from behind them.

"*Jah*, Teacher Minerva says we can come, if it's all right with you," another boy called out. "She knows we won't be able to pay attention to our lessons."

"And besides," another boy added, "the girls got out of school for their painting, so it's our turn!"

Monroe turned and laughed. The three Peterscheim

boys and Lowell Kurtz were all gazing eagerly at him from the porch. "Did you men fill the troughs with water and put hay in the feeders, like I asked you to?" he quizzed them.

"*Jah*, Bishop, we did!" Lavern replied.

"Finished your horse chores this morning before school," Menno chimed in. "And we've been painting your fence, too."

"*Jah*, we should have it all painted white in the next couple of days," Lowell said proudly. "We've been working every day after school."

"Fabulous! You might as well come along so my horses can get used to you," Monroe said. "Run ahead and open the barn doors—and then stand off to the side. They'll be in a hurry to get out of the trailers when they smell the hay and water."

"We want to watch, too," Lily chimed in as she and Fannie came outside. "The schoolroom's all but empty with the boys out. And Teacher Minerva wants to come along. It's a big day for Promise Lodge!"

Monroe chuckled. "As long as you ladies stay outside the pasture fence—and stay quiet—you're all welcome," he said. "These horses are gentle, but they're huge. They'll spook easily if you make any racket."

Fannie drew her fingers across her lips as though she was zipping them. Smiling at each other, the girls followed the boys off the porch.

"Hey, Bishop, need some help with your Clydesdales?" Roman called over as he and Noah approached from their homes. Queenie raced around them, barking excitedly when she caught the scent of the horses.

"The more the merrier," Monroe replied. "If some of you fellows will go ahead of us and open the pasture gates, that'll be a big help. I'll meet you up there, Truman," he called out, waving at the first big truck. "Edgar, why don't you follow him?"

The two drivers waved. They put their trucks in gear and eased the big horse trailers up the road. The kids, Noah, and Roman were already jogging toward Monroe's place, tossing sticks to Queenie as she ran ahead and circled back to them so they'd throw again. It gratified Monroe that everyone was so excited about the arrival of his horses, and that the young men had worked so hard to make this big day possible.

Monroe turned to Ralph. He was nearing seventy, but he still ran his blacksmithing business and was muscular and fit. "Ready to walk up the hill, Bishop?"

"*Jah*, I need to stretch my legs after that long ride—and it'll give me a chance to look everything over. This is quite a nice place," Ralph remarked as he kept stride with Monroe. "Looks like you've got men who're *gut* with their tools, to build these homes with such nice porches and siding."

Monroe waved at Preacher Amos as he and Mattie came from their house, and he saw Lester standing on his front porch, too. Up the hill, Preacher Marlin and Harley were coming from the barrel factory to see what was going on. "You'll get a chance to meet all of our carpenters and the fellow who owns the window and siding business before we even get to my place. Looks like all our men heard the rumble of the trucks and are coming out to help," Monroe said. "Hardworking people here—women and men both—with a variety of skills and businesses."

"Sounds like a recipe for success and happiness," Bishop Ralph said. "*Denki* for inviting me to play a small part in the future of Promise Lodge."

* * *

Christine grabbed her jacket and joined Minerva in the parade of folks who wanted to see Monroe's Clydesdales. By the time they got outside, Mattie was walking up the hill ahead of them, talking with Noah's wife, Deborah, as well as Mary Kate, who carried baby David in a basket. Gloria and Frances Lehman fell into step with them, too.

"This is exciting!" Gloria said.

"We've got to be really quiet!" Lily called back to Gloria. "No screaming, or the horses might stampede."

As they approached the two stock trucks, Christine heard the stomping of large hooves against the trailers' metal floors. Truman was backing around so the gate of his truck's trailer was between the pasture gates that Roman and Noah were holding open. Several impatient whinnies came through the slots in the trailers, and just as the other women reached the pasture fence, the Clydesdales began stepping down the metal ramp Monroe had pulled from the bottom of the trailer.

"Those are the biggest horses I've ever seen," Mattie said, awestruck.

Christine couldn't take her eyes from the huge, muscled brown horses as they filed into the pasture, their white-blazed noses in the air, sniffing. Their black manes quivered, and as they trotted into the pasture, the longish white hair that covered their hooves floated with each tentative step.

"Go for the barn, Patsy," Monroe called out, pointing toward the two red structures down the hill. "Go on, girl— we're home now."

One of the mares—probably Patsy—gazed steadily at Monroe and followed the direction of his hand. With a shake of her large head, she took off at a canter, and the other horses followed her. Their hooves thundered against the ground as they negotiated the pasture's gentle slope, some of them nipping and frisking with each other along the way.

"That's the most magnificent sight I've ever seen," Minerva said.

Hearing this, Monroe strode toward the fence, where the ladies and girls all stood in a row, watching the horses between the white fence planks. Christine couldn't miss the happiness lighting his face as he glanced back at his Clydesdales. "They *are* magnificent," he agreed reverently. "Can't tell you how good it is to smell them again, to run my hands over their glossy hides . . . to see the intelligence in their gentle eyes as I work with them. It's been a long four months without them."

Christine reached between the white planks to squeeze his shoulder. "Don't let us keep you from your work, dear. We know you're eager to get your horses settled in."

Monroe blessed her with a boyish grin. "Means a lot that you ladies came to welcome them," he said. "I'll see you all later—"

"I was thinking we should have a special supper tonight so everyone can welcome Ralph," Christine suggested.

Monroe stood absolutely still, gazing raptly at her. "*Denki* for that fabulous idea, sweetheart. I'll spread the word." He glanced toward the gate as Truman drove down the hill and Edgar finished positioning the second trailer. "Gotta go. Now that the mares are unloaded, the stallions and the geldings will need a little more attention. You know how it is with guys."

Christine and the other women laughed. Standing on her toes on the bottom slat of the fence, she leaned forward to watch Monroe pull the metal ramp from the underside of the second trailer.

"Easy, boys," he repeated as he approached the trailer gate. "Mind your manners, now. Folks are watching you."

When he opened the gate, three stallions bolted into the pasture with whinnies and snorts. They sniffed the ground, saw the mares eating hay from the round metal feeders between the barns, and took off at a gallop that made the ground tremble. "My word, these horses are even bigger!" she exclaimed.

"Not a breed for a short man to work with," Mattie remarked beside her. "You can see how comfortable Monroe is around them, though."

Maybe he'd heard Mattie talking, and maybe he just felt inspired when three geldings came out of the trailer and surveyed their new domain. Monroe whispered something to the nearest Clydesdale, stroking its thick brown neck. The horse nickered eagerly and gracefully knelt on its front legs. With a secretive smile lighting his face, Monroe slipped out of his boots.

Christine held her breath when Monroe straddled the gelding and sat down, taking sections of its luxurious black mane in both his hands. The horse rose, quivering with excitement, and then took off in an easy canter. As Monroe circled the pasture on his huge mount, he appeared to be having the time of his life guiding the Clydesdale into figure eights. When he'd pointed the horse toward the gate again, Monroe rocked forward, got his legs under him, and stood up, his arms extended to help him balance as his mount continued to canter.

"Oh my word," Christine whispered, her heart pounding against her rib cage. "I had no idea he was a trick rider."

"And a fine one, too!" Mattie agreed as they watched the horse and rider approach.

When the men and boys broke into applause, Christine and the other ladies joined them. Monroe slowed the huge horse with a quiet command until it stopped directly in front of her. He lowered himself until he was sitting on the horse again, towering above them all.

"This is Gabriel," Monroe said as he stroked the horse's broad shoulders. "He's my personal mount, and I use him to train the younger Clydesdales that will eventually perform in show rings and competitions."

The horse whickered as though he knew he was being praised.

"Can you teach *us* to ride like that, Bishop?" Lowell asked eagerly.

"*Jah*, that was awesome!" Lavern blurted.

Monroe swung one leg over Gabriel's neck and dismounted, as nimble as a man half his size. "I don't see why not," he replied. "Gabriel's trained, so it's a matter of you boys learning to give him the correct commands—"

"Maybe with a saddle, until you boys get the hang of handling such a huge horse," Preacher Marlin said. "Bishop Monroe makes it look easy, because he's obviously been riding and training Clydesdales for a long time."

"*Jah*, since I was about your age, Lavern," Monroe said, smiling at the slender thirteen-year-old. "Took my share of tumbles, and I'm really lucky that I rolled out of the way before I got trampled—more times than I care to remember. We'll start you boys slow and work you up, so your parents don't have heart attacks when they watch you."

Christine laughed along with everyone around her. For a golden moment, Monroe focused on her as though he didn't notice anyone else was around. Then he nodded at the crowd gathered at the fence.

"This friend who came back from Macomb with me is Bishop Ralph Byler, and we're having a special supper at the lodge tonight to get acquainted with him," Monroe announced, gesturing toward Ralph. "He'll be performing the wedding ceremony for Christine and me this Saturday morning—and you know that means the Kuhns, Christine, and her sisters will be cooking up a storm to get ready so quickly. If all your families could bring food to share tonight, we'll have a wonderful time."

Christine smiled at Mattie. "Did I find a *gut*, thoughtful man, or what?" she teased.

Mattie hugged her. "I think we both did well, sister. Now we need to help Rosetta work things out."

Chapter Twenty-Six

Rosetta had her head in the mudroom's upright freezer, carefully removing pies, when she heard the outside door open.

"Oh! I—I thought you'd be gone to see the horses with the other ladies."

Maria. Rosetta's heart began to pound as she carefully backed out of the freezer with a stack of pies in her arms—purposely blocking the kitchen doorway. Maria had been noticeably absent the past few days, and her statement confirmed Rosetta's suspicion that the blonde had been avoiding her. "Christine's getting married Saturday," she explained, praying for patience and a civil tongue. "Since Truman's and my wedding was canceled, we're using the pies we'd baked for that occasion."

Maria's eyes darted toward the kitchen, but there was no escape from the mudroom when Beulah and Ruby came to stand in the doorway. "I—I have no idea why you called off your wedding," Maria protested in a tight voice. "Truman was really upset when you—"

"Truman isn't my concern right now." Rosetta handed her stack of frozen pies to Ruby and turned to face Maria, her pulse accelerating with pent-up frustration. She'd wondered how she would handle this conversation with her tenant, and the words she'd tried out dozens of times in her mind suddenly evaporated like mist rising from Rainbow Lake. "I want to know why you had your arms around him, Maria. You knew Truman and I were engaged."

Maria's blue eyes resembled saucers. "I—I was just thanking him for finding another store that wants to sell my pastries."

"And what was Rosetta supposed to think about that?" Beulah muttered. "If it had been me walking in on you and my fiancé, I'd have started throwing things, young lady."

"*Jah*, you're young, but you're certainly old enough to know when to keep your hands to yourself," Ruby put in. She and her sister filled the doorway, crossing their arms as they awaited Maria's reply.

Maria's face turn deep pink as she clasped and unclasped her hands.

"I suspect you've left early and come in late these past few days because you knew I was upset with you," Rosetta said, holding Maria's gaze. "Or maybe you just stayed at Truman's house, like you did when his *mamm* was sick. How do you like that dining room furniture I picked out? Have you been trying out the new bedroom set, as well?"

Maria gaped. "It's not that way, Rosetta! Truman and I have been friends for years—"

"And every time I've seen you in the same room with him, you've had your hands on him—or he's had his arm around you," Ruby remarked. "If I were Rosetta, I'd be wondering if you didn't intend to marry him yourself."

Rosetta wanted to hug the Kuhn sisters for supporting her—for expressing all the disturbing thoughts she hadn't had the nerve to say out loud.

Shock had overtaken Maria's flushed face. "*Marry* him?" She spat the words as though she'd taken a bite of something sour. "Truman's old enough to be—well, he's just *old*!"

Deep down Rosetta felt relieved, but she didn't relax her stern stance. The blonde was probably ten or eleven years younger than Truman—not an insurmountable gap in age, but the idea of marrying someone who was thirty-three obviously didn't appeal to Maria. "So how are you and I to go forward, considering that your apartment is next to mine and your business is on my property?"

Maria's chin quivered. "I . . . I don't know," she whispered. "I'm really sorry, Rosetta. I didn't know I was out of line."

Rosetta softened a bit, but Maria hadn't really answered the question—and probably had no idea what to suggest about their future relationship.

"If it were me," Ruby said, "I'd find every way possible to prove my intentions toward Truman were nothing but honorable—"

"And I'd do everything in my power to make it up to Rosetta . . . and maybe find someplace else to go," Beulah added in a low voice. "It's serious business when a wedding is canceled over such a misunderstanding. The couple's entire future—their love and trust for each other—has been destroyed."

Maria let out a sob. "I'm sorry," she blurted. "I—I just want to go to my apartment now—"

When the Kuhn sisters stepped back into the kitchen, Maria bolted up the stairs, her rapid steps echoing in the stairwell.

Rosetta let out the breath she'd been holding. "*Denki* so much for your help," she said as she took Ruby and Beulah in her arms. "Maybe I overreacted to—"

"You caught them together and you called it like you saw it," Ruby reassured her.

"High time somebody held that girl accountable,"

Beulah insisted as the three of them eased away from one another. "Maybe she'll be more aware of how she comes across to other folks now. And maybe Truman will man up and explain his part in it, as well."

Rosetta sighed. She was glad she'd be cooking for the rest of the day. It gave her a chance to reevaluate the scene she'd witnessed in Maria's bakery—and to mull over Maria's reaction to the idea of marrying Truman.

Guide me in the way You'd have me go, Lord, she prayed. *Now it's up to Truman and me to figure this out—and we need Your help.*

Saturday morning was barely a glimmer on the horizon when Christine awoke. The aromas of coffee and bacon made her stomach rumble as she peered out her window. The pearl gray of the approaching dawn had a hush about it, a sense that a glorious day was about to bless everyone at Promise Lodge as they attended the wedding ceremony at Monroe's new home and enjoyed the meal in the lodge dining room. Christine slipped into an old dress for a trip to the barn, smiling with joy—and a secret. Not only was she marrying their handsome, compassionate bishop today, but she was also the bearer of a sealed envelope she dropped into her apron pocket.

"*Gut* morning, dear friends," Christine said as she reached the bottom of the back stairway. "*Denki* a hundred times over for the wonderful-*gut* food you're cooking today."

Ruby and Beulah turned to smile at her. Work aprons covered their finery—Ruby sported a new purple dress with big pink polka dots, and her sister glowed in a splashy print of pink, orange, and purple tulips. "It's your big day, Christine, and I wish you and Monroe all the happiness your hearts can hold," Beulah said cheerfully.

"It's an honor to prepare your wedding meal, dearie," Ruby put in as she placed the lid on a blue enamel roasting pan. "We have Maria to thank for the boxes of breakfast pastries we can enjoy and share with your guests from Coldstream."

· "Glad to hear that," Christine said, patting her apron pocket. "Rosetta's in the barn milking her goats, so I'm going over to deliver this letter Truman slipped to me last night."

The sisters' eyes lit up. "What's it say?" Ruby whispered gleefully.

Christine laughed. "I didn't steam open the seal, but I suspect we'll all be able to read Rosetta's face later today," she replied. "I certainly hope it's a note of encouragement, since Truman and Rosetta will be facing each other all morning, as our side-sitters."

"*Jah*, it wouldn't do to have them glaring at each other while you and Monroe exchange your vows," Beulah said. "Take a plate of those pastries to sweeten the visit."

On the way through the dining room, Christine placed a couple of cream cheese Danish, an apple fritter, and a chocolate cake doughnut on a plate. When she stepped out onto the lodge's front porch, she paused to take in the beauty of the morning. Rays of the sunrise glimmered on the white blossoms of the serviceberry trees near Rainbow Lake as two pairs of mallard ducks splashed down into water that reflected the morning sky. In the wooded areas, redbud trees and dogwoods were starting to show off their springtime colors. Her Holsteins lowed in the red barn where Roman was milking them. As Christine headed for the smaller white barn, her heart thrummed with the beauty of the day—and with the hopeful feeling Truman's letter gave her as it rustled in her pocket.

She stepped carefully between chickens pecking at grain and entered the barn. Rosetta was seated at the milking stand with Gladys. The other four goats lifted their ears and approached Christine, bleating their greeting.

"And *gut* morning to you girls, too," she replied. She held her plate of goodies higher as she scratched between the curious goats' ears.

Rosetta turned to face her, rhythmically splashing milk into her pail. "I wasn't expecting to see the bride out here on her wedding day," she remarked. "Whatever you've brought has certainly sparked Gertie and Blanche's curiosity. Be careful, or Bernadette will bump you while Betsy catches what falls off your plate. They're partners in crime, you know."

Christine laughed as cream-colored twins Bernadette and Betsy seemed to follow Rosetta's prediction. "I know what you girls are up to," she teased, walking toward the milking stand. "But I'm not sharing Maria's goodies, because I can see your rations in that pan over there."

Rosetta glanced at the pastries. "Are these the ones Beulah bought a while back and put in the freezer?"

"Nope. This morning Maria provided two big boxes of fresh rolls and doughnuts for us and our guests." Christine waved the plate in front of her sister, watching for her reaction.

"She's doing penance after the Kuhns and I put her on the spot the other day," Rosetta said. "It's a nice gesture. Give me a bite of that chocolate cake doughnut, please."

Christine detected no undercurrent of bitterness or frustration in her sister's voice—a definite improvement over Rosetta's earlier moods. She held the glazed cake doughnut so Rosetta could bite into it. Christine chose a Danish for herself and set the plate on a nearby feed cabinet. "Whatever you said to Maria must've cleared the air, *jah*?"

"Thanks to the Kuhns, she knows she crossed the line," Rosetta replied after she'd chewed and swallowed. "The best part was the expression on her face when Ruby hinted that maybe Maria wanted to marry Truman. You'd have thought we'd washed her mouth out with lye soap."

Christine relished a big bite of her pineapple cream cheese Danish, pleased that her sister's sense of humor and perspective had returned. "Speaking of Truman," she said as she reached into her apron pocket. "He asked me to give you this. If you'd like to read it now, I'll be happy to finish milking Gladys for you."

Rosetta's brown eyes widened. "I'm finished," she said. When she moved the milk pail and released the head gate, Gladys hopped away to join the other goats. "So you're passing notes, like we used to do in school?"

Christine handed her the large yellow envelope, which bore Rosetta's name inside the outline of a heart. "I have a feeling this is the most important piece of writing I've ever delivered. I'll leave you to read it in private, if you want."

Rosetta gazed at the heart and her name, and then ripped open the envelope. "What did Truman say when he gave it to you?"

Christine smiled. "He implored me to get this to you before the wedding so there'd be no eyes sending daggers between the two front rows during the ceremony."

Rosetta waved her off. "Truman would never—oh, look at this pretty card," she said with a wistful sigh. "'Can you find it in your heart to forgive me?'" she read from the front, and when she opened it, a folded letter fell out. "Well, it's a *gut* sign that he doesn't expect the card to do all the talking."

Christine stuffed the rest of her Danish into her mouth, hoping Truman's message was as sweet and satisfying as the pastry. Rosetta read silently, quickly skimming the tight lines of Truman's handwriting. She blinked back tears, and by the time she'd read the back of the second page her chin was quivering.

"Oh, Truman, why did I ever doubt you?" Rosetta murmured as she wiped her eyes with her apron. She looked up at Christine with a tremulous smile. "He says he's as much to blame as Maria for upsetting me, and—and he's asked me to be patient. He's checking into a café that's now for sale in Cloverdale, where she can reopen her bakery without moving her building," she said in a rush. "He wants me to have no doubt about his love for me . . . and he's asked if we could talk this afternoon, after your wedding."

"That's the best news I've heard in a long while," Christine said. "What do you think, sweetie? Does he deserve a second chance?"

Rosetta sniffled, but she was chuckling. "I want to see the look on Maria's face when Truman informs her of his plan," she said. "She might be in for a shock."

"Or she might recognize an opportunity to expand her business in a bigger town."

Rosetta sighed happily, holding Truman's letter to her heart. "If anyone can make this happen, it's Truman—and truth be told, I'd be willing to buy the bakery building if she leaves it behind."

"If she leaves her appliances, maybe Deborah or my girls will want to open a bake shop," Christine mused.

Rosetta stood up with a big smile on her face. "I think we should get ourselves dressed for your big day, Christine. Before you know it, it'll be time to walk to Monroe's place!"

Chapter Twenty-Seven

Rosetta finished dressing and twisted her hair into a fresh bun. She glanced in the dresser mirror to place her new *kapp* on straight, liking what she saw. Christine had bought fabric in a deep shade of teal for her and Mattie's dresses, to complement the celestial blue of her wedding dress. The rich color flattered Rosetta's brown hair and eyes.

Will Truman like it? Will he think I'm as pretty as—?

Rosetta laughed at herself, refusing to finish the comparison. She'd been foolish to believe that the man she loved would find Maria more attractive, more desirable than she was—but perhaps calling off their wedding had inspired a worthwhile change of heart and a major change at Promise Lodge. Rosetta wanted to like and trust Maria—wanted to forgive and forget, as the Ordnung prescribed—but her heart would always remember the scene in the bakery. She grabbed Truman's note to read it one more time before she left for Christine and Monroe's wedding.

My dearest Rosetta,

I hope you can forgive me for being oblivious to your needs and feelings. I count myself even more to blame than Maria for your heartache, because

*I'm old enough to know better, to realize how
inappropriate any displays of affection with her
appear. Please believe that although Maria is a
longtime friend, she's the last woman I would want
for a wife. From the moment I met you, Rosetta, my
heart knew you were The One.*

Rosetta sighed wistfully. "I'm the one who needs to be
forgiven, Truman," she murmured. "I jumped to a stupid
conclusion."

*If you can accept this written apology, I'd like to
spend the rest of the day with you after Monroe
and Christine's wedding, to apologize in person . . .
to figure out how we can point ourselves toward
the altar again after we kiss and make up.*

Rosetta smiled. Only a dead woman wouldn't respond
to Truman's soulful kisses, and just the thought of him
pressing his lips to hers made her shiver with anticipation.
She'd heard folks joke about squabbling just because
making up was so pleasurable—but she hoped she and
Truman would never trivialize their affection by purposely
disagreeing, or so one of them could be *right*. She was old
enough to believe that being happy and loved trumped
being right and in control.

Rosetta smiled at the next paragraph, because she'd read
it a dozen times.

*If you can be patient, dear Rosetta, I'm hoping
to acquire the café that's up for sale on the square
in Cloverdale. A lot of folks there miss Maria's
bakery—and she has more friends there, anyway—
so I'll convince her that moving back is the best
thing for her business and her personal life.*

*Please don't get the idea I'm buying this building
for her as a gift because I love her! I believe you'll
be happier if she moves on, and I bet we can find a
new use for the bakery building at Promise Lodge.*

Rosetta was willing to buy the building and appliances
Maria would leave at Promise Lodge so Truman wouldn't
be paying for Maria's future out of his own pocket. She had
no doubt that Laura and Phoebe—or even Allen or the
Helmuths' cousins—could find a way to adapt the building
for their own use.

*I will always love you, Rosetta. If you'll give me
the chance, I intend to prove beyond a shadow of a
doubt that you and I belong together forever. Can't
wait to gaze at you from the newehocker benches
during your sister's wedding . . . can't wait to stand
with you before Bishop Monroe someday soon and
exchange our own vows. With all my love, Truman.*

Rosetta let out a long, gratified sigh. It was such a relief
to know she wouldn't be doubting Maria's intentions anymore. It was even better to know that Truman's love for her
had never wavered despite her fearful doubts about his
feelings for Maria.

She tucked the letter and card into the yellow envelope
with a smile. *Today's the first day of the rest of our lives,
Truman,* she thought as she went downstairs to wait for her
sister. *I'm ready to make the most of it.*

As Christine sat on the front pew bench beside her two
sisters, her body vibrated with nervous excitement. It was
a thrill to be sitting in Monroe's new home—soon to be her
home—for this wedding, instead of in the meeting room at

the lodge. She listened patiently during the church service as Preacher Marlin and Preacher Eli spoke about God's eternal promise to lead His people in love, and about the sanctity and responsibilities of marriage. She recalled hearing similar sermons when she'd exchanged vows with Willis Hershberger so many years ago . . . when she'd been too young to fully understand the words *until death do us part*.

She gazed around the front room, which had been expanded by the removal of some portable interior walls and was filled with her friends and family. Monroe's deep green eyes held hers. He looked very handsome—if a little nervous—in his best black trousers and vest, wearing a new white shirt she'd sewn for him. Preacher Amos and Truman sat on either side of him as his side-sitters. Christine still had to pinch herself to believe that when all the pew benches had been removed and the interior walls were put back into place, she would be sharing this beautiful, spacious home with the most caring, handsome man she'd ever met. It seemed that all the love she'd poured into her marriage with Willis had only been the preparation for this day, this holy relationship Monroe had asked her to share.

After the final hymn of the church service, Bishop Ralph rose from the preacher's bench, smiling at her and at Monroe. "It's an honor to be conducting this ceremony for Bishop Monroe Burkholder and Christine Hershberger," he began in a resonant voice, "and we're happy all you folks could join us for this blessed occasion. Now that I'm acquainted with the residents of Promise Lodge and their livelihoods, I can't imagine a finer place for this couple to begin their new life together."

Bishop Ralph's sermon reminded everyone that the marriage between a man and a woman was akin to Christ's taking the church as His bride—a love that had withstood the test of centuries. Christine folded her hands in her lap so she wouldn't fidget with her white organdy apron or her celestial blue wedding dress. She exchanged glances with Mattie and Rosetta, grateful for the love only sisters could share—a love that burned brighter on the special days of their lives. As Bishop Ralph brought his remarks to a close and nodded at her, Christine's heart fluttered like humming-bird wings.

Monroe rose from his bench, and Christine did, too, barely able to breathe. He looked at her with intense devotion, and she hoped her expression moved him as deeply. When he clasped her hand and they faced Bishop Ralph, Christine felt like a young girl again, lightheaded with joy.

As the age-old phrases were spoken, Christine was aware of repeating them effortlessly, without fear or hesitation, even though she felt as though she were floating above the scene, watching rather than participating. Monroe's mellow voice rang confidently as he followed Bishop Ralph's lead in a ceremony he'd performed dozens of times, yet she sensed his responses came from the deepest part of his heart and soul. Bishop Ralph pronounced them husband and wife, and for brief, shimmering seconds, Christine felt so caught up in Monroe's loving gaze that everyone around them ceased to exist.

"Christine, I love you so much I can't find words," Monroe whispered. Before she could reply, he pulled her close for a kiss that stirred her soul.

"Oh, Monroe," she murmured when their lips parted, "you've made me the happiest woman on earth."

When he kissed her again, applause filled the room and a few of the younger men whistled enthusiastically. They eased apart, and as Monroe slipped his arm around her so they could face their family and friends, Christine felt loved and cherished beyond measure. What a joy it was to see so many happy faces surrounding them, celebrating their union—and to see Phoebe and Laura beaming at them, too. It was a dream come true to be Mrs. Monroe Burkholder.

"Looks like Truman's not giving Rosetta a chance to escape," she murmured as folks filed between the pew benches. Truman had made a beeline behind the bishop to grasp her sister's hands.

Monroe smiled. "They'll get their act together one of these days," he predicted. "Personally, I'm glad the courting and questioning are behind us so you and I can move on to the good stuff." His smile intensified as he held her gaze. "Upstairs. First chance we get today. Are we on the same page, sweetheart?"

Christine's face flushed, but she'd never felt happier or more desirable. "Same page, same chapter," she replied. "I can't wait to fill the book of our life together with all manner of adventures, Monroe, starting with this very moment."

From the Promise Lodge Kitchen

Rosetta Bender, Christine Hershberger, and the Kuhn sisters love to cook—and with so many weddings at Promise Lodge, they'll be in the kitchen constantly to keep guests and family members fed! In this recipe section, you'll find down-home foods Amish women feed their families, along with some dishes that I've concocted in my own kitchen—because you know what? Amish cooking isn't elaborate. Plain cooks make an astounding number of meals from whatever's in their pantry and their freezers. They also use convenience foods like Velveeta cheese, cake mixes, and canned soups to feed their large families for less money and investment of their time.

These recipes are also posted on my website,
www.CharlotteHubbard.com.
If you don't find a recipe you want,
please email me via my website to request it—
or to let me know how you liked it
or any of my other recipes!

~Charlotte

Cranberry-Date Bars

These bars are chock-full of fresh cranberries and chopped dates, a filling that needs no added sugar! And because the crust contains whole grain oats and cornmeal, these bars are as good for breakfast as they are for a dessert. They freeze well, too.

Filling

 1 12-oz. bag fresh cranberries (thaw, if frozen)
 1 8-oz. box chopped dates
 2 T water
 1 tsp vanilla

Crust

 2 cups old-fashioned oats
 1½ cups brown sugar, packed
 ½ tsp baking soda
 1 cup melted butter
 1 cup flour
 ¼ cup cornmeal

Glaze

 2 cups powdered sugar
 2–3 T orange juice
 1 tsp vanilla

In a medium saucepan, simmer the cranberries, dates, and water until the cranberries pop. When thickened, remove from heat and add the vanilla.

Meanwhile, preheat oven to 350°. Stir all the crust ingredients together until well moistened. Press half the mixture into a sprayed 9" x 13" pan and bake for 8 minutes. Remove from oven and spread the filling over the crust, then dot the filling with clumps of the remaining crust. Bake another 25–30 minutes, until the bars feel almost firm in the center. Cool on a rack. Mix glaze and drizzle over the top.

Kitchen Hint: _You can replace half of the flour with whole wheat or white whole wheat flour._

Rosetta's Best Chocolate Chip Cookies

Soft, chewy, and full of chips and nuts, these cookies are irresistible!

   1¼ cups brown sugar, packed
   ¾ cup butter-flavored shortening (not butter)
   2 T milk
   1 T vanilla
   1 egg
   1¾ cups flour
   ¾ tsp baking soda
   1 12-oz bag dark chocolate chips
   1 11-oz bag butterscotch chips
   1 cup chopped walnuts or pecans

Preheat oven to 375°. For best results, cover cookie sheets with parchment paper. Cream the brown sugar, shortening, milk, and vanilla until light and fluffy. Beat in the egg. Combine the flour and baking soda in a separate bowl and mix into the creamed mixture until just blended. Stir in the chips and nuts. Drop onto cookie sheets about 2 inches apart. Bake 8–10 minutes, or until cookies are just starting to brown. Cool the cookies on the pan for a few minutes and then finish cooling them on a rack. Makes about 4 dozen cookies. Freezes well.

Cream Cheese Cake Mix Cookies

Recipes abound for cookies that begin with cake mixes, but the cream cheese adds a new dimension of YUM. There are as many variations of this recipe as there are cake mixes! The cookies bake up soft and chewy, and your favorite chips, nuts, and other add-ins make them uniquely yours.

    1 box cake mix, any flavor
    8 oz cream cheese, softened
    ¼ cup butter, room temperature
    1 egg
    1 tsp vanilla or other extract
    2 cups baking chips, nuts, coconut, raisins, etc.

Preheat oven to 350° and either spray cookie sheets or cover them with parchment paper. Place cake mix, cream cheese, butter, egg, and extract (which should enhance your cake mix flavor) in a large mixing bowl and beat until batter is smooth. Stir in the chips, etc., of your choice. Drop by large spoonsful onto baking sheets, 2 inches apart. Bake about 12 minutes, or until bottoms start to brown (center will still be a bit soft). Cool on a wire rack. Makes 3 dozen. Freezes well.

Cheesy Egg Muffins

An easy make-ahead breakfast entrée that's high in protein and can be customized with the veggies you add! You can squeeze it between English muffin halves for a sandwich.

1 dozen eggs
1 tsp salt or sea salt
Pepper, dill weed, parsley, to taste
1 cup fresh or frozen spinach
1 cup thinly sliced mushrooms
¼ cup chopped onion or sliced green onion
2 cups shredded cheese (your favorite kind),
    more for topping

Preheat the oven to 350°. Spray each cup of a 12-muffin pan. Crack the eggs into a large liquid measuring cup and whisk with salt and other seasonings. Divide the spinach, mushrooms, onions, and cheese between the 12 muffin cups and then carefully pour egg mixture over the vegetables, leaving a ¼" space at the top. Stir with a fork so egg mixture is distributed around the vegetables. Top with extra cheese if desired.

Bake for 20–25 minutes, or until pick comes out clean from the centers. Muffins will sink a bit—let them rest a few minutes in the tins. Use a rubber spatula to remove the muffins to a platter. Eat immediately or cool and transfer to a resealable plastic bag. Keep in the refrigerator up to a week, or freeze for a month.

Kitchen Hint: *You can substitute other vegetables for the spinach, mushrooms, or onion. Keep the amount the same so they'll fit into the muffin cups.*

Ruby's Special Chocolate Cake

When it comes to desserts, busy Plain cooks are happy to start with a box mix and "doctor it up." This formula is especially good with a chocolate cake mix, but it works for any flavor you choose! Makes a 9" x 13" cake, two 9" round layers, or 24 cupcakes.

1 cake mix, following the directions except:
Replace the water with the same amount of milk
Replace the oil with melted butter—and double the amount (½ cup becomes 1 cup)
Add an extra egg
(For instance, the cake I make has 4 large eggs, ⅔ cup melted butter, and 1 cup milk.)

Pour the batter into sprayed pan(s) and bake according to package directions!

Mocha Buttercream Frosting

This recipe is nothing short of fabulous! It frosts/decorates a 9" x 13" layer, top and sides, and the frosting is dense and rich. I use Ghirardelli chocolate, but any brand of 100% cacao that's unsweetened will work well.

2 tsp instant coffee or espresso powder
2 T boiling water
1 4-oz 100% cacao unsweetened chocolate baking bar, melted
⅔ cup butter, softened
4–4½ cups powdered sugar
¼ cup milk
1 tsp vanilla extract
dash of salt

Dissolve the instant coffee in the boiling water, then stir into the melted chocolate. In a separate large mixing bowl, beat the butter until soft. Gradually add 4 cups of the powdered sugar, milk, and vanilla, beating until smooth. Beat in the melted chocolate mixture until well blended. For decorating, you want the frosting to form peaks/ridges that hold their shape, so you might want to add that other ½ cup of powdered sugar.

Sweet & Sour Four-Bean Salad

This is one of my mom's recipes, and I always looked forward to family gatherings when she served it. Amish cooks (and Mom and I) use a pint jar of home-canned green and wax beans for each can in the recipe. A great way to get your veggies—and it keeps several days in the fridge.

⅓ cup canola or salad oil
1 tsp each salt and celery seed
Black pepper to taste
⅔ cup white vinegar
¾ cup sugar
1 onion, chopped
1 red or green bell pepper, diced
1 15-oz can yellow wax beans
1 15-oz can green beans
1 15-oz can red kidney beans
1 15-oz can garbanzo beans
1 15-oz can whole kernel corn (optional)

In a large bowl, mix the oil, seasonings, vinegar, and sugar. Add the onion and bell pepper. Drain the canned vegetables and stir into the dressing, coating well. Refrigerate, stirring after several hours. Best made the day ahead. Makes about half a gallon of salad.

Chocolate Beet Bread

You'll think you're eating chocolate cake for breakfast—
yet you're also eating whole grain flour and beets and
antioxidant-rich cocoa! Best served warm, so the chocolate
chips are gooey (I use Ghirardelli 60% cacao chips).

1½ cups + 2 T all-purpose flour, divided
1½ cups whole wheat flour
1 cup unsweetened cocoa powder
¾ cup sugar
2½ tsp baking powder
½ tsp each salt and nutmeg
2 15-oz. cans sliced beets
1 cup buttermilk
3 large eggs
½ cup olive oil
2 T orange zest
1 T vanilla
1 cup dark chocolate chips

Preheat oven to 350°. Thoroughly spray a Bundt pan. In a
large bowl, mix the flours (reserving the 2 T for later),
cocoa, sugar, baking powder, salt, and nutmeg. Drain the
beets and puree them in a food processor or grinder. Place
the beet puree in a medium bowl with the buttermilk, eggs,
olive oil, zest, and vanilla—blend well, and gently pour
into the flour mixture. Toss the chips with the 2 T flour and
stir into the batter. Pour batter into the prepared pan and
bake about 40–50 minutes, or until a pick inserted in the
center comes out clean. Cool in the pan 15 minutes. Invert
onto a serving plate.

Yield: 12–16 servings.

*Don't miss Charlotte Hubbard's next Amish romance,
the second in her Simple Gifts series,
set in Willow Ridge, Missouri.*

A Simple Wish

*The Amish residents of Willow Ridge share their talents
at the Simple Gifts crafts shop—and share the blessings
of faith, hard work, and love with their community—even
when family secrets bring unexpected challenges . . .*

Making rugs for Simple Gifts has taught Loretta Riehl
that an unassuming pattern can reveal surprising depth.
People, too, have a way of defying first impressions.
Drew Detweiler came to Willow Ridge under a cloud,
but the handsome craftsman has gained
the community's respect for his upholstery skills
and commitment to making amends for his mistakes.
As her new brother-in-law's twin, he's joining the family
for dinners and Sunday visits at the Riehl house,
and Loretta can't deny enjoying his attentions.

If only her *dat* were willing to let a little joy into his life.
Cornelius Riehl grows more stern with each passing day,
and Drew suspects there's more to his moods than
missing Loretta's late *mamm*. Hoping to fulfill Loretta's
wish to live in a peaceful, happy home again, Drew sets
out to learn the truth. It's a journey that will bring to
light painful realities—but also the chance to forge a
new, honest, and loving future together . . .

Ordinarily, the shaded front porch was the coolest place to spend a July afternoon, but the sweat trickling down Loretta Riehl's back had nothing to do with Missouri's heat and humidity. Will Gingerich, her former fiancé, sat on the other end of the porch swing from her, and his back-and-forth motion was becoming so quick and jerky that she could barely guide her toothbrush needle through the loose knots of the rag rug she was making.

"The biggest mistake I ever made was to let your *dat* end our engagement, Loretta," Will said urgently. "I should've stood my ground. I should've believed that our love was strong enough to withstand my losing the farm to my brothers."

Loretta swallowed hard, fearful of where this conversation was leading. She'd been devastated when Dat had come between her and Will a couple of years ago, but she'd accepted it as her father's will—which was second only to God's will. "Who among us has ever stood up to Dat and won?" she asked in a tight voice. Her hands were trembling as she drew the strip of sage green fabric through the next rug knot with her homemade needle. "I cried my eyes out and pleaded with him again and again, but he was convinced you weren't *gut* enough—that you could never provide me a home."

"He was wrong!" Will declared. "I should've insisted that you and I could live at your place—back when we were in Rosewood—the way a lot of newlyweds do until they have the money for a home of their own."

Loretta stifled a sigh. Why was Will thinking this way when they both knew they would've been miserable living under Dat's roof after Mamm had died? Even with her sisters, Edith and Rosalyn, to support them, their marriage would've gotten off to a rocky start.

"And the other monumental mistake I made," Will continued fervently, "was latching onto Molly Ropp too quickly after your *dat* severed my relationship with you. Why didn't I realize Molly's parents were too eager to get us married?"

"How could you have known Molly was pregnant?" Loretta pointed out. "We don't like to believe that any young Amish woman would succumb to temptation—or keep such secrets—"

"And how was Molly supposed to know that it was Drew Detweiler who fathered her twins rather than Asa?" Will demanded. As he raked his light brown hair back with his fingers, he appeared lost in his own world—not really hearing anything Loretta said. "Molly was deceived. *I* was deceived—"

"You paid dearly for that, Will. And that episode's behind us now—although I sense you're still mourning Molly's passing," Loretta put in quietly. She rested her hands in her lap, no longer able to concentrate on her rug. "But God saw to it that some *gut* came of your trials and tribulations, ain't so? Little Leroy and Louisa are a joy to us all—the light of Edith and Asa's marriage. And once Drew confessed and apologized to everyone for masquerading as Asa, he's become an accepted, forgiven member of our church district and the Willow Ridge business community. That's real progress, to my way of thinking."

When Loretta looked across the road, she noticed that one of the Detweiler brothers was coming out of the stable in an open buggy pulled by a tall, black Percheron. Asa and Drew, identical twins, owned matching horses, so it was impossible to tell which one of them was heading down the long lane toward the road.

She held her breath. Was it her imagination, or was the driver of that buggy looking right at her?

"I—I've never forgiven myself for turning my back on the love we shared, Loretta," Will said again. He stopped the swing so suddenly that Loretta's long, loose strips of rug fabric fluttered to the porch floor. "We both knew we had a love that would have seen us through a lifetime together. I was so upset about your Dad splitting us up that I didn't realize Molly was coming on to me too fast, too soon," he lamented, gazing at her with the soft, brown eyes of a begging dog. "I am so sorry, Loretta."

Loretta was feeling more unsettled by the second, because Will's soul baring was leading her down a path she no longer wanted to follow. How could she tell him she wasn't interested in rekindling their relationship? It would break his heart and depress him further while he still mourned the death of his wife and their misguided marriage.

Sighing, she chose her words carefully. "God has a reason for everything He does—every stumbling block He places in our paths—"

"But I see the world so clearly now!" Will blurted out. "I've prayed over these things night and day since Molly died and left me with her six-month-old twins. And while I never wished that cancer would take her, her loss gave me hope that you and I could—"

Loretta stood up, dropping her unfinished rug onto the swing between them. As the Detweiler buggy approached the road, coming toward her, she realized that Drew surely must be driving because Asa and Edith were inseparable—they went everywhere together and took the twins with them, in their baskets. Her pulse quickened. Drew was gazing right at her, pulling out of the Detweilers' lane and stopping the buggy on the roadside in front of her.

"Loretta, I've got a *gut* steady job now, farming for Luke and Ira Hooley," Will was saying, oblivious to the buggy. "Soon I'll be planting a vineyard for them—can you imagine that? And I'll be asking the Brenneman brothers to build us a house—"

"Hey there, Miss Loretta!" Drew called out from the buggy. "I have an errand to run. Want to come along?"

For a moment, Loretta felt lower than a worm, but she couldn't allow Will to believe he could take up where they'd left off. He hadn't heard a word she'd said as she'd gently countered his suggestions. Loretta nipped her lip, glancing apologetically at the handsome young man who'd gone through such an ordeal these past several months. Without a word, she hurried down the porch steps and across the front yard toward Drew Detweiler.

Grinning, Drew dropped down from the buggy. As he clasped Loretta's hand and escorted her to the other side of his open vehicle, she wondered if he was leading her down a path riskier than Will's and far more dangerous. A path more daring . . . and passionate.